Bunyan
and
Henry
or,
❧ THE ❧
BEAUTIFUL
DESTINY

BUNYAN

AND

HENRY

OR,

 # THE

BEAUTIFUL

DESTINY

Mark Cecil

PANTHEON BOOKS

NEW YORK

Copyright © 2024 by Mark Cecil

All rights reserved. Published in the United States by Pantheon Books, a division of Penguin Random House LLC, New York, and distributed in Canada by Penguin Random House Canada Limited, Toronto.

Pantheon Books and colophon are registered trademarks of Penguin Random House LLC.

Library of Congress Cataloging-in-Publication Data
Names: Cecil, Mark, author.
Title: Bunyan and Henry; or, the beautiful destiny / by Mark Cecil.
Description: New York : Pantheon Books, a division of
Penguin Random House LLC, 2024.
Identifiers: LCCN 2023013886 (print) | LCCN 2023013887 (ebook) |
ISBN 9780593471166 (hardcover) | ISBN 9780593471173 (ebook)
Subjects: LCSH: Bunyan, Paul (Legendary character)—Fiction. | Henry, John (Legendary
character)—Fiction. | LCGFT: Mythological fiction. | Adaptations. | Novels.
Classification: LCC PS3603.E3426 P38 2024 (print) | LCC PS3603.E3426 (ebook) |
DDC 813/.6—dc23/eng/20230707
LC record available at https://lccn.loc.gov/2023013886
LC ebook record available at https://lccn.loc.gov/2023013887

pantheonbooks.com

Map by Rhys Davies
Jacket illustration by Chris Wormell
Jacket design by Mark Abrams

Printed in the United States of America

First Edition
2 4 6 8 9 7 5 3 1

For Henry, Wyatt, Aubrey, and Ronan, who heard this story first.
And for Dede, who made it all possible.

Bunyan

AND

Henry

OR,

THE

BEAUTIFUL
DESTINY

A Long Time Ago, in an Age of Monsters and Mystery . . .

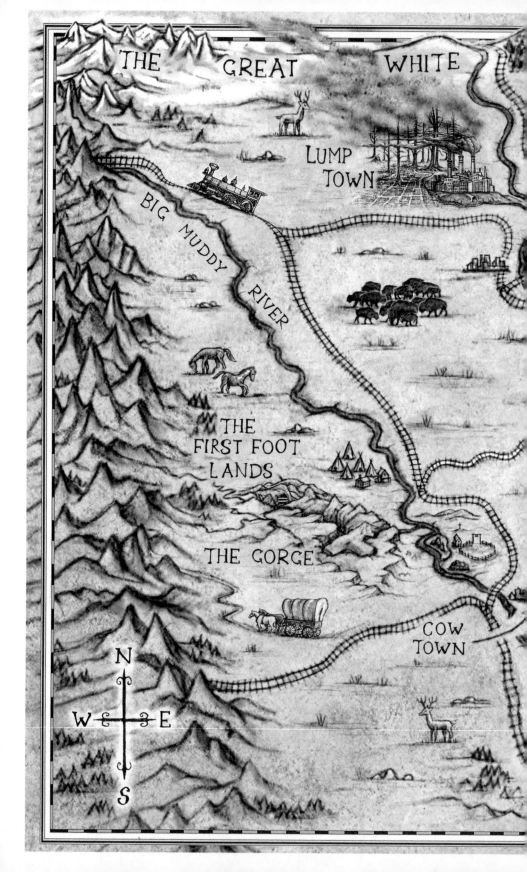

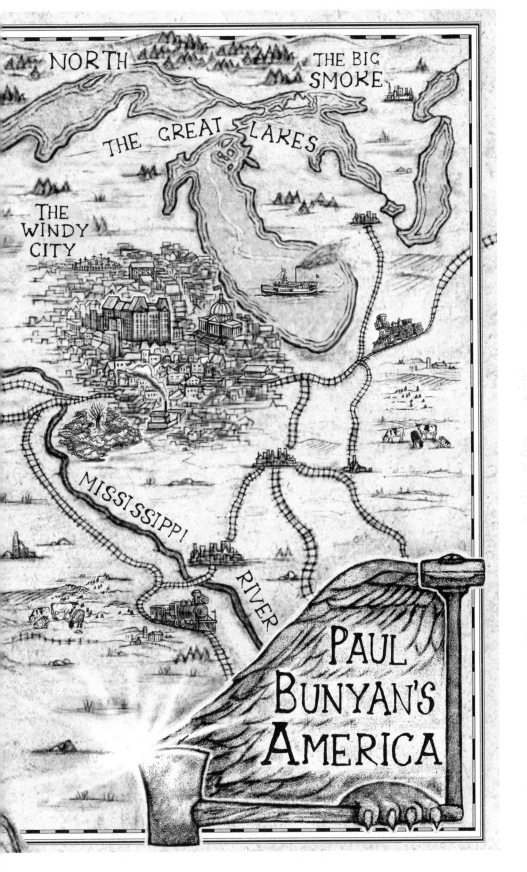

THE CHILALI

When Paul Bunyan was a young boy on the vast, windswept plains of America, his mother told him stories about a magical creature called a Chilali.

The Chilali, Sue Bunyan said, was a tall, handsome, and somewhat mischievous being that lived in the woods. They had the voice of a human, great brown wings like an eagle's, and the spotted legs of a jaguar. According to Sue, the Chilali always arrived at a particular moment in a person's life.

"The Chilali loves someone at a crossroads," Sue said. "The moment when a person can shy away from change or walk the Twisty Path toward the Beautiful Destiny."

Year after year, as winter gales rattled the windows of their log cabin, or on lazy summer days when the sun baked the open prairies, Sue told her son these strange, entertaining tales. And Chilali stories were *quite* entertaining. They all had one quality in common: in order to follow the Chilali's advice, the hero had to change their life in the most shocking way.

In one of Paul's favorite tales, a baseball player had to intentionally strike out in order to win the girl he loved. In another, a businessman had to live the life of a beggar to save his dying brother.

When telling the stories, Sue delighted in making her characters knock on all the wrong doors before the right one opened, tying themselves in terrible knots before at last they got untangled. The Twisty Path was never obvious, or safe, or straightforward. It involved delays, backtracking, and confusion. These were stories of quests, bloodshed, and true love.

Sue told her son other tales, too: of Noah, Moses, and Jesus; of Hercules, Odysseus, and Beowulf; of fantastical dwarves, terrible trolls, and benevolent wizards. But in the end, it was the stories about Chilalis that young Paul loved most. The boy became certain that one day he would meet a Chilali himself.

Paul's family had come to the Midwest in a covered wagon following the War for the Union. His father, Augie, was a veteran who'd taken out a large loan to buy both cattle and land. Across a small creek from the family ranch stood a grove of trees, and on warm days, as the cows lowed in the distance and the wind snaked through the golden grass, Paul walked to this grove, climbed the branches, and tried to spot a Chilali.

This was a nearly impossible task, it should be said, for Chilalis were clever, elusive, and always just outside the boundary of one's vision. As Sue told it, if a person ever turned to see one face-to-face— *whoosh*—the creature would be gone.

Nevertheless, day after day, young Paul went into those woods, scanning the branches like a spy. He'd search as he chopped firewood with his dad in the afternoon. He'd search at night, too, when the prairie wind blew so strong the house creaked. Lying in his bed, young Paul would stare across the moonlit stream, wondering, *When will I be at a crossroads, so the Chilali will speak to me?*

One thing was certain: a life without a Chilali was not a life worth living.

In any case, despite the fact he had not met a Chilali—*yet*—the boy was largely happy, climbing trees, chopping wood, and listening to stories, there with his mother, his father, and their great herd of cattle, far out on the American plains.

This happiness, however, would not last.

Paul was twelve years old when the first cow grew sick. The disease was horrifying. Tongues turned hard as wood. Yellow pus dripped from blistered mouths. Locusts swarmed over their hides. Worst of all, the animals lost their minds, charging at their owners as if they were strangers.

One evening, Paul came back from the grove to find his father in the paddock, tending to one of the sick cows. A storm was moving in and rain had begun to fall. Suddenly, thunder clapped. A stampede broke out. The beasts raced around the paddock, bellowing with a terrible sound Paul would never forget—

BRRRRAAWWWWWWW

Paul shouted and ran to his father, but a bull knocked him to the ground, stomping on his foot. As he cried with pain, the boy saw a flash of light—*just there*—in a gap amid the charging beasts. He dashed along the path of the light, sprinting despite his injury toward the fence and diving through it, just as a bull's horns slammed into the post behind him. As Paul grasped at his mangled foot, he turned back, searching for his father.

There he lay, facedown. Round and round the cattle charged, and as the thunder boomed and the rain lashed his cheeks, Paul screamed for his father to move, to get up, to *please, please get up*. In time, he felt himself being pulled back into the house.

"Stay here," said his mother, pushing him through the door.

Paul watched from the window, through the downpour, as the stampede at last subsided and his mother, drenched with rain, dragged the limp body of her husband from the mud.

For the rest of his life, the image of his father's lifeless body, chin hanging down on his chest, would return to Paul's mind. And every time it did, he straightened his spine, turned his head away, and let out a mighty sigh.

The next day, they buried Augie under a small wooden cross behind their home. Then Sue shot every last sick cow dead. Paul never forgot that sound. Bullet by bullet, blast by blast. In the house, he covered his ears with a pillow.

Needing money, Sue took a sample of the cattle meat to town. But the beef had an unnatural, silvery hue and gave off a strange, metallic odor. It frightened the butchers. No one bought it. Desperate for money to pay off the family loan, Sue tried to sell the ranch. No one would buy that either.

Soon after, a pair of bankers paid a visit. One was tall, with squinty eyes and a patchy beard. The other was short and fat, with a ruddy face.

"You've got two options," said the tall one. "Pay it back, or go to debtors' prison."

Young Paul sat beside his mother at the kitchen table, holding her hand.

Sue asked, "How long will it take to pay it off?"

"In monthly installments, and at a rate you can afford, ninety-nine years."

Sue looked down at her son and stroked his hair. To Paul, his mother was the most beautiful woman in the world. Her hair, pulled back into a bun, was the color of golden wheat. She looked like the figurehead on the prow of a ship—steady and graceful, eyes on the horizon, even in the tempest.

"Excuse us for a moment," said one of the bankers. "Nature calls."

The two men went to the outhouse. Sue said to Paul, "Why don't you go fetch them water, so they can wash their hands?"

Paul's foot still hadn't healed properly from the stampede. On his crutches, he went to the well, where, hidden around the corner, he overheard the bankers talking.

"She'll never pay it off," said the fat one. "Best to lock her up now."

The taller one scratched his beard. "You sure?"

"They're white trash. Can't even keep their cows alive."

Young Paul felt like he wanted to throw up, knowing these men had the power to put his mother in prison.

"Never easy to break up a family," said the tall one, heading into the outhouse.

"Bah," said the fat one. "These crackers can get used to anything."

In the end, Sue convinced the bankers her word was good. She signed the documents, promising she would pay the same amount every month.

Days later, she and young Paul left behind the homestead for good.

From the back of a covered wagon, Paul watched as the wooden cross marking the grave of his father receded into the distance. Behind it stood the grove, where the wind blew in the empty boughs.

So began the scrap meat years.

Sue did odd jobs up and down the Midwest, working two, three, sometimes four at a time. She scrubbed floors, folded clothes, baked biscuits, packed sausages. The pain in Paul's lame foot often kept him from working. He played the harmonica in the streets for extra pennies. For a holiday treat, Sue bought bits of scrap meat from the butcher. For years, she found ways to make the monthly payment.

But then the markets crashed. A depression swept the country. Suddenly, there were no jobs to be found.

One morning there was a knock on the door of the Bunyans' dingy one-room apartment on the outskirts of Cow Town.

"Who is it?" said Sue, sitting up in bed.

"Open up!"

Just hearing those voices, Paul already knew. Sue slid the locks off the door and opened it. In the hall stood the same two figures, one tall, one fat. This time a police officer stood with them.

"You'll have to come with us," said the officer to Sue.

Young Paul saw the gun on the man's belt.

"Please," Sue begged. "Don't take me from my child."

"You want us to lock him up, too?"

Tears raced down Sue's cheeks. In her final moment of freedom, she embraced her son, hugging him so hard she might have broken him in half.

"Never, *ever*, let them crush your spirit," she said in her son's ear. "Do what you must, believe what you must, become what you must, to keep your soul alive."

The officer put Sue in handcuffs and led her downstairs, where he shoved her into the back of a police wagon.

"Mom!" Paul shouted, standing in the road. "Mom!"

As the wagon pulled away, Sue peeked out from a small square window. The expression on his mother's face showed a bottomless sorrow. Then the wagon turned the corner and she was gone.

Alone in the street, Paul beat the walls of the tenement till his knuckles were bloody. His mother was all he had. Some way, somehow, he had to get her free. But what could be done?

It was only a few months later that Paul first heard about Lump Town.

Lump Town—the vision of the industrialist El Boffo. Lump Town—where they mined the miracle mineral, which was lighter than oil, burned hotter than coal, and was more potent, they said, than any substance known to man. Lump Town—where the streets were covered in soot, the trees had gone dark from pollution, and the Factory stacks, mighty as volcanoes, blew rivers of smoke into the sky, so much that the sun no longer shone.

In Lump Town, the pay was meager day-to-day. But El Boffo made a big promise to all his workers: after ten years of service, you get a house and a gold bar. A gold bar was more money than a cracker like Paul could imagine. And it would certainly be enough to set his mother free.

And so, Paul took the train north. There, in the hinterlands of America, he saw the gray and yellow smog. He saw the ashen roads. He saw the smokestacks belching smoke. Thinking of his mother, locked in a prison, he took a job in the Lump Town mines.

To his surprise, Paul Bunyan thrived in Lump Town. Always a quick study, he learned the Lump Town ropes. He grew powerful, and adept at managing his foot, still lame from the bull stampede. He thrived so much, in fact, that on the day *this* story begins, he had muscled his way into an annual contest called the Lump Town Finals. The Finals were a perilous event, featuring each step of the Lump extraction process; miners sometimes died competing in it. But the risk was worth it. If you won, you didn't have to wait the ten years; you got your gold bar and your dream house right then.

And as for Chilalis? Up in Lump Town, Chilalis were a matter of ridicule. "A children's story," scoffed the miners. And they could barely hold back a laugh if anyone used a phrase so naïve, so idealistic, as "the Beautiful Destiny."

Whenever Bunyan recalled his own youthful obsession with these magical beings, he'd just smirk to himself and think, *I'm a beat-down man in a hard, hard world. I've got no time for nonsense.*

But things were about to change.

We all have at least one great journey in us, and Paul Bunyan was about to embark upon his. By the time the sun set on this very day, he would be forced to question a great deal of what he had come to believe about the world.

Especially when it came to the Chilali.

CHAPTER 1

THE CONTENDER

Paul Bunyan had grown into a hulking man with a broad forehead, a beard down to his collarbones, clear eyes, and rock-solid shoulders. Now well into his twenties, he was so tall he had to duck under most doorways, and because of his heft people often assumed he could really lay a man out.

"Just look at those arms," they'd say. "Bet you could break a man's jaw like *that*."

Bunyan would only shrug. "If it ever came to that, I suppose."

The fact was, though Bunyan had lived in some rough spots, he had not once in his life been in a fistfight. Which isn't to say Bunyan was afraid of fights—he'd broken up plenty. Nor did he shy from pain generally—he'd faced his share. He simply lacked a natural desire to punch another man in the face, and, as yet, no one had ever tried punching him in his.

Yet to call Bunyan soft just because he'd never smashed in someone's nose would be a mistake. For buried deep in Bunyan's core was a keen ferocity of will. His favorite saying, passed down to him from his father, was *Discipline destroys misery*.

This very ferocity of will was on display now, on the morning of the Lump Town Finals, as Bunyan sat in his bedroom, chilling his lame foot in a bucket of ice water. He was nervous, but the nerves were only telling him to prepare. He stirred his leg in the frigid slush and saw the championship run in his mind's eye.

"All right," Bunyan said to himself, letting out a long breath. "Let's go over this one last time."

Stage one. Five minutes. Get the Lump.

Set the oil lamp at your feet, far enough away so the backswing won't knock it. Find three targets before the whistle blows. Know your first, second, and third strikes. Mark each with the pick, X, X, X. When the whistle sounds, keep count in your mind. Thirty swings per seam. Count off two minutes, then load the cart.

Stage two. Three minutes. Up the shaft.

A hundred fifty steps from the pit to the floor. Count with your breaths. Odd numbers in, even numbers out. The burn in your thighs will start halfway up. Push through it—the pain won't kill you. Above all, don't tip the cart.

Stage three. Two minutes. Pack the oven.

Biggest load of coal possible for each toss. Watch the temp. When it hits a thousand, cool off, then three more quick loads. Dump the cart.

Stage four. Four minutes. Crank the gear.

Your foot will be throbbing and you'll be well off the lead, but no one cranks harder—not Mad Dog, not anyone, not ever. Crank up, lean far, pull down, chin back. Lock in that rhythm till the gear's blowing breeze. Careful about your chin.

Last stage. Sixty seconds. Drop the hammer.

If you drop the hammer all at once, the crusher's gonna hit the pan hard and the platform's gonna jolt. Just hold the gear tight, and—

"Paul?"

The bedroom door swung open and Bunyan yanked his foot in the ice tub to one side, hiding it around the side of the chair. The move was so quick that much of the icy water sloshed onto the floor.

"It's just me," said Lucette.

"Sorry. I was just . . . preparing."

After all these years, Bunyan was still self-conscious about his lame foot, even in front of his new wife.

"Almost time," said Lucette. "Morning whistle any second."

Her shining brown hair fixed in a ponytail, the energetic Lucette passed Bunyan swiftly on the way to the dresser in the corner. From the bottom drawer she lifted her husband's wood and leather brace, then sat before him on the bed.

"All right, let's have it."

The chair creaked under Bunyan's weight as he hoisted his right leg out of the icy tub and set it on her lap.

There it was: Old Junk Foot.

Crushed beneath a bull's hoof the day his father died, it had healed poorly and only seemed to have gotten more deformed with age. The foot bent inward at an unnatural angle, with the bones fused awkwardly beneath the skin. Ugly as it was, the bigger problem was functional. Without his brace, the bulky limb would easily roll. Before he'd come to Lump Town, the foot had been getting worse, a source of daily pain. Only when he met Lucette did things change.

Lucette, that clever woman! So deft with her hands, so inventive. Not only had she constructed for Bunyan a new brace, she'd discovered a way of massaging away the pain, using her elbow. Though Bunyan was shy about his foot, Lucette herself had never once been squeamish. Without her, he wouldn't have made it to the Finals at all.

Lucette dried off Bunyan's wet, cold foot with a towel.

"Ready?"

Bunyan raised his eyes to the ceiling and blew out three quick breaths.

"Okay," he said. "Go."

Clamping the foot with her left arm, Lucette drove the point of her right elbow into the knot of Bunyan's muscles. Bunyan hissed in pain, but Lucette didn't let up. She made tight circles, deeper and deeper into the ligaments, making his toes involuntarily spread apart. Deeper she drove still, till the pain was so sharp Bunyan feared his wife might break his bones. At last, she stopped.

"Try it."

Bunyan wriggled his toes and rotated his ankle. Old Junk Foot felt—remarkably—loose and pain free.

"It's good."

Lucette picked up the brace: a tube of leather sewn into a right angle that covered the bottom of Bunyan's calf down to his toes. A wooden splint ran along each side, with four metal buckles strapped across the front. Lucette fastened it on.

Gingerly, Bunyan got up. His foot was now iced, massaged, and strapped in. He put weight on it. He walked back and forth. He stood on his tiptoes, then ran in place, his legs popping up quick to his chest.

"Feels all right."

The whistle blew. One hour to be at the Factory gate.

Lucette stood and gave her husband a quick peck on the lips—something she had to get on her tiptoes to do—then patted him on the chest. "Breakfast is ready."

Bunyan thought he noticed a bit of worry in his wife's eyes but wasn't sure.

As Lucette slipped downstairs, Bunyan put on work clothes—overalls and a flannel shirt. A locomotive screeched from the streets below. Walking to the window, he pulled back the curtain to let in the dim Lump Town light. A film of overnight ash clung to the panes.

When he'd first arrived years before, there was still a bit of sunlight filtering through the smog above the valley. Now the haze was all-enveloping. Even in late spring, when it was likely a bright day elsewhere in America, the sun could not be found.

A few blocks away on the train platform, men unloaded crates of milk, barrels of water, and palettes of eggs. All the food had to be shipped in; nothing grew here anymore. There were no cattle or pigs to eat either, an odd upside for Bunyan, who feared bulls more than anything in the world. In Lump Town, El Boffo forbade animals of any kind.

Bunyan let the curtain fall and turned toward the stairs. Suddenly, he froze.

There, by the door frame, he saw it. The familiar silvery light.

The Gleam.

"Oh no," he muttered. His stomach seized up with anxiety.

The Gleam had first appeared to Bunyan the day his father died.

There in that stampede amid the trampling bulls, this silvery light had glimmered like traces of molten metal on the ground, guiding him to safety.

Since then, the Gleam had appeared at unexpected times. It haloed around objects, lit up people's faces. Most often, it did what it was doing now—it formed a kind of beckoning trail. But beckoning toward *what*? Bunyan never knew, never wanted to know. Though it had saved his life years before, the Gleam was above all a reminder of the terrible day that sealed his family's fate. What's more, it made him feel crazy—like there was something not quite right about his mind.

Bunyan sighed.

"I'm a beat-down man in a hard, hard world," he said to the Gleam. "I've got no time for nonsense."

Bunyan made one more tour of the room, testing out his foot. He felt ready.

Despite his handicap, despite the Gleam, despite his father's death and mother's imprisonment, he'd grunted, ground, and groaned his way into the Lump Town Finals. He'd chiseled the Lump, climbed the shaft, cranked the gear, inhaled the smog, and every step of the way, he'd dreamed of his distant goal. He'd get to the Finals, get the gold, get the house, then, side by side with Lucette, he'd get his mother free. He'd hated Lump Town, but he'd borne it. Now he was on the doorstep of freedom.

Fifteen minutes of focus.

Fifteen minutes of pain.

He rallied himself, deep in his heart. *Fifteen minutes and we're out of here.*

CHAPTER 2

THE DREAM QUILT

As he was heading downstairs, Bunyan passed their small laundry room. The door was open a crack, and amid the clothes, baskets, and buckets, just below the window, something caught his eye. He pushed open the door.

There, sitting on Lucette's worktable, beside the sewing kit, was something he hadn't seen in months:

The Dream Quilt.

Not only was it unfolded, Lucette had added a patch to it. Bunyan approached, taking in his wife's astonishing artistry.

The Quilt was sewn in a five-by-five grid, with room for twenty-five squares in all, twenty-three finished before today, all of them prompted by "the Voice." The Voice was unpredictable. It would be silent for months, then in an unexpected moment it would reveal a new image to Lucette. She would then quickly sew the image and attach the new square to the rest of the Quilt's top.

"When the Voice speaks, it's like I'm giving birth," she told him once. "I have to sew till the image is out. Till then, I can't think of anything else."

The Quilt's details were rendered in gold, turquoise, scarlet, and magenta. It was full of sound and smell—a crashing sea, a lush bed of flowers. Birds, meteors, stars, butterflies. Apples, mountains, storms, thrones. Here in Lump Town, where not a single bird flew, nor a single blade of grass grew, Lucette's visions harkened to the vibrant world beyond.

"I am just a gateway," she would say, "and the Voice passes through."

The Voice didn't merely offer visions of strange beauty. The Voice also hinted at the future.

One patch featured a meteor charging toward Earth through space, on a collision course. Lucette had sewn it just before she'd met Bunyan.

Lucette's interpretation: *You were a meteor that struck my life, making one world out of two.*

In the depths of winter two years before, she'd sewn a circle of burgeoning fruit trees amid a vast tundra. This was right before Bunyan had proposed.

Lucette's conclusion: *In this bleak world, you sheltered me in a ring of joy.*

Yet another square showed a giant egg hatching. Out of it extended a lone, huge, muscular leg. The same week she'd sewn it, Bunyan was promoted from the pit up to the Factory floor.

Lucette's interpretation: *A new life begins for you, even with just one good leg.*

Lucette didn't always completely understand what she sewed—at least at first. The twenty-third square, for example, showed a mysterious man with dark hair, seated in a chair. To his left lay a hammer; to his right, an anvil. In his lap lay an axe, which seemed to be glowing.

"I don't know what this one means yet," Lucette said. "But I'm certain that axe isn't merely an axe."

Presently, Bunyan leaned over the worktable. His fingers were perpetually soiled with the oil, grease, and ash of the Lump Factory. Not wanting to leave a smudge on his wife's work, he wiped his hand on his overalls and carefully dragged the Quilt by one corner toward the dim light of the window.

There, in the twenty-fourth square, sewn onto the rest of the Quilt's top overnight, he saw the latest image from the Voice:

Two birds, flying together over an open sea. The waters below them were as silverdark as Lump. No land in sight.

He looked closer.

The bird on top was actually *holding* the one below. The bottom bird looked limp, not flying at all.

Its eyes, Bunyan saw, were closed.

———————— • ————————

The Bunyans' cramped home was one of several in a long row of flimsy shacks. All were identical, with two rooms up top and two on the bottom. A patch of yard in back was just a blanket of uniform soot.

Downstairs, Bunyan found Lucette in their small kitchen, dishing onto a plate what she'd fried in her skillet: eggs, salted meat, and canned beans. She poured a cup of coffee and set it on the table, then, without lifting her eyes, went to the wash bucket to scrub the dirty pan.

Bunyan went straight for his wife. "Lucette."

The moment she turned to him, he saw that her eyes quivered with hidden thoughts.

"I saw the Dream Quilt."

Lucette wiped her hand on the towel. "I—I'm sorry."

Bunyan held her by the hips, keeping her close, then pushed a strand of hair off her brow. Lucette's face could tell a thousand stories. Whether it was a stitch between her eyebrows, a slight smirk, or the tiniest tilt of her head, she could render judgments, reveal moods, or deliver a joke. Bunyan was an expert at reading his young wife's face, and today, the stitch in her brow meant trouble.

"You weren't going to tell me?"

"Of course I was. It's just . . . the Voice has never . . . shown me something like that."

Bunyan gently placed his knuckle beneath her chin. "Luce, I don't have a chance in the Finals unless we are like *this.*" He pressed two fingers together—no space between them.

Lucette smoothed the fabric of Bunyan's shirt with her palm. "The birds . . . I think the one on top is you. I'm the one on the bottom. You're carrying me . . . and"—Lucette's lips pressed together—"I'm dead."

"Dead? No. That can't be what it means."

The Factory whistle blew again. Forty-five minutes.

"I'm sorry. And on today of all days. But that sea . . . it was just so . . . endless."

Lucette coughed. Bunyan fetched her a glass of water.

"Thank you." As she drank, she pointed to his food on the table. *Eat.*

Bunyan went to the table and took a bite. Lucette sat on a stool and dropped one leg, then the other, into her tall work boots.

"Hold on a second," said Bunyan, putting down his fork. "I think I know *exactly* what the Voice is trying to say."

"You do?" Lucette rummaged in her workbag and took out her gas mask.

"So today is the Finals, right?"

"Yes."

"And I'm matched up against Mad Dog."

"Indeed."

"Mad Dog Mahoney, three-time reigning Lump Master. Mad Dog Mahoney, your former suitor."

"Stop," Lucette said, wiping a bit of ash from the gas mask lens with a rag.

"I believe Mad Dog has been waiting *years* for just this moment, to crush me head-to-head, so he can fully settle the score with the upstart kid who stole his bride-to-be."

"I wasn't anything-to-be when it comes to Mad Dog Mahoney."

"He's gonna have a big house one day."

"Ha." Lucette tucked her pants into her boot tops. "Mad Dog's the only man in Lump Town who doesn't want to leave."

"He never got over you."

"He never got over his dog."

"*Here's* what the Quilt is trying to say," Bunyan went on. "The bird on top is me. The bird on the bottom is Mad Dog. And today"—Bunyan flexed his biceps and tapped it with his finger—"I'm not *only* going to crush him physically"—he tapped his temple—"I'm going to crush him mentally. And most of all"—Bunyan gamely raised an eyebrow—"I'm going to crush that little dream of his that you picked the wrong hubby."

"Is that so?" said Lucette, examining the hose of her gas mask. She drove her finger down into it and fished out a piece of debris, which she flicked onto the floor.

"It is very much so," said Bunyan, taking a bite of bacon. "And after the Finals, I'm going to have to *yank* Mad Dog Mahoney up off the ground and *carry* him off the Factory floor. That, my darling, is what the Voice has foreseen."

Lucette crossed the room, rubbing Bunyan's neck affectionately for a moment on her way to the coatrack.

As Bunyan finished his breakfast, the face of Mad Dog Mahoney surfaced in his mind. It was a brutal, repellent sort of face, as if Mad Dog were a cold stone amid the currents of the world's emotions, absorbing none of its tender pains. He'd gotten his nickname because of the dog he'd smuggled into town years ago. The dog quickly grew sick and irritable, and began barking, howling, and biting his master at all hours. The scars on Mad Dog's hands, legs, and neck looked savage, but in fact they were evidence of how hard he tried to keep his pet alive. If there had ever been mercy in Mahoney, it died with that dog.

A knock came on the door.

Bunyan looked out the ash-covered window to see the Filter Brigade had arrived. Each of the ladies was equipped with the same uniform and gear as Lucette: smocks, boots, and gas masks. All of the women in town worked in either the Water Refinery or the Filter Brigade. In Lump Town there were no days off, but on the day of the Finals, the ladies got a break to watch the contest.

Lucette slipped on her FILTER BRIGADE CAPTAIN armband, then went to the wall and turned the crank of the house filter. The fan, which had to be turned several times per day, sucked out the ashes and dust.

At the door, Bunyan gave his wife a half dozen rapid kisses on the forehead. He breathed in the sweet, faint, floral scent of soap in her hair, a smell that always relaxed him.

"Where would I be without you?" he said, pulling her close.

"Making some other woman very happy?"

"In the gutter, that's where."

Lucette smiled as best she could and smoothed the fabric on his chest. "I'll be in the front row. Be safe."

Lucette slipped her gas mask over her head, perching it up on her forehead. Bunyan always thought she looked adorable like that. He took her hand and kissed it. As he did, he noticed a dark bruise on her finger. It looked like a smudge of ash. He tried to wipe it clean, but it didn't come off.

"Hopefully your last day on the job," he said.

"Yours, too."

"You won't miss your friends on the Filter Brigade?"

"If I have you, I have the world." Lucette thumped her husband on the chest three times. "Pump that Lump."

"Ain't no chump," he answered.

She slid down her gas mask, tightened the straps, and opened the door into the dim, ash-blown streets.

"Morning, Captain!" said the women of the Brigade, waiting outside.

"Morning!" said Lucette.

Bunyan followed his wife out. "Morning, ladies!"

The Brigade waved. Bunyan watched as Lucette walked off. A few steps away, she turned and blew a kiss to him through her gas mask.

Good woman. Great woman. *Best* woman. In times of stress, Bunyan always reassured himself with this thought: if Lucette had chosen him, he must be doing *something* right. His mother had once told him, "There's no clearer test of a man's character than who he chooses for his wife." *Judge me by my wife anytime.*

The Factory whistle blew again. Thirty minutes.

Standing in his doorway, Bunyan noticed the American flag hanging just beside him had grown dusty. He clapped the flag till its red, white, and blue colors showed more brightly, then set off toward the Factory.

He kept his head down as he wove through the gridlike streets. He walked along the polluted Moses Creek, then past the soaring petrified tree at the center of town, the silverdark Christ Trunk. The ever-present scent of Lump filled his nostrils: both sweet and sour at once, almost like bread baking; a smell that promised to nourish but never could.

Soon, Paul Bunyan took his place amid the huddled masses gathering by the bridge over the creek. He raised his eyes to see, above the Factory gate, a proclamation in cast-iron letters:

THE FUTURE IS IN YOUR HANDS

An hour later he was deep in the pit and nothing was going as planned.

CHAPTER 3

BLEED FOR THE PURE

Four minutes in and Mad Dog had already loaded his cart, while Bunyan was crawling on all fours, collecting what Lump he could. The original spot he'd X'd out was a false deposit—looked like Lump but was only rock. The second deposit hadn't yielded much either. Frustrated, he increased the force of his swings but accidentally knocked over the lamp, which broke.

Mad Dog stood over him at the base of the shaft, the web of scars on his neck lit by his lamp. "It's not your turn, cracker," he said. "It's never gonna be your turn." With that, he snuffed out the light.

As Mad Dog began to climb the shaft, Bunyan gathered as many chunks of raw as he could, dumping them in the cart by the handful. By the time he'd gotten enough and pushed his cart onto the track, Mad Dog was nearly halfway to the top.

Stage two. Up the shaft.

He breathed as he'd practiced: odd numbers in, even numbers out. *One, two. Three, four. In, out. In, out.* Fifty steps and his thighs were burning.

He was furious with himself. Marking two bad spots, then losing a whole minute on the dig? What was wrong with him? Had Lucette's dream thrown him off? By his sixtieth step, his legs were ready to give out. A vague roar echoed down the shaft. Mad Dog was already on the floor.

Seventy-five, seventy-six—halfway up.

Then, on the seventy-seventh step, it happened. A bolt of pain shot up his leg.

"Ah!"

The cart slammed against his shoulder and nearly careened down the shaft. Jamming his foot on a rail tie to stabilize the load, Bunyan looked down to see what he feared most: Old Junk Foot twisted loose in his brace.

Propping himself on his one good leg, Bunyan barely had the strength to hold on. He had begun to slip down the slope, back into the pit, when—

There.

A flash of light upon the track.

The Gleam.

No time to question. He planted his foot just where the Gleam shined, and there he found a solid hold. Secure, he propped the cart on his massive back and worked his bad foot out of the boot. He managed to unbuckle the broken brace and fling it aside, then jam his Junk Foot back into place.

He put weight on it—*Arggh*. No broken bone. Just a bad twist. Pain, but he could manage. As the crowd rallied for Mad Dog above, Bunyan laced his boot back up.

He was hopelessly behind. He had to go and go hard. *Discipline destroys misery.* Rotating back into position, Bunyan heaved himself into the next step, thrusting the cart upward once more.

Seventy-eight. Seventy-nine.

Faintly but surely, he could hear the crowd's chanting. They were chanting for . . . *him*.

"Bun-yan! Bun-yan! Bun-yan!"

He heard women's voices. The ladies of the Filter Brigade, perhaps. Lucette, probably, had whipped them into a cheer.

By now Mad Dog had no doubt loaded the oven; he might even be at the gear.

Hundred fifteen, hundred sixteen—just get out of the tunnel.

Hundred thirty-four, hundred thirty-five—grind for the Pure.

One forty-eight, one forty-nine—bleed for the Pure.

One fifty—go!

The moment his cart edged onto the floor, the crowd rallied. Above him the ceiling soared over the row of gigantic vats, side by side like great ships in a harbor. Each had been fitted with an oven, a platform, and the gear to power the crusher. The gear alone was two stories high.

Foot blasting with pain, Bunyan limped to his oven and began to shovel it full of coal. After fifteen loads, the fire was so hot it scalded his skin. When he hit thirty, he dumped his cart on the belt, and for the first time he saw his haul. More Lump than he'd expected. *Lucky.* He could make plenty of Pure from that. With his load on the belt, he staggered up to the platform and the mighty gear.

As he did, Bunyan saw, out of the corner of his eye, the white dress in the front row.

Lucette.

It *was* her chanting, and there she was, chanting still, passion in her face. *Belief* in her face. "Bunyan! Bunyan!"

Fifteen minutes and we're outta here.

Bunyan glanced to his left: Mad Dog's gear was spinning quick, his crusher rumbling and the blades whipping deep in the vat. Overhead, his cylinder was nearly half full with the superheated Lump, the silverdark Pure.

Not out of it yet, thought Bunyan, taking the crank in hand.

Bunyan growled as he leaned in and pulled back, flexing his gear into motion. With his Junk Foot stable, Bunyan lowered the hammer and felt the crusher pummel the raw deep in the vat.

"Pump that Lump! Pump that Lump!"

Crank, lean, pull, back. Crank, lean, pull, back.

At a dozen turns, the gear was whipping and Bunyan's body rocked with it. Round and round it went in the circular rhythm. Like an oarsman in a crew, Bunyan strained each last muscle, deep in harmony with the machine that surrounded him.

Faster now.

With one hand, Bunyan dropped the hammer further and felt the sputter of hot raw pelting the vat walls.

Crank, lean, pull, back.

Bunyan was only faintly aware of the crowd stomping and clapping, lost as he was in his work, knowing his machine intimately, fully extending on the push out, then pulling back just as the iron crank swept up with terrifying force.

Suddenly, the crowd erupted. Bunyan glanced up. The first drops of Pure had hit the bottom of his cylinder.

"Drop! It! Drop! It!" the crowd chanted.

The hammer controlled the height of the crusher. The lower it went, the harder the grind. The risk in dropping it too soon was that the chunks of raw would still be too big and could cause a jam, making the gear stop cold, rocking the platform and even hurling Bunyan into the axles below.

Bunyan glanced left. Mad Dog's own hammer was still only halfway down. *What?* Bunyan couldn't believe it. He'd been at the gear a full five minutes and hadn't dropped the hammer all the way?

Mad Dog's playing it safe.

Bunyan looked up at the cylinders. Mad Dog was at three-quarters, Bunyan just one-third, but rising fast.

The whistle blew.

One minute left.

"Ham-mer! Ham-mer!"

No choice now.

With one hand on the fast-whipping crank, Bunyan reached for the hammer and yanked it down, from PEBBLE all the way to POWDER.

His crusher hit the pan and smashed the raw just as Bunyan threw his body weight against the gear and absorbed the jerk. The slam of the crusher nearly threw Bunyan off his feet, but when the crank came round again, he flexed his arms, leaned his body forward, and—

The gear still spun.

The crowd roared as Bunyan sucked in the sweet-sour Lump fumes and felt the blades whipping hard just behind the vat wall—*whoomp whoomp whoomp*—pulverizing the raw as the Pure gushed forth.

Forty seconds.

Whoomp whoomp whoomp

With every rotation of the gear, Bunyan gained on Mad Dog. Lost in the ecstasy of competition, he lifted his eyes to see the Pure pouring fast as water from a faucet. Mad Dog at last dropped the hammer, but Bunyan knew it was too late.

Twenty seconds.

Whoomp whoomp whoomp whoomp

"Pump! That! Lump!"

Bunyan's body seemed to sing as he rocked to the beat of the rotation, his muscles having internalized this rhythm long ago. *Crank, lean, pull, back! Crank, lean, pull, back!* At this speed, if the crank struck him it would tear his head clean off, yet he let it pass just a finger's width from his beard.

"Bun-yan! Bun-yan!"

Whoomp whoomp whoomp

Bunyan tasted drops of sweat pouring into his mouth as the hot Lump melted just on the other side of the wall . . .

Crank! Lean! Pull! Back!

Whoomp whoomp whoomp

Come on . . . Bunyan spoke in his heart to his machine, like he could coax the Pure right out of the vat. *Come on* . . .

"Bun-yan!"

Whoomp

This was for his mother.

Whoomp

This was for Lucette.

Whoomp

And if the crusher jammed, no better way to die than this, rising where they said he'd fall, racing where they'd called him trapped, the cracker who came from nothing but made good. Bunyan's body was floating up, hardly even his, the perfect harmony of muscle, machine, and spirit, as if he were no longer a man but an anthem, a mist of light now rising high—

Everything you've got.

Whoomp

Everything you've got!

"Ohhh!"

As the whistle blew, the crowd erupted with a mix of cheers, boos, groans, and shouts. Amid the bedlam, Bunyan pressed the brake with his foot and the gear screeched and he raised the hammer to release the tension on the crusher.

Bunyan bent over, hands on his knees, catching his breath, his arms trembling, his thighs like jelly, pouring sweat onto the platform below. At last, he raised his eyes to the cylinders.

Mad Dog's cylinder was at nine-tenths.

Bunyan's was full to the top.

A moment later, he felt arms around his neck. "You did it!"

Lucette had raced up on the platform and leapt on him, sweaty and filthy as he was. The joy streamed from her eyes.

"I always knew!" she said. "I always knew!"

Arms around his neck, Lucette dug her fingers into his sweaty hair, pressing her body against him.

Still panting for breath, Bunyan looked up again at the two cylinders, just to make sure.

Yes. The result stood. He'd won it all.

She kissed him on the lips.

"We're outta here," she said, smiling, radiant, beautiful.

The gold bar. The house. His mother. Lucette. "Yeah," said Bunyan. "We're gone."

"Ladies and gentlemen!" announced Dedrick, the Factory manager, from the bridge over the vats. "We have a new Lump Master!"

CHAPTER 4

THE LUMP MASTER

Bunyan sat on a bench outside Dedrick's office. Beside him lay a copy of the House Book.

"The Future Is in Your Hands!" read the words on the cover, repeating the Factory slogan.

When an employee completed ten years in Lump Town, the deal was they got two things: a gold bar—also known as "the Lump Sum"—and a new house. The House Book had grainy photos and descriptions of all the homes from which employees could one day choose.

There was the Riverside Bungalow (page 4), the Mountainview Ranch (page 11), the City Walk Apartment (page 25). Everyone in Lump Town had their favorite, and many even had ranked them, front to back. No one in Lump Town was living their "real" life yet; that would begin later, far from Lump Town, in one of these pleasant abodes.

Bunyan and Lucette had theirs picked out, too. It was on page 17: the Country Farmhouse. Bunyan had looked at the photos of the Country Farmhouse probably a thousand times. The curving driveway up to the front steps. The painted shutters on the windows. The smoke curling from the chimney. The wraparound porch with rocking chairs. The fields rolling out to the horizon. "Your tranquil home in the heartland!" said the copy.

And now, amazingly, it would actually be his. Perhaps even within a week's time, he would be sitting on those rocking chairs, his mother and his wife alongside him. The only thing left was the paperwork.

From inside the office, the voices of Dedrick and Mad Dog spiked in anger and Bunyan overheard Dedrick snap, "When I need your advice I'll ask for it."

Maybe Mad Dog couldn't quite stomach the loss.

After a final glance at the Country Farmhouse, Bunyan closed the House Book and raised his eyes to see a familiar face hanging on the wall: El Boffo.

Railroad baron, Factory owner, and bestselling author, El Boffo had a full head of white hair and small, hard eyes. Yet the most striking feature of the portrait was his mouth: a bushy white mustache ran above a smile so big it showed his top *and* bottom teeth. El Boffo's smile appeared so aggressive, it looked like it might colonize the rest of his face.

Below his picture was printed a saying from his book, *Awaken the Capitalist Within.*

#124: IF YOU AREN'T MOTIVATED BY A DEEP DREAM, ONE DAY YOU WILL FIND YOURSELF UP AGAINST SOMEONE WHO IS. THAT PERSON WILL DEFEAT YOU.
—*EL BOFFO*

Upon being hired, all Lump Town employees received a copy of *Awaken the Capitalist Within.* Throughout the Factory, in bathrooms, at workstations, and in hallways, various quotes from *Awaken* ran under the same photo.

#9: OPTIMISM ISN'T JUST AN ATTITUDE TOWARD REALITY, IT IS ITS CREATOR.

#25: IF YOU KEEP YOUR EYE ON THE MONEY INSTEAD OF YOUR DREAM, YOU'LL END UP LOSING BOTH.

#28: AN IDEA NOT PUT PRACTICALLY TO USE DOES NOT YET TRULY EXIST.

#89: YOU HAVE A CHOICE: MAKE WEALTH OR TROUBLE. CHOOSE WEALTH!

#121: THE MAN WHO CANNOT BE STOPPED, EVEN BY RUIN, INSPIRES.

#160: SHOW ME A MAN'S HERO AND I'LL SHOW YOU HIS FUTURE.

#202: IF YOU REFUSE TO SHAPE YOUR OWN DESTINY, DON'T WORRY, SOMEONE ELSE WILL.

#233: FEW HAVE THE RIGOR TO WALK THE STRAIGHT PATH THROUGH LIFE'S DIVERSIONS. THOSE WHO DO FIND PROFIT.

Sitting on the bench, Bunyan studied the photo of El Boffo. Despite the smile, Bunyan detected a certain energy behind his eyes, that of the primitive beast on the savannah, squaring off for the only negotiation that mattered: *Who's gonna survive—me, or you?*

Mad Dog stepped out of Dedrick's office and stood over Bunyan. "Dedrick will see you now."

Bunyan rose to go in, but Mad Dog blocked his way. Solid as a chest of iron drawers, the gigantic three-time Lump Master stood with his arms crossed and a gun on his hip. Bunyan was himself a large man, but he only came up to Mad Dog's neck.

"Got your house all picked out?" said Mad Dog with a smirk.

Bunyan only then realized he was still holding the House Book. "Yeah," he said. "Just like everybody else."

"Not me. The only place I want is right there." Mad Dog nodded toward Dedrick's office. "One day, Lump Town's gonna be the richest city in America. And Dedrick will be long gone."

"You enjoy your house," said Bunyan, pitching the House Book back onto the bench, "I'll enjoy mine."

Bunyan again moved to go in, but Mad Dog stepped in front of him so Bunyan was face-to-face with a few of the scars he'd gotten from his old, sick dog.

"You know what I laugh about sometimes?"

"What's that?"

"The two of you. You, walking around the streets. Thinking. Staring into space. Reading your books. Her, with that Quilt of hers. 'The Voice.' You two really do deserve each other. See, Lucette had a chance to marry the future Lord of Lump Town. I tried to warn her."

"Warn her about what, exactly?"

"Smart women choose takers, not dreamers."

At that, Bunyan grabbed Mad Dog by the shirt and shoved him against the wall—he'd never been in a fistfight before, but maybe today was the day. Mahoney pushed him right back across the corridor, slamming him against the other wall. Each man had a hand on the other's neck when Dedrick called out from his office.

"Bunyan? Come in here, please."

The two let go.

"Just stay out of my way," said Mad Dog.

"I'll send you a letter from my new house."

Mad Dog began to laugh. "Your new house!" He laughed harder as he walked down the hall. "Keep dreaming."

Bunyan opened the door and walked in. Dedrick's office was neat. Spare. On one wall were several awards, each one citing the Lump Town Factory as the "Safest Factory in America." Directly behind the desk was yet another photo of El Boffo with a caption below it:

#I: AMERICA IS FOR THE TAKERS. TAKE IT WHILE YOU CAN.
—*EL BOFFO*

Sitting behind his desk, Dedrick was, as always, immaculately dressed. His every detail radiated precision: His shoes, polished. His white shirt, pressed. His jacket, sleek. His jaw, clenched.

Dedrick was a remarkable figure in Lump Town. For one, he was one of the few Black men there. Certainly, he was the only Black man to walk around the dusty streets in a three-piece suit. Beyond this, he had a striking life story. Abandoned as a child, Dedrick had grown up as a penniless shoe shiner on the South Side of the Windy City. One day, he happened to shine the shoes of El Boffo, who had spotted in Dedrick a rare, perfectionist grit. El Boffo hired Dedrick straightaway and over the years assigned him various jobs of increasing importance, eventually putting him in charge of all aspects of Lump processing. By now, Dedrick's grip on the administration of the Factory was such that just to see him walking down the street could make a man's spine straighten. His nickname was the Lord of Lump Town.

Presently, the Lord leaned back in his chair and offered Bunyan his habitual chilly smile.

"So. The new Lump Master. Happiest day of your life?"

"Still hard to believe."

"I've had my eye on you for some time, Bunyan. I think you've got it in you to become a real 'taker.' And in Lump Town, like all of America, takers win."

"Thank you" was all Bunyan could manage to answer. He knew he'd be leaving first thing tomorrow. To fill the silence that followed, he cleared his throat.

At that, Dedrick's expression changed. "Is that a cough I hear?"

"No. Just something caught in my throat."

Dedrick squinted ever so slightly at Bunyan, then the concern vanished and he resumed his icy smile. "How about that reward, then?"

"That would be terrific, sir."

Dedrick stood and walked to the wall. He spun a combination into a safe and took out a sack.

At first glance, this sack looked much smaller than what Bunyan expected. Beyond that, it didn't seem to hold a bar. It looked like it held coins. But no matter—as long as whatever was inside the sack had the *value* of one gold bar. Maybe it was diamonds . . .

"There you are," said Dedrick, laying the small sack on the edge of the desk.

Bunyan reached out and picked it up. Very light. He gently emptied the contents into his enormous hand to see . . .

Six silver pieces.

No. He counted again.

Five.

His stomach dropped.

"I should probably explain," said Dedrick, retaking his seat. "The thing is, this year, there's been some strain across the El Boffo Industries portfolio. Just a confluence of matters. Fluctuations in the railroad business. Interest payments. A bit of belt tightening all around."

Bunyan stared down at the coins. He didn't want to look up, knowing the mortification his face would show. At last, he said, "But . . . what about the gold bar?"

"Lump Town is just one of El Boffo's many investments. A high tide brings all ships up. A low tide brings them down. Just a low tide this year. That's all."

"But I earned that gold bar . . . It was part of the deal."

"Well, I think certainly by next year—"

Bunyan cut him off, emotion in his voice. "My mother is in debtors' prison. The gold bar would get her out. That's why I came to Lump Town in the first place."

At that, Dedrick's face tightened. "Given that your mother is in prison, that's all the more reason to stay and win again next year. It's very likely that by then the award will be back up to the full amount."

Bunyan pawed his beard with his hand. He felt sick. Like when the men in suits came to get his mother.

"And what about the house?" said Bunyan.

"Right." Dedrick pulled open a desk drawer and took out a large volume with a photo of a stately manor featured on the front. "What I'm about to show you is between me and you."

"I've seen the House Book."

Dedrick shook his head. "The House Book is for common workers. This is the *Mansion* Book." He pushed the volume across the desk. "Only for the eyes of Lump Masters."

Bunyan took the book in his sooty hands and flipped through the pages. The homes were breathtaking: The Petit Château. The Colonial Estate. The Avenue Town House. The Secluded Island. The Beachfront Villa.

"Stick with me and you'll have your pick," said Dedrick.

Bunyan couldn't concentrate. He didn't need any of these houses. What would he do with grand pianos? Sculptures? Private beaches?

Dedrick went on. "As Lump Master, feel free to come here and look through the Mansion Book any time you like. Mi casa es su casa, as they say."

Bunyan dropped the book back on the desk. "I don't need the house. I need my mother out of prison."

"Like I said, just a momentary softness in the numbers. But don't worry. This ship will right itself. When you pay into the system, the system pays into you. The gold is gonna come. For you. For me. For everyone."

"And what if it doesn't?"

Dedrick put the Mansion Book back in his desk drawer. His voice grew colder. "If the gold doesn't come, then I'm a bigger fool than anyone. All right?"

Bunyan felt his face getting hot. He felt the shame of having been duped. "There's rules ... you can't just change the rules."

Dedrick cleared his throat. "It's all in your contract. Page seven, I believe." He quoted from the contract without breaking eye contact. "'The Factory reserves the right at any time and for any reason to change the monetary award for the Lump Town Finals.' At any rate, tomorrow morning, I'd like you to join us on the Factory floor and lead us in the Lump Pledge. As the new Master, you'll have certain obligations. You'll be the face of the town, in case any lawmakers or journalists arrive and ask questions ..."

But as Dedrick went on speaking, Bunyan's mind spun down into a hole. *Of course it would be this way.* Folks like Bunyan fought with blood and sweat. Those above him fought with ink and paper. Ink and paper always won. All these years icing his foot. All these years risking his life. And for all that, nothing but five lonesome pieces of silver. The mountain of his mother's debt would remain.

A knock came on the door.

"Just a second," said Dedrick.

Mad Dog answered from the hallway. "It's a matter of urgent import."

At that phrase, Dedrick's posture changed—he seemed to sit up more straightly in his chair. "A matter of urgent import?"

"A matter of urgent import."

Bunyan could see thoughts moving behind Dedrick's eyes.

"I'm sorry," Dedrick said to Bunyan, "but we'll have to cut this meeting short."

Bunyan slid the five silver pieces back into the sack. Really, he hardly needed a sack at all. His pocket was big enough.

Dedrick stood and came around the desk. At the door he said to Bunyan, "We're not so different, you and I. I came from the bottom, just like you. I have my eye on the gold, just like you. The straight path pays. Just keep the faith." He winked. "The gold comes tomorrow."

As Bunyan walked out of the office, he brushed past Mad Dog in the hall. Standing with him was a man wearing a wide-brimmed rancher hat, dusty leather pants, and tall boots. The stranger cut an unlikely figure in Lump Town; he looked like he'd been swept in from the prairie on a horse.

As the pair walked in, Bunyan heard Dedrick say, "You'd better have something for me. In a few days, time will have run out . . ."

CHAPTER 5

THE ROOTED AXE

As Bunyan stepped out of the Factory into the late afternoon, the sour-sweet stench of Lump again filled his nose.

The gold comes tomorrow, Dedrick had said.

A man can die before tomorrow comes, Bunyan reflected.

Dreams never died in Lump Town, but they never seemed to get born either. In Lump Town, there were two kinds: leavers and lifers. The leavers sized the place up quick and fled. As for the lifers, none of them wanted to be here, but none of them knew how to go. The longer you hold on to the dream, the harder it gets to release. What starts as a reward ends up as a chain.

Standing below the Factory sign—THE FUTURE IS IN YOUR HANDS—Bunyan didn't know what to do, where to walk, what to say, who to see. Noise came from the center of town—a bit of evening carousing had begun, part of the Lump Town Finals festivities. Between the contest, the ceremony, and the long wait to meet Dedrick, most of the day was already gone. He headed the other way, mindlessly putting one foot in front of the other along the ashen, gridlike streets. He limped on his braceless Junk Foot, stiff and sore from the contest.

So what, then, stay another year? Get ripped off again? What would he write to his mother in prison? What would he tell Lucette?

The Factory reserves the right at any time and for any reason to change the monetary award for the Lump Town Finals.

America *was* for the takers. It was for people like Dedrick and El Boffo. People like the bankers who put his mother in prison. Maybe next year he'd get a sack of acorns.

As he turned the corner, Bunyan raised his eyes to see the central feature of Lump Town, Christ Trunk.

The story went that the first settlers had seen this gigantic tree from a hundred miles out, extending a thousand miraculous feet into the heavens. Amid a forest of giant spires, this one soared even above the rest, five horses in diameter, fifteen horses around at its base. In awe, they named it Christ Trunk and called the town itself Eden.

Bunyan had often wondered what a lush land this must have been, with creatures darting in the woods and the bright waters of Moses Creek bending like glass over the stones. On the opposite side of the creek would have lain a lazy meadow, with butterflies flitting among the bending green ferns.

By now, of course, there was no meadow, but rather the gigantic, muscular cliffs of the Factory and its trio of volcanic smokestacks. Christ Trunk's leaves had long since gone. Its bark was petrified and its upper reaches were engulfed in smog. Its hue was the hue of everything in Lump Town: silverdark.

Moses Creek, meanwhile, was choked with the Sludge. The Sludge was a sticky, glistening, silverdark goo, the runoff of Lump processing. The Sludge had one remarkable quality above all: it was indestructible. It didn't evaporate. It couldn't be reduced. Its creation was irreversible. Once made, Sludge was a permanent feature of the Earth. The only thing that could be done with the Sludge was to throw it away, and in Lump Town, that meant pouring it in Moses Creek. No one would dare step in those waters, much less drink them untreated.

Eden was gone.

Bunyan turned up a back street. On the edge of town, near the boundary of the silverdark woods, he passed an old church with broken stained-glass windows, a relic of bygone times. Scrawled on the side of the church was an old limerick:

One day Good Sam met a Chilali,
He left his home to chase his folly.
On bent roads he wandered,
His fortune all squandered,
He died lost in deep melancholy.

Around the edges of the words Bunyan saw the faint wink of the Gleam.

The Gleam. As if Bunyan needed further proof today that he was a freak, a fool, a failure. He was a beat-down man in a hard, hard world, and at this moment of all moments, he truly had no time for nonsense. If he was ever going to spring free from the trap of Lump Town, he'd have to stamp the Gleam from his soul entirely. Be rational. Be clear. Walk straight. Learn to take. Learn to milk. Milk the world like a good American. Milk it for all it's worth.

Back at home Lucette would be packed and ready to go. She'd already be living in the future—a future that would never come.

Let her stay in that happy place a bit longer, he thought. Bunyan walked further into the woods. The ancient, majestic trunks soared around him. The forest floor was covered in a snow of ash.

In time, he arrived at a boulder, where he beheld a sight that never failed to astonish him: the Rooted Axe. Ages ago, this great, mysterious tool had somehow been wedged into the side of the rock, its handle extending horizontally over the ground. Its dimensions were enormous, beyond human scale: the shaft ten paces long, its head alone as large as a wheelbarrow. The grip hovered at Bunyan's chest level, suggesting that once—inexplicably, miraculously—someone about Bunyan's height had driven the giant thing into the stone.

Bunyan laid his hands on the handle to attempt again what he had attempted so many times before. With all his might, he pulled, then pushed, then pulled again, his whole body's weight behind it. He yanked and tugged and leaned, pressing his foot against the rock, anything to dislodge it even a centimeter.

The Rooted Axe didn't budge.

As he stood back from it, Bunyan saw a flash of light upon the head. The Gleam again. He sighed. He'd seen the Gleam more today than he had in years. He didn't know what it meant.

Something caught his eye overhead. A single bird broke through the dense haze of smog. Seeing the lifeless woods below, the bird turned up and flew into the sky above once more.

Bunyan thought of Lucette's Dream Quilt. *One bird carrying another across the endless seas.*

The meaning of the Quilt was another mystery. Perhaps the bird on the bottom was his dear mother, left to perish in prison. But who would carry her?

Tears welled in Bunyan's eyes. Deep in his being he felt a despair that had no answer. Lump Town was a trap. The world was a trap. His life was a trap. His soul was a trap.

I would do anything, believe anything, become anyone, if only I could find a way out, he thought.

Bunyan heard a distant clap of thunder. Evening was falling. Time to get home.

But just as Bunyan turned back toward town, he stopped short.

Above him, standing upon the head of the Rooted Axe, staring directly down at him, was . . .

Great God.

Instinctively, Bunyan knelt. He lowered his eyes to the forest floor. He'd only glimpsed them for a moment, but that was enough.

The jaguar legs. The giant wings. *How could it be?*

Kneeling, Bunyan pressed one hand to the earth, as if to make certain he was still securely in the world and not in some fantasy. Then, ever so slowly, he raised his eyes.

The Rooted Axe was vacant.

Bunyan's blood beat wildly in his neck. His back was drenched in hot sweat. The woods around him were silent. They seemed empty. Perhaps he'd only imagined the being.

Cautiously, he stood. He looked left, then right. Then he caught himself.

Yes, the Chilali was there. He could *feel* their presence.

"Are you lost?"

The Chilali's voice came from just behind Bunyan. It was calm yet ironic. Powerful yet charming.

For a moment, Bunyan couldn't find his own voice. At last, he managed to whisper, "Who are you?"

"*Hmmmmmm.*"

The sound was like a deep vibration. It felt like acknowledgment. An understanding of sorts. Yet also, a gentle prodding.

Then the Chilali said, "My question is, who are you?"

Out of the corner of his eye, there on the sooty forest floor, Bunyan spotted a jaguar foot. Moments later, he heard a flutter of wings. The foot vanished.

"What is it you want?" asked Bunyan.

"*Hmmmmm*," repeated the Chilali. "What is it that *you* want?"

Another question to answer Bunyan's question. *Strange!*

"You're . . . a Chilali," he said quietly. "Isn't that so?"

Bunyan heard the snap of sticks on the forest floor. The Chilali spoke from behind him. "Have you looked about yourself, to see who I am?"

Looked about himself? Bunyan searched the floor of the woods. He saw some old, silverdark pine cones. Some twigs. An ashy branch. Then . . . oddly, he saw a peculiar arrangement of sticks. Bunyan tilted his head, studying them. Astonishingly, the debris on the forest floor seemed to form . . . letters. He sounded them out.

"M . . . O . . . K . . . I. Moki? Is that your name?" Bunyan pronounced it to rhyme with *smoky.*

"*Hmmmmmmmm.*"

Again, that sound! Bunyan couldn't tell if it meant yes, no, or maybe.

This has got to be a prank. Bunyan closed his eyes and steeled himself. No need to be afraid. This was all fake. Probably Mad Dog Mahoney's work.

Quickly, he whipped around to where he thought the Chilali was perched. "Aha!"

But the forest was empty.

"I get the joke!" Bunyan yelled, looking behind the trunk of another tree. "Very funny!"

Yet no sooner had those words escaped his lips than Bunyan saw once again, just at the limit of his vision, two jaguar legs hanging down from a branch above.

Again, instinctively, he averted his eyes. Bunyan thought back to the stories his mother had told him in his youth.

The Chilali loves someone at a crossroads.

"Am I at a crossroads? Is that why you have come?"

Moki answered with another question. "Have you ever wondered why it is you see the Gleam?"

Not a single person on earth, other than Lucette, knew about the Gleam. That was *his* word for it.

"I don't think it means anything. It comes when I'm afraid."

"Does it come when you are afraid? Or are you afraid when it comes?"

Can't Moki just answer with a simple sentence? "The Gleam is proof my mind's not right. There's something wrong with me."

Bunyan sensed the being just behind him, by his right shoulder, equal to him in height. Enormous. Graceful.

"Is the Gleam proof there is something wrong with you?" asked Moki, this time very close to Bunyan's ear. "Or is it proof there is something right with you?"

When Bunyan didn't answer, Moki went on, "Have you ever wondered what would happen if you followed it?"

"*Followed* it? What do you mean, followed it? It's just . . ." Bunyan waved his hand before himself. "Craziness. It's . . . nothing."

"Do you see the Gleam now?"

Bunyan got tense just *thinking* about the Gleam appearing. His first recollection, any time he saw it, was his father's shout for help. The thundering hooves. The mangled body. The mud.

He sighed. "No, I don't see it."

"Are you looking with the eye of your belly?"

"The eye of my belly? What does that mean?" Again, Bunyan looked around. Again, nothing. "I don't see it. I don't want to see it."

A branch snapped behind him. "Will you try looking now, this time with the very anchor of your being?"

Bunyan closed his eyes and took a deep breath. He did his best to follow this strange advice, locating his being's so-called anchor. At last, he opened his eyes.

Nothing.

"Sorry. I can't see it."

"Will you try once more, looking from the endless place, the timeless place, the fearless place, the place that does not move, below the belly and before the spine, from the very eye of your soul?"

Bunyan closed his eyes and tried again.

And to his shock, when he looked, this time, he saw it. Just a few spots at first, but soon they grew in number, like small dollops of pearly, molten light. The path of the Gleam led straight to the trunk of an enormous nearby tree.

"The Gleam has never come when I asked for it," said Bunyan.

"And *have* you ever asked for it?"

Bunyan rubbed his eyes. When he opened them again, the Gleam was still there, pulsing on the ground, stronger than before, like gobs of a metallic rainbow, swirling with inner life.

"Do you remember the stories you heard, long ago, about the Twisty Path?" said Moki.

"Of course," said Bunyan. "It leads to the Beautiful Destiny."

"Could it be the Gleam has been trying to show the way to the Beautiful Destiny all along?"

"I don't know . . . I've been seeing it a lot today."

"Could it be you have come to the moment when you can delay no more?"

The Gleam grew brighter still, leading up the trunk into the yellowish smog above. The sheer vertical face of the tree was dizzying.

"So, I'm supposed to climb that? I haven't climbed a tree since I was a child."

"*Hmmmmmm.*"

"It's just . . . following the Gleam . . . I've always thought it was a curse. A kind of illness."

"And what if the Gleam was not a curse, nor an illness, but instead, your one true gift?"

The Gleam seemed to beckon specifically to one particular ridge of bark. Bunyan walked to it and put his hand upon it. Another ridge glowed brighter, just above.

"It's becoming brighter, the more I follow it."

"*Hmmmmmm.*"

Just then, the air seemed to chill. Night would soon fall. Until now, this magical being had seemed wise, charming, sly. But suddenly Moki seemed . . . *menacing.*

Bunyan pulled his hand off the tree. "I can't climb that. It's too high. I'm not strong enough."

The answer came from over his left shoulder, cool and ironic. "How can you say how strong you are, when all your life you have ignored your greatest power?"

Bunyan felt afraid. "Sorry, I've got to get back. It's just . . . Lump Town isn't a place for the Twisty Path. It's a place for . . . takers."

"In the end, is it better to take from the world or to give yourself to the Twisty Path?"

Bunyan struggled to find a response. A phrase of El Boffo's came to mind. He repeated it aloud. "'Few have the rigor to walk the straight path through life's diversions. Those who do find profit.'"

Somewhere in the branches above, Moki answered, "And what happens when the straight path fails?"

Another clap of thunder. The Gleam vanished.

"Moki? Moki?"

The Chilali was gone.

CHAPTER 6

THE STORM

Bunyan looked about on the forest floor for the place where the word *Moki* had been spelled. He couldn't find it. His whole body gave a shiver, as if he were trying to throw a snake off his back.

It's all crazy, he thought. *You just need a good night's sleep.*

Leaving the Rooted Axe behind, Bunyan walked out of the woods to the hillside that overlooked Lump Town, where the gas lamps glowed orange in the dim grid of streets.

Rain began to fall. Before Bunyan had even taken a few steps onto the road, the skies opened and the waters poured down.

Bunyan sprinted past the abandoned church, down onto Main Street, past those who were still gathered outside the Factory, then on past Christ Trunk and Moses Creek, splashing through the leaden slop all the way back to his doorstep, where he leapt over a final puddle, ducked through the doorway, and . . .

All was quiet. All was calm.

Only the deep muffled patter of the rain on the roof could be heard. A low fire burned in the stove. A lamp flickered on the kitchen table.

Bunyan went to the wall and turned the filter crank a few times to suck out the evening ash. On the table by the lamp, he noticed a folded note. He opened it and read:

Congratulations, Paul!!!!!
So now the whole world knows (at last) what you always have been,
Today a thousand eyes have seen what I always have seen.
What I knew in an instant, each last one has finally learned:
That you're a champ. Now have some pie. I hope it's not too burned.

And no matter what, remember this:
A BUNNY LOVES LETTUCE

Bunyan smiled. This was their old riddle game, one they'd played from the very start of their courtship, always trying to stump each other.

Taking a bite of pie, Bunyan sat down with the pencil and on the back of the page tried to crack it by rearranging the letters.

A Bunny Loves Lettuce . . .

Lusty, Unbeaten . . .

Beauty Love Tunnels . . .

A Cutesy Novel . . .

None of those were right. He thought a moment more, then—

Ah! He solved it. He wrote down the answer.

Bunyan polished off the piece of pie in a few quick bites, then climbed the stairs. As he did, his mind cleared.

All told, no matter what, they still had each other. They'd think it through, side by side, come up with a new plan. *If I have you, I have the world.*

Upstairs, he stepped into their bedroom.

"Behold, your new Lump Master," he announced.

But the room was empty. The sheets were neat—Lucette had not slept in them yet. He went to the laundry room.

Ah! There he saw her, sitting at her chair, the Dream Quilt in her lap. Bunyan crept up behind her and embraced her, putting his cheek next to hers.

"A Bunny Loves Lettuce . . . ," he said. "I think there's two answers! Of course, on the one hand, it's 'Lucette Loves Bunyan.' But you could do it the other way around, too, 'Bunyan Loves Luce—'"

But he stopped short.

His wife . . . something was wrong. She hadn't budged. She hadn't looked. He went round her to see—

Her eyes were wide open—alarmed. As Bunyan watched help- lessly, she tried to speak.

"*Prr . . . Paulrrggghh . . . Prrrr!*"

Her veins—the roots of her hair—her cheeks—*Oh God!*—they were turning silverdark!

"Oh no, no, no, no—"

Lucette gagged. Froth formed on the side of her mouth. Bunyan quickly scooped her up and carried her to the bedroom. She strained and spit the whole way.

"Don't choke!" He feared he was harming her. "Breathe easy!"

Setting her down on the bed, Bunyan wiped her mouth, then arranged her limp arms and legs. He tucked a pillow beneath her head, his panic rising, but even as he did her eyes rolled back—

"Lucette! No! Stay with me!"

Fluid struggled up and down her throat, her belly rising and fall- ing with spasms, her eyes searching frantically, as if seeking within for the cause of her pain. *Oh, the terror in her eyes!*

"My hands are so cold . . . ," she whispered. "My skin . . . I can't feel it!"

Even as Bunyan tried to warm her fingers, he saw the silverdark aggressively filling them, like a dye advancing through a glass of water. What was happening?

"I have to get the doctor." He kissed her on her cold forehead. "Two minutes!" In a blind panic, Bunyan was already bounding down the stairs, shouting back over his shoulder. "Just hang on!"

He blasted through his door into the rain and sprinted down the darkened street as thunder clapped overhead, racing through puddles in a blur, down Main Street and up a block till he pounded on the door of Dr. Niebuhr's house.

"Open up!"

Even in those few seconds that the doctor didn't come, Bun- yan felt like his mind was coming apart. He pounded again. "*DOCTOR!*"

At last the door opened as the old doctor fit his glasses on his nose. "What is it?"

"My wife—her skin is turning silverdark!"

The doctor's eyes widened. "How long has it been?"

"Just now. It just started now."

"Have you moved her?"

"Moved her?"

"Whatever you do, don't move her! I'll get my things."

Bunyan was off running again, hurling himself toward home, imagining Lucette closing her eyes once and for all, never to open them—*Faster!*

At home Bunyan banged through the door and ran upstairs and with a few leaps—three steps at a time—he was in his room.

"Luce!"

Her eyes were still open, though her skin had now darkened almost completely. Bunyan's body felt light with terror. His wife looked like an iron statue! Drops of rain fell from his hair as he stroked his young wife's frigid, silverdark cheek. All had grown strange, all but her eyes.

Those eyes now found her husband's as tears released over her temples. "My hands," she whispered, "they're all gray!"

"Oh, darling!" His voice broke. "The doctor is coming. Let me get you blankets."

Bunyan rushed to get the blankets from the next room, grabbing everything he saw. He came back and laid them on her, with the Dream Quilt on top.

He heard Dr. Niebuhr enter, downstairs. "Hello?"

"Up here!"

The doctor rushed up.

"Her skin!" said Bunyan. "Look!"

Gingerly, Niebuhr sat on the bed. He was a slight, bald man who always looked anxious, as if he were certain that one day a brick was going to fall on his head and kill him, though he couldn't tell just when. In the disaster that lay before him now, it looked as though his perpetual dread was well founded.

"Has she been coughing today?"

"Yes, this morning."

He fit a stethoscope in his ears and placed the bell on her heart. "Did she show little bruises?"

"Bruises?"

"Markings on her arms. Her body. Anywhere."

Bunyan racked his brain. He remembered seeing the ash-colored stain on her finger this morning. "Yes, I think so. What is this? What is happening?"

Pulling back the blankets, the doctor felt her hands and touched her forehead with his fingertips.

Bunyan went round to the other side. He stroked her cheek. By now, only her hair remained brown. His wife! Silverdark!

Moving nothing but her eyes, Lucette searched the doctor's face for an answer.

"Don't be afraid," Bunyan said, carefully holding one of her hands in both of his own, trying to warm it.

At last, Niebuhr stood and rubbed his glasses, still fogged from the rain. He pulled the blankets once more over her body.

"So . . ." The doctor seemed to struggle to find the right words. "None of what I am about to say can be repeated."

"Talk straight to me! Can you cure her?"

He cleared his throat. "From now on, we cannot move her. If she shifts even an inch, she'll gag. Soon, she will pass into a coma."

"A coma?"

Dr. Niebuhr mastered his voice. "She is on the verge. These next few minutes are all we may have left."

Another inky wave of silverdark had suddenly, aggressively, crawled up Lucette's neck, staining it deeper than before.

"The verge of what?" said Bunyan. "Look at her skin!"

Lucette let out a cry.

"Try to remain calm. Speak to her. Say what's in your heart."

"You do something! You stop this from happening!"

"It cannot be stopped. Please, speak. While there's time."

Perplexed, enraged, defiant, horrified, Bunyan sat beside his beloved wife. Gently, he kissed her forehead, then her icy, grayish lips.

"Darling!"

Lucette looked up at her husband wildly, as if her soul were trying to break free from the prison her body had become. "I am so afraid . . ."

He nodded, stroking her cheek, her hair. "Just hold on. I am here. I am right here."

She grimaced, as if at some sharp pain deep within her. More tears rolled down her cheek. "I am not finished. I haven't even begun."

"We are not finished." Bunyan's voice broke. He stroked her cheek with his knuckle. "*We* have only just begun."

Her eyes searched about. "The Quilt . . ."

"It's here."

"The Voice . . ."

"Yes?"

Lucette's eyes closed, and Bunyan feared she was gone. Gently, ever so gently, Bunyan slid his arm beneath her neck.

Lucette opened her eyes again, but this time, sleepily. Unfocused. Her brow stitched up between her eyes, as if she were bewildered by something. "So warm . . ."

Eye to eye, nose to nose, they gazed at each other. Bunyan felt his love pouring out—as if that love alone might have the power to push out the invading silverdark.

Then her eyes closed.

"Darling?" he whispered. "Lucette?"

Bunyan's heart sank.

"Have mercy," said the doctor.

Lucette's chest rose and fell with her breath, but her eyes remained closed.

"No!" Bunyan gazed incredulously down upon his wife. "No!" he shouted, as if forbidding what had already occurred. "I was just talking to her!"

Unable to bear the sight of his silverdark wife, Bunyan bent down and embraced her again, delicately stroking her hair over and over and muttering, "No, no, no, no," as he gently kissed her by her ear, "No, no, no," as the doctor buried his face in his hands, "No, no," as Bunyan kissed her cooling skin, "No," as the rain overwhelmed the gutters below and broke into the streets. "No."

CHAPTER 7

A VISITOR
IN THE NIGHT

Even then, as Bunyan embraced his wife's frigid, silverdark frame, there came a violent knock upon the door.

Bunyan and the doctor froze to listen. The pounding came again. Louder still.

"Let me get it," said Niebuhr.

The doctor went down. From the floor below, Bunyan heard a low, tense conversation. Moments later, Niebuhr returned.

"It's Dedrick."

"What's he doing here?"

"It's his job to know things."

Bunyan grabbed the slim doctor by the shoulders. "You tell me what is going on here!"

Niebuhr's anxious eyes looked as if they masked four or five different thoughts. His answer was succinct. "You'd better speak to him. I will watch over her."

Confused, Bunyan descended. There, in a trench coat with a black briefcase in one hand, stood the Lord of Lump Town. But he wasn't alone. Beside him was the towering figure of Mad Dog Mahoney.

"Good evening, Lump Master. I am sorry to have to make this visit. I understand there is an illness in the house."

Bunyan almost flew out of his skin. "That's right, there is! My wife's skin turned silverdark, and she won't wake up!"

"We should sit," said Dedrick, stone-faced as ever.

Bunyan didn't sit. "We need a cure! What's the cure?"

With a handkerchief, Dedrick blotted his forehead, wet from the rain. He remained controlled and gestured toward the table. "Please."

Bunyan did sit, but only on the edge of the chair. As he did, to his own surprise, he felt rational, in full command of his mind. Ignoring Mad Dog, he focused on Dedrick. "She's not the first to fall ill, is she?" He rapped the table with his knuckles, hard. *Thump, thump, thump!* "And it's the Lump that's causing it, right? That's why there's no animals here."

Dedrick took off his coat, hung it on a hook by the door, then sat. "Rest assured, the health of our employees is of utmost importance. At this moment, we don't know what causes this condition. We are studying the matter closely."

"I don't need you to study it, I need you to save her! What's your plan for that?"

Dedrick remained unrattled. "I'll tell you what I know. And for now, it must remain between us."

"Between us?"

"Will you keep this between us?"

"Speak!"

As Mad Dog hovered by the door, Dedrick explained. "It is a rare condition called the Stucks. In the few cases we have seen, the patient falls into a coma. During that time, we can maintain the patient with broth. Dr. Niebuhr will help with that."

"The *cure*," said Bunyan. "What is the *cure*?"

Dedrick proceeded carefully. "I can promise you, you're in good hands with Niebuhr."

"We need to take her to the Windy City. We'll put her on the morning train."

"I'm afraid she must stay just where she is. Moving her at all could cause irreparable harm. Given the gravity of the situation, you will need to quarantine, here in the house with her. She cannot have visitors. I will handle all necessary communications with the Factory and the Filter Brigade."

"So, I'm supposed to sit here and do nothing?"

"We don't want to cause unnecessary panic."

"*Unnecessary?*"

At that, Dedrick set the briefcase on the table and snapped open the shining brass buckles. Out of it, he took what looked like a large brick, enclosed in a velvet sack. He loosened the strings upon the bag and pulled from it a sight Bunyan could hardly believe:

A gleaming bar of gold.

Only in his dreams had Bunyan seen so much wealth.

From the briefcase, Dedrick then pulled two sheets of paper. "To get the gold bar, all you have to do is sign here. One copy for me. One for you."

More ink and paper.

Before Bunyan could respond, Niebuhr came downstairs. "I'm going to get a few things for the patient. I will be back shortly."

"Thank you, Doctor," said Dedrick.

"Her condition is stable. Better than the others."

At that, Dedrick gave the doctor a sharp look. Niebuhr's lips parted, as if he knew he'd just said something in error, but he shuttled out the door without a word.

Bunyan scanned the document, hardly understanding what he read. "So . . . you're paying me because my wife is sick?"

"Much of this was spelled out in general terms in your original contract. 'If workers are injured, they shall be fairly compensated by the management.' This gold bar is your family's compensation. El Boffo cares deeply for the inhabitants of Lump Town."

For Bunyan, it didn't add up. Men were constantly being injured in the Factory, then told to get to work the next day or risk being fired and denied the Lump Sum. Why such generosity now?

Dedrick loudly cleared his throat into his fist and turned to Mad Dog. "May I have a glass of water?"

Mad Dog huffed but shuffled to the sink.

Bunyan stared down at the terms written into the contract.

. . . must remain in his home for the course of a month . . . must remain in Lump Town for one year from the date of the onset . . . must not ever speak of the nature of the condition, for risk of asset seizure and clawback . . .

Bunyan wondered, *If the disease is so rare, how did Dedrick have such a document ready so quickly?*

"What is this . . . asset seizure? Clawback?"

Mad Dog put a mug of water before Dedrick. It had a floral print and happened to be Lucette's favorite.

Dedrick drank. "In essence, what the document is saying is: Don't talk about this illness. Stay here one more year. Then the gold bar and the house are yours."

"Don't talk about it ever?"

"You want your mother out of prison. If you sign this, she will be out in one year's time. Guaranteed. You won't even have to compete in next year's Finals."

Bunyan stood and paced. "You didn't have that gold for me earlier. But you have it now?"

"There are funds for absolute emergencies. There is a system, Paul. You'll have to trust this system."

"It's the system that made her like *that*!" Bunyan pointed toward where Lucette lay upstairs. "*Lump* made her like that!" Bunyan pawed at his beard, his mind racing. "I've got to get out of here. I've got to get her help."

"That may be your instinct at first," said Dedrick calmly. "But if you leave Lump Town, all the work you've done, all you've earned, will have been for nothing."

"What about the six years I've already put in toward the Lump Sum?"

"You must stay, or everything goes to zero."

Mad Dog was wandering around by the stove, poking at Bunyan's things.

"Hey. Can you get this man out of my sight?"

Dedrick turned in his seat. "Mad Dog, could you give us a moment?"

Mad Dog stared at Bunyan with a sneer, as if to say, *Only because he ordered me to.* He stepped out.

Alone with Bunyan, Dedrick took out his handkerchief and blotted his forehead once more. He seemed to soften, offering a faint smile of empathy. "There are times this place feels like hell. I know it, Paul, more than you can imagine. The long climb to get the gold, well, sometimes it hardly seems worth it. But know this: if you go outside the system, I can't help you anymore."

Dedrick reached over and gave Bunyan a squeeze on the hand. Then he returned the gold bar to its velvet sack and tucked it away in the briefcase. He stood, put his handkerchief away, and put on his coat. He left one copy of the agreement on the table.

"I'm going to leave Mad Dog here tonight, just to keep an eye on things. When I come back in the morning, I hope to have a signed agreement." Dedrick gave Bunyan a pat on the shoulder. "There's nothing more you can do. If you stay put, I can be your ally. Don't throw your six years away. Think of your mother in that prison cell."

Dedrick stepped out into the rain. Moments later, Mad Dog came back in.

"I don't need you in this house," said Bunyan.

Mad Dog sauntered over to a chair, sat down, and hoisted up a grimy boot. It landed with a *thunk* on the kitchen table.

"Orders from the boss."

He then reached into his pocket, pulled out a bag of sunflower seeds, bit into one, and, without breaking eye contact, spit out the shell at Bunyan's feet.

Bunyan was about to leap on him in fury when he remembered Lucette was lying alone upstairs. Panicked, he raced up.

In the bedroom, Lucette lay as she had before, still as stone, eyes closed, chest barely rising and falling beneath the Dream Quilt.

Bunyan leaned down and whispered into her ear. "I'm here, Lucette. I'm not going anywhere."

As he gently embraced his wife, Bunyan heard the front door open and shut, followed by the sound of someone mounting the stairs. He turned to see a soaking-wet Niebuhr.

Entering, the doctor set down his bag, then closed the bedroom door. He pulled up two chairs and motioned for Bunyan to sit beside him.

"What is it?" Bunyan asked.

"You haven't been told the truth," the doctor said in a hushed voice.

"The truth about what?"

Niebuhr glanced over his shoulder at the door, pushed up his glasses on his nose, then leaned in still closer.

"The race for information is a deadly one. And you are now right in the middle of it."

CHAPTER 8

THE SALVATION LIGHT

Quietly, the slight, bald, and ever-anxious Niebuhr went on, "If word gets out about what I am about to say, I will deny I told you. Do you understand?"

Bunyan nodded.

Niebuhr rubbed his palms on his thighs. "Do you have any idea why all of this is here? The Factory? Lump Town? Do you have any idea about the real purpose of Lump?"

Bunyan shrugged. "Energy? Profit?"

"Energy and profit are a sideshow. The real reason we're here," Niebuhr whispered, "is salvation."

The doctor stopped talking a moment and turned his head toward the door, listening again for Mad Dog. When all was quiet but for the rain tapping on the roof, he resumed.

"In my old life, I was a professor of natural sciences at the University of the Windy City. I'd published extensively on mineralogy. El Boffo approached me, promising gold to join his secret project. The money was too much to refuse, and soon I was working in his lab. It's where he builds his Lump-powered devices, everything that goes in the Wondertorium."

Bunyan had heard about the Wondertorium, an enormous showroom with scores of fantastical vehicles and inventions.

"The Wondertorium gets all the attention. But El Boffo's true aim is building a device called the Simulorb."

"The Simulorb?"

"A globe made of iron and glass, with Pure Lump at its core. Under the right pressure and with the proper rotation, the Pure begins to emit a certain radiation. This radiation has special powers. Healing powers."

"Healing . . ."

"That's right. I initially imagined his goal was to introduce a competitor to coal and oil. But in a private meeting he explained his ultimate ambition: the panacea. He wanted to cure disease. Mend bones. Heal wounds. The applications seemed infinite. I was mortified at first. I was a respected professor. Had I thrown away a good career to make snake oil for a crank? Even so, I stayed. If he was paying me so much, I reasoned, it had to be real. No one would plow such a fortune into a scam."

The doctor adjusted his glasses and went on. "The Simulorb project was separate from the rest of the lab. When I came on board, everything was already under way. Other scientists had been working for years. They were flummoxed. Many of them doubted the device could be built. None of the scientists knew where El Boffo got his initial ideas. His ambitions seemed, frankly, outlandish. But when we reported our failures, he reassured us, 'The Simulorb has been built before, and by people with a lot less schooling than you.' When the scientists couldn't get the result he wanted, El Boffo would fire them. In time, that's what happened to me. He forced me to finish out my contract in Lump Town in order to get my Lump Sum."

Niebuhr shook his head, vexed. "When I began this work, I was idealistic. Or at least, open-minded. Coming to Lump Town, I see where things are headed. Here we make waste, and throw that waste away. But as our species crowds the planet, one man's 'away' is another man's 'here.' Even if the Salvation Light *can* be made, and even if it *is* a miracle, our Earth is a miracle, too. So we destroy one miracle to make another. To fix life, we break it. We are a parasite on the verge of killing its host. To put it another way, 'progress' is not progress when you're heading in the wrong direction. I fear in times to come our age will live in infamy as the generation that laid waste the Earth."

Niebuhr stood and went to the door. He opened it a crack, peeked through the opening, then gently closed it again. Returning to the chair, Niebuhr pulled a newspaper from his bag and opened it to an inside page with the headline:

EL BOFFO TO REVEAL LUMP-POWERED "HEALING" DEVICE AT THIS YEAR'S WONDERTORIUM GALA!

"Apparently, there's been a breakthrough," said Niebuhr. "The gala is next week. If El Boffo has indeed succeeded in building the Simulorb, it will change the course of history. The technology will be irresistible. The appetite for Lump will be insatiable. The world will soon become one dark and smoking Lump Town, end to end, its rivers, lakes, and oceans slicked with Sludge. But more important for you: if the device works the way El Boffo claims it should, it's the one thing that could cure your wife."

"She can't go to the Windy City. Dedrick said she can't be moved at all."

"You'd have to convince El Boffo to bring the device here."

The doctor took a pair of scissors from his bag and clipped a lock of hair from Lucette's head, close to the scalp. He laid it across Bunyan's lap.

"Look."

Bunyan held the lock of hair below the lamp on the dresser. Most of it was Lucette's natural light brown color. But at the roots he could see a trace of silverdark.

"The hair is like a clock," said Niebuhr. "When the silverdark has traveled from the roots to the tips, she will die. Some patients remain in the coma for thirty days. Others don't last nearly as long."

"Has anyone survived it? Even once?"

The doctor shook his head.

Bunyan dug his fingers into his beard. "So, the whole reason El Boffo is poisoning the earth, petrifying the woods, pouring Sludge in the river, and blotting out the sun is so we can invent this . . . healing machine?"

"This is El Boffo's bet," answered Niebuhr. "He will turn the green world black, but ultimately, he thinks no one will care. The Simulorb will cure disease, heal wounds, reduce pain, and extend life. He calls it 'the Salvation Light.'"

"And you're sure it can cure her?"

"The science suggests it may be possible. As of yet, theory has not become reality. But it is your only hope."

"If El Boffo heard she was sick, surely he would come."

"Getting him here will be an uphill battle. If the device works, his investors will be first in line. All lives are worth saving. But some are worth saving more than others."

Bunyan leaned back and looked up at the ceiling, trying to sort through it all.

"Whatever you do now, you must be extremely careful," said Niebuhr. "There are enormous fortunes at stake. Lives and reputations, too. One might say the future *itself* is on the line. Dedrick is in charge of intelligence—both gathering the useful and stamping out the threatening. In the race for knowledge, many have been silenced. There are eyes all around. Do you understand?"

"If the race is so dangerous, why are you sharing this with me?"

Niebuhr wiped the fog from his glasses. "I owe a special debt to your wife. When I first came to Lump Town, I was without a friend, without a clue. My health was poor. It was Lucette who showed me the ropes: how to filter the air, where to get good eggs and fresh apples. She even arranged for me to get the cleanest water from the refinery. She did me many a kindness I never had a chance to repay."

Putting his glasses back on, Niebuhr nodded toward Lucette's silverdark body. "El Boffo believes even *this* is acceptable collateral damage, as long as he gets his device. I myself have looked the other way many times. It's gone too far."

A restless feeling dawned in Bunyan—hope.

"If I went to the Windy City, how would I find El Boffo?"

"On the first Friday of the month, there's a cash fight on the outskirts of town. It's run by a woman named Eleanor Throttlecock. She has a company called . . ." Niebuhr tapped his finger on his lips. "Sasquatch Productions. In the entire time I worked for El Boffo, he never missed a fight. The next one is a few days from now."

"So, I'll talk to El Boffo there?"

"Easier said than done. He is the most famous man in America, always surrounded by guards. You can't just walk up to him."

"Then how?"

"El Boffo loves winners—thinks they rub off on him. He dines with whoever wins Throttlecock's brawl. Prevailing in that ring is the only way."

"But if I went . . ."

"I will look after her here. I've seen several—"

Suddenly, the doctor held up his finger and froze. Bunyan heard the sound of someone coming up the stairs. The door opened.

"Lots of chatter up here," said Mad Dog.

The doctor stood. "I was just leaving. I will return to check on the patient in the morning."

Mad Dog watched the two men suspiciously as Niebuhr put the rest of his things in his bag. Before he left, Niebuhr stood before Bunyan and gave him a look of peculiar intensity.

"Be careful with this disease, Paul. The enemy in this room is very aggressive. What it wants most is for victims to stay *right where they are*. Even just the smallest move, and our opponent will attack."

Niebuhr held Bunyan's glance an extra moment to be sure the meaning of his words landed. Then he walked down the stairs.

"You've got to stay quiet in Lump Town. The quieter you are, the faster you rise," said Mad Dog before he closed the door.

When he was alone again with Lucette, Bunyan's heart nearly came apart. He leaned on the post at the end of the bed and tried to sort through his options.

Option one: Sign Dedrick's document. Watch Lucette die. Stay in Lump Town a year. Get the gold bar. Set his mother free.

But even this seemed deeply uncertain: How could he be sure that gold bar would come? Dedrick had ripped him off once; couldn't he do it again? Worse still, how could he sit here, helpless, as this disease invaded his wife's every cell?

Option two: Go to the Windy City. Try to meet El Boffo. Beg him to bring his secret device here.

But that seemed so improbable as to be ridiculous. A cracker couldn't just show up and expect to meet an emperor. And even if he *could* meet El Boffo, he'd still have to convince him to bring the Simulorb to Lump Town. Further still, what if the machine didn't work? He'd have nothing, then. No Lump Sum. No job. No wife.

Turning these ideas over in his mind, Bunyan picked up the paper Niebuhr had left. He scanned the headlines:

MARKETS PANIC AT SPREAD OF MYSTERIOUS METAL MEAT CATTLE PLAGUE

GROVE HIKER CRUSHED TO DEATH BY SO-CALLED TREE OF LIFE

He saw a picture of El Boffo, with his aggressive smile.

WONDERTORIUM WIZARDRY WOWS WINDY!

Then he noticed something strange. At the bottom corner of the page was an advertisement with huge bold letters.

$$$$$ CASH REWARD $$$$$

FOR THE APPREHENSION OF ESCAPED CONVICT

JOHN HENRY

DESCRIPTION: BLACK. MUSCULAR BUILD. QUICK WITH A HAMMER.
DISTINCTIVE SCAR ACROSS HIS CHEST.
CONSIDER ARMED AND VERY DANGEROUS.

Beside the wording was a roughly rendered picture of a man with close-cropped hair, a thick neck, and haunted eyes.

IF SEEN, PLEASE REPORT TO:
PULASKI & LYNCH, 111 ADAMS ST., THE WINDY CITY

WANTED ALIVE

$$$$$ PAYMENT UPON CAPTURE $$$$$

F.O.L.

Yet what struck Bunyan about this advertisement was not the wording, nor the picture itself, but rather . . .

The Gleam.

It surged all around the picture of this man, as if to say, *Take heed!* But take heed how? And do what? Bunyan didn't know. He put the paper aside.

As he gazed once more upon his wife, a pang of grief struck his heart. He saw the patch of the Dream Quilt with the two birds flying over the sea.

You're carrying me, she'd said.

Bunyan stood and paced, then sat, then stood and paced some more. Plans, fears, hopes, and instincts advanced, recoiled, and wrestled in his mind. There was risk in doing something. There was risk in doing nothing. There was risk every way he looked.

Late into the night, weary from his circling thoughts, Bunyan at last sat in the chair, closed his eyes, and fell asleep.

Bunyan awoke with a start. Outside, dim dawn had come.

Quickly, he pulled his spare leather brace from his drawer and secured it on his foot. He grabbed his old harmonica from the dresser and shoved it in his pocket. Standing by the crack in the open door, Bunyan heard Mad Dog snoring at the kitchen table below.

Bunyan leaned over Lucette's silverdark body and kissed her cold cheek. His heart stirred within him.

"Hold fast, darling," he whispered in her ear. "I will carry you to that distant shore. There, you will awaken."

Moments later, he walked to the laundry room, opened the window, and leapt out, landing in the sooty yard behind their little home.

He advanced cautiously along the streets. Niebuhr's coded warning had been clear:

The enemy in this room is very aggressive. What it wants most is for victims to stay right where they are. Even just the smallest move, and our opponent will attack.

Bunyan hurried up to the squalid shacks and run-down buildings along the outskirts, then moved past the abandoned church, where he slipped into the petrified woods.

Soon, he was standing by the Rooted Axe. The words of Moki were in his mind:

How can you say how strong you are, when all your life you have ignored your greatest power?

He closed his eyes and searched within himself for the endless place, the timeless place, the fearless place, the place that does not move, below the belly and before the spine, the very eye of his soul.

When he opened his eyes, the Gleam was not there.

Come on.

Bunyan tried again. He thought of all he had been through, all the suffering and wasted time, the thankless work and dire risk that had led him to this crossroads.

But when he opened his eyes a second time, still he saw no Gleam.

Bunyan pressed his eyes shut and clenched his jaw. *I will do anything, believe anything, become anyone, if only I can find a way out!*

When he opened his eyes the third time, he saw it. The molten, pearly light blazed a path up the tree, high into the smog above.

He laid his hands upon the huge ridges of the trunk and began to climb.

CHAPTER 9

THE TWISTY PATH

Bunyan scaled the gigantic tree high over the earth. With each ridge of bark, the Gleam grew brighter, showing the path ahead.

At last he came to the haze that formed the ever-present helmet over Lump Valley. Minute shards of floating Lump residue cut his throat as he inhaled. He buried his mouth in his shirt to breathe, but there was no escape. Inhaling this toxic fog was like sucking quicksand.

As he rose, the smoky stew about him grew hotter, filled with the trapped heat of the sun. Bunyan coughed. He was suffocating. Dizzy, he buried his face again by his shoulder, trying to filter out the bad air. *Hurry!*

Squinting to see the Gleam, Bunyan ascended as rapidly as he could, feeling the sun's light growing brighter all the while—that sun that he had not seen in years. He began to feel an almost physical craving for it, drawn up to the light like a child toward the face of his parents. His arms worked faster, pulled harder, till—

Ahh!

The open air!

Out of the Lump smog at last, Bunyan spotted a branch that, even at this height, was broad as a sidewalk. He gulped huge breaths of clean air, then gradually raised his eyes.

Expanding about him in every direction was the sky's brilliant blue dome. In the distance there gathered stately clouds, puffed up high, erupting upward into the day.

As his sight adjusted to the brightness, Bunyan observed another stark detail: the lacquered, silverdark tops of the giant trees poking up here and there from the swamp of smoke. A graveyard of massive trunks. Spellbound, he looked on in silence, till suddenly, he heard a voice.

"So, you have decided to embrace your true gift?"

The voice came from behind and above him, cool and ironic as it had been the day before.

"The straight path has failed," said Bunyan. "But I cannot do this alone."

Gripping the bark, he noticed one hulking, skeletal tree, so much larger than the rest, soaring above the lake of pollution that enveloped it.

"That must be Christ Trunk," Bunyan said.

"*Hmmmmmmmm.*"

A smell soon struck Bunyan's nose. A strange smell. A delectable smell.

"What *is* that?" Bunyan eagerly looked about, his mouth watering.

Moments later Bunyan saw, growing from a crack in the branch, something he had not seen in years: soft, fresh, green, living . . . *life.* It appeared to be a vine of grapes. They were strange-looking grapes— small, withered, hard. But they were growing nonetheless, fighting for life here in the smallest of crevices.

He knelt and took one in his hand. A tiny, perfect green sphere. He placed it in his mouth and pressed his teeth down upon it. He felt a cool eruption of juice, followed by overwhelming sweetness. For years, what had he eaten? Crumbly bread, smoked and salted meats, beans out of the tin. He found another, this one misshapen like an eggplant. He ate. More juice. It was ecstasy.

Just then, Bunyan heard the distant moan of a train whistle. He didn't have much time. He could see the tip of the Chilali's great brown wing just beside him.

"My wife is sick. If I do nothing, she will die. If I try to save her, I risk all I have worked for."

"When your mother told you stories about the Chilali," said Moki, "were they stories of those who stayed safe?"

"No."

"Were they stories of those who became rich?"

"The opposite."

"Or who had it easy?"

"Of course not."

"Were they stories of pleasure?"

"Not really."

"Or guaranteed success?"

"No."

"In all the stories your mother told, what was the one guarantee of the Twisty Path?"

"The Beautiful Destiny."

"*Hmmmmmm.*"

"So there really are no certainties with the Gleam," Bunyan said.

"Would you prefer the certainties of Lump Town?"

Far off to the south, Bunyan could see a broiling light, a kind of fountain within the sky, nearly as bright as the sun.

"What is that light, there?"

"Doesn't it tell you what you already know? That the Twisty Path leads to the Windy City?"

Bunyan stared into the light, which seemed to be the very hue and substance of the Gleam. The longer he gazed upon it, the more his worries fell away. Suddenly, he was filled with the urge to follow the Gleam completely, fearlessly, and not squander a second more. The clouds, the sky, even the dead, skeletal trees in this toxic lake of Lump smog, all seemed to bear a single message: *Strike forth.*

"Will you swear something to me?" asked Moki.

"What is it?"

"Will you swear to give yourself to the strange way, the hard way, the absurd way, the unconventional way, the courageous way, no matter what the Gleam asks?"

"I swear."

"Will you swear to become something new, since becoming is what the Path requires?"

"I swear."

"*Hmmmmm.*"

In some faint, distant way, Bunyan was aware that what lay before him was difficulty, danger, perhaps even death. But all he could see now was this new dawn, surging with light.

———•———

Soon, Bunyan was back on the floor of the woods. He'd have to avoid town. Mad Dog would be looking for him. He passed the abandoned church on the outskirts, then a row of shacks. Somehow he'd have to get across Moses Creek to the tracks on the other side.

"There he is!"

Quickly, Bunyan turned to see Mad Dog pointing at him from down the street. Dedrick stood beside him. As Mad Dog reached for the gun on his hip, Bunyan took off running.

First he dashed toward the train, but then . . . he saw it.

The Gleam!

It looked bright as a puddle of molten metal, forming a path not toward the train, but directly into town. Bunyan hesitated for a moment, not wanting to backtrack. But then again . . .

What happens when the straight path fails?

He followed it.

"Stop!" shouted Dedrick. "*Lump Master!*"

As he ran, the Gleam only grew brighter, blazing a path through the town as if the earth itself were on fire. Bunyan wove through the weary throngs on their way to the Factory, zigged down a side street, zagged down another, then shot down a passage between two shacks as Mad Dog chased behind.

Bang!

The bullet whistled past his ear.

Sprinting back out on Main Street, Bunyan could see the train across Moses Creek had pulled into motion. But instead of leading him directly there, the Gleam again sent him zigging through yet more alleys, under clotheslines, every which way except the straight way through the grid of Lump Town's streets, till suddenly he emerged alongside Moses Creek, running parallel to the tracks, only the river between him and the train.

Bang! Bang!

As the shots cracked behind him, Bunyan sped alongside the Sludge-filled stream. Up ahead he saw a bend. He'd have to get across. The train was only gaining speed.

As he reached the river, Bunyan lost sight of the Gleam. He stopped. Before him was the toxic Sludge of Lump residue, dangerous to even touch. But after another moment, he spotted it. Crooked. Shimmering. Radiant. Beckoning. The Gleam upon the waters.

Take heed!

Bunyan dove.

Down he went, kicking and flailing underwater, not daring to open his eyes in the foul Sludge, nor come to the surface to open his mouth for even a single breath and expose himself to the gunfire. With *one! two! three!* more strokes, he at last put his foot down on the opposite shore and came up for air.

Bunyan scrambled onto his feet and turned back to see Mad Dog standing beside Dedrick across the water. Mad Dog aimed his gun. He had a clean, open shot. But by now, a crowd had formed. The dirty denizens of Lump Town had gathered along the banks of Moses Creek. Still more stared at the scene from the Factory bridge beneath its familiar sign:

THE FUTURE IS IN YOUR HANDS

Dedrick reached over and gently pulled down Mad Dog's arm.

Bunyan ran for the last carriage on the train, ignoring the pain in his Junk Foot as he leapt for the ladder on the rear car. He grabbed hold and pulled himself aboard.

The wind cooled his soaking clothes as the train gained speed, and Bunyan looked back one final time to see Dedrick, Mad Dog, and all the workers gathered, spellbound and staring.

As the train clicked and clacked away from the smokestacks, the squalid shacks, and the soaring, silverdark wood beyond, Bunyan knew his Lump Sum, his Lump Master title, and his time in the straight grids of Lump Town were done.

All he had now was the Gleam.

CHAPTER 10

THE WINDY CITY

"All aboard!"

Bunyan woke to the sound of a shrill whistle. For a moment he had no idea where he was. He had been sleeping in one of the boxcars between some crates. He cleared his throat, blinked his eyes, and tried to orient himself. Half sitting up, he looked through the carriage slats and beheld an astonishing sight:

A heaving, pumping, thriving, muscular flood of humanity. Enormous buildings made of brick and stone formed a blufflike boundary along a boulevard. Scores of men, hundreds of them, thousands, all in bowler hats and suits, rushed in and out of doorways, shouldered through the throngs, and dodged the carriages while bicycles wove their way among the buggies.

Bunyan spoke through a slat to a man on the platform. "Hey! What stop is this?"

It took the man a moment to realize where the voice was coming from. At last seeing Bunyan through the crack, he said, "The Windy City."

The Windy City?

"Last call!" shouted the conductor from the platform.

Bunyan scrambled up and leapt down to the train platform just as the train lurched back into motion.

In the brilliant midday sun, a riot of smells struck Bunyan's nose: fried fish, roasted chestnuts, newspaper print, a woman's perfume, armpit odor, stained leather, locomotive smoke, fresh-cut lumber, the manure of stockyards. Across the steaming street stood an astonishing variety of stores: the Painter and the Glass Bender, the Bricklayer and the Architect, the Butcher, the Grocer, the Grainery, the Coffee and Tea Emporium, the Tobacconist, the Druggist, and the Saloon, and on down the block to the Seamstress, the Tailor, and the Hat and Cap Boutique. Further up, Bunyan saw a glistening river, clogged with chugging steamboats blowing black smoke all the way out to the shimmering lake beyond.

Amid the bustling of the train platform, Bunyan saw something that caught his attention. Nailed to a wooden post was a sign:

$$$$$ CASH REWARD $$$$$
FOR THE APPREHENSION OF ESCAPED CONVICT
JOHN HENRY

It was the same notice he'd seen in Niebuhr's paper. And again, the Gleam was positively surging around the lettering and the rendering of the man. *Take heed!*

Bunyan ripped down the sign and jammed it in his pocket. Then he turned to a vendor behind a fruit stand.

"Pardon me. I'm looking for a place called Sasquatch Productions . . ."

———— • ————

Two hours later, Bunyan stood on a downtown street, looking up at the sign in the window:

SASQUATCH PRODUCTIONS
CONNOISSEURS OF EXQUISITE VIOLENCE
"Behemoths are our business."

Peering through the glass, Bunyan could see scores of men behind desks, round the sides of desks, at the corners of desks, forming a second row encircling the desks, all bartering, gesticulating, accusing, pointing, shouting.

"Excuse me," said a voice behind Bunyan.

A gigantic man stepped past him; he wasn't a single inch shorter, nor an ounce less girthy, than Mad Dog Mahoney. With the opening of the door, a thunderous noise burst from the interior.

Moments later, a stocky young man with red curly hair walked up the street.

"Hi, hello, pardon me," Bunyan said, stepping in front of him. "I'm here to see Eleanor Throttlecock."

The fellow had a great wad of chaw in his lip, as well as a squint in his eye that suggested he'd walked directly from yesterday into today without sleep in between.

"Looking for a fight?"

"No, um, I'm actually looking for El Boffo. The thing is, I need to speak with him. You see, I'm on a mission for my wife."

The young man's face brightened as if, in the course of a few moments, he'd registered the precise steps by which Bunyan would transform into a business opportunity.

"The name's Sully O'Connor." He smiled. "Follow me."

Inside, the office roared with huddles of men berating each other as a "cheat," a "liar," a "lowlife," "scum," yet in the very next breath, laughing and doling out tumblers of bourbon while clapping each other on the back, saying, "Good to see you again," and "Another day, another deal." It was just before nine in the morning.

Off to one side, a hulking, bronze-skinned man with piercings in his ears and nose was being weighed on a scale and sized with a tape measure round the belly.

"Watch your step," said Sully.

Bunyan looked down just in time to hop over the legs of a man doing push-ups with a cinder block balanced on his back.

"You from around here?" said Sully, ducking between two sparring partners.

"Lived all over. Lump Town most recently."

"Lump Town, eh? Don't see many of those." Scooting past a desk, Sully punched a seated coworker on his shoulder, then spit some chaw juice into his trash can. "What's it today, Carl?" said Sully. "On the deals or on your heels?"

Carl raised an eyebrow. "Ah, Sully. Having you here is like having two people out sick."

"Everyone knows you're not afraid of hard work, Carl," answered Sully with a smile. "After all, you sit next to it all day."

Moving along, Sully winked back at Bunyan. "We ain't got culture in the Windy City, but we sure eatin' regular."

Sully led Bunyan into an office along the back wall where the slat blinds were lowered and smoke clung to the ceiling. Over a paper-cluttered desk, two men stood locked in an intense debate. A tall man, skinny as a birch tree, leaned over the desk. He had long gray sideburns, a bowler hat, and a sneer on his face.

"I'll tell you what, Abe," he said. "Five minutes in the gutter and I could find a snake with more spine than you."

The seated man sported slicked-back wavy hair gleaming with oil, a loosened necktie, and a pencil tucked neatly behind his ear.

"And I'll tell *you*, Lenny, if I had a penny to murder, I'd shove it up your ass and watch you pinch it to death."

At that, Lenny and Abe stared at each other in an apparent stalemate. Though Abe's face said, *My bones despise you*, the brightness in his eyes said, *No place I'd rather be.*

At last Lenny broke off the stare and grabbed a fountain pen from the desk. "All right, it's a deal."

Both signed, then vigorously shook hands.

"Always a pleasure. Love to the missus."

"Don't be a stranger." Lenny tipped his hat to all in the room and departed.

Abe turned to the new arrivals. "And the cat drags in another. How goes it, Sully?"

"Same as always. Can't tell if I'm kicking ass or getting my ass kicked. Allow me to introduce . . ."

"Paul Bunyan," said Bunyan.

Abe eyeballed the newcomer. "Big fella, eh? Look at those shoulders. Bet you could really lay a man out."

"If it came to that, I suppose. Listen, I'm here to see Eleanor Throttlecock. See, I need to speak with El Boffo—"

"El *Boffo?*" said Abe, half amused, half intrigued.

"Yes. I've heard he eats with whoever wins your fights. Of course, the ideal scenario would be if there was a way to meet him *without* fighting. You see, I'm on a mission for my wife. She's very sick and—"

"Meet him *without* fighting?" scoffed Abe. "Sure! Why don't we all go meet him? We'll just walk arm in arm over to the Palace Hotel and whistle up at his window. I'm sure he'll pop right down."

Sully gave Bunyan a squeeze on the shoulder. "If you wanna meet the big man, you're gonna have to run the table."

Bunyan looked around the office. Boxing gloves lay on a few squalid shelves jammed with folders, papers, and old trophies. On one wall hung a drawing of a hairy beast, savagely gripping the bars of a cage.

"So . . . what does it mean, run the table?"

Abe leaned back in his chair, fingers laced thoughtfully across his trim belly. "It means you knock down every man we put in front of you. No less than three, no more than five. An honest evening's work."

"Right, well, I'm not exactly a fighting man. I prefer to solve conflicts socially. Discussion. Compromise. Gathering different points of view . . ."

Ignoring this, Abe fished around in a box on the floor, then tossed a pair of boxing gloves across the desk. "Put these on, will you?"

Bunyan slid his hand halfway into the glove. It didn't fit.

Abe tossed over a new set of gloves. "Try these?"

Bunyan did his best to work the next pair on, but again his hands were too massive.

Sully, meanwhile, had begun shadowboxing in front of a mirror against the wall, making a *pah, pah, pah!* sound with his punches. "Got a feeling Mr. Lump Town's gonna be my big score." *Pah, pah!* "I've got the eye, Abe. Just like Ellie."

Abe shoved the box of gloves away, as none of them fit. "Anyway, what do you do for work?"

"I'm a miner from Lump Town."

"Work in a factory?"

"Do a bit of everything. Blast the pit. Run the shaft. Crank the gear."

Abe leaned back in his chair, musing. "The God of the Gears."

Sully snapped his fingers and pointed. "The Factory Freak!"

"The Factory Freak?" asked Bunyan.

"Eleanor loves a good ring name," said Sully, pulling a poster from a shelf and handing it to Bunyan.

FRIDAY FIGHT FEST!
"Get in the Barn!"

FEATURING:
HELLCAT MAGGIE · "OLD IRONSIDES" BENNY BUCKFACE ·
SWEET DADDY WOODSHED · BILED OYSTERS MALLOY ·
"GATLING GUN" GOEMPERS · MICKY FACEWRECK ·
MUSH RILEY, A.K.A. THE RIVER PIRATE · BOBO CASH ·
THE PATSY CONROY GANG

"A whole *gang?*" muttered Bunyan as he went on reading:

HAVANA HECTOR · MISTRESS SMOTHERSQUAT ·
STEEL-DRIVIN' JOHN · NECK-SNAPPER MCNULTY ·
SADIE THE GOAT, A.K.A. THE ONE-EARED BITCH ·
THE BEHEMOTH

"You poor?" said Abe.

"Poor?"

"White trash. You know, a cracker?"

"Trying to make my way like everyone else."

"How about King Cracker?"

"The Redneck Rumbler," said Sully, who'd stopped shadowboxing and sat on the edge of the desk. He looked at Bunyan and smiled. "The Honky Hulk."

"The *Hillbilly* Hulk."

"You know who he really reminds me of?" Sully appraised Bunyan.

"Bluebeard?"

"The Chopper."

"Chopper had no discipline," said Abe. "All horse and no rider. Never been a student of the game, have you, Sully?"

Bunyan interjected, "So I'll have to beat three of these guys? Maybe five?"

Sully ignored him and went on speaking to Abe. "Just to be clear, and in the presence of *a witness*, can we at least agree on the greatest of them all?"

"You mean Behemoth," said Abe matter-of-factly.

"Steel-Drivin' John. Johnny ate Behemoth *up*."

"Had his number that night, I'll grant you. But I'm talking about those of presently known whereabouts."

"Who's Steel-Drivin' John?" said Bunyan.

"Oh, nobody but the fastest, most dangerous, most indestructible fellow with a pair of fists ever to walk the face of the earth," said Sully. "Came into town maybe a year ago. Mowed down a dozen in a row." Sully stood up to demonstrate. *Pah, pah, pah, PAH!* "Just like that."

"But a lot faster than that," said Abe. "Anyway, he's gone." Abe rolled his index finger forward, suggesting a proven thesis. "Ergo, Behemoth is the best."

"I'd like to agree with you, but then we'd both be wrong. Behemoth's days are numbered."

"Oh, here we go." Abe rolled his eyes. "Sully's 'secret sauce.'"

"Just need a man to roll the dice. A man with an appetite for *risk*." Sully clapped Bunyan from behind on both shoulders. "A man like the Hillbilly Hulk!"

Bunyan cleared his throat. "So, can I get in the fight or not?"

Suddenly, the ruckus in the office outside went quiet. Abe stood up quickly and went to the slat blinds.

"That depends on the lady of the house"—Abe straightened his tie and peeked out the office window—"who has just arrived on the premises."

CHAPTER 11

RUN THE TABLE

Bunyan approached the slatted blinds, through which he saw a remarkable sight:

The scores of men in the office, boisterously haggling moments before, now stood mute as a cluster of mussels on a tidal rock. A few tipped their hats, though most remained utterly motionless until Eleanor Throttlecock had passed all the way through their ranks and opened the door to her corner office. The moment she closed it, the room erupted in dealmaking once more.

Abe whipped a comb from his pocket and dashed to the mirror, where he began working it through his wavy hair. Sully fished his chaw from his lip; flicked it into the bin, where it landed with a *thunk;* then ducked in front of Abe to check his teeth.

"Get back to work," said Abe to Sully. "Cracker, you come with."

"Oh no you don't," said Sully. "This is *my* recruit. *I* get to present him."

Abe was flustered but couldn't disagree. Moments later, Abe, Bunyan, and Sully entered Throttlecock's office.

Sitting behind her desk, Eleanor Throttlecock wore an embroidered, powder-blue dress with a matching broad-brimmed hat. Upon the desk she'd dumped a finely stitched leather bag and a parasol. She appeared, to Bunyan's scrap-meat eyes anyway, to be some kind of aristocrat. As she tugged a long, cream-colored glove off one hand, she examined a contract on her desk.

"I thought I said I wanted my contracts bulletproof." Throttlecock spoke with a posh, Old World accent. "What you gave me is Swiss cheese."

Abe grudgingly picked up the contract. "I'll work on it, ma'am, no problem."

"I think the fire under your ass needs a fire under *its* ass." Throttlecock noticed Bunyan. "Who's this?"

"My new recruit," intervened Sully. "Wants to run the table and meet El Boffo."

Throttlecock's glare was so invasive that Bunyan felt as if imaginary, ocean-cold tentacles had slithered into him and enveloped his heart. At last, her thin lips curled into a smile.

"The train station," she said. "This morning."

"How do you mean, ma'am?" said Bunyan.

Throttlecock worked the second glove off. "I saw you from a block away. I never forget a pair of shoulders."

"He's on a mission for his wife," said Sully, excited.

Throttlecock raised an eyebrow, then walked around the desk to Bunyan.

Slight, short, and full of electricity, Throttlecock only came up to Bunyan's chest, where she smoothed the fabric of his shirt and felt the muscles beneath. She pinched his biceps. Bunyan felt like a steer being prepped for a trot at the fair.

"He's from Lump Town." Sully cranked an imaginary gear in the air. "The Factory Freak."

Bunyan cleared his throat. "Right, well, the thing I need is to speak to El Boffo. I don't *necessarily* need to get into the ring."

Bending down, Throttlecock gave Bunyan's thigh a light tap with her knuckle. "Who do we have on tonight?"

"Let's see . . . ummm . . . we've got Bobo, Gatling Gun, Hector. Behemoth, of course."

As Abe listed the fighters, Throttlecock grabbed Bunyan's left hand and studied his massive, calloused palm, then turned it over to examine his knuckles.

Bunyan took back his hand. "Sorry, as I was saying to these two earlier, if these are all experienced fighters, I'm just not sure . . . See, I've actually never been in a fight before."

"Never been in a *fight?*" said Abe with a smirk. "Hell of a find, Sully. Fresh meat for Behemoth."

Throttlecock took a few steps back and squinted at Bunyan, looking him up and down. "Turn around?" He turned. "Hands over your head?" He reached up. "Your foot. What's wrong with it?"

Bunyan couldn't tell how Throttlecock had noticed Old Junk Foot so quickly. "An accident, when I was a child."

"You have a brace?"

"Yes."

"Face me?"

Bunyan rotated again.

"Jog in place."

This was getting ridiculous.

"Jump up, knees high so they hit your chest."

As Bunyan jumped, he glanced through the slats in the office window at the dozens of men going through similar trials. "Are all of those men out there fighters, too?"

Throttlecock let out a sharp laugh, like a flock of birds bursting from a tree. "*Fighters?* Stop jumping."

Stepping up close, Throttlecock studied Bunyan's frame a moment more, then returned to her seat at the desk. "Tell me something . . ."

"Paul."

"Tell me something, Paul. How many true prospects do you think are out there?"

Bunyan peered through the slats at the grunting, sweaty men. "Thirty?"

"Try again."

"Forty?"

"I have a precise number in mind."

"Forty-three?"

"I would say the number of true *fighters* out on that floor is exactly zero." Throttlecock gave Abe the side-eye. "Not a single one of the men out there strikes me as having . . . *it.*"

"You can tell just by looking?"

"Do you see the house behind me?"

Bunyan looked out the window to the street.

"No," said Throttlecock. "In the photograph above my head."

Bunyan looked at the photograph of an enormous mansion with pillars, wrought-iron gates, and a sprawling, manicured landscape. "That's a big house."

"It is big, and it is mine," said Throttlecock. "Can you guess how I came to own such a house?"

Bunyan shrugged.

"Because I have the *eye*. And what my eye noticed at the train station this morning, and what I am confirming now, young man, is that *you* have *it*. There is something unusual about you. Something that just might work in my ring."

Sully gave Abe a little punch on the shoulder and flashed his eyebrows. "Got the eye."

Bunyan shook his head. "There's got to be a more direct way. I just . . . my wife is sick, you see, and I—"

"Enough about your *wife!*" snapped Throttlecock. "Now, listen to me. El Boffo is one of the most illustrious figures in the world. There are gates, guards, locks, moats, and walls separating crackers like you from gods like him. But the fact is, he has dined with the champions of my Fight Barn on the first Friday of every month for twenty-three years straight. Why? Because he, like me, is obsessed with the gritty, gutty gladiator. He is a connoisseur of 'it.' If you want to meet El Boffo, then gird up your loins and climb through my ropes. *There is no other deal.*"

———— ✦ ————

Sully walked Bunyan out to the street.

"Fresh meat for the Behemoth?" said Bunyan, concerned. "Is that what Abe said?"

"Don't worry about Abe," said Sully. "Opportunity is a mirror to a man's soul. It always seems small to the small and great to the great. You got food?"

Bunyan emptied his pockets. All he had was his harmonica. In the rush to leave Lump Town, he'd forgotten to bring the pieces of silver he'd won in the Finals. "I've got nothing."

"Here." Sully put some change in Bunyan's hand. "Buy yourself a sandwich."

As he said this, Sully looked up and down the street. Determining that no one was watching them, he stepped around the corner and motioned for Bunyan to follow. In privacy, Sully put one hand on Bunyan's shoulder.

"Tell me something, big fella, what kind of man are you?"

"What do you mean?"

"Are you one of these straight-and-narrow types? Or are you a man willing to think a bit . . . *roundabout?*"

"I just want to meet El Boffo."

"Right. Well, here's the thing. Only one man's ever beaten the Behemoth, and that's Steel-Drivin' John. From the looks of it, you're no Steel-Drivin' John. But maybe you've got a different asset. Shall we say, an openness to the untraditional."

Bunyan had no idea what Sully was talking about. The redhead went on, "Think about it. Who takes a two-day trip from Lump Town with nothing but a harmonica, then signs up for a Throttlecock death match, just to meet a plutocrat?"

"Death match?"

Sully laughed. "'Mission for my wife'! God, I love a romantic." He fished a bit of chaw from his tin and fit it in his lip. "I'm gonna be frank with you, cracker. You're not gonna meet El Boffo, you're not gonna run the table, you're not gonna beat the Behemoth, and you're probably not even gonna get out of that ring alive, unless you do *exactly* as I say. For it to work, you have to follow my instructions precisely . . ."

CHAPTER 12

CHANGE OR DIE

Lying flat on his back, looking up at the spinning rafters of the Fight Barn, Bunyan could hear, as if through leagues of water, the bloodthirsty crowd, stomping and chanting.

"Bo-bo Cash! Bo-bo Cash!"

When he was a boy, Bunyan's father told him stories about the War for the Union. *In battle, you can see the bullets coming,* Augie said. *The problem is, you just don't have time to get out of the way.*

So it had been with Bobo's left hook, which Bunyan had indeed seen coming, but only too late.

"Five! . . . Six! . . ."

Bunyan felt nauseous. Disoriented. Stunned. Sully had offered him a ploy for dealing with the Behemoth, yes, but at this moment it looked like Bunyan wouldn't even get past the first fighter.

"Seven! . . . Eight! . . ."

Lucette's face appeared in his mind. How many times, and in how many different ways, had this angel of a woman lifted up his meager life? And now she lay on their bed, stone cold, on the edge of death! The least he could do, for her sake, was get up.

"Last chance, big fella . . . Nine! . . ."

Feeling like a sopping wet blanket dredged from a swamp, Bunyan drew himself to his feet, just before the count of ten.

In the other corner, Bobo Cash pumped his fist to the crowd as the Barn kept chanting, "Bo-bo Cash! Take out the trash!"

The ref summoned the fighters to the center. Bobo, tattooed from his neck down to his feet, flashed a gap-toothed smile.

"You're gonna die tonight, cracker."

"Boxers ready?"

Eleanor Throttlecock's ring felt wobbly as the deck of a ship in a squall. Bunyan blearily put up his fists. Then—*ding!*—the bell rang and Bunyan shambled back to his corner.

"All right, kid. Sit down and put your chin up!"

Sully had assigned Bunyan a cut man named Mac to dress his wounds between rounds. Mac had several wooden teeth, a towel over his shoulder, and a glare so hawkish it could have picked a lock.

"Can't hide who you are in a fight!" Mac said in a half shout as he washed Bunyan's face with a rag pulled from a bucket of filthy water. "Out in that ring, each man's only fighting one opponent: himself!"

The Fight Barn was located on the outskirts of the Windy City, over an hour's ride from downtown. A crowd of a couple thousand had jammed in, a cross section of Bunyan's countrymen: three-piece-suited bankers slumming for a thrill; a bunch of warehouse cronies in overalls; grim farmers and their bored wives; a pack of railroad workers feasting on ribs; a trio of sharply dressed Black friends in suspenders and hats taking bets from all sides.

The smell of barbecue was thick in the air. By the Fight Barn door stood a pair of burly cooks sweating over a smoke pit the size of a baby whale. Scores of beef ribs lay across the grill, their ample grease dripping into the spitting fire below. With massive tongs, the cooks poked and flipped the marbled meat, now and then dragging a slab off the grill, which a cleaver man walloped with a sharp *bang! bang!*, dropping the pieces into a newspaper and slathering on a dollop of sauce. An order cost a nickel, watermelon on the side.

By the ring, a marching band of drums and trumpets blared out tunes between the rounds. Beside these musicians, Bunyan saw Sully gesturing to him.

"You got him, big fella!" Sully threw a couple of punches in the air. "Uppercut down Main Street!"

Dazed, Bunyan gazed over at his opponent's corner, where Bobo gleefully dragged the thumb of his boxing glove across his throat.

Mac slathered more grease on Bunyan's cheeks to help the punches slip off. "What's wrong with you, kid? Every time you throw a punch you look like you want to say *sorry!*" Mac grabbed Bunyan's massive arm. "Feel that? All the strength a man could want! You're fighting like you've never fought before!"

"Well, I haven't!"

"You haven't? Then let me tell you how it works, kid: you've got to *hurt the other guy!*"

"Just not made for this kind of thing, I guess . . ."

Mac furiously squatted before Bunyan like a home plate umpire. "Hey!" Bunyan didn't look up, so Mac smacked him on the cheek. His intensity poured through his face like flames licking the grate of an iron grill. "I don't give a *damn* if you think you're made for this. You've got to *become* made for it, *right now!*"

"Then tell me what to do!"

"What's your job in the Factory? Quick!"

"I swing the pick. I push the cart. I shovel the coal. I crank the gear."

"All right," said Mac. "When you punch, swing the pick. When he stumbles, push the cart. When he hits back, shovel the coal. When you finish, crank the gear. And keep that chin out of the way. Got it?"

Ding!

"It's change or die out there, kid!" Mac shouted as Bunyan shuffled into the ring. "Change or die!"

Smelling blood, Bobo trotted from his corner and unleashed a swarm of blows.

When you punch, swing the pick.

As if he were swinging his hammer down on the chisel in the pit, Bunyan let fly a hook. Bobo blocked it, but Bunyan immediately let fly another, then another, then another, just as if he were pounding a spike into a rock wall. At last Bunyan landed a left on Bobo's ear and he watched his opponent stagger back.

When he stumbles, push the cart.

Bunyan lunged at Bobo with both arms, as if he were pushing the cart up the shaft. Bobo tried a wild uppercut but it missed, and Bunyan flung him on the ropes.

When he hits back, shovel the coal.

Like he was pitching fuel in the Factory oven, Bunyan shoveled uppercut after uppercut right through Bobo's guard, hitting his chest, then his ear, then his head.

When you finish, crank the gear.

Then, as if he were right back in the Lump Day Finals, Bunyan mimicked the motion of spinning the gear as he slammed an overhand right square into Bobo's eye. Bobo spun and fell facedown, one arm tangled in the ropes.

"It's all over!"

The ref jumped in front of Bunyan to push him back as Bobo lay senseless on the mat, blood pumping from his nose.

"Get the stretcher!"

As Bunyan made his way back to his corner, the crowd offered a mix of cheers and jeers. Row by row, money changed hands as at ringside, the marching band blasted out an upbeat number.

"You did it, kid!" said Mac, rapping Bunyan on his shoulders. "You became what you had to become!"

"Ladies and gentlemen!" sounded a voice from overhead. "We have a *winner*! It is our challenger, the God of the Gears, the Factory Freak, Paul Bunyan!"

Bunyan raised his eyes to see Eleanor Throttlecock, high over the ring. She stood in a kind of crow's nest, a huge barrel sawed off about waist high, hanging from the rafters. Looking prim as ever in a lace-trimmed dress, Throttlecock shouted over the crowd through a giant cone that served as a megaphone.

"Can we *hear it* for our newcomer?" Her posh voice had grown raspy due to her nonstop yelling through the evening's earlier fights. "I *told* you I have the eye!"

As Throttlecock screamed, Bunyan noticed a scene developing in a special box, about twenty rows up:

El Boffo had arrived.

He wore a dapper top hat and suit and was flanked by a few bodyguards. Bunyan recognized him from the photo—the white hair, the colonizing smile. The legendary investor offered a wave here and a fist pump there. He wiggled his fingers to the ladies. A teenager ran up to get an autograph but El Boffo's entourage kept the kid at bay.

Bunyan considered jumping out of the ring right then, but he didn't see a path through the crowd.

"Our *next* fighter is one of your *all*-time favorites," announced Throttlecock, her voice blasting through her cone. "The Potentate of Pounding, the Beast of Bullets, that most vicious veteran! *Meine damen und herren*, Gatling Gun Goempers!"

The marching band snapped into a military tune as Goempers climbed into the ring. He had no hair and a handlebar mustache, and as he put on his gloves, Bunyan noticed a missing pinky.

Yet no matter how many battles old Gatling Gun had seen, when the bell rang, he was no match for Bunyan's barrage.

When he hits back, shovel the coal.

Halfway through the first round, Bunyan sprung from a crouched position with an uppercut that connected dead center on Goempers's chin. The hit was so clean, Bunyan felt it in the roots of his toes.

Goempers fell back, sprawling on the mat like a snow angel.

"That's how it's done, kid!" shouted Mac when the fight was over.

Next came Havana Hector, who entered the ring to a peppy Caribbean number.

Ding!

Though Hector tagged Bunyan with a quick left on the first punch, the rest of the fight took just thirty seconds.

When you finish, crank the gear.

Bunyan sent Hector to his knees with a rock-solid right to the ribs.

Again, Mac leapt like a leprechaun into the ring. "That's it, kid! Now, let me fix that face!"

As Mac stitched up Bunyan's bleeding brow, the chants rained down from the bleachers, low and steady at first, then growing louder, till they consumed each last member of the crowd . . .

"*Be-he-moth! . . . Be-he-moth! . . .*"

Bunyan's soul filled with dread. *What must I become now?*

CHAPTER 13

THE BEHEMOTH

With three opponents down, Bunyan didn't want to fight anymore. He went to the ropes and shouted, "El Boffo!" He waved his arms. "Sir! I need to talk to you!"

At last, El Boffo seemed to notice Bunyan. The magnate cupped his hand to his ear. "I can't hear you!"

"Mr. Boffo! Please! I'm from Lump Town!"

El Boffo said something to his bodyguard, as if to confirm what Bunyan was saying. Then he burst into laughter.

"If you want to talk to me, sonny boy"—he put up his fists in a fighting stance—"then *win!*"

Up above, Throttlecock paced in her barrel as she gloried in the rising chants. "Let me *hear you*, my chickadees! Who do you want?"

"Behemoth!"

"Who pops joints like popcorn?"

"Behemoth!"

"Who cracks skulls like pomegranates?"

"Behemoth!"

Throttlecock extended her hand ceremoniously toward the band's drummer, who began a slow beat. The crowd stomped along, slowly, menacingly.

Stomp! Stomp! Stomp! Stomp!

They began their chant:

Rip his guts, Behemoth! Smash apart his hips!

Stomp!

Shatter every bone, Behemoth! Tear apart his ribs!

Stomp!

Chop him down, Behemoth! Chop him to the deck!

Stomp!

Then tear off his finger, and put it on your neck!

Stomp!

"Enter the Four Horsemen!"

At Throttlecock's command, the rear doors of the Fight Barn swung open. Four men entered, dressed in black hoods and gowns, carrying a cage upon their shoulders.

"So, he's in that cage?" said Bunyan to Mac, doing his best to mask his terror.

"Not he," said Mac. "It."

Arriving at the edge of the ring, one of the hooded Four Horsemen unlocked the door and the creature leapt out.

What first struck Bunyan was the Behemoth's size, several feet taller than himself. Wearing nothing but a loincloth, the pasty, sickly-skinned creature slumped forward, with arms so long they dragged along the canvas mat. Its tangled hair fell over its filthy face as one eye drifted in a different direction, giving it a drugged look.

Next, its head. A normal forehead stood upright, like a wall round the brain. But the Behemoth had no forehead at all, just a low-slung hill retreating from its apelike brow. Its teeth protruded like a goat's. Its massive maw stretched from one ear to the other.

Presently, one of the hooded Four Horsemen stepped into the ring holding a live chicken. The Behemoth eyed the bird lazily at first—with its good eye—but the instant the Horseman dropped it on the mat, the Behemoth shot after it with astonishing agility, like a spider racing low across a web. One arm snapped it up and with a flick broke its neck; then the thing bit into the breast and a spurt of blood shot forth. The Behemoth made a quick meal of the guts, then carelessly lobbed the feathery carcass across the ring, where it plopped at Bunyan's feet. Bunyan eyed the dead chicken without a word, till Mac kicked it into the front row.

"Not fully human," said Mac, "not fully not."

Bunyan noticed the Behemoth was wearing a kind of necklace, strung with what at first looked like grayish-purple carrots. Having heard the Behemoth's chant, Bunyan now understood these for what they were—severed fingers. He remembered Gatling Gun Goempers's missing pinky.

"If he wins, he takes a finger?"

Mac nodded grimly. "Tradition."

"Ladies and gentlemen!" blasted Throttlecock overhead. "It has been *months* since we have found a worthy challenger. And our sweet Behemoth—he looks *ready*, doesn't he?"

Money furiously changed hands between the rows as bets were laid down.

As Mac fiddled with Bunyan's foot brace, trying to loosen it and refasten it, Bunyan felt his resolve unraveling. Then he hiccupped. *Hic!*

For a moment, Bunyan considered the so-called plan Sully had laid out for him earlier that day. He spotted Sully at ringside, gesturing at him.

"Don't wait!" He gave the thumbs-up. "Use the secret sauce!"

No way, thought Bunyan. *It's suicide.*

"Open your mouth." Mac proffered water from a metal cup. "Drink."

Bunyan drank. *Hic!* "How do I beat him?"

"Look me in the eyes."

Bunyan did. *Hic!*

"That bell's gonna ring any second, kid, and it's no different now than it's been your whole life. The day you were born, you came out of the womb and figured out how to survive. Some point along the line you got this lame foot and figured that out, too. You weren't born knowing how to spin the gear in the Factory, but you learned it well enough. And all throughout, at any step along the way, you could have said, 'Nope, it's not in me, I give up.' But I've seen it tonight, kid. What you've got in here"—Mac slapped Bunyan's chest three times hard—"is a heart big enough to win. It's *got* to be big enough."

"But that's a monster—" *Hic!*

"It doesn't *matter* if it's a monster!" shouted Mac. "A fighter only ever becomes the fighter he's *forced* to be. Only when you're up against a nightmare will you learn to face the nightmare—not a moment before!"

Hic!

Ding!

The Behemoth advanced toward Bunyan, its knotty long hair swaying on either side of its face. In the middle of the ring, it tilted back its head and roared.

"Yaaaaarrrrrrrr!"

Its teeth were brown and slimy, still stringy with raw chicken meat. Its breath smelled like rotten fish.

Bunyan circled the creature, looking for a punch to throw. Round and round he went till at last he tried a jab. Behemoth swatted it away. He tried another. This time Behemoth caught his hand in midair, crushed his knuckles, then struck Bunyan with a hook to his exposed ribs so hard that Bunyan fell to one knee to catch his breath.

"One! Two!"

Sully O'Connor yelled from ringside. "Come on, man! Do it!"

At nine, Bunyan got up. *Hic!*

Bunyan circled the monster again, but this time the Behemoth reached in with its lengthy arms, grabbed Bunyan by the hair, and flung him so hard against the ropes that he slid out of the ring and crashed on the ground by Sully's feet.

"You're not gonna get another chance!" shouted Sully.

Ding!

The round mercifully finished, Bunyan crawled back to the stool in his corner. Mac gripped Bunyan's head with both hands. "Can you see me?"

To Bunyan it appeared there were several Macs, one floating up and to the right, another down and to the left, all of them mixing with one another.

"I do hate quitting, kid," said Mac. "But if you got to quit, I understand."

As the Fight Barn rocked with wild chanting, Bunyan gazed across at the drooling, rancid creature hunched on its fists, its putrid goat-jaw hanging slack below its sloped forehead.

Sully had explained the plan in the alley that morning:

So, about a year ago, I head to the North Side to see where Throttle-cock keeps the Behemoth in its cage. Around sundown, Behemoth's trainer comes in. Now, Behemoth's a bit testy before its dinner. Starts thrashing around, spitting, chewing the bars. Runs the trainer right out! Well, a short while later, this little girl shows up. Couldn't be more than ten. I panicked. I thought, What's this girl doing? The Behemoth's gonna kill her! But this little girl, she just walks in the cage and starts singing the old lullaby "Danny Boy." Well, lo and behold, the moment she starts singing, Behemoth calms right down. Stops thrashing. Stops spitting. Lies right there in the cage, harmless as a puppy. The little girl lays down the plate of food, but the thing doesn't even eat! It's fast asleep! The girl even gave it a little pat on the head. So here's the deal, cracker: You sing that tune and Behemoth will go down. You won't even have to throw a punch.

There was only one problem: Bunyan had never been able to carry a tune. If he tried, he'd probably just enrage the beast.

But maybe, Bunyan thought—just maybe—there was another way.

Bunyan took a deep breath and swallowed.

"Take off my gloves."

"I understand," said Mac. "No shame in knowing when it's time to quit."

"I'm not quitting. Just take them off."

"I'm here to protect you, kid. If you want out, I'll throw in the towel. But—"

"Hey!" Bunyan said, grabbing Mac by the back of the neck with his glove. "I've got a plan. Just take off the damned gloves!"

Mac stared at Bunyan, incredulous, but after a moment he began unlacing the gloves as he muttered, "This is crazy, kid. Just crazy, crazy, crazy . . ."

Mac pulled them off just as the bell rang.

Ding!

From his spot at the front, Sully leaned forward, too excited to even speak. He nodded at Bunyan in solidarity.

Bare-handed, Bunyan stepped into the center of the ring, where the Behemoth met him with another nauseating "*YYYYAAARRRRR!*"

Bunyan held up his hands to show he had on no gloves. The monster watched him curiously.

With one hand—still keeping the other up—Bunyan reached into his pocket and slowly pulled out his harmonica. Ever so carefully, so as not to startle the Behemoth, Bunyan raised the harp to his lips and began to play the old song that he knew so well, one that his mother had sung to him as a child:

Oh, Danny boy, the pipes, the pipes are calling
From glen to glen, and down the mountain side . . .

The crowd grew hushed. The Behemoth tilted its head to one side like a listening dog. As Bunyan cupped the harp in his hands, the notes bent and returned, climbed and tumbled, mixed and rang out clean.

But come ye back when summer's in the meadow,
Or when the valley's hushed and white with snow . . .

Now the creature's two eyes were focused on Bunyan—the second eye was no longer drifting off—and as Bunyan played another verse, the Behemoth began to howl in plaintive agony along with the tune, all the way through to the final verse, when the creature raised its chin up toward the roof and let out a forlorn cry as Bunyan ended the song:

For you will bend and tell me that you love me,
And I shall sleep in peace until you come to me.

With that, lethargically, the Behemoth lay down upon the mat.

From the corner, Mac whispered to the referee. "Start the count."

The crowd looked on in stunned silence as the ref began. "One . . . two . . ."

Bunyan slipped his harmonica back into his pocket and retreated to his corner, leaning back against the ropes as the ref finished.

"Nine . . . ten! It's all over!"

There, on the bloody canvas, the mighty Behemoth slept.

The ref scratched his mole-covered head. "Gotta hand it to you, kid. Never seen a fight like *that*." He turned to the Four Horsemen. "Get the cage!"

CHAPTER 14

THE GLEAM

The job had been done, the table had been run. He'd fought, he'd suffered, he'd changed, he'd won. The Twisty Path was not for the faint of heart, but Bunyan had made good on his oath to Moki and followed it to the last.

Time to speak to El Boffo.

Ringside, Sully O'Connor collected money from all sides. "And I thank you . . . A big thanks to you . . . and a *special* thanks to you . . ." Sully turned to Abe. "Oh, ye of little faith . . ." Abe dug deep in his pockets for a wad of cash and slapped it into Sully's palm.

Bunyan shouted up at Throttlecock in her perch. "I beat them all! It's over!"

Too stricken to respond, Throttlecock watched from her perch as the Four Horsemen packed her slumbering creature away, its hairy arms hanging out between the bars.

The crowd, disappointed at the lack of a fight, jeered and booed. Crumpled newspapers and watermelon rinds rained down on the ring. A half-eaten rib, tossed up from the audience, struck Throttlecock in the chest, then rolled down her dress, slathering barbecue sauce over the lace.

"Rip-off!"

At that, Throttlecock seemed to regain her senses. She rang her cowbell. "Will you *listen* to me?"

"Bring back Behemoth!"

"Will you just be *quiet*!"

She rang the bell so hard it looked like she was trying to shake a feral cat off her arm. At last the crowd grew still.

"Now then!" she shouted over the throng. "Do you actually think that I, Eleanor Throttlecock, would *ever* let you down? Do you think I could have risen to the very *height* of my profession if I didn't know how to deliver the *goods*?"

More jeers and boos.

"The Factory Freak has shown heart, yes he has! He's been clever. Unpredictable! But to run Eleanor *Throttlecock's* table, the challenger must defeat *five* fighters. And by my count, we've only had four."

"What is she talking about?" said Bunyan to Mac. "I defeated Behemoth! The Behemoth is last!"

Throttlecock paced around in her sawed-off barrel, possessed with new purpose. "Tonight, my friends, I have something *special* in store. Oh yes! Tonight, you shall witness unstoppable force against immovable object! Tonight, the unbreakable spear meets the impervious shield! The paradox unthinkable! The pairing irresistible! Black versus white! Night versus day! Undefeated contra undefeated!"

"What's going on?" said Bunyan.

"Oh no . . . ," muttered Mac.

Throttlecock lowered her hand toward Bunyan. "In this corner, our newcomer, the Lump Pumper, the God of the Gears . . ."

As she spoke, the crowd stood on its toes, searching the Fight Barn for whoever was next.

"And in the opposite corner, for our final bout of the evening, I present to you the Romulus of the Rail Yards, Mr. Lightning Fist, and all of this—*all of this!*—because I would never, *ever* let you down . . ."

"It can't be . . . ," said Mac.

Throttlecock blasted the name into her cone. "Steel! Drivin'! John!"

The roar was deafening. The crowd, transported. The ecstasy, universal. A blur of frenzied activity consumed each last man, woman, and child—getting odds, making bets, better odds, more bets, double down, triple down, all the money, all on this. Sully and Abe hugged each other and jumped with joy.

"She can't do this," said Bunyan. "I beat Behemoth! I ran the table!"

High overhead, Throttlecock paced about, egging the crowd on. "Are! You! *Ready?*"

Amid the fanfare, a rather nondescript Black man stepped into the ring. Bunyan wasn't sure who it was—maybe Steel-Drivin' John's advance man? No shirt, black shorts, black boots. He sat on his stool. About the same age as Bunyan, he looked calm. Subdued. Almost polite.

"Who's that guy there?" asked Bunyan.

Mac stared at the man, awestruck.

"Hey, Mac! Who is that?"

"It's him . . . It's . . . the champ."

Wait—that face. Bunyan remembered it. The sign. The newspaper. The train platform. All lit up with the Gleam. JOHN HENRY— WANTED ALIVE. Could it be?

Bunyan looked to the man's chest. There, upon it, was a scar, right over his heart. *Distinctive scar across his chest.* It had to be.

Their eyes met. Steel-Drivin' John's expression radiated the confidence of a judge in a courtroom, whose power was both earned and absolute. *Welcome to my world,* said the look on his face. *You may not get what you want, but you'll get what you deserve.*

He slowly turned his chin to the right, then the left, cracking his neck.

All around, wagers were settled. "Bunyan lasts a round?" "No." "Half a round?" "No." "Thirty seconds?" "Less."

Throttlecock violently rang her cowbell again. "Yes, yes, *yeeeessssssss*," she said with verve, almost flirting with her minions. "You were *angry* with me, weren't you? Well, are you angry with me *now?* Ask and ye shall receive!" The crowd roared back its approval as Throttlecock paced about, riddled with new energy.

"Quick, what do you know about this guy?"

Mac shook his head, seeming overcome. "I thought he'd vanished . . ."

"The bell's about to ring."

"You've been clever all night, kid. Got any more tricks?"

"No. You?"

Mac quickly slathered gobs of grease on Bunyan's face. "Just try to stay out of the way. Uppercut is quick as a bolt."

"What about hitting him?"

Mac smacked Bunyan encouragingly on both shoulders. "Yeah. Try that!"

Ding!

As the first round began, Steel-Drivin' John strode across the canvas mat with measured calm, like a cat from his lair, creeping toward his prey with neither a sound nor a footprint. As they circled, Bunyan experimented with a few jabs, but his adversary only pulled his neck back ever so slightly, measuring Bunyan's reach.

Bunyan thought back to what had worked with Bobo Cash: *When you punch, swing the pick. When he stumbles, push the cart. When he hits back, shovel the coal. When you finish, crank the gear.*

He tried it all. Swing, push, shovel, crank. Everything whiffed.

Halfway through the round, Bunyan stormed in with yet another desperate flurry, but Steel-Drivin' John just kept his own gloves down by his waist, not even bothering to put up a defense. He leaned back on the ropes and kept his chin out of the way, twisting his torso left to right, bobbing and weaving as each effort missed the mark. At the end of the flurry, the wearied Bunyan clung to his opponent, panting for breath, desperate just to stand up.

"Don't make it hard on yourself," Steel-Drivin' John said in Bunyan's ear. "Better to just go down quick." He gave Bunyan a shove back into the middle of the ring. "When you want it to stop, just take a knee."

The first punch was so fast and exact, it struck Bunyan dead in the middle of the forehead, like a piston hammering. Then came another, followed by another, the strikes so quick they were nearly invisible, like Bunyan was fighting a ghost. Here a sting on the ribs, there a blast to the gut. Bunyan suddenly felt like he was in a barrel rolling down the side of a mountain, pitching end over end. He dropped to one knee.

Steel-Drivin' John—who still hadn't broken a sweat—bent down. "Just stay there and nobody gets hurt."

The ref counted. "One . . . two . . ."

Bunyan squeezed his eyes shut, then opened them again, trying to see straight.

"Three . . . four . . ."

I'm doing all I can, he said in his heart to Lucette. *I don't know what I've got left.*

"Five . . . six . . . seven . . ."

If I have you, I have the world. Ah, Lucette!

At nine, Bunyan stood.

"Unwise," said his opponent.

Bunyan's whole body hurt. "I'm fighting for something more important than my life."

Steel-Drivin' John raised his fists. "So am I."

"Fight!" said the ref.

Bunyan again swarmed his opponent with punches, hook after hook after hook. But his fists only struck blank air. Meanwhile, like the iron-armed hammer man he was, Steel-Drivin' John drove punches into Bunyan's ribs, arms, and ears, like he was blasting nails into stone.

Bunyan dropped to his knee a second time, sucking wind.

"One! Two! Three!"

In the middle of the count, Bunyan heard a welcome sound.

Ding!

Bunyan wobbled back to his stool, where Mac assessed his bleeding face and couldn't tell where to begin.

"I've got no chance in there!" said Bunyan. "It's like a squall of scorpions! A fog of hammers! A tornado of vipers!"

"Calm down!" shouted Mac. "The only way to win is to be calm. Only the calm fighter can see clear!"

Bunyan closed his eyes and spoke to Moki in his heart:

I'm going to die in there if you don't help me.

If the Chilali was near, they did not speak. The bell rang again.

Ding!

Drained of all but his most primitive will, Bunyan charged at his opponent. He rained down blow after blow after blow after blow. He offered the best and last of his energy.

And not a single punch hit.

Crafty, cool, and quick, Steel-Drivin' John trotted energetically about his target.

"I asked you twice to go down. I'm not gonna ask a third time."

The bedraggled Bunyan felt like a scarecrow after a hurricane. The inevitable was closing in.

Yet just as Steel-Drivin' John came in to throw a punch, Bunyan saw something:

A spark of light in the air . . . just to the right.

The Gleam.

Bunyan threw his head toward it and at the same moment felt the light breeze of a missed punch. Instantly, he saw another spark, this one down by his own knee. He crouched and felt another punch miss his ear.

Another spark, another duck. Another step, another miss. Suddenly, the air was filled with a kind of fireworks erupting in sequence; all Bunyan had to do was follow it along—*step, slide, duck, lean, slide, duck, lean, step*—and put his head where the next light flashed.

After a dozen straight misses, Bunyan smirked. "What's the matter, John?"

Steel-Drivin' John squinted, frustrated. "Can't run forever."

Now it was Bunyan who grew relaxed. *Slide, duck, lean.* The molten airborne map of the Gleam lit the way before him as he feinted, slid, and high-stepped around the ring.

"Swing and a miss!" Bunyan announced after another whiff. "Strike three!"

Just as the two came face-to-face, Bunyan saw the Gleam light up his foe's forehead. After an instant, the light vanished. But seconds later it appeared on his ribs.

Bunyan let his left hook fly, and for the first time in the fight he felt the sweet thud of connection. Steel-Drivin' John was so stunned by the blow he skittered sideways across the mat and crashed into the ropes, where he fell on all fours.

The crowd went silent as the ref began his count. "One! . . . Two! . . . Three! . . ."

"Get up, champ!" shouted Abe, running from his seat to the side of the ring. "Get up!"

Mac laughed with joy and disbelief. "You got him, kid! I don't know how, but you got him!"

"Six! . . . Seven! . . ."

Wincing and stretching his bruised torso, the mighty boxer at last rose to his full height, just as the ref reached eight.

At that, Steel-Drivin' John's expression changed. He was in pain—that was clear. He was doing his best to mask that pain—this was clear, too. The knockdown had infuriated him—that was most clear of all.

And so the two great men set upon each other once more. Two rounds turned to three. Three to four. Four to ten. They passed the hour mark. The cut over Bunyan's eye gushed blood. A welt the size of an egg puffed up on John's cheek. Mac got a sack of ice and chilled Bunyan's face between rounds.

But even with the help of the Gleam, Bunyan still couldn't bring his opponent down, so peerless and flawless a fighter he was. Twenty rounds. Twenty-five. Time after time, Bunyan muttered to himself, "Just make it these three minutes." The round would end and he'd deliriously, nauseously, take a seat. Then, a minute later, when he heard the bell for the start of the new round, he'd think of Lucette, lying silverdark on their bed, and say to himself, "Just one more."

At the end of the twenty-ninth round, Bunyan and Steel-Drivin' John were tangled in the corner, leaning on each other just to stay up.

"Tell me," said Steel-Drivin' John, "why won't you quit?"

Bunyan clung to him, one arm around his neck. "My whole life I've been shut out, turned down, and left for dead." He panted for breath. "But I got something I can't give up, something I won't let go, something I'll never deny." The pair stumbled across the ring and together crashed into the ropes on the other side. "Why won't *you* quit?"

Steel-Drivin' John rested his forehead on Bunyan's sweaty, bloody shoulder. "I've been locked up and put in the hole, I've fought the law and lost, I've lived my whole life in the shadow of a lie. But I got something I can't forget, something I won't forsake, something I've got to save."

Hugging each other like two bloody bears, the men drifted into the center of the ring. The crowd started to boo.

"Fight!" they shouted. "Kill him!"

"Last night, I dreamed there was a boulder in my path," said Steel-Drivin' John, panting for breath. "That boulder is you."

Bunyan gripped his foe to stay up. "I won't go down."

"I won't go down, either."

"I can't knock you out."

"I can't knock *you* out."

As the crowd tossed rib bones and watermelon rinds at them, at last Steel-Drivin' John said, "What must be must be. Just follow my lead."

At that, Steel-Drivin' John took Bunyan's glove in his own and raised it up high at the center of the ring, as if they both were victors. The pair bowed, first to one side of the audience, then the next, till they'd bowed to all four sides of the Barn.

From above, Throttlecock shouted down into her cone. "Keep going, you two! Punch! *Punch!*"

She slid down a rope from the crow's nest and landed in the center of the bloodstained ring.

"Just *what* is going on here?" She looked to the ref, who himself had wearily taken a seat in the corner. "These men need to *fight*! Someone needs to win!"

Throttlecock grabbed Steel-Drivin' John's gloves and held them up. Then she propped up Bunyan's fists. "Come on! Go!"

But the men threw no more punches.

"It's a draw," said Steel-Drivin' John, working off his gloves.

"We're even," said Bunyan.

"There are no *draws* in a Sasquatch Productions fight," shouted Throttlecock. "Someone wins! Someone loses! Who won?"

"Neither."

"Both."

"You signed a *contract*." Throttlecock jabbed a finger in Steel-Drivin' John's face. "It's in *writing*. You think you're getting paid for this? You get *nothing*!" Then she wheeled around to Bunyan. "You think you're meeting El *Boffo*?"

A crumpled-up newspaper struck Steel-Drivin' John's calf and a watermelon rind hit Bunyan's arm as the fans got up and began to leave.

Throttlecock ran to the ring's edge. "Stay! Wait! They'll keep fighting!"

Up in his special box, El Boffo stood, shook his head, and headed toward the exit. Seeing this, Bunyan hopped out of the ring and tried to push his way through the throng. "El Boffo!" he shouted. "Wait!"

But the crowd was thick, Bunyan's energy was gone, and moments later, El Boffo had vanished into the streets.

CHAPTER 15

F.O.L.

A nd what do I get, for all I've given?" Bunyan lamented to himself, seeing El Boffo go. "Nothing! Nothing! Nothing!"

"Don't be down, kid," said Mac, a bit misty-eyed as he patted him on the back. "You did great. All I ever wanted was a kid with heart who'd listen to me . . ."

But just at that moment, Bunyan's mind was elsewhere. On the other side of the Fight Barn, he spotted Steel-Drivin' John heading for the exit. Strangely enough, his opponent was positively smoldering with the Gleam, as if he were a star fallen to earth.

Bunyan chased after him. Outside, the early spring air smelled of rich soil and the smoking wood of the barbecue pit. The Gleam lit a path, clear as a shining river, straight to where Steel-Drivin' John was washing his face in a rain barrel.

"Quite a fight," Bunyan said, walking up.

No response from his opponent. Bunyan took a step closer to him and lowered his voice. "Hey, so . . . are you John Henry?"

He looked at Bunyan sharply. "Where did you hear that name?"

Bunyan produced the bulletin from his pocket.

$$$$$ CASH REWARD $$$$$
FOR THE APPREHENSION OF ESCAPED CONVICT
JOHN HENRY

Steel-Drivin' John snatched it. As he looked over it, Bunyan studied the differences between the picture and the actual man. The crude neck and haunted eyes of the drawing made John Henry appear to be barbaric and frightening. In reality, even after a brawl, his face was intelligent, handsome, subtle.

"Where'd you get this?"

"The train station. It's you, right?"

"Yeah." John Henry stuffed the sign into his pocket and looked around to see if anyone was watching. "Are you one of them?"

"One of who?"

John Henry grabbed Bunyan's forearms, examining them. "A man on the top of the pyramid."

"No, I don't think so . . . I . . ." Bunyan struggled to think of how to explain. "I'm from Lump Town. I'm here to meet El Boffo, and . . . well . . ." Bunyan realized how bizarre it all sounded. "I'm on a mission for my wife."

Stepping back from the barrel, John Henry kept an eye on Bunyan as he changed from his fighting clothes into clean pants and a button-down shirt. Bunyan noticed a knife strapped around his calf, concealed in a sheath.

"Throttlecock told me this was your first fight," said John Henry. "You expect me to believe that?"

"It's true."

"Right." John Henry threw his bag over his shoulder. "I may be a lot of things to a lot of people. But I'm no fool."

John Henry walked off. As Bunyan watched him go, the Gleam only shone brighter around him.

Bunyan began to mutter out loud to Moki, almost growling at them. "Well, what do you want me to do, *follow* him? He doesn't want to talk to me. This is ridiculous."

But the Gleam kept pulsing urgently along the ground like a living thing. With no better plan, Bunyan trotted after John Henry.

"Back in the ring, you said you were fighting for something more important than your life." Bunyan hustled up beside him. "What is it?"

John Henry kept walking beneath the trees. Even though they were at the outer limit of the Windy City, it was still a crowded stretch of road, filled with saloons, card houses, and dance halls, packed with buzzing fans who'd poured into the night straight from the Fight Barn. John Henry kept glancing about himself, as if in fear of being followed.

"I'm really sorry to keep bothering you," Bunyan went on. "It's just, I think you and I need to work together."

At that, John Henry turned. "I don't know what you're up to, man, but there's only two people I stick my neck out for in this world. And you're not one of them."

As John Henry tried to leave, Bunyan grabbed his arm. "Please. Will you just talk to me?"

John Henry pulled his arm free and, without a further word, dashed across the street, where he darted down an alley behind a general store.

Bunyan jammed his hands into his pockets. "And that is that," he grumbled under his breath, as if to Moki. "The Twisty Path comes to an end."

Where would he go now? He had no idea.

As Bunyan was standing there along the road, staring at the place where John Henry had vanished, he suddenly got shoved in the back so hard he almost fell over. He turned to see a scuffle spilling into the street.

A circle had formed around a white man and a Black man. The white man, with a wide-brimmed hat, a patchy beard, and a smug grin, squared off with the Black man, who was tall and lean, with focused eyes and a barely concealed fury. The white man had a bandolier full of bullets and a gun on his hip. The Black man didn't have anything but a glare.

"The trouble is," said the white man with a southern accent, "the more you tamper with America, the more you corrupt the original."

"The *real* trouble," said the Black man, "is that the original *itself* was corrupt. Tampering's our only chance."

"A pyramid turned on its head falls down."

"Better for it to fall than stay faulty."

As the crowd cheered on the barbs, Bunyan noticed the white man had a fabric band around his arm. The symbol upon it was a pyramid, broken in the middle. The top portion was white, while the larger, bottom portion of it was black. In the gap between were the letters "F.O.L."

He'd seen those letters a few times before—on the bottom of the John Henry Wanted poster.

"I'm just fighting so the past doesn't get lost," said the white man, raising his voice.

The Black man answered, "The past ain't nothing but dead weight."

"When America changes, she dies."

"When America changes, she'll finally get born."

Just when it looked like the two would come to blows, another white man jammed his way into the circle. This one had a large nose that divided his face like a blade. He, too, had an F.O.L. band on his arm.

"Pulaski!" he said. He grabbed the bearded white man by the shoulder. "I marked him. Come on."

At that, the pair hustled out of the skirmish, mounted two waiting horses, flicked the reins, and charged down the street.

The name was unmistakable.

IF SEEN, PLEASE REPORT TO: PULASKI & LYNCH, 111 ADAMS ST., THE WINDY CITY

No doubt these were the bounty hunters after John Henry.

Bunyan broke into a jog, then a run, then a sprint, past the general store and down the dim alley, just in time to see the horses of Lynch and Pulaski vanish into the graveyard up ahead.

Crack!

A gunshot. Shouts.

Bunyan dashed toward the noise, his Junk Foot chafing painfully in his brace as he rushed in among the moonlit graves to see Pulaski and Lynch up ahead, already dismounted. They had pistols pointed at John Henry, who stood with his hands up. Unseen, Bunyan crept behind the gravestones.

"Well, well, well," said Pulaski.

"Just missed you in the Burgh," said Lynch. "Almost had you in the City of Brotherly Love. Old Man Duncan's been missing you on the gang."

"Black Betty's been missing you, too."

Bunyan was now just a stone's throw away, hidden behind the statue of an angel. On the ground, he spotted the silvery path of the Gleam, leading right up to John Henry.

He remembered his oath to Moki.

Will you swear to give yourself to the strange way, the hard way, the absurd way, the unconventional way, the courageous way, no matter what the Gleam asks?

Bunyan racked his mind. It was impossible. The men were armed; he was not. He scanned the scene. The two horses stood next to a wide hole in the ground, an empty grave.

Suddenly, he got an idea.

Bunyan stood up straight, walked into the open, and after a few steps was face-to-face with Lynch and Pulaski.

"You got one, huh?" said Bunyan.

"Move along, pal," said Lynch. "This ain't no business of yours."

Bunyan flashed his eyebrows at him. "The more you tamper, the more you corrupt the original."

Pulaski squinted, confused at hearing the words he'd just spoken out in the street.

Bunyan walked over to Pulaski and gave him a pat, right on his F.O.L. armband. "Turn a pyramid on its head and it falls," he said with confidence. "If America changes, America dies."

"Damn straight, brother," said Pulaski. "But we'll take it from here."

Lynch took handcuffs from his hip. He was about to lock John Henry up when Bunyan stepped in his way.

"You wouldn't mind if I searched him first, would you, patriot?"

Lynch cocked an eyebrow. "Say, weren't you that fella in the ring?"

"You bet I was. Couldn't take him down in there. All the more reason to take him down out here." Bunyan shook his head. "Just wanna
make sure he realizes the past isn't past."

Pulaski thought a moment, then pushed his hat back on his head.
"All right. Go on."

As Bunyan approached, John Henry kept his hands in the air and
eyed Bunyan carefully. Bunyan began patting down his legs, his chest,
his arms, making a big fuss the whole time.

"What are you hiding here, big boy? Knife in the belt? How
about a gun? Sometimes these types like to hide a gun right in the
armpit . . ."

Quick, Bunyan shoved his hand in John Henry's armpit. Finding
nothing there, he worked his way around till they were face-to-face,
chatting the whole while.

"They get more clever all the time, don't they?"

Then, just as his face was turned away from both Pulaski and
Lynch, Bunyan spoke quickly under his breath in John Henry's ear.
"*When I clear my throat, be ready.*"

He immediately resumed his chatter. "Crafty fellas, these run-
aways. Can hide a shiv anywhere."

"Hey, wrap this up, all right?" said Lynch. "We've been on him for
months. He's our prize."

"Just finishing now, my brother . . ." Bunyan moved around to
John Henry's back and knelt down by his boots. Then he froze. "Well,
won't you look at this?"

"What?" said Pulaski.

Bunyan shook his head. "You just hate to see it. But it really is no
surprise . . ."

"What'd you find?" Lynch approached cautiously with the cuffs.

Still squatting, Bunyan waved Lynch over. "Come look!"

Lynch stepped toward Bunyan as Pulaski seemed to get more
excited. "Hey, I want to see, too."

As John Henry kept his hands in the air, Bunyan motioned eagerly
for Lynch to squat down. Lynch holstered his gun and crouched,
right by John Henry's boot.

There, Bunyan pulled John Henry's concealed, gleaming, eight-inch knife from its sheath.

"Well, I'll be damned."

It was just then that Bunyan loudly and distinctly cleared his throat.

"Look more closely," said Bunyan. "Check out what it says on the handle."

"What's it say?" said Pulaski, trying to look himself and only limply holding up the gun.

Lynch leaned in, and by the dim light, he read the letters on the handle of John Henry's knife. "F . . . O . . . F? What's that mean?"

"Hmmm," said Bunyan. "I think it means . . . *Now!*"

In a flash, Bunyan grabbed Lynch by the side of the head, shoved his face on the ground, and had the knife on his neck. John Henry didn't miss a beat, snatching the gun from Pulaski, right out of his hands.

"Hey!" shouted Pulaski, but John Henry turned the gun on him quick and shot him in the leg—*crack!* Pulaski grabbed his thigh and screamed, crumpling on the ground. John Henry hoisted him by the belt and dragged him to the empty grave, pitching him in.

"Stay down or I shoot again," said John Henry.

Bunyan dug the knife tip into Lynch's flesh. "Drop the cuffs. Stand up."

Finished with Pulaski, John Henry approached Lynch and pointed the barrel of the gun directly between Lynch's eyes, so it touched the top of his nose.

"Easy, boy," said Lynch. He dropped the cuffs. "Here."

"Ain't nobody's boy," said John Henry. He nodded to the empty grave. "Get in."

Bunyan removed Lynch's gun from his holster, picked up the cuffs, and gave Lynch a shove into the grave, where he toppled onto Pulaski, who screamed even louder.

John Henry pointed the gun down at them. "Facedown."

As the pair of bounty hunters squirmed in the hole, John Henry took the cuffs from Bunyan and threw them in. "Put these on. One for each wrist."

The bounty hunters handcuffed themselves to each other.

As Bunyan tucked Lynch's gun in his belt, he saw, gathering at the edge of the graveyard, half a dozen men gawking and pointing. He handed John Henry his knife. "We gotta go."

The pair dashed off, creeping behind crypts, stepping past sepulchers, ducking among vaults, then at last hustling through the moonlit mounds and monoliths of the dead and hopping a fence out on the main street, which was still crowded in the aftermath of the fight.

They tried to blend in but hadn't run ten strides down the road when *crack! Crack!* A pair of shots split the air.

"Gotta hustle," said John Henry.

They sprinted down the street, looking for a place to duck into a store, mix in among the pedestrians, anything to get out of sight.

Crack!

"Stop!"

They turned back to see the handcuffed bounty hunters running together. Lynch pulled out a tiny pistol he'd hidden under his arm.

"Where to?" said Bunyan.

John Henry eyed the storefronts. "Here. Right here."

Bunyan looked up. There, on the porch of a saloon, stood five Black men. One had his arms crossed. One leaned on the rail. Another glared. The fourth grinned. The fifth eyeballed the two men. Each held a weapon: a shotgun, a pistol, a handgun, a rifle, and a revolver, respectively.

John Henry bounded up the stairs. "Got a bit of white heat on us," he said to the one with the shotgun.

"Go on," the Black man at the door said. He put his fist on Bunyan's chest. "This boy straight?"

"Yeah," said John Henry. "He's all right."

The men cleared the way, then stood in front of the entrance. From inside the establishment Bunyan heard the handcuffed bounty hunters shouting in the street.

"John Henry!" Gunshots. *Crack crack crack!* "John Henry!"

"They're not getting in here," said the Steel-Drivin' Man.

Safe inside, Bunyan spotted a sign overhead:

GABRIEL'S PARADISE ROADHOUSE
A Full Supporter of Second Amendment Rights
BLACK CLIENTS PREFERRED—FIREARMS WELCOMED
BLACK-ON-BLACK CRIME—STRICTLY PROHIBITED
BLACK-ON-WHITE CRIME—IT'S YOUR MESS TO CLEAN
WHITE-ON-BLACK CRIME—GOOD LUCK

"Come on," said John Henry. "Let's grab a drink."

CHAPTER 16

GABRIEL AND THE SAVANT

Inside Gabriel's Paradise Roadhouse, surrounded by Black patrons, the two battered, gigantic men took a seat. A woman with a towel on her shoulder and a pistol in her belt sidled up.

"What'll it be?"

"Couple beers," said John Henry.

The waitress, also Black, took a moment to size up Bunyan. "This cracker straight?"

"Plenty straight."

The waitress yelled out to the bar for two beers and moments later banged them down on the table.

"If you'd like, I can seat him in the rear," the waitress said to John Henry.

"Appreciate the offer. We're fine for now."

From a stage in the back, a band ground through a hoedown, the musicians glistening with sweat as they played with a washboard, a trumpet, a fiddle, a standing bass, and a pair of wooden spoons.

Bunyan was about to start talking when another man appeared beside the table, this one with a double-barreled rifle slung over his shoulder and a cigar wedged in his mouth. He took out the cigar to speak with John Henry.

"Any problem here?"

"No problem."

"He know which way the wind blows?"

"Think so."

Immediately, yet another man, this one clearly a bit buzzed, came up laughing with a young woman.

"Make it a double," he shouted after her as she kept walking toward the bar.

Seeing Bunyan, the man stopped cold and stared for what seemed like minutes.

At last, he leaned in, almost nose to nose with Bunyan. "Long as you're in here, try to be a credit to your race."

"Yes, sir," Bunyan answered. As he walked off, Bunyan shifted uneasily in his seat. "Never been in a place like this."

"A place like what?"

"It's like the color of my skin makes me a target."

"Can't imagine." John Henry had already knocked back his beer and motioned to the waitress for another. "Anyway, thanks for the help back there. You're pretty good at playing the part. Could have fooled me."

"So, you're a railroad man?"

"Family man."

"And this Pulaski and Lynch . . . they're bounty hunters?"

"Right. That Wanted sign you found at the railroad station is bad news for me. Clock is ticking."

"I saw the bands on their arms. The pyramid. What is F.O.L.?"

"Fraternal Order of Liberty. Bunch of thugs pretending to be patriots." John Henry shook his head and took another swig. "For hate to go out in public, it has to dress like an ideal. Been on my back for years."

A portly man approached the table—overweight and gloriously so. He wore a bounteous apron and a chef's cap and had a pistol hanging low off his belt. He warmly shook John Henry's hand with both of his own.

"I'm Gabriel. Welcome to Paradise. Any cause for concern here?"

"We're all right," said John Henry. "Tell you what, though. I could use an escort downtown. Street's a bit hot."

Gabriel smiled. "We ran those boys off. They won't bother you a bit. Escort's coming right up."

Onstage, the hoedown had ended and a lone young blues singer took the stage with a guitar and slide. He sang low and easy and pure, and at the end of each line the crowd called out, "That's it!" "Go on!" "What else?"

John Henry drank his beer and focused back on Bunyan. "So, what's your deal, man? You went up against the Behemoth, then me, just to talk to El Boffo? Got to be an easier way."

"If there is, I couldn't find it. You've run the table before, right?"

"Couple times."

"Then you must have had dinner with El Boffo."

"Wouldn't break bread with the man if you paid me."

"Why's that?"

"I've got family I'd rather eat with. It's men like him that kept me in the chain gang in the first place."

"El Boffo did that? I just thought he was . . . you know . . . a capitalist."

"The fire of capitalism burns with the fuel of Black men. He's got a taste for cheap prison labor. The sweat of my brow, the blisters on my hands, the blood on my back—in the end, it all lined El Boffo's pockets. Labor makes the money. Money makes the laws."

Bunyan thought this through. "So I guess you and I both worked for the same man . . . Maybe that's how we're connected."

"Connected?"

Bunyan didn't know how to say it, other than to say it. "Right. So . . . what it boils down to is . . . well . . . I believe you're part of my destiny."

John Henry nearly spit out his beer. "Your *what?*"

"You see, there's something I call the Gleam. Ever since I was a kid, well . . ." But Bunyan trailed off. He felt mortified, ridiculous, so much so that he was relieved when another patron came up to the table.

"This white boy with you?" The man had a brutal-looking swamp knife sheathed on his belt.

"He's all right," said John Henry. "Got me out of a jam just now."

"If you say so. No devils in paradise."

As the man walked off, Bunyan tried to resume, though he felt sure he'd already lost his audience. "You see, the Gleam, it's kind of like an instinct, a conviction. I see it on people, on things. When I saw the Wanted sign, it lit up all around your face. Then tonight, remember in the second round, when suddenly you couldn't hit me?"

"No way this was your first fight."

"But it *was*. That was the Gleam helping me then, too. It showed me where to move, where to punch. Then after the fight, the Gleam appeared again. It's why I followed you to the graveyard."

John Henry smirked and shook his head. "Gimme a break, man."

"You ever heard of a Chilali?"

John Henry thought. "Maybe. Old legend. I think my wife told me about them once. She studies those things. Has eagle wings, jaguar legs? And there's the thing about, what do you call it . . ."

"The Beautiful Destiny," said Bunyan.

"Right. Fairy tale."

Behind Bunyan onstage, the singer hit clusters of notes while pounding on the guitar with the heel of his palm for the beat. "Go on!" the crowd shouted. "Go!"

"Well . . ." Again, Bunyan paused. It was hard to say such things to another grown man, especially a sharp-eyed one like John Henry. "The fact is, I saw a Chilali myself, a few days ago outside Lump Town. They told me that the Gleam is my special power. It helps me see the Twisty Path to the Beautiful Destiny. As it so happens, you're on my Path."

At that, John Henry laughed. Then he laughed some more. Eventually he laughed so hard there were tears in his eyes.

"I'm sorry," he said at last. "I'm sorry. I just . . . with all that I've been through, sometimes it's nice to hear a good joke."

Bunyan raised his hands and let them crash on the table, as if the whole thing sounded just as preposterous to him as it did to John Henry. "What can I say? To me, the Gleam is real. I left everything I had to follow it. My job. My pay. My future. My wife is sick, and I'm trying to save her life. Right now, the Gleam is all I've got."

Another man walked by and glanced suspiciously at the pair. John Henry raised his palm with a gesture that said, *No problem here.*

John Henry drummed his fingers on the table, thinking it through. "I've heard a lot of wild stories in my time, and I've even believed some of them. But this story, well, even if it *is* true, about this light, this ..."

"Gleam."

"Even if it's real, I still don't see what any of it's got to do with me. I'm on the run, and my plan is to leave this country on the next boat that'll have me. So, I don't see how it's even possible we work together."

Bunyan pulled the lock of Lucette's hair from his pocket. The silverdark had crept a third of the way up. "I only have a few days myself. When this silverdark gets to the tip, she'll be gone."

Gabriel returned. "Escort's outside. Anywhere you want to go."

John Henry glanced at Bunyan. "Where you staying tonight?"

Bunyan shrugged. "Nowhere."

John Henry drained the last of his beer. "Come on. You'll stay with me. You may be crazy, but you stuck out your neck."

The two got up to leave. At the door, Gabriel stopped John Henry and nodded quick at Bunyan. "You *sure* this boy's okay?"

John Henry nodded. "A bit crazy. But okay."

Gabriel pulled up his sleeve and showed John Henry his wrist. It was scarred, as if chains had been on it. Quietly, he said, "I'm here to help any man who's been on the gang, in any way he needs. We clear?"

"*Mighty* clear."

"Paradise has always got to keep moving. But I'll be here a minute, I reckon. If you need us, give a holler." Gabriel shook John Henry's hand. "We always got room for Lions."

The last comment seemed to catch John Henry by surprise. After a moment, he nodded, still shaking Gabriel's hand. "Friendship over fate."

Gabriel grinned. "Ain't that the truth."

Outside, Bunyan and John Henry got into a waiting carriage, driven by two men with shotguns over their laps. Behind them, the crowd went on hollering in the Roadhouse as the young singer's voice poured gold into the night.

———————•———————

It was well past one in the morning when Bunyan climbed the stairs to John Henry's fourth-story tenement, so it was very strange to see that, outside his door, there was a line of finely attired white men.

"This is the place," said John Henry.

Bunyan and John Henry—so big they couldn't walk side by side down the hall—squeezed past these men and ducked inside.

The layout of the apartment was tight but neat. In one corner stood a stove, a washing bin, a few jugs of drinking water, and an icebox. Curtains covered the window, though through a slit Bunyan could see a clothesline extended to a tenement opposite, the sheets hanging from it lit up by the brilliant moon.

"Who were those guys outside?" asked Bunyan.

"You'll see."

Standing in the kitchen, Bunyan spotted in the next room a Black woman of about thirty and a burly white man of about sixty, sitting across from each other at a table. The man had thinning hair and an enormously bushy white goatee, and he appeared to be a touch bewildered. The woman, with a bright face and an alert posture, noticed the pair and raised an eyebrow at John Henry, as if to say, *Hello.*

"Remember how I said I didn't stick my neck out, except for two people?" said John Henry. "That's my wife, Polly. She's one."

"Who's the white guy?"

"The governor."

"The governor? As in, the *governor?*"

John Henry smirked. "I'll be back in a minute. Stay here and listen. You might learn something."

John Henry walked across the room and vanished through a doorway on the other side.

As he did, Bunyan noticed a certain smell and found his mind flooded with visions of old, yellowing pages and big, black type. He had memories of words: rhyming words, debated words, strident words, comforting words, words that shaped him as a child, words that sustained him as a man, new words, old words, ancient words, words older than the oldest living things . . .

It was the smell of . . . *books.*

Here in John Henry's apartment, Bunyan suddenly noticed there were books everywhere. Books on the floor, in the corners, by the walls, in the nooks, and piled high behind Polly. For a moment it seemed as if John Henry's small apartment were *made* out of books. It occurred to Bunyan that if John Henry was to be considered "armed and very dangerous," as the Wanted poster stated, then the pen must truly be mightier than the sword.

After taking in the sheer volume of volumes, Bunyan's gaze returned to Polly. She was focused on a piece of paper between herself and the governor, trying to lead him along, though the poor man was clearly struggling.

"Right . . . so . . ." The governor scratched his head. "I think I get it. It's very good, of course . . ."

"By this point in the speech, you've divorced them from their old beliefs," said Polly. "Now you must wed them to a new direction."

"And add some gravitas," added the governor with a hopeful smile. "They just love gravitas."

"Perhaps a quote."

"Oh yes, a quote! Maybe Pericles." He smiled. "Or Demosthenes."

It seemed to Bunyan that Polly's intellect surrounded the governor's like a vast sea encircling a rudderless boat. She tapped her finger on her lips. "How about . . . 'It is easier to build strong children than repair broken men.'"

"Ah, Aristotle," said the governor.

"Douglass," Polly corrected him. She was about to jot it down, then stopped. "Or, wait. Even better: 'The soul that is within me no man can degrade.'"

"Ah, surely *that* is Aristotle," said the governor rapturously.

"Douglass again."

"Wonderful."

"Yes, I do think it does the trick," said Polly. Penciling in the quote, she handed the finished document back to the governor.

"Yes, yes, yes, it's all perfect." The governor stood, bowed his head, and dropped a nickel into a small dish on the side of the table. "A little extra today."

"Till next week?"

He nodded eagerly. "They're just *gobbling* this stuff up."

The moment the governor left, the next man from the hallway entered and sat. He wore a wrinkled suit and spectacles and he appeared a touch on edge as Polly gazed over his document.

"So . . . ," Polly said at last, "the idea is that, in the future, people would live on this . . . *boat* . . . and . . . never return to land? For generations?"

"Correct." The man looked as nervous as a chef explaining his dish to a forbidding restaurant critic. "The ship is self-sustaining."

"And this is important because"—Polly flipped back to the first page—"'the lands of the Earth will no longer be inhabitable'?"

The man nodded. "Humans will have polluted the land. They will be *forced* to live on the sea."

Polly studied a diagram on another page. "And what happens when they have also polluted the sea?"

The man shrugged. "Cross that bridge when we come to it."

Polly stood and walked along the bookshelf behind her, eyeing the books with a breezy command. She took down a hefty volume and opened to a page in the middle.

"Goldblum and Rossier have suggested something similar." She pointed to the page. "Here. The Generational Ship."

The man quickly scanned the article, his leg bouncing anxiously below the table. "Oh no . . . oh no, no, no. If it's already been patented . . . that won't work at all. In the Bubble they expect *original* ideas." He ran his hand through his hair. "Thank you for alerting me to this."

He dug into his pocket and dropped two pennies in Polly's dish, then briskly exited.

A third man now entered, this one with a bohemian air. His shirt was untucked, his knickers looked baggy, and his expression suggested an inner squabble between unbridled purpose and fragile vanity. He set his pages down before Polly with a bold flourish.

"Zair you are, instructrix," he said with a heavy accent.

Polly smiled. "Good evening, Johann. How's the play?"

Looking like he might vomit, Johann sneered, "Lesen und sehen. Read and discover."

As Polly looked through Johann's work, John Henry reemerged from the rear room and came to Bunyan's side.

"So let me get this straight," said Bunyan in a hushed voice. "Your wife, Polly, is an expert on politics, patents, *and* playwriting?"

"Three of her plays are being staged right now," said John Henry. "Each one written by a different white man."

"And for this, she gets paid pennies? Makes a man want to scream."

"If you feel like screaming, you're beginning to understand. Come on, there's someone else I want you to meet."

CHAPTER 17

THE LIBRARY WITHIN

Bunyan ducked under the door frame into a small back room. A lean bed stood off to one side, sandwiched between yet more stacks of books. A desk—equally fortressed around its edges with volumes—stood on the other side of the room, with a trio of suitcases in the corner beside it. One wall was covered in maps: the Midwest, the Old World, and the Windy City. Another map showed the entirety of the Great White North.

"Newton?"

From behind the stack of books on the desk came a voice. "Yes, sir?"

"Come out here."

A slender boy emerged from behind the books—no question he was John Henry's son. He had the same broad forehead, large hands, and subtle look in his eyes as his father, though the boy's were behind a pair of glasses.

Seeing Bunyan, Newton looked hesitant.

"Don't worry. He's a good one," said John Henry.

Approaching carefully, Newton fixed the round-rimmed glasses on his nose, then extended his hand to Bunyan for a shake. "A pleasure to meet you, sir."

The boy had a firm grip, though the flesh was tender, nothing like his father's tough and meaty hands.

Bunyan crouched down. "How old are you?"

Again, the boy looked to his father.

"Go on," said John Henry.

"Eleven, sir."

John Henry kissed his son on the head. "He is my whole world, though I only first met him a year ago."

John Henry walked to a small, framed picture on the wall, a charcoal etching of a toddler. "Polly drew me this. For ten years I carried it in my pocket, right here." He patted his heart.

"Ten years . . ." Still crouching, Bunyan turned to Newton. "So, do your parents read you all these books?"

The boy smiled at the mention of the books, loosening up a bit. "I read them myself."

"Oh, you do, do you?"

Bunyan scanned a nearby stack. *Updated Views on the History of America's Settling. The Religions and Prayers of American Natives. The Languages and Heritage of Africans.*

"Part of raising a child well is telling them the right stories," said John Henry. "Stories are the stuff souls are made from."

"My mother taught me the importance of words," said Newton. "The power of ancestors is stored up in them."

Bunyan gazed about at the books. "But you can't have read *all* of these. There's so many."

"Oh, I don't read them *anymore*." Newton tapped his temple. "Now they're in here."

"He's memorized them," said John Henry, putting his arm around the boy's shoulder and squeezing him again with pride. "He has his mother's mind."

"*Memorized?*"

"More or less," said John Henry, pulling up a plank in the floor. "And these, too."

The space beneath the plank revealed yet more books underfoot. John Henry swung a plank loose on the wall. More books there. Then he lifted up the map of the Midwest to show yet another hidden bookshelf.

Bunyan kept scanning the titles. *The Untold History of Far Eastern*

Immigration. Ziggurats, Astronomy, and Mathematics: The Civilization of America's First People.

"So then," said Bunyan to Newton, "it's a whole library, all inside you."

"That's right!" Loosening up still more, Newton hopped on top of a huge suitcase in the corner. "Memory is the only way to transport our library to the Great White North. We're leaving tonight!"

"Is that so?"

A rat darted out from behind one of the suitcases and scurried into a hole along the wall.

"We're not taking the rats, though," said Newton.

Just then, Polly swept through the door. She looked radiant, as if walking on air, and despite their humble circumstances, her demeanor had a dash of cosmopolitan elegance. She rushed to her husband and embraced him, burying her face in his neck. John Henry rested his chin above her head.

"So," said John Henry, "untie everybody's knots?"

"Did my best." Polly set her coin dish down on the desk, with a pile of nickels and pennies in it. "Problem is, soon as they leave here, they just tie them right up again." She turned to Bunyan. "Who's this?"

Bunyan detected a note of mistrust—just like he'd first felt from Newton, and for that matter, everyone at Gabriel's Paradise Roadhouse.

"Polly, this is Paul Bunyan. He helped me out of a jam tonight."

"What jam?"

"Bounty hunters. F.O.L."

Polly's hand clapped over her mouth. "They found us?"

"They've put up signs." John Henry pulled the Wanted bulletin from his pocket and showed it to his wife.

"Did they follow you here?"

"We lost them. Took the long way around."

"And him?"

"He helped me escape."

Polly gazed over at Bunyan, reevaluating him. She squinted at his forehead. "Who gave you those lumps?"

"Courtesy of your husband," said Bunyan. "Pretty good with his fists."

"Wait—you met in the *ring?*"

Bunyan nodded. "I was trying to speak to El Boffo."

"And why on earth would you want to do that?"

"I'm on a mission for my wife."

"A mission for your wife?" Polly laughed. "Well, I suppose that's the best thing to be on a mission for." She turned back to her husband. "Anyway, no more El Boffo for *us*. Let me show you what I got."

Polly walked briskly over to the luggage in the corner, where she kissed Newton on the forehead, holding his face in her hands. "Tonight is the night!"

"Yes, Mama!"

From a side pocket of one of the suitcases, Polly withdrew a small folded leaflet. "Bought it today for a penny." She held it up. "A pocket map of the Big Smoke!" She pointed to some of the different locations in this, the biggest city in the Great White North, situated across the Great Lakes to the east. "Queen's Park. Fort York. The Distillery. And look here, the university!" Polly rubbed Newton's head. "Everything packed?"

"Everything!"

Hands on her hips, Polly gazed affectionately at the titles lining the walls. "I'll miss these books. They're like old friends. In the Big Smoke I'll be relying on you, Newton, to jog my memory."

Outside, a bell struck twice for two in the morning. Polly rubbed her palms in front of her chest. "No sleep tonight!" To John Henry she said, "How much did we win?"

At that, John Henry's expression was careful. Polly picked up on it immediately. She cocked her head. "What's wrong?"

"Come here," said John Henry, extending his arm.

Worry spread over Polly's face, chasing out the joy. "You're scaring me. Did the bounty hunters take it?" She pointed at Bunyan. "Is it because of him?"

John Henry shook his head. "It's because of him I'm here at all."

"But the money. Where is it?"

Again, he calmly motioned to his wife. "Come here."

"We still have to pay Mr. V."

John Henry took in and let out a deep breath. "The money is gone, Polly."

"How much is gone?"

"All of it."

Polly laughed sharply. "What do you mean, all of it? Throttlecock said the challenger was some factory kid. Never fought before."

John Henry glanced over at Bunyan. "Meet the factory kid."

Polly looked between them, incredulous. "*Him?* John! We've got to leave tonight. There won't be another boat for *weeks* that can hide us. If the bounty hunters found you at the Fight Barn, they'll find us here."

"They don't know where we live." John Henry again beckoned. "Please. Polly. Come sit."

Still she didn't go to him, but walked to the mattress, lifted a floorboard, and took out a book. To Bunyan's surprise, it was a copy of *Awaken the Capitalist Within*. Inside, the pages were hollowed out. Polly fished out some money—only a few coins.

"You bet *everything?*"

"Just like we agreed. The full wager was the only way to afford Mr. V."

"But how could you lose"—she looked at Bunyan with disbelief— "to him?"

"Well, technically speaking, it wasn't a loss. It was a draw."

"A draw? So did you get the money back?"

John Henry shook his head. "Polly, even if I *had* won, it wouldn't have made a difference. Without Paul, the F.O.L. would've taken the money and me both. I'd be on my way back to the South right now."

Polly was still sorting it through. "And you're *sure* he's not with them?"

"He had to run the table to get to me. He had to beat the Behemoth. He put a knife to a man's throat and got shot at to boot. That's a lot to go through."

Polly stared blankly with her hand over her mouth. Newton ran to her.

"It doesn't matter, Mama. If we don't have the money, we'll just pay Mr. V when we get to the other side."

"I'm afraid it doesn't work that way, Newt," said John Henry. "Mr. V won't do a thing for us till he has all the money. No passports. No fake identification. No working papers. No hideouts. Not even a trip across the lakes."

Tears fell down Polly's face. "I can't keep doing this, John. Oh God, I just can't stay on the run, always looking over my shoulder, always wondering if you'll come back the next time you leave."

Again, John Henry extended his arm toward his wife. "Please?"

At last Polly went to him and sat on his lap. She wiped away her tears and sniffed. "I just can't keep living this life where I'm waiting for our real life to begin."

Newton ran to his parents, slamming into them to form a three-person hug.

"We're still together. We're still free," said John Henry, holding the only two people for whom he'd stick out his neck.

Bunyan slipped out of the room, leaving the family to their moment.

———————◆———————

A while later, John Henry came into the kitchen, pulled a bottle of bourbon and a pair of tumblers from his cabinet, and set them on the table. Together the two rock-shouldered men dwarfed the table between them.

Bunyan tried to think of something helpful to say. "Maybe we can have a rematch. Get in Throttlecock's ring again, so you can make the money you need."

John Henry shook his head. "The F.O.L. would find us if we did. Besides, I don't think Eleanor would have us back after tonight."

"Why can't you just sneak onto a boat? There's probably loads of boats going across the lakes every day."

John Henry poured the bourbon, downed his shot, and sucked his teeth. "If the bounty hunters can track me here, they can track me in the Great White North. Mr. V's the only option. V is for *vanish.*

He'll get us new birth certificates. New citizenship in a new country. But he's not cheap."

Bunyan grimaced at a flash of pain in his Junk Foot. The muscles were tight and the skin on his ankle was raw.

"Let me get something for that," said John Henry. "I saw you limping on it in the ring."

John Henry shoveled some ice into a bucket and set it on the floor. Ashamed of how his lame foot looked, Bunyan angled his body away as he dropped it in.

"How about some dinner?" asked John Henry.

Soon there was rice, beans, and pork shank simmering on the cast-iron stove top. John Henry seasoned the meal with chilies, butter, salt, and a bit of brown sugar. In another pan he heated up hunks of yellow corn bread in bacon fat.

They wolfed the meal down without a word, drinking an entire pitcher of iced tea along the way. When they'd finished, John Henry took a tin half-filled with peach cobbler from the shelf, which they split into wedges.

Done with the meal, John Henry poured another round of bourbon, then opened the window beside him, letting in the cool spring air. He reached his arm out the window and waved it around.

"You know what this is?"

"Tell me."

"Freedom. You can forget how good it feels if you've never lost it." He moved his muscular arm slowly back and forth in the night. "It's like stirring a pot of gold."

"I seem to have gotten off on the wrong foot with your family," said Bunyan, shifting his foot in the ice bucket.

"My wife and son are suspicious. Newton has nightmares about the Thin-Lipped Ghost Man, come to get his Daddy again."

The breeze gently lifted the curtain as if it were a woman being swept off her feet by her dance partner.

"How is it, then, that Newton is eleven years old, and you hadn't seen him till one year ago?"

As John Henry sipped his bourbon, he told Bunyan his desperate tale.

CHAPTER 18

THE LIE

My grandpa was born a slave and came north after the War for the Union. Toward the end of his life, his greatest joy was caring for the pigeons on the roof of our apartment in the City of Brotherly Love.

"The pigeon is the humblest of creatures," he said. "Any old place is good enough for them. They sleep in the alleys and eat scraps of food. When there's trouble, they don't fight or stick out their neck; they just fly away. There's wisdom in the pigeon."

My grandfather was a quiet man, a loner with few friends. He worked the same job in a textile mill for years. The only time he would ever open up to me was when he was on that roof, with the pigeons around him, eating from his hands.

"Think of the lion. The lion is handsome, the lion makes a big noise. When the lion comes, everybody looks. But what does the lion get? Only blood and strife. The lion is hunted. The lion is put in a cage. I'd rather be a pigeon any day."

My grandfather lived into deep old age. In his final days before he died, he spent nearly all his time on that roof.

"If I ever came back to this world, I would come back as a pigeon," he said to me. "No one desires them. No one has any use for them. Everyone looks right past them. Because of that, they live in peace."

I tried at first to be like my grandfather. Small. Humble. Quiet.

Content with a life on the fringes. But I just wasn't cut out for it. I had a big smile, a big stride, a big swagger, and a big voice. I knew about the darkness my grandfather lived through. But America was in a new time, and I was a new kind of man. I was going to make a big noise.

It all came easy to me. I could fire a baseball past any batter. I could croon a love song onstage. I always had a girlfriend. And by the time I was a teenager, when I strolled down my block in the City of Brotherly Love, all the mamas and the papas called out, "Here comes John Henry!"

I met Polly when I was seventeen. She avoided me at first. She was neat, clean, and bookish—always with her nose in a book! When I came up to her, she'd always put on this serious face and pepper me with questions.

"What books do you read? What job do you want? What political party do you support? And why in God's name do these people always shout, 'Here comes John Henry'?"

"Because I'm a man's man," I told her with a smile.

"And what's a man's man?"

"A man's man is whatever he needs to be to get the job done."

The girl was whip-smart, and for me intelligence was the key. She was a beauty, sure, but choosing a girl based on how she looks is like picking a bird to eat based on the color of its feathers.

In those days I passed my time in the pool joint and the dance hall, places like Bubba's Ballroom and the Greasy Preacher. I'd always take the long way home past her place, hoping to bump into her. One day I found her standing outside her house.

"There's a snake in there," she said. She was clutching a book to her chest.

I ran in and couldn't get it with my boot. So I got a frying pan and whacked it on the head. I carried it outside, dangling like a rope.

"What did I tell you?" I said. "Whatever it takes to get the job done."

Soon after, I informed her we were getting married.

She laughed. "Is that so?"

"It is so. And it is final."

"We'll see about that."

Next day, I told her again. Next day, same thing, till eventually she said, "Boy, if you want to marry me, no more Bubba's, no more Greasy Preacher. You've got to start reading books."

"Is that so?"

"It is so," she said, "and it is final."

After that, boy, I got on those books quick.

Back then, the future was bright. I almost wanted time to stop, there were so many choices. Polly wondered: Would she be a scholar? A historian? The first in her family to go to college? For me it was: A politician? A fire captain? Maybe I'd open my own store. The future was like an orchard in autumn—so many fruits, pick as many as you want; the only question was if you had a bucket big enough.

Polly and I married one afternoon at a white church with a bright white fence, a little graveyard round back. We were happy for four precious weeks.

Then, fate struck.

See, my grandfather had warned me about ever going south. But I wrote him off, headstrong as I was. Thought he was too stuck in the old ways. When my country told me "all men are created equal," I believed it.

So I took a train south to visit my cousin. I was at a grocery store when a white man, passing me in the aisle, drove his shoulder into me.

"Why you jostling me, boy?" he said.

There it was, you see, right from the start—a lie. I hadn't jostled anyone. *He* bumped into *me*. That was the first of the ten thousand lies that would follow, each lie an offspring of the great Lie, which says that the man who stands behind the Black skin is less than the man who stands behind the white.

Lie though it was, I kept calm. I apologized and put my head down. But as I walked toward the exit, the man picked up a shovel and pushed me from behind.

"Run back home, buck."

My grandfather had also warned me to keep cool, especially with white people. "Your anger will depart, but what you do in your anger stays forever."

I turned to face my assaulter. I could see his face was ugly with rage and the Lie had spread its roots deeply within him. He'd probably drunk it in with his mother's milk. Again, I apologized and moved to the door. But he wasn't done.

"I thought I told you to run!" he shouted.

I felt the blow on the back of my head and I stumbled to the ground. He tried to hit me again, but I was quick and snatched the shovel from his hands.

He was wild then, raging like a man can only do if he's never paid a price for his rage. Spitting and cursing, he threw punches at me that I blocked with the shovel head. He squealed to the shop owner, "That boy attacked me!"

My stomach sank. I knew already the situation was out of my hands.

"Keep that buck here," said the owner. "I'll get the cops."

At that, three white men standing by in the store wrestled me down and knelt on my back.

If I've thought about that moment once, I've thought through it a thousand times. Should I have fought them off and run?

My hesitation was enough to seal my fate.

A pair of officers arrived. The lies multiplied. One witness fibbed, the next repeated it. Soon enough, the lies stopped seeming like lies at all. My so-called attack on the man wasn't a lie anymore, it was just "their side of the story." And when I told the officers it was *me* who'd been attacked—the plain truth everyone had seen—that became just my "version" of events.

Like we say on the gang, white hands can't be made dirty and Black hands can't be made clean. Within minutes, I was in chains, loaded up in the wagon. I spoke to my new wife in my heart: *Oh, Polly, I am sorry.*

That night in the cell I still had faith. "By morning, someone will speak up." Morning came and went. I kept believing. "By evening, someone will speak up." But no one said a word.

They assigned me my "lawyer."

"Tell the judge how you hit him and you're sorry," he advised me. "He'll show you mercy if you do."

That was the idea, see. It's easier for everyone if you just go along with the lies. Makes the machine run smooth. And it's not only easier for them, it's easier for you, too. It hurts less if you start to think, *Yeah, I've probably done enough bad in my life to deserve what's coming to me.* You can bear the weight of the world if you feel the burden is just. But if you know you've been cheated, the weight of a single hair is too much.

Again, I thought of my grandfather. *Don't stick out. Fly from trouble.* But my pride rebelled.

"I'll tell them the truth," I told my lawyer. "Not a word more, not a word less."

I'd heard things were bad in the courts. Just how bad, I soon found out. As the trial began, I was astounded at the lies. These were elaborate, arranged, rehearsed, coordinated lies—a *symphony* of lies. Each white man swore to God he'd tell "the whole truth and nothing but the truth," then the lies poured forth like a river. And why not? When you've got the gun and gavel both, the truth is yours to shove around. They lied so well I almost believed it myself.

At last came my turn on the stand.

My grandfather had something to say about truth telling, too. My grandfather, if you hadn't guessed, had something to say about pretty much everything. *Be careful with your words,* he told me. *In virtuous times, the truth is cherished. In uncertain times, the truth is heroic. But in evil times, the truth is suicide. For the Black man in America, these are evil times.*

Yet as I put my hand on the Bible, I thought, *If I lie, I'm no different from them.*

So, I spoke it all. Spoke it clean. Spoke it clear. Spoke it loud. I spoke the truth right to the face of every last man in that room.

Pretty quick, I could see it wasn't working. When the white men testified, the judge and jury all leaned forward, focused, nodding, ready to agree. But when I talked, they all leaned back, yawned, looked away, and checked their watches.

The lawyer for the other side approached me. "Are you sorry for what you've done, boy?"

"Am I sorry for telling the truth? I am not."

The lawyer turned to the jury and scoffed. "Listen to that! Incapable of honesty! Incapable of remorse!"

That's when something else became clear. This trial wasn't about what happened in that grocery store. No, it was about these white men putting on a show. See, they wanted to *show me* how easily a Black man's life gets crushed. Not crushed because of evidence and truth. Crushed *despite* the evidence and the truth. Crushed for sport. *That* was the message. I knew it, they knew it, they knew that I knew it, too. It was just a plain delight for them to demonstrate how easily they could make a lie into the truth. It's a black magic they practice in those courts—white magic, if you will. If twelve men on the jury say you did something, well—*poof*—you did.

The sentence came. Five years for assault.

After the sentencing, one of the guys on the jury came up to me. He showed me a tattoo on his forearm. A pyramid—white on top, black on the bottom, the letters F.O.L. in the middle. It was the first time I'd ever heard about the Fraternal Order of Liberty. It wouldn't be the last.

"That's always been the shape of America," he said, pointing at the tattoo. "And that's how it's gonna stay."

Polly was there. As they chained me up and pulled me away, I asked the bailiff if I could hug her one last time.

He answered with a shove. "Get in the wagon, boy."

My eyes met Polly's. I tried to throw my whole soul into that glance so she could keep it with her five long years.

They shipped me to prison and within days I was out on the gang. El Boffo needed railroads built, so he cut deals for the cheapest labor. And so, under the blazing sun out on the open prairies, I learned to lay El Boffo's tracks.

On the gang we said we worked from "cain't to cain't"—cain't see in the morning to cain't see at night. Breakfast, lunch, and dinner never changed: fried dough, pig fat, and grits. End of the day, we washed up. One bucket of water and one bar of soap for a hundred filthy men. We played checkers till we slept.

The track boss was a man named Duncan. Tall man. Hard man. Ambitious man. And because of all the kickbacks he got on his cheap labor, Duncan was also a rich man. Duncan kept a thick whip on his belt, a cat-o'-nine-tails nicknamed Black Betty. "Show me your lip and I'll show you my whip," he said. "Black Betty don't speak loud, but her lessons are remembered."

One morning I dropped my spoon at breakfast. Duncan tied me to a post, whipped me with Black Betty, and left me in the sun.

That evening, he came back. "Anything I can get for you?"

"A drink of water," I said.

Duncan brought over a dog dish. He let his dogs slurp their fill. "Go on," he said. "Have the rest."

I got real hot then. But on the gang you have to learn to set anger aside like a hot coal. If you don't, it cooks you from the inside.

And so, every day I took my hammer, every day I whopped it down. Took it up, whopped it down. Took it up, whopped it down. We sang through the day, old spirituals and gospel songs. I think we would have died without those songs. Singing loosens a man up, unties knots nothing else can reach. We chanted to keep the time.

"Came this far already," we said. "Ain't hardly gonna die."

Not too fast, not too slow, we spoke with every strike.

"Came this far already." *Whop.* "Ain't hardly gonna die." *Whop.*

The days spread before us like the sea. Never ending, never changing. We learned to tell the time by our shadows. Ten o'clock, two o'clock, four o'clock. We'd become human sundials.

Early on, I nearly lost my mind, thinking about my case. I knew I was innocent. I said that word over and over in my heart: *innocent, innocent, innocent!*

But innocence didn't matter. Think of how the laws get made. Far away in the old white buildings, the old white men write the rules. They write 'em strict, write 'em cruel, then they pop champagne. "You're the toughest on those dogs!" "No, *you're* the toughest!" They slap each other on the back. "Lock 'em up for good!" "Lock 'em up for life!" That's the first step.

After that, they round us up. Run us in for standing in the wrong place, looking the wrong way, saying the wrong word, thinking the wrong thought. Run us in for no reason at all. That's step two.

Once the Blacks are in jail, El Boffo starts to hire. He buys our labor at half the rate and in no time the sweat of prisoners starts to turn a profit. Racism, you see, deep down, it's always just been good business. Nothing lives in America unless it turns a profit, and nothing dies as long as it does.

Last step, El Boffo completes the cycle. He takes half the cash he made from our labor and mails it back to the politicians. Flush with money, the same crew gets reelected and they begin it all over again. Make the laws. Make the arrests. Assemble the workforce. Reap the profits. Split the dough. Turn the screw again.

The Lie is there, presiding over every step. The Lie keeps the lawmakers blind. Keeps the cops agitated. It keeps the heart of the capitalist clean. They'd never let it happen to one of their own. But as for us? Conscience is just friction in the machine. The Lie is there to grease those wheels. Don't worry about the Black folks, they deserve what they get, way down at the bottom of the pyramid.

And so, pen pushers grind lives to bits. It's not just the convict's life they grind. They grind his mother. Grind his father. Grind his children. Grind his whole world.

Anyway, I learned with time to stop thinking about that word, *innocent*. Facts are just footnotes in a story this big. Remembering my innocence just kept the wound fresh.

One day Polly wrote me a letter. In it she included a charcoal drawing of a baby boy.

This is our son, Newton.

By that point I'd grown half-dead inside. It was so bad I could see a man collapse and I'd envy him because he'd got off the gang. But when I saw Polly's drawing, that little face, the chubby cheeks, the big eyes, I wasn't dead anymore. It put fuel in my soul, good to burn a thousand years.

A plan formed in my mind. I'd be just like my grandpa. Keep my nose clean. Avoid trouble. Work hard. Keep my mouth shut. Be the pigeon I had to be to get free.

Funny enough, it was around this time I met someone who didn't believe in keeping quiet at all. His name was Elijah.

Elijah was a new transfer, sent to Duncan's gang for trouble he'd caused at other prisons. He became my shaker. All the hammer men need a shaker to set up the spikes. Elijah set up mine. Elijah was the best shaker I've ever seen. But Elijah was proud, too. Dangerously proud. He kept his head up high—high as the nail that gets hammered down.

The guards beat him down again and again. "Too uppity," they said. But Elijah didn't seem to care. He'd get his whipping, get sacked in the hole, and come out with his chin up just like before. Somehow, the guards couldn't lay hands on his spirit. He took his meals at a table with a few other men. They kept their chins up, too.

One day, while we were out hammering, I asked Elijah about it.

"Why are you always going around with your chin up? You like those whippings?"

"I choose to be a lion," said Elijah. "And for that I pay a price."

I shook my head. "My grandfather always said, a lion gets blood and strife, but a pigeon steers clear."

"It's true, I do get blood and strife. But what does a pigeon get? Only scraps and bits."

I hammered down another nail. "Is that what you talk about at dinner every night with those fellas? Being a lion?"

"We talk about the Code," said Elijah. "A man without the Code ain't nothing but a jellyfish."

We stopped talking as one of the guards passed by. When he was gone, I asked, "What's the Code?"

"The Code's the only thing stronger than the Lie. The Code's what helps a man live a full life."

"A full life, huh?" I whopped down another nail.

"The world's upside down," said Elijah. "Lions won't stop fighting till it's right-side up."

Just hearing that word, *fight*, made me uneasy.

"You ever want to find out more about the Code, let me know," said Elijah.

I shook my head. "I've got a wife and a son I've never seen. I don't want any trouble."

Elijah nodded, like he'd heard that answer before. "Before a man's ready, he can't be moved. After a man's ready, he can't be stopped."

Later on, Elijah and two other men tried to escape. Duncan chased them down, brought them back, and gave them a whipping so bad he almost killed them. They stayed in the hole for three months.

While Elijah was in the hole, Duncan pulled me aside. "If I were you, I wouldn't mix with his type. You want to see your wife and kid, right?"

"Yes, sir."

"Then just keep your head down."

I did what I was told. In those days, I worked like never before. I could drive my hammer from cain't to cain't, as sharp at dusk as I was at dawn. I forgot betrayals, forgot injustice, forgot the past, forgot the word *innocent*. My future with Polly and Newton was all I saw.

I was so determined in those days, Elijah sometimes said, "Slow down, John! Hold back!"

But I didn't listen. I *needed* to get lost in my work, just to make the time go by. I could simply *feel* it—the arc of my hammer coming down, like the unbroken edge of a circle. Then I started doing two twenty-pound hammers at once.

Came this far already. Whop. Ain't hardly gonna die. Whop.

Word began to spread. I was the leader of the fastest gang in the South. When I came out on the track it was like I was back in the City of Brotherly Love. "Here comes John Henry!"

Duncan got real prideful about it. He even invited his buddies to watch. They all had that pyramid tattoo—Fraternal Order of Liberty.

"That's my boy right there." Duncan pointed at me. "Trained him up myself."

Trained me up? Duncan never did a thing but whip and watch. But I couldn't get mad about it. On this side of the Lie, anger's just another temptation.

Finally, the day approached. At last, I'd crossed the desert of those five years. With my release date in sight, for months my guts had been twisting up in me, squeezing with joy, so much I could hardly sleep. All I could think about was holding my Polly and lifting up my Newton.

One week before my release, Duncan called me before a judge. He was quick about his business.

"Unfortunately, the inmate made an escape attempt last week," Duncan said. "I recommend making a stern example."

I didn't understand. "Sorry, what's this about?"

Duncan kept his eyes on the judge. "I've got witnesses. I'd say at least a few years is reasonable for what he's done. He's inspiring others to insubordination. He's even been talking with the Lions."

A few years? For what? For who?

"I'm surprised at you, John," said the judge. "I'd heard you were doing so well."

Wait . . . they were talking about me?

I couldn't contain myself. "I never tried to escape once! I never did anything but sweat and bleed on those tracks!"

Duncan seized on that. "Still denying his crimes, just like at his trial."

"It's a lie! Everything has been a lie. Right from the beginning, a lie!"

"I've heard enough," said the judge.

"You can't do this to me!"

Duncan signaled to the guards. "Put him in the wagon. Bring him to the hole."

I lost my cool. I punched a guard, knocked one out, then another. It took four of them to at last get me in cuffs.

"I've always been straight!" My soul came apart within me. "Every day of my life I've been straight!"

Into the hole I went. Next morning, a guard came to the slat and gave me the news. "You got another five, John."

"Five what?"

He waited a long moment, then he said, "Another five years."

CHAPTER 19

THE CODE

John Henry poured another round of bourbon as the night breeze blew through the window. Bunyan sat spellbound as he finished his story.

———◆———

"Five more years."

It took the judge a moment to think it, a moment to say it, a moment to write it. But for me, it was five years to live it and a thousand years to feel it.

There in the cell, I lost my mind. I paced and punched walls. Again, the desert of time extended before my soul. I bit steel bars with my teeth. Insanity was a relief.

Right there, I decided to make an end to it. I took off my belt and hung it from a rafter for a noose. As I fit that belt around my throat, I was ready to escape the Lie once and for all, the Lie I knew I could never defeat.

But just as I was about to do the deed, I noticed a note, slipped under the cell door. I stepped down and opened it.

"The soul is like a vine," the note said. "It will crawl in any direction you let it. The Code is a wall that keeps the vine upright. More tomorrow."

I sat on the floor and read it again. Then again. Then again. I read it all that night, as if these words were the cord that tied me to this living world. And it wasn't only the words that saved me. What saved me was the fact that Elijah had found a way to get that message to me, just when I needed it most.

The next day, another note. "If you are part of us, we are part of you. If we are part of you, you are part of us."

And the next: "The full life has five stages. First, to seek. Then, to learn. Then, to build. Then, to preserve. Then, to give. You are forbidden to leave this life till you have fulfilled every stage."

And the next: "A man's soul is like wax. Fear is like a flame that melts the wax. Since the Lion stamps out the flame of fear, the Lion keeps his shape."

Deep in the hole, those notes kept my spirit afloat.

When at last I got out, Duncan put me back on the tracks. He approached me cautiously, Black Betty on his hip.

"Sorry about this trouble, boy," he said, keeping his distance. "You're the best hammer I got. Couldn't afford to let you go."

If my hands weren't in chains, I might have torn his head clean off.

And so, I began my new life, my life within the Code. Duncan split me up from Elijah, my shaker. But I found ways, here and there, to talk to him and the other Lions. We kept our chins up. We weren't gonna get sucked dry.

Capitalism makes everyone a sucker, see? There's some who suck the resources—suck the rivers, the ground, the people. El Boffo—he's that kind of sucker. Then there's those who *get* sucked—the ones can't save up, get up, or get out. That's us on the gang, and every working stiff, too. Capitalism always sucks—only question is what kind of sucker you'll be.

In time, Elijah converted most of the men to Lions. He started working on a plan. "One man in the hole, all men in the hole. Duncan can't punish us all. He needs our work to make money. If we hold firm, we'll break him."

Well, the very next time a man got sent to the hole, we all sat right down on the ground. Didn't move an inch. Duncan went around whipping us, but we held firm. Duncan said he wouldn't feed us till we got up. Still, no one budged, all day and all night. In the morning, Duncan took the man out of the hole. He fed us and we got back to work.

I felt such pride. I couldn't believe it. I saw our men were willing to starve to win. Even die to win.

But the good feelings were short-lived. A few days later, the man who'd gone to the hole was found in a ditch by the tracks, dead, with a rag in his mouth. We pulled the rag out. On it were the words we knew so well.

Fraternal Order of Liberty.

After, Elijah spoke with us. "A Lion has sacrificed for you. Now you must sacrifice for another. Friendship over fate." He was adamant about that, more than anything else. *Friendship over fate.*

One night a fortune teller named Baba Ruski came through camp. An old woman, she spoke in paradoxes: everything was a riddle, containing its own contradiction. Yet somehow, her crooked truths explained the world better than the straight ones.

Reading my palm, Baba Ruski told me the exact place I would die: in a tunnel, deep under the earth.

"Your hammer will set you free," she told me. "But it will be the death of you—and well before your time."

"I can't die young," I said. "I've got people waiting on me."

She answered again, just as cryptically. "Death can stop you from living, but it can't stop you from giving. The more you give away, the less death has to take."

"If it's like you say, I just won't pick up the hammer anymore."

But Baba Ruski answered, "Be careful. For the more you run from your fate, the quicker it will come."

I tried to make sense of her words. The hammer, the tunnel, an early death. But where? When? Death had never haunted me like that before. It was like a window had broken in my soul: death's cold air was always blowing in.

I decided I couldn't wait any longer. I had to get back to Polly and Newton now.

There's four ways to get off the gang: live out, buy out, run out, die out. Live out—I couldn't wait any longer. Buy out—I had no money for a pardon. Die out—I wasn't gonna die in chains. That left one option—run.

Only a week after Baba Ruski left, Elijah and I tried our first escape: we commandeered a prison wagon. Duncan caught us and put us in the hole. Next time, we sawed through the floor of the prison house. In the hole again.

After another attempt, Duncan lost his composure. He tied me to the whipping post. Normally, he whipped prisoners on the back.

"Turn him to the front," he told his boys. "I want to see his face."

Duncan whipped me till he was out of breath. That's how I got these scars over my heart. I chose to be a Lion. For that I paid the cost.

After those escape attempts, Duncan had eyes on me at all times. Weeks turned to months turned to years. Those were the darkest times. Wake, hammer, lunch, hammer, dinner, checkers, fight, bed. I fought a lot in those days. We'd do anything to kill the time. We juggled hammers, even threw rail carts. I could throw an empty rail cart further than anyone. I also spent a lot of time in the hole. As for the hole—it's not worth describing. Those who know it don't want to remember. Those who don't can't understand.

Time was my real enemy. Uncertainty makes a journey twice as long; hopelessness makes the load twice as heavy. See, time is a man's only true currency. He trades it for money. Trades it for love. Trades it for stature. Trades it for memories. But imagine just wanting to burn your time, to throw it away from yourself so far you can't feel it anymore. Killing time is a sin against life. But it's a sin I committed.

Came this far already. Whop. Ain't hardly gonna die. Whop.

Then came the day that changed my life. Funny enough, it was the day we got new chains.

The new chains were weak chains. Chintzy chains. I guess Duncan and El Boffo weren't making enough money, so they bought some bargain bondage. Looking at these chains, I got to thinking about the words of Baba Ruski. *Your hammer will set you free.*

I went to Elijah. "We can beat the shackles any which way," I said. "Watch."

I showed him how a hammer blow could bend the chains. A few

quick strikes was enough to let your foot slip out. By that point Duncan had whipped and shipped so many men that Elijah and I were the only two Lions left. We agreed to run the next day.

In the morning, I said to Duncan, "Sir, I'm feeling up to my old work again. Mind if I go ahead?"

Duncan was happy to see it. "Been waiting for your work ethic to come around, boy."

As we got out in front of the gang, Elijah and I started blasting like the old days. One spike up, knock it down. Next spike up, down it went.

Half a mile up, I waited till the gang was chanting real loud—*Came this far already! Whop! Ain't hardly gonna die! Whop!*—then I set my shackle against the rail of the track and with a mighty blow I smashed it with my hammer. The shackle drove into my flesh and crushed against my bone, but I swallowed up my scream. Again and again I pounded the steel—*Came this far already! Whop! Ain't hardly gonna die! Whop!* Next I did Elijah—I beat his shackles into ovals, too. Then we did our wrists.

Elijah had stolen a tin of lard from the kitchen. Quick and sly as we could, we greased our feet and hands.

"Ready?" I said.

"Ready."

Next moment, we threw our tools down and wrenched our greased limbs free. I could hardly believe it, but suddenly, our chains were on the ground and we were running.

Just a ways up, a ledge extended over a river below. We sprinted straight for it.

"Stop!"

Duncan chased on horseback. He fired shot after shot, blowing his whistle and shouting at us as he gained. We were just twenty paces from the cliff when one of Duncan's bullets hit Elijah in the shoulder. He stumbled and I reached down to help. That gave Duncan enough time to catch up. He held us at gunpoint as he slipped off his horse, Black Betty on his hip.

"Won't you ever learn, John Henry?" Duncan said to me. "You ain't never gonna live that full life."

But in just that one minute I'd breathed too much freedom to give it up again. Fearless, I ran at him. Walloped him. Purest punch I ever threw. He shot and missed. I struck his gun from his hand and kicked it away, then ripped Black Betty off his belt.

In that moment, the spirit of my grandfather returned to me. *What does the lion get? Only blood and strife.*

But after nine years of prison, there's one thing I learned for sure: I wasn't no good at being a pigeon. I whipped Duncan up and down. Whipped him across his chest, his back, whipped him a hundred times.

"Come on," said Elijah. "We gotta go!"

But it felt like boiling water passing out of me, purifying me, cleansing me. At last, I whipped Duncan on the face, right across his eyes.

As he clutched his face, bleeding into his hands, Duncan screamed, "I'll kill you, boy, if it's the last thing I ever do!"

The other guards were catching up. I threw down Black Betty, and Elijah and I ran for the cliff. We jumped, sailing through the air and crashing into the waters below. When we popped up downstream, we were clear.

Elijah's shoulder was okay—just grazed by the bullet. The next few days, we slept by swamps and in cotton fields, anywhere out of sight. We kept moving at night, knowing they'd be on us soon.

Elijah and I had a pact. If one of us got caught, we'd make sure the other got free.

"Friendship over fate," we swore.

On the fourth night, hiding out in an old abandoned barn, I awoke to the sound I dreaded to hear: bloodhounds. They'd tracked us.

As the dogs barked in the dark, I looked for Elijah. He was gone. Next thing I knew, I heard his voice outside. Elijah was speaking to the bounty hunters real loud.

"It was a mistake to run, sir!" he shouted. I knew he was speaking loud so I would wake up. "I'll be glad to get back on the gang, sir!"

"Tell us where John Henry is and we will set you free," I heard the bounty hunters say.

"John Henry's over there," said Elijah, "in the tall grass!"

As Elijah led them away, I had just enough time to slip out through a loose board. I ran downwind so my scent wouldn't travel to the dogs. But with every step I went, my heart broke a little more. Elijah could have turned me in. But he was true to the Code. A Lion to the end.

I kept moving north. For weeks I hopped trains, slept under bridges, waded through marshes, slunk into cities, the dream of my Polly and Newton in my heart.

Came this far already. Ain't hardly gonna die.

I tracked down an old friend in the City of Brotherly Love. He told me she'd gone to the Windy City.

And so, a year ago, on a warm, pleasant evening, I arrived here. Out in that very hallway, my heart beat so fast it might have broken through my ribs. My arm, which had lifted a twenty-pound hammer ten thousand times, trembled like a baby's as I raised it up to knock.

Polly answered from the inside. "Who is it?"

Oh, how a cry broke from me as I heard that voice!

"It's John," I tried to say.

My Polly—too sharp to miss a thing—she knew who it was. The door flew open. She leapt upon me, no hesitation, put her hands all over my face, crying and moaning and saying my name. I lifted her off the ground and crushed her against me. How can I explain, how it hurt to feel that much joy? It was like shards of glass cutting me from the inside.

We needed a moment to size each other up. Ten years of stories we had to tell, but suddenly, no words to speak!

"Your muscles are so hard!" she said. "Your baby fat's all gone!" She felt the scar on my chest and cried.

She took me to see my boy. I never felt the taken years like I did that moment I laid eyes on Newton. His first words, taken. His first steps, taken. The tender years, all taken. Here he was, almost a grown man, and this was my first minute with him.

My son!

It was like a thousand birds sleeping in my heart had stirred from the branches, beating their wings all about my chest.

"Newton," Polly whispered.

He woke up quick and alert, my bright-eyed boy. His jaw went slack. I was a stranger to him. He looked carefully at his mother.

"It's your father," she said.

He gave me a tentative hug, not used to my face, not used to my smell. I pulled him against me. He was so tender. So lithe. So light. Nothing like my hard, scarred self! My voice broke like a croaking frog's.

"Newton, oh, Newton. You don't know me, but I've been thinking of you, every second of your life."

We talked all night, this new family, this old family. By morning, my little Newt had got more used to me. After that, for almost three days straight, he wouldn't let me go. He hugged me round the waist before bed, hugged me when I got up. When I sat down to eat, there he was again, hugging me. This strange family, this familiar family. After all these years, we were suddenly like three strings of a guitar, plucked as one chord, vibrating side by side. At night I didn't want to close my eyes to sleep, for fear my joy might end.

As for Polly and I, well . . . whenever partners reunite, they're like two spinning gears that have to approach, then separate, then approach and separate again, until they learn again to spin together. She prodded and probed just like the old days—all her questions. Soon enough, our gears met. At night we lay so close, you couldn't have slipped a dollar bill between us.

Polly explained what she'd done over those ten years. "I was not idle with you gone—not for a minute. I fought with the only weapon I had—words. I read a thousand books, I wrote a thousand letters, I begged and pled with the law, all to spring you free. I sent my latest letter to a judge the morning you returned."

In those first weeks, my joy fit in my heart no better than a waterfall in a thimble. It was joy so huge, it felt almost like fear—as if I'd been handed a priceless diamond and I was afraid I might somehow misplace it, lose it, drop it.

These days, I sometimes see men—free men—who squander their lives, fritter away their time, sit about and kill the hours—kill them like I used to. What would I give to be able to buy their squandered hours and add them into my own life?

I've learned that hope can bury itself, hibernate deep down within a soul. But hope isn't sleeping in me anymore. They'll have to kill me before I surrender.

Anyway, such is how I came here. I've got to keep running. I don't have any love for the Great White North, but if America wants to have its Lie, it can't have my family, too.

By the time John Henry finished the story, the bourbon was gone and it was nearly dawn. For a long time, Bunyan was silent.

"A lot of white folks don't know how it is on this side of the Lie," said John Henry. "Now you know a little bit. One day they'll wake up and realize, we're Americans, too."

Bunyan knew the pain of a family member in prison—his mother was there still. He knew what it was to have your life crushed by pen and paper—the bankers had taken it all. And he knew what it was like to feel you are the trash the world wants to throw out—he and Lucette were nothing but two crackers at the bottom of the barrel.

But John Henry's story was so very large, so very dark, and so very sad, Bunyan simply had no words to speak.

In the small living room where Polly had written speeches for the governor earlier that evening, John Henry prepared a makeshift bed out of blankets. At last, one question did occur to Bunyan.

"Did you ever hear what happened to Elijah?"

Setting down a pillow, John Henry shook his head. "What he did was heroic. Many times, I've looked within myself, and to be honest, I don't know if I would do the same. My wife, my boy. I can't put anything between them and me." John Henry sighed. "Elijah was the ultimate Lion. And he paid the ultimate price."

A few hours later, Bunyan woke to the bright light of day. He checked Lucette's lock of hair.

The silverdark had crept further along. No time to waste.

Before he left, Bunyan said goodbye to John Henry. "I still believe somehow we will work together."

With a weary smile, John Henry shook Bunyan's hand. "You seek your destiny. I'll face my fate."

CHAPTER 20

THE WONDERTORIUM

I need to speak to El Boffo," said Bunyan to the man at the ticket counter. "Where can I find him?"

The Wondertorium was a massive, block-long, Old World–style structure, with a glittering crystal dome for a ceiling and an American flag waving on top. Inside, the scene was wall-to-wall action, where attendees ate popcorn, snarfed cotton candy, licked lollipops, and slurped drinks as they crowded about exhibitors, entertainers, salesmen, and lecturers of every stripe, all touting the latest and greatest applications of the miracle mineral Lump.

The man at the ticket counter looked at Bunyan, befuddled. "I'm sorry, you mean, where is El Boffo . . . *himself*? I certainly have no idea." He looked past Bunyan. "Next!"

Bunyan walked past a lemonade peddler toward a stage where a young woman's head emerged from a metal pod called the Lump-Powered Oscillating Bathtub. She maintained her smile as the rattling pod occasionally splashed hot water on her cheek through the neck hole.

"Her muscles are growing more relaxed by the moment!" said the presenter, in a top hat. "And when the body relaxes, the mind soon follows."

Bunyan waved to the presenter, who looked a bit miffed at being interrupted.

"Sorry, can I help you?" he said at last.

"Yes, hi. I'm from Lump Town, on a mission for my wife. Do you know where I can find El Boffo?"

"El Boffo?"

"Yes. Have you seen him?"

The presenter smiled. "Well, if you want to find El Boffo, young man, just look around. El Boffo is everywhere!" With that, he turned back to the tub. "How are you feeling *now*, Ursula?"

The contraption shook beneath her as she answered, "W-w-w-w-w-w-onderf-f-f-f-f-ful!"

Bunyan shouldered on toward a locomotive-like vehicle, over which a banner read:

THE LUMP-FUELED STEAM HAMMER

This gargantuan contraption was an amalgam of disparate industrial parts—gigantic steel wheels, a protruding exhaust snout, a massive drill at its tip. Two steel picks extended along each side of the drill, as if the entire contraption were some squat, prehistoric, tusked elephant.

An excitable, dapper man with greased-back hair leaned debonairly against the massive drill.

"Not concrete, not granite, not the mountains *themselves* can slow down this little baby. El Boffo and his family have built railroads from coast to coast. One day, he'll drill straight through the center of the *earth*."

The man knelt down before a boy in the front row, who was eating a hot dog. "And do you know where it will end up?"

"The Far East!" said the boy.

The showman stood and laughed. "Correct! *Ni hao*, anyone?"

A newspaper reporter scrawling notes beside the stage raised his hand. "Sorry, but can I ask, what about the enormous black cloud that is spreading across the middle of the continent?"

The dapper man smiled. "Does your newspaper not like progress?"

"It's not that . . . It's just there are legitimate concerns. Fumes, toxicity, sunlight, heat . . ."

"Ladies and gentlemen, I think I've spotted an anti-Lumper!"

The crowd laughed.

"Remember, everyone," said the presenter, "Lump poverty is *actual* poverty."

"Excuse me," Bunyan interrupted. "Where can I find El Boffo?"

The presenter ignored Bunyan and went on. "And as if conquering the terra firma weren't enough, Lump will soon also conquer the skies! Look up, ladies and gentlemen, and behold the Lump-Lit Hyper-Balloon!"

Bunyan raised his head to see, several stories above, slowly circling beneath the crystal dome, a blimp as big as a mansion.

He moved on, zigging and zagging through the Wondertorium, trying to find anyone who knew where El Boffo was.

At one point, he passed a stage on which stood a young woman with two huge canisters on her back and a small cannon in her arms. Overhead the banner read:

THE LUMP FLAMETHROWER

A little sign at the foot of the stage said NEXT DEMONSTRATION IN . . . The clock next to it read twenty-three minutes.

Behind her, a discreet sign over a door read, WEAPONS TECHNOLOGY—PRIVATE. Two guards stood outside. A man in a suit was permitted entry, but only after showing a large, special-looking ticket.

Nearby, Bunyan noticed a small book stand. It appeared there was only one book for sale: *Awaken the Capitalist Within*, though in dozens of different editions.

Ladies' Book Salon Edition (With Questions to Spark Conversation!)
Decorative Display Edition (Empty Inside!)
Unabridged Edition (The Ultimate "Musket Ball Stopper"!)
Sunday Service Edition (For the Enterprising Pastor!)

Standing next to a rotating stand filled with Wondertorium postcards was a bored teenager with a green visor on her head and her hair in a ponytail.

"Hi, hello, hi," said Bunyan.

Seeing him, the girl launched into something of a half-hearted sales pitch. "Are you ready to be Awakened? Because here at the Wondertorium Bookstore we aren't just selling books. We are selling a way of li—"

"No, sorry. I don't want to buy anything. I'm just hoping you can help me."

She continued unabated in her memorized speech. "Reading El Boffo's classic masterpiece is a great way for any self-starting young man to pull himself up by the bootstraps—"

"Listen, I don't want a book."

"Postcard?"

"Do you know if El Boffo is in the building? I need to speak with him."

"Speak to him? Nobody speaks to him."

Bunyan grimaced. "But is he here, in the building?"

"He might be. I think he's due to give a presentation in"—she looked down at a schedule card by the register—"about fifteen minutes."

"Fifteen minutes? In person?"

"Mm-hm. It's sold out, but they always keep a few extra tickets at the door."

"Great! And where can I get those?"

"All you have to do is stand in that line there."

Bunyan turned to see a mass of people on one side of the hall, below a sign that read, WONDERTORIUM THEATER. It was not so much a line as a mob. There were hundreds crushed up against the theater doors.

Bunyan took a spot at the rear. Just beside him two children sat and played a board game. One kid moved a piece across the board and yelled, "Took it!"

The other moved his own piece. "Took it!"

The red, white, and blue–colored board appeared to be a map of the world. One area said, "Gold!" Another area said, "Fresh water!" Another, "Farmland!" Another, "Gas!" The labels went on: "Oil!" "Coal!" "Ice!" "LUMP!"

Back and forth the kids went shouting at each other. "Got it!"
"That's mine!" "Took it!" "Took it back!"

On an adjacent table, Bunyan saw a stack of the games for sale:

TAKE IT!

TAKE IT! IS EL BOFFO'S ALL-AMERICAN BOARD GAME!
PREPARE YOUR CHILD FOR REAL LIFE IN AMERICA, AND SPEND HOURS OF
FUN TOGETHER WHILE DOING IT!
BANKRUPT, CONQUER, AND ELIMINATE YOUR RIVALS!
TAME, HARNESS, AND EXPLOIT NATURE!
POSSESSION MIGHT BE NINE-TENTHS OF THE LAW,
BUT IT'S 100% OF TAKE IT!

REMEMBER:

"JUST BECAUSE THEY HAVE IT DOESN'T MEAN YOU CAN'T TAKE IT!"
Ages 4 and up.

Just then, a bright-faced young woman swerved in front of Bunyan
on a bike with a smoke-spewing motor attached to the back. A sign
round her neck read, ASK ME ABOUT THE LUMP-FIRED VELOCIPEDE!

Stepping out of the way, Bunyan nearly backed into yet another
display:

HOLD A PIECE OF LUMP IN YOUR OWN HAND!

Upon the table was a chunk of raw, the kind Bunyan handled in
the mines all the time. One after another, people lit up with smiles as
they stepped up and handled the stone.

"It's so heavy!" said one boy.

"Here, let me try," said another.

"Wow!"

Two guards, each with a billy club and a WONDERTORIUM PATROL
badge, oversaw the handling, as if it were a matter of great concern
that someone might run off with the rock.

A boy of about nine looked up at his mother. "Am I old enough to
work in Lump Town?"

"A few more years," said his mother. "Then we'll all go."

A voice shouted over the crowd. "The next presentation of *Awaken the Capitalist Within* will begin in five minutes! Advance ticket holders, please form a single-file line at the—"

But before the announcer could finish, the mob crushed its way toward the door. The line was unruly, full of shouts and shoving and accusations. "Back of the line!" "You weren't here!" "No holding spots!"

Bunyan, at the rear, hardly moved an inch, and after what seemed like only a minute, the announcer called again over the throng. "That's all for today, no more admittance! Please come back tomorrow!"

Amid the groans that followed, Bunyan spotted, out of the corner of his eye, a custodial entrance at the rear of the theater.

Quick as he could, he made his way to the side door and grabbed the knob, then, when it didn't give, he simply tore it clean off.

Behind him he heard someone yell, "Hey! You need a ticket!" The man grabbed Bunyan's shoulder just as he got through. "You can't go in there."

"What can I say?" Bunyan tossed him the broken knob. "I *took it*."

He slammed the door shut and moments later had mixed into the crowd in the dark auditorium, where he waited for the show to begin.

CHAPTER 21

THE COLUMBUS OF CAPITALISTS

The space was enormous: a capacity of thousands, packed to the brim, standing room only, electric with energy. Everyone chattered:

"Have you seen him before?"

"Third time."

"My fifth."

"My eighth."

Two teenagers behind Bunyan were in the midst of what sounded like a recitation contest from *Awaken the Capitalist Within*.

"One ninety-four," said the first. "'Hard work guarantees you nothing, but without it you have no chance.'"

"One twenty-three: 'If you buy what's unimportant, soon enough, you'll be forced to sell what *is* important.'"

"Two hundred eight: 'The boss can fire his employees. Only the customer can fire the boss.'"

"Three thirty: 'Mankind can engineer itself out of any crisis. Especially one of its own making.'"

"Eighty: 'Fools use statistics like drunk men use lampposts. To prop them up, rather than to light their way.'"

"Oh! Seven: 'Statistics are like women's undergarments. They appear pleasing but hide what's most important.'"

"Good one!"

The lights dimmed and a disembodied voice sounded through the room.

"Ladies and gentlemen. Welcome to the live presentation of *Awaken the Capitalist Within.*"

The crowd fidgeted, whispered, shushed.

"Give us El Boffo!"

"To begin today's session," the voice went on, "if you will direct your attention to the front of the theater."

Into the stage lights walked a white girl with long, perfectly combed blond hair, a white dress, a blue sash, bright red lipstick, and a sparkling tiara. Her face beamed with unalloyed joy.

"Please join me in welcoming this year's Little Miss Windy City, Darlene LaLibertay!" The crowd applauded and whistled. "Darlene will now give us her award-winning speech, 'Manifest Potential: The History of Lump.'"

Darlene smiled, waved, and began. "Long ago, the First Foot people were hunters and gatherers. They ate buffalo, fished, and lived in little tents. They hardly ever entered into Giving Mother Cave, a place filled with Lump . . . Lump that nobody was using! One day, the First Foot chiefs met the technologists of El Boffo Industries. That day, they learned what riches lay right below their feet!"

As Darlene went on with her story, a young woman in front of Bunyan said to her friend, "I'll bet Darlene will marry a Bubbleman."

"Lucky her."

Darlene continued, telling of negotiations, trades, feasts, and treaties, at last finishing up her tale.

"And that is the true story of how Lump made its way to the Wondertorium! In cooperation with the First Foot people, we have created many jobs on Native lands, so they never have to hunt and fish again!"

After a round of applause, the announcer piped up. "Ladies and gentlemen, Darlene will now sing a song."

An organist beside the stage trotted out a peppy intro. Then Darlene extended her arms toward the audience and sang with conviction.

My country, 'tis of thee,
Lump and the Factory,
Of thee I sing!
Lump that my father plied!
Lump that's our children's pride!
From the deep mountainside,
Let new Lump spring!

As the crowd clapped, someone threw a bouquet that Darlene deftly snatched out of the air. She waved and smiled on her way to the wings.

The voice of the announcer returned. "Disciples! Workers! Capitalists! The moment has come!"

Cheers.

"He's been called the Napoleon of Net Worth, the Bismarck of Business, the Plato of Profits, and the Rembrandt of Revenue. He is the Electrifying Entrepreneur, the Wilderness Wildcatter, a man who can recycle, improve upon, multiply, and utilize just about *anything* in Nature . . ."

"We love you, El Boffo!"

"He is the Darwin of Debt! The Galileo of Gross Margins! The Beethoven of Bull Markets! The Stradivarius of Stocks! And most of all, he is *all yours* for the next forty-five minutes! Ladies and gentlemen, I give you the Columbus of Capitalists, the one, the only, Elllll Boffooooo!"

In the tumult that followed, men threw their hats onstage and two girls in front of Bunyan screamed with such shrillness Bunyan had to cover his ears. Amid the bedlam, the stage remained dark and empty, till at last, the mob grew quiet.

"Shhhh! Shhhhhh!" This shushing went on for some time, until even the occasional screaming girl had been silenced.

At last, out of the void, emerged a question:

"Who here has a *dream?*"

"We do!" thundered the crowd in unison.

"And who is ready to seize that dream . . . *today?*"

"We are!"

"Just one more question . . ."

The people all around Bunyan were electrified—eyes bulging, chests heaving, temples sweating.

"Who is ready to . . . *Boff! Your! Life?!*"

The roar that followed was so great Bunyan's clothes vibrated.

As the lights came up, onto the stage jogged the energetic, stocky El Boffo in a jacket and tie. Despite his white hair, he bounded youthfully from one side of the stage to the other.

"You!" He pointed at someone. "Boff your life!" He pointed at another. "You! Boff your life!" He hustled elsewhere. "You! And you! And you! Boff! Your! Life!"

Suddenly the whole crowd was chanting it. "Boff! Your! Life! Boff! Your! Life! Boff! Your! Life!"

After a lasting swell of ecstatic chants, the crowd finally piped down.

"Welcome, welcome, welcome!" El Boffo rubbed his hands together. "I'm telling you, today I can almost *smell the Boff!*"

Screams.

"In my book . . . Has anyone here bought my book?"

More screams.

"In my book, I taught you to awaken the capitalist within."

"Yes!"

"But that was just the foundation. We innovators, we instrumentalists, we *ambitionists*, we must keep building from that foundation. We can't come to the top of the mountain and pat ourselves on the back! We must arrive at the summit and grow *wings*." He suddenly froze dead in his footsteps and looked at the crowd from the corner of his eye. "Let the fools have the beauty . . ."

The crowd finished off the well-known saying: "We'll take the money!"

El Boffo leaned low and clenched his fists, whipping up a new chant. "This . . . is how . . . the world . . . works! This . . . is how . . . the world . . . works!"

The audience boisterously chanted along with him, getting louder with each line: "This . . . is how . . . the world . . . works! This . . . is how . . . the world . . . works!"

Like a conductor, El Boffo motioned with both arms for more volume, more ferocity . . .

"THIS . . . IS HOW . . . THE WORLD . . . WORKS!"

Then, with a cut of his arm across his chest, he silenced them. Sweating, he took off his jacket and threw it on the back of a chair, stage right. He loosened his tie.

"Do you know what phrase I hear a lot these days? 'Sinister industrialist.'"

"Boo!"

"In the papers they call me a modern-day pharaoh." He pretended to crack a whip. "A slave driver!"

"Boo!"

"That got me thinking." El Boffo wagged his finger. "What *is* the signature building of the pharaoh? The pyramid?"

"Yes!"

"Well, let's consider the pyramid. Zero economic purpose. People couldn't even go inside! At least in the cathedrals of the Old World, you could get shelter from the rain."

Laughter.

"So, the pyramid—just one big gravestone. What the Egyptians didn't understand is that the only *meaningful* human activity is *economic* activity. If it can't be traded for a dollar, don't spend a second doing it."

"Yes!"

"Now let's talk about America's signature building: the skyscraper."

Applause.

"The skyscraper is a waterfall of wealth! The architect—enriched. The engineers—enriched. The builders—enriched. And how about the businesses housed *within* the skyscraper? All of them . . ."

"Enriched!"

"Yes! The American skyscraper is the golden goose, my friends!" El Boffo stacked one hand on top of the other, all the way up. "Wealth, multiplying wealth, multiplying wealth!"

"Boff your life!"

"They say capitalism causes problems."

"Boo!"

"But you know the answer to capitalism's problems?"

"More capitalism!"

"Who said that? You?" He pointed. "Yes! If there's a problem with capitalism, well, pay the man to fix it! If there's another problem, pay the next! Pay! Pay! Pay!"

"Yes! Yes! Yes!"

"A pharaoh *destroys* creativity by enslaving his people. I *unleash* creativity by employing mine!"

The crowd went wild.

"It's the American Way, friends! They call me an exploiter. But the way I see it, if I'm exploiting you, it's a compliment. I only exploit the *worthy*. If you're being exploited, that's how you know you've finally *made* it."

Laughter.

"As Darlene said—and wasn't Darlene lovely?"

"We love you, Darlene!"

"I love her, too . . . As Darlene said, we must develop the *potential* of this beautiful land, not sit idly upon it. Why, friends, is America so beautiful? I'll tell you why. *Because of its potential!* A fool looks at Nature and sees a scenic view. Mountain, meadow, stream. But a shrewd man looks at Nature and sees a cow!" El Boffo squeezed his hands before him. "Milk, milk, milk!"

The crowd went along. "Milk! Milk! Milk! Milk!"

"If you're smart, you gotta squeeze it dry," said El Boffo. "Because the truth is: if you don't squeeze it, someone else will."

Cheers.

"It's all in the Bible," said El Boffo. "Just exercising my dominion like the next fella. The bee has its hive. The beaver has its dam. And humans shall soon have, sea to shining sea, this one, uninterrupted electric garden."

As the crowd nodded and chuckled, El Boffo shook his head, satisfied. "They don't like how I talk in the press. But you know me.

Whatever happened to calling a spade a spade? They talk theories, I talk reality. They talk books, I talk life. The truth can be bitter, but drink it quick, and it'll put hair on your chest."

El Boffo took a moment to wave to a few people in the crowd. For all his burly bluster he had an almost cutesy way of waving with just his fingertips.

"Yes, yes, yes. God bless America, right?"

"Yes!"

"The world looks at our country from across the seas and wonders, why do they work so much, sweat so much, toil from dawn to dusk? Why in God's name are they always chasing, chasing, *chasing*? But this American hustle has transformed our species. Today, human beings are gods of power. Gods of splendor. The clothes we wear, the lights we see, the building we're in, all of it came from . . . where? I'll tell you where: from some man or woman caught up in the hustle. And honestly, if you're not chasing *something*, are you really an American at all?"

More laughter.

"The chase doesn't just make one man rich. It makes all men rich. And that brings us to our present moment." El Boffo settled himself. "Ladies and gentlemen, my father, a great railroad pioneer, built the arteries of this nation. The question remains—what shall we pump through these arteries? What shall we, together, *do*? Well, I have a notion."

"El Boffo for Senate!"

"What my engineers have discovered is the most remarkable form of energy ever known to man. My ultimate aim—because I never aim low—is the salvation of mankind. What we shall pump through these veins, my friends, is *Lump*."

A girl screamed.

The crowd laughed as El Boffo winked at her. "So much love today! Fantastic. I must say, it was a long road for me. But you know what I did when I was at rock bottom?" He gave the audience a wry look. "That's when I realized what needed to happen . . ."

The organist struck a low, minor chord, full of tension . . .

"That's when I decided to awaken something . . ."

"Yes!"

The organist kept creeping upward . . .

"That's when I decided to resurrect something . . ."

"The capitalist!"

Creeping higher still . . .

"That, ladies and gentlemen, is when I decided to . . ."

"YES!"

"Boff! My! Life!"

The organ ripped into a robust tune as El Boffo did a little duck-walk, hands on his hips, getting low and sticking out his chin as the crowd clapped in rhythm.

As Bunyan watched all of this, he couldn't help but be swept up in the show. Back in Lump Town he'd sometimes advised himself, *The less you question, the easier it is.* Indeed, without any thoughts at all, what a fun, bold, triumphant world the Wondertorium seemed to be.

Presently, he forced himself to remember his purpose. He had to get El Boffo's attention. Maybe shout a question? Just blurt it out: *Sir, my wife is sick in Lump Town, and you need to help her!*

But the crowd around him was too loud. He had to get closer.

"Excuse me, excuse me, sorry . . ." Bunyan began to push his way to the front.

"Hey, watch it, creep."

"Sorry, it's just that I need to speak to El Boffo . . ."

"Yeah, we do, too."

"I'm on a mission for my wife . . ."

"Stop pushing! No one cares about your wife!"

Suddenly El Boffo frantically waved to the organ player, who cut off his tune. El Boffo raised his index finger to his lips, signaling the crowd to be quiet. As the crowd silenced, he held out one arm.

"Look!" he said in a stage whisper. "A mosquito! Right on my arm!"

Bunyan kept angling his huge body through the crowd, whispering, "Sorry! Emergency. Sorry!"

El Boffo went on. "You know what the anti-Lumpers would tell us? Set the mosquito free!"

The crowd laughed, but El Boffo waved again so they'd be silent.

"Don't disturb the mosquito!" He raised his hand to his mouth, as if he were confiding a secret to the audience. "After all, what about its mosquito children? What about its mosquito *culture?*"

By this point the crowd was nearly bursting with titters and suppressed laughter. El Boffo flashed his eyebrows at them. "Well, you know what I say?"

He raised his free hand up in the air and . . .

Whack! He slapped the mosquito and shook his arm so the dead insect fell on the stage.

"I say: Humans first!"

The crowd roared and laughed and clapped.

"It's true," he said, blotting sweat from his forehead, having a laugh about it himself. "They say I'm polluting the world, even as they ride my trains, or eat the food those trains conveniently brought to their doorstep. Really, they could just say 'Thank you.' No, I'll never understand these anti-Lumpers. We are transforming the world, after all." He beat his chest with his fist. "We are transforming *ourselves.* To be anti-Lump is to be anti-human. To be anti-Lump is to be pro-bug!"

"He should be president," said a man in front of Bunyan.

"He should be emperor."

As the organist wrapped up another little tune with a blitz of the keys, El Boffo stood at the front of the stage. "I wonder, is there anyone here, today, who wants to Boff their life, right here, right now?"

People screamed and waved their hands. "Meeeee! Meeeee!"

Bunyan, having at last reached the edge of the stage, raised his own arm and waved it.

"I can't heeaaarrrr you . . . ," said El Boffo playfully.

At last, El Boffo picked a young man on the other side of the auditorium. "You! Get on up!"

Security helped the fellow up onstage.

"You look like the enterprising sort," said El Boffo.

The skinny young man had a pale face and trembling hands. "I am, sir."

"Let me ask you something," said El Boffo. "If the opportunity to truly Boff your life was presented to you, would you take it?"

"I—I believe I would, sir."

"Well then, I am going to make you an offer. Are you ready?"

"I am, sir."

El Boffo reached into his pocket and withdrew a piece of paper. He waved it in the air. "I hold in my hand a train ticket to Lump Town. Young man, I am offering you, no questions asked, a full-time position in my Lump Factory."

Oohs and *aahs*.

The young man reached for the ticket, but El Boffo yanked it back. "The condition is, you must leave for Lump Town straightaway. No goodbyes. No turning back. The train departs in . . ." El Boffo looked at his watch. "Thirty-three minutes precisely. So. What'll it be?"

Trouble fell over the young man's face. The crowd started to chant. "Take it! Take it!"

"Young man, this is your opportunity to be the next Lump Town millionaire." El Boffo goaded him on. "Remember: one can never achieve unconventional outcomes by making conventional choices."

"Boff your life!"

"Last chance . . ." El Boffo pulled a lighter from his pocket and lit it below the train ticket. "Three . . . two . . . one . . ."

"Could I ask a question?" said the young man abruptly.

El Boffo seemed confused by this. He lowered the lighter. "A question? I suppose. Why not?"

"What is it like in Lump Town?"

"What is it *like*?"

"Well, I've read it's polluted. That people get sick."

A look of annoyance crept into El Boffo's face. "Well, you can't believe everything you hear, can you?" He flashed his eyebrows to the crowd. "Of course, I have my enemies in the press."

Laughter.

The magnate went on, "All you need to know is that you'd be on the straight path to the Lump Sum if you took this ticket. America is for the takers, young man. Take it while you can."

"But why is it that people don't ever come out?" asked the young man onstage.

An awkward silence fell across the theater.

"What is he *talking* about?" whispered someone next to Bunyan.

El Boffo cleared his throat. "Are you a plant? A muckraker? Did the *Times* send you here?" El Boffo seemed to be waffling. "Anyway, I thought you came up on this stage because you had *ambition*."

The young man nodded. "I did. I do. Sir, I'm sorry. It's just that it's ... you know ... ten years ..."

Just then, Bunyan spoke up. "I can tell you what it's like in Lump Town!"

The whole crowd turned to face him.

"I'm *from* Lump Town!"

Thinly veiled alarm could be seen on El Boffo's face as Bunyan—without being invited—climbed up onto the stage. He'd taken only a few steps when a guard rushed in from the wings and took him roughly by the arm.

"Wait," said the young man imploringly to Bunyan. "You can tell me what it's like? What it's *really* like?"

As the guard began to drag him away, Bunyan answered, "Indeed I can! I'm the Lump Master!"

The young man turned to El Boffo. "Sir, can we hear what he has to say?"

The crowd looked on, restless.

"Well, of course," said El Boffo uneasily. "I would love to have our Lump Master answer. Guard, please."

The guard let him go as El Boffo squinted at Bunyan, seeming to recognize him. He said quietly, "Wait ... didn't I see you ..."

Bunyan answered in a whisper. "Yes, in the Fight Barn last night. I've been trying to talk to you."

Registering this, yet still seeming unsure, El Boffo turned to the crowd. "Well, ladies and gentlemen, let's have a warm welcome for our Lump Master!"

The crowd offered a tepid applause.

The young man cleared his throat. "Do you like working in Lump Town? Is it safe?"

"Well ..." Bunyan began.

Safe? He thought of Lucette, silverdark in her bed. He gazed out at the crowd. He could hardly see a thing in the bright lights.

"See, the real truth about Lump Town is ..."

El Boffo's eyes widened.

Then Bunyan smiled. "The truth is that Lump Town is the finest place I've ever worked!"

El Boffo's expression eased with relief. "See that?" he said. "Right there from the horse's mouth!"

Bunyan put his hand on the young man's shoulder. "You ask why people don't leave. I'll tell you why. It's because they don't want to! Did you know the Lump Factory is the safest factory in America, seven years running?"

"It is?" said the young man.

"Amazing, isn't he?" said El Boffo to the crowd.

"How often do you get to work in a place where you feel the future is truly in your hands?"

"Do people *ever* get sick?"

Bunyan swallowed the truth. "Not that I've seen."

"What about the trees turning dark? The smog."

Bunyan nodded, as if he'd spent time thinking about this grave and meaty matter. "I'll tell you what I believe: Mankind can engineer itself out of any crisis. Especially one of its own making."

"How about that?" said El Boffo. "Our Lump Master is truly awakened! I swear, this was not rehearsed!" To the young man, El Boffo said, "Last chance. Do you take the ticket or not?"

The young man did not hesitate. "Yes!" He grabbed it, then shook El Boffo's hand. "Thank you!" He turned to Bunyan. "And thank you, Lump Master!"

As the crowd clapped with approval, Bunyan shook the young man's hand. Bunyan kept smiling and nodding, even as he thought of the deadly, ashen streets the young man would soon walk.

"And *that's* how you Boff your life," said El Boffo. "That's how you *take it!*"

More cheers.

"Now, my dearest disciples, if you don't mind, I must be going. We've got a train to catch! I will see you all again soon. Till then, as always, stay hungry, stay greedy, and stay . . ."

"Awake!" they screamed.

"Let's hear it then!" El Boffo raised his arms like a great conductor as the entire crowd chanted together:

"*What I dream in my mind this morning, I will work for by this evening, and will hold in my hands tomorrow!*"

The organ blasted to life once more as chants of "Boff your life!" followed the Columbus of Capitalists, the young man, and Bunyan to the wings.

The moment they were offstage, the delight dropped from El Boffo's expression and he glared at Bunyan. "Just who the *hell* are you?"

CHAPTER 22

THE UNDYING WOUND

Before Bunyan could answer, El Boffo unceremoniously sent the young man off to the train station.

"Make sure he checks out, passes the test, and signs all the documents," El Boffo snapped to one of his men. "He doesn't get inside till Dedrick's grilled him."

"Of course, sir."

El Boffo turned back to Bunyan. "You. Come with me."

Bunyan followed El Boffo down the corridor toward the outside, but just as they were about to emerge onto the street, El Boffo came face-to-face with a tall, lean, elderly man in a top hat.

"Excuse me, Harrold."

It took him a moment, but at last, a flicker of recognition passed across El Boffo's face. "Ah, Cornelius Rockerford! I hardly recognized you, you look so young." El Boffo offered an instant, hollow smile. "Sorry about the lunch the other day. I had reached out to your office . . . Anyway, how is the new home? Big home! One of the biggest in all Windy, I hear."

Cornelius wasn't having it. Coolly, he evaluated El Boffo. "I'm going to be in the front row at the gala. If I don't see what you promised, the spigot of cash turns off for good. The entire investor group is behind me."

"And it will be *marvelous*," said El Boffo. "Your investment will pay off tenfold. A hundredfold."

"Funny. I've been thinking this is the worst investment I've ever made. I'm beginning to see you less as a businessman and more as a kind of . . . quack."

When he said that, El Boffo shot a glance around to see if anyone was listening. He reached out and forcibly shook Cornelius's hand.

"Cornelius, what you are going to see at the gala is nothing less than a miracle. A real *science* miracle. I *promise*. After all, you can't put a price on health, can you?"

Cornelius took his hand back, then with a long, bony finger pulled down his collar, showing a rash on his neck. "I didn't pay millions for a placebo."

"Oh, that will clear right up!" exclaimed El Boffo. "Bright skies ahead. Bright skin, too! I'll have my people reach out about that lunch!"

With that, El Boffo continued outside to his carriage, Bunyan following right behind. The carriage had been stained the exact hue of the silverdark trees in Lump Town. Across the rear of the vehicle was engraved, in gold leaf inlay, EL BOFFO.

The enormous Bunyan squeezed into a seat as the Galileo of Gross Margins settled onto the cushion opposite and the carriage pulled into traffic.

El Boffo let out a sigh, seeming relieved to be free of Cornelius Rockerford. After a few moments, his gaze settled on Bunyan. "So, what are you doing on the outside?"

"Sir, I just needed to speak to you."

"Does Dedrick know you're here?"

"More or less."

"He approved it?"

"Not exactly approved . . ."

"You realize that in leaving Lump Town, you're likely forfeiting your Lump Sum, as well as your Lump Master title."

"I do."

Bunyan tried to stay focused but felt disoriented by the celebrity sitting before him. El Boffo seemed like a photo come to life.

El Boffo shifted in his seat, still trying to piece it together. "And you also were at Ellie's fight . . ."

"Like I said, I've been desperate to speak with you."

The magnate rapped on the window slat over his shoulder, which immediately slid open.

"Tea!"

Moments later, a pair of hands gently guided a small thermos through the slat. El Boffo unscrewed the top and sipped.

"For my vocal cords. All the money I've ever made, I've made with my voice." He took a sip. "You want to talk? You've got one minute."

Bunyan regained himself. "Sir, I'm on a mission for my wife. As we sit here, she is lying on our bed in Lump Town. Her body is cold as ice. Her skin has turned silverdark."

Bunyan pulled the lock of hair from his pocket. He was alarmed to see it was nearly half discolored. To keep a cry of despair from escaping, Bunyan put his fist over his mouth and cleared his throat.

"When the silverdark gets to the end of the lock, she will die. Only you can save her."

El Boffo looked at the hair. "Save her?"

"Well, I understand, sir, that you have built a device, the Simulorb. This device . . . it could help. Or so I've heard."

"Hm." El Boffo looked out the window.

Desperate, Bunyan awkwardly got down on one knee in the space the carriage provided. "Sir, I know you've got people in line ahead of my wife. Rich people. Important people. People like Cornelius Rockerford. But I . . . you see, I love my wife. Anything you want from me, I would do it, if you could just take that device to Lump Town."

El Boffo seemed disengaged, craning his head to observe a scene on the street corner in which a peddler was dressed up like a doctor at a medicine show. The man held up a crystal container as he barked at the passersby.

The sign overhead read:

<u>DAFFY'S WIZARD OIL</u>

Miracle Tonic! Cordial Liniment!
Purging Electuary! Electromagnetic Effects!
"The Silver Bullet!"

CURES FOR:

NOXIOUS HUMOURS · DROPSY · SCURVY ·
CANINE MADNESS · LA GRIPPE · GROCER'S ITCH ·
SPLEEN & GREEN SICKNESS · BABY STONES & RICKETS ·
FITS OF THE MOTHER · THE WIFFLE-WOFFLES, MUBBLE
FUBBLES, & THE MORBS · WORMS & SWAMP GUT ·
COLIC & DISTEMPERS · BRAIN WATER, LOCKJAW,
MILK LEG, TOOTH ROT, & SCABBY BOTTOM ·
PUKING FEVER · QUINSY · TRENCH MOUTH & DRAGON
BREATH · SCRUMPOX · BOWEL GRIPING & FOUL WIND ·
THE RUNS

At the bottom of the sign appeared the testimonial:

"VINDICATED AGAINST ALL COUNTERFEITS AND NOTORIOUS
SUGGESTIONS!"

—*Hamlin's Almanac*

El Boffo scowled. "Now *that's* a quack. Mendacity in a bottle."
Bunyan cleared his throat again. "Sir?"
"Hm?"
"She's captain of the Filter Brigade. We are two of your most loyal workers."
At that, El Boffo looked at Bunyan thoughtfully. Almost tenderly. "Get up, son."
Bunyan got off his knee and sat beside El Boffo. El Boffo looked Bunyan up and down. "Over there, if you don't mind."
"Of course." Bunyan returned to his spot on the other side.
El Boffo sipped his tea. "You care for this girl very much, I see."
"I do."
"I think a person must choose what he will take seriously in life: work or love. For me, it's always been work."

"If she could be cured, it would be a miracle. Imagine what the world would say! You'd be a hero."

El Boffo took another sip of tea, then screwed the lid back on. A hardness came over his face. "Well, I wish I could help you, son. But I can't."

"I understand it's secret. I won't say a word about anything."

"Tell me something. You ever play chicken with fate?"

"How do you mean?"

"Bet the whole farm on something? And I mean, the *whole* farm."

"I can imagine."

"My father, he built a railroad empire. But it's not enough, see? I needed something for *myself*. Something *I* built. I have my *own* juice. That's the thing about Cornelius. It's all his daddy's money. No juice of his own. There are the great men of history, and there are the rabble. The great men have the juice; the great men walk upon the rabble."

El Boffo sighed. "So, I bet the farm. And not just my farm. Lots of farms. Cornelius's farm. Everyone's farm. Well, as some fool once said, better to have gambled and lost than to never have played the game."

"I don't understand. Do you mean . . . you don't have the device? But the newspaper. There was an announcement."

"Oh, that. Well, you've got to motivate people any way you can. I wanted my team to know that their failure—if they did fail—would be quite public. The Windy City would be watching. The *world* would be watching."

"Did they fail?"

El Boffo gave Bunyan a sad smile, his fingertips laced over the top of his thermos. "Just a fantasy, in the end. The fantasy of a hunchbacked janitor and an Indian." He twisted the pronunciation of the last word to rhyme with *engine*.

Bunyan wasn't sure what he meant. "But even if you're close to completing it, we—"

El Boffo rapped again on the slat by his head. It slid open immediately. "Pull over."

As the carriage jerked to the side of the road, El Boffo opened the door for Bunyan. "I'd like you to report back to Lump Town immediately. Best of luck with your situation. And please—adhere to the contract. No talking. The world's about to come down on me. Don't let it come down on you, too."

"Please . . ."

"Out."

Bunyan descended into the street and watched, helplessly, as the carriage and its distinctive gold letters merged into traffic.

"Grrrr-ahhhh!"

Half scream, half growl, the sound Bunyan made was so loud, someone nearby jumped away, startled. He set off walking down the street, hands jammed in his pockets. He cursed Dr. Niebuhr, cursed Moki, cursed the Gleam, cursed everything that had gotten him where he was. Most of all, he cursed himself.

"So that's it, huh? Give up everything to get nothing! What a mess! What a jackass I am! Grrrrr-ah!"

But Bunyan had hardly gotten going with his cursing when he noticed, in the display window of a hardware store, the Gleam shining upon an axe.

"Oh, wonderful! Here we go again! The Gleam on an axe! Great clue! What am I supposed to do with that?" He muttered all this as if he were berating Moki. "You want me to steal that axe? That's the only option, mind you, because I sure can't buy it! Remember? I quit my job to come here! Maybe I'll get so broke they'll take me to debtors' prison! Reunited with Mom at last!"

Grimacing and muttering, Bunyan kept walking down the street. As he turned a corner, he lifted his head and saw something he couldn't believe. The Gleam, again! This time, the molten, silvery hue shined upon the head of a person across the street. Bunyan squinted.

Wait . . .

The posture, the wristwatch, the hat . . . an impeccably dressed Black man in a three-piece suit.

Dedrick?

Maybe the Lord of Lump Town had come to hunt him down. Fire him. Maybe worse.

As the Gleam shined upon Dedrick, Bunyan resumed chattering aloud with Moki. He sounded like a madman. "So, I should follow him? That's what you're telling me?"

brrrrraaaawwwwww

As if all these obstacles weren't enough, Bunyan now beheld, in the road between himself and Dedrick, a massive herd of cattle. He began to tremble.

Cattle—his oldest, deepest fear.

He looked up and down the block. The herd extended in both directions. He stood on the boundary of that street like a man on the bank of a deadly river.

"And I'm supposed to chase Dedrick through this herd?" he muttered. "*That's* where the Beautiful Destiny lies? This is insanity."

But what other option did he have? If the Gleam was his only hope, he had to go now.

Bunyan took a deep breath, then stepped in among the herd. It was the closest he'd been to a cow since he was a child.

Calm down. They won't stampede. That was only once, and it was a long time ago . . .

Bunyan sidestepped around the sharp horns of one bull as another jostled into him. A third bucked, and suddenly Bunyan's mind flooded with images more real than the world around him—

His father lying beside a cow, his arm deep in the animal's mouth. A cloud of locusts on the hide. "You have to soothe their pain . . . Be gentle, even when they are furious. Gentle to the last . . ." Then the clap of thunder and BRRRAWWWWWW—

The old, undying wound.

Terrified, Bunyan weaved and shoved and hopped his way back through the herd to the sidewalk where he'd started. Stepping on the curb, his Junk Foot twisted awkwardly, jolting out of his wooden brace as he stumbled. Lightning bolts of pain shot through his body as he limped to the side of a building, where he slumped to the ground.

His body felt cold. His legs were covered in mud. He was breathing fast, like that same scared twelve-year-old from all those years ago. Dedrick and the Gleam were gone.

"Idiotic! Completely idiotic!"

For some time, Bunyan sat there, muttering to himself, till at last, he regained his composure and worked off his muddy boot. He tried to massage his Junk Foot with his thumbs, but the muscles had gone tight as rocks. At last, he rebuckled the brace and stood.

When the herd had finally passed, Bunyan crossed the road to the place he'd seen Dedrick. He stood before a stately building, from which hung a dozen regal-looking flags. A line of elegant horse-drawn carriages idled along the road outside. Bunyan looked up to see the imperial words carved in stone:

THE PALACE HOTEL

The name rang a bell.

Abe had mentioned this place, back in Throttlecock's office. The Palace Hotel. The home of El Boffo. This had to be where Dedrick had gone.

Bunyan tidied himself up. He brushed off his boots, picked the mud from his pants, tucked in his shirt, and ran one hand through his hair. Then he boldly walked into the lobby and scanned the scene:

Frescoed ceiling, grand stairway, scarlet carpet. Ball gowns, hoop-skirts, parasols. Top hats, satin vests, polished boots. Ashtrays, leather sofas, all deluxe.

No Dedrick.

"Excuse me . . . *sir?*" Quick as a bird from branches, a man shot out from his perch behind his desk to determine just what this cracker was doing amid the finery. "Is zare something I can help you with?"

Bunyan looked down to see a squat, balding man, dressed in white gloves and a gray frock coat. He was gazing at Bunyan the way one might gaze at a fly in a bowl of soup at a restaurant—certainly its presence was a mistake, one that could be forgiven only if promptly rectified.

"I'm just . . . looking for someone."

"Indeed, you have found someone," the man said in a thick Old World accent, tapping a placard on the desk that read:

BENEDICT SOUSLATABLE
Palace Hotel Concierge

"Benedict Souslatable." Bunyan sounded it out so it rhymed with *inflatable.*

"Souslatable." Benedict corrected the pronunciation so the end sounded more like *aw bluh.* "Perhaps you are seeking a colleague in zee carriage house? Or perhaps in zee plumbing? I can ring zee relevant staff."

Bunyan resumed scanning the lobby. "There was a man who walked in here earlier. His name is Dedrick. I need to find him."

"And for what purpose, may I ask?"

"I need to—" Just then, Bunyan spotted Dedrick heading into a restaurant in the back. "There he is. I'll just go meet him there."

"Ahhhh, so zis is zee Dedrick you mean," said Benedict, moving to block Bunyan. "Well, Mr. Dedrick is dining in zee private quarters at zee Lineage Club. So, if you could just follow me ziss way, toward zee—"

But Bunyan stepped around him and kept going as Benedict called from behind, "Sir? *Sir!*"

In a few moments Bunyan was face-to-face with the Lineage Club maître d'.

"Hi, I need to have a word with that man who just walked in, Dedrick . . ."

Bunyan craned his neck into the restaurant to see crystal glasses, porcelain plates, and linen-covered tables. Again, Dedrick had vanished.

"Please, remove him from zee hotel," said Benedict, arriving from behind.

"Guys, come on," said Bunyan as a security guard approached him—the second one that day. "I'm on a mission for my wife, you see. I just need to—"

"Zee regulations are *very clear,*" said Benedict, pointing to a sign on the wall.

Bunyan looked and read:

THE LINEAGE CLUB
Pedigreed Feasting for the Fittest One Percent

"And you"—Benedict looked Bunyan up and down—"are not zee one percent!"

Bunyan felt a hand beneath his armpit and a minute later he was back out on the street.

CHAPTER 23

A REMINDER

Bunyan walked around the side of the Palace Hotel to an alley. He sat on an old milk crate in the shadows.

"What am I even *doing?*" he said out loud, tugging at his own hair. "If I had never left Lump Town, at least then I could have stayed by Lucette's side. I could have held her hand. Comforted her. And now . . . let's be honest . . . I've completely lost my mind!"

"Hmmmmmm."

Hearing the sound, Bunyan turned his head a few inches to see, just to his left by the brick wall, the jaguar foot of the Chilali. Bunyan lowered his head in reverence, though he was fuming.

"Why am I here following Dedrick? What would I even say if I got to him? And the Gleam on that axe in the window? What are these clues? You've led me astray. That's all there is to it."

"Hmmmmmmmm."

"Oh yes! Very helpful, that sound of yours! You know something? There's a reason I avoided the Gleam my whole life." Bunyan kicked a bean tin on the ground. "Remember Good Sam? 'He died lost in deep melancholy.'"

Old Junk Foot had started to throb again. Bunyan reached into his boot to readjust his brace. As he fixed it, he noticed a hole in the bottom of his sole.

"And my boot is ruined, too! Perfect! All this 'giving oneself to the Path'... Listen, life is for the takers, and that's just that." Bunyan yanked off his boot, took off his brace, and stretched his toes. "It's all too late for me. Maybe if I had started following the Gleam at a young age. But not now."

"What is more important, your place upon the map, or the road that you are on?"

Bunyan went on, hardly listening. "I should have stayed where I was—on the beaten path. This Twisty one must come to an end."

Moki flapped their wings and landed on the other side of Bunyan, just behind his shoulder. The being calmly interrogated him. "Tell me, then, have you yet heard a thousand nos before hearing a single yes? Have you yet searched the utmost corners of your soul, to find your final effort? And even then, after all has been given, have you found a way to give again?"

Bunyan listened in silence, massaging his foot.

"And tell me, Paul Bunyan, in your time on the Twisty Path, have you borne what you never thought you could bear, yet still kept true to the compass of your soul? And have you, Paul Bunyan, amid all the battles with the obstacles outside you, yet contended with the obstacles within you?"

Moki spoke right by Bunyan's ear. "And in your fear, Paul Bunyan, in this, your terrible hour of fear, have you proven you can wait out the dark and, when daylight comes, step into the gusting winds once more?"

Still Bunyan made no answer.

Moki went on, growing even more forceful, "And have you yet learned to keep the faith, that at the end of all your suffering you will find a door? Have you yet learned that even with a hundred backward, sideways, and painful steps, the Twisty Path will *still* deliver you to Beauty in the final moment? And have you yet realized that every *second* you have spent on the wrong path has prepared the way for your ultimate deliverance?"

Still Bunyan kept quiet.

"And if you have not been and done and known these things, Paul

Bunyan, how can you say you know the Twisty Path? How dare you say the Path is at an end? How dare you say you are anything but a beginner?"

Bunyan reviewed his entire life till now. His father dead. His mother in prison. His time in Lump Town. His love for Lucette. Every decision he'd ever made had been sound at the time—the best decision he could make, knowing what he knew. And all of it, *all of it*, had led him inexorably to this moment, in a Windy City alley where the straight path had failed and he had no friend but the Chilali.

"So I have come this far, just to begin?" he asked the being.

"*Hmmmmmmm.*"

Bunyan put his foot back in his brace and shoved it into his boot. "All right, then. If there is something more to show me, then show me."

Bunyan felt Moki close to him then. One of their jaguar feet was visible, just beside him. "What have you done so far, upon the Path?"

"I've been brave. I've been strong."

"If you have been brave and strong, is it perhaps time to be small and humble?"

Bunyan shook his head and scoffed. "Small and humble. So this is what the Twisty Path means—that you must be everything."

"*Hmmmmmm.*"

Bunyan took a deep breath and closed his eyes. He tried to locate the endless place, the timeless place, the fearless place, the stationary place, below the belly and before the spine.

The moment he opened his eyes, he saw it. The Gleam, bright and clear as day, glistening unmistakably around . . .

. . . a row of Palace Hotel trash cans. Bugs and critters blanketed the filthy containers. A raccoon stuck its head up under a lid.

"Of *course* it's the trash."

Bunyan looked closer to see cockroaches smothering the cobblestone and a pair of rats squabbling over a scrap of meat. The Gleam shone furiously around one of the trash can lids.

The more Bunyan stared, the more he understood that—disgusting as it was—there was simply, and yet again, nothing else to do but follow.

With a groan, he pulled his shirt over his nose to block the smell, approached the trash can, and picked up the lid. Inside were innumerable shadowy insects, together making a repulsive whirring sound. He gagged.

In the corner of the bin, covered in flies, was a discarded apron lit up brightly with the Gleam. Bunyan grabbed it, shook off the bugs, and slammed the lid shut.

"All right," he muttered, turning back toward Moki, "now what?"

But the alley was empty.

Seconds later, a door banged open. A man carrying a huge pot of steaming stew approached the cans.

"Lift that for me, will you?"

Bunyan opened the trash as the man poured the hot contents into the bin, sending rats scrambling out from a hole on the bottom. As he walked back to the door, the man turned to Bunyan.

"Well, you gonna put that thing on and get back to work or what? Break's over."

Moments later, Bunyan had tied on his apron and stepped into the kitchen of the Palace Hotel.

CHAPTER 24

A MATTER
OF URGENT IMPORT

B unyan grabbed a broom and got to work.

The hubbub in the kitchen was like a riot. Everywhere cooks chopped, fried, seasoned, tasted, stirred, whipped, poured, baked, flipped, and chopped again. The back-and-forth chatter of dozens of chefs mingled with the clanging, sizzling, and rumbling of a hundred pots, pans, and plates. The savory aroma made Bunyan's gums pinch.

Sweeping his way about the noisy kitchen in his apron, which barely fit around his girthy waist, Bunyan spotted the door to the main dining hall. Beside it stood a lengthy steel counter with a row of plated meals upon it. Beneath each meal was a slip of paper with a scrawled table number: *Table 34, Table 3, Table 19 . . .*

Two ripely charred pepper steaks hit the counter, each accompanied by a dollop of mashed potatoes, a trio of fat asparagus stalks, and a burgundy-hued ring of jus lapping about the base. The cook slipped a note beneath: *Private—E.B.*

Bunyan caught sight of the Gleam winking around the plate's rim, and in the next instant, a tuxedoed waiter scooped up the plates and backed out of the swinging dining room doors. Bunyan followed him out.

Through the sumptuous tables they weaved, among the glamorous, between the mannered, behind the luxurious, then on they strode before a chamber quartet, where Bunyan got a disapproving eye-bulge from another waiter sailing by with a tray over his head. At last, they arrived in a dim hallway, decorated with a paisley wallpaper. Here, the waiter deftly slipped through a small swinging door.

The filthy, aproned Bunyan stood against the wallpaper, inconspicuous as a rhino amid the daffodils. A minute later, the waiter emerged and spotted him.

"What in *God's name* are you doing out here? And where did you pull that apron from, the trash?"

"Actually—"

"If I see you out here again, I'll have Benedict *throw* you out. Understood?"

"Yes, of course."

The waiter rushed off down the hall. "Get back in the kitchen pronto!"

Quickly, Bunyan slipped into the private room. There, directly in front of him, sat El Boffo and Dedrick. Luckily, their table was on the far end of the room, and their seats were angled toward a small fireplace. For a moment Bunyan stood undetected, not knowing quite what to do. He considered announcing himself, but El Boffo was in the midst of vigorously making a point.

"...gave me that news *right* before I went onstage. Lecker's dropped *every single ball* I've thrown at him. 'The Formula!' he tells me. 'A few more weeks is all I need!' It's lies. The device will *never* be ready ... He's had *years* ..."

Bunyan spotted the Gleam glowing under a linen-covered table that stood just beside him.

Perhaps it is time to be small and humble.

Quickly, he crawled beneath the table and squeezed his giant body into a ball, then watched the conversation through a slit in the fabric.

El Boffo lifted up a hand and let it crash on the table, rattling the crystal and silverware. "I've got a pack of millionaires counting on the Salvation Light, and Lecker's making me look like another huckster with a dream. All my debt's coming due this year. I'm about to be more liquidated than a pound of chuck in a meat grinder."

Dedrick cleared his throat. "Sir, I believe I have some news on this . . ."

El Boffo sniffed the air. "Did you change your clothes, since coming here?"

"I haven't had a chance."

"Smells like Lump . . ."

The waiter zipped back into the room, whisked over to the linen-covered table where Bunyan was hiding, scooped up a water decanter, then whooshed water into El Boffo's and Dedrick's glasses.

"Anything else I can get for you gentlemen?"

Dedrick turned to the waiter and said firmly, "If you don't mind, we'd like some privacy. I need to ensure that absolutely no one else enters the room."

"Of course. I will notify Benedict as well. Let me just wheel the table over to you, sir, so you have everything you need."

Oh no.

Moments later, the waiter gripped the water table and began to move it. Crouched beneath like a squirrel, Bunyan scurried along on all fours, keeping just out of sight beneath the linen.

"Just ring the bell if you need anything else." The waiter withdrew.

Bunyan had broken into a sweat. Painfully contorted, trying to keep silent, his eyes were just inches from Dedrick's perfectly shined patent leather shoes.

El Boffo took a gulp of wine and wiped his mouth—Bunyan was close enough to actually *hear* him swallow. "You know the *Times* is trying to pin Metal Meat on us, too? And on top of everything, did you know there is a Lump Master running around the Windy City?"

"I realize. If I could, sir—"

But El Boffo spoke right over him. "Anyway, you've probably guessed why I summoned you here. I did you the courtesy of waiting till after the Finals."

"Sir—"

"The fact is, your job was not *merely* to run Lump Town but also to help me win the race of information. I would have taken any intelligence, really. Lump deposits. Research. A stolen document or two."

El Boffo cut off a bite of steak and put it in his mouth. "Of course, there's Mad Dog Mahoney, too, a man ready to step into your shoes any day. Seems to me he's hungry like you used to be, back when I found you in the streets. Remember that? Back when they called you Shine?"

"I do have something to share—"

"No sense delaying it." El Boffo gulped more wine. "I tried to be fair. I warned you, too. All your benefits—eating in restaurants, taking the elevator, even coming through the front door—well, these privileges are contingent on results. The F.O.L.'s growing stronger every day in this country, and you can imagine what *their* opinion is—"

"If you'd just let me tell you—"

"I always fended them off, saying, 'No, no, really, despite what you might think, he's up to the job—'"

"It's a matter of urgent import!"

At last, El Boffo paused. "A matter of urgent import?"

"Yes. A matter of urgent import."

After a long moment, El Boffo said quietly, "Well, why didn't you say so?"

"I have been trying, sir. I would have brought it up sooner, but I needed to make sure we had complete privacy."

"Go on, then. Spill it!"

"Four days ago, a woman in Lump Town acquired the Stucks."

"I heard. This Lump Master running amok told me all about it. He even knew about the Simulorb."

"The night she grew sick, she was treated by the town physician, Dr. Jacob Niebuhr."

"Niebuhr . . ."

"He used to run the laboratory."

"Right! I never trusted that man. Real egghead. A pound of action is worth a ton of theory, I promise you."

"The doctor's behavior that night struck me as suspicious. The next day, I had his home searched. Mahoney turned up something interesting, at the bottom of one of his drawers: a letter."

El Boffo took another bite of steak. "What kind of letter?"

"It appears to contain information concerning the Simulorb. The letter may even have been written by one of the Simulorb's original inventors."

"The *janitor?* That *Indian?*" El Boffo again drove an accent into the word to make it rhyme with *engine.*

"Yes. It seems the Tome does exist, after all."

For this, El Boffo apparently had no words. All Bunyan heard was a utensil striking the plate.

Under the table, Old Junk Foot was throbbing. Bunyan feared if he tried to move it, it would disturb the linen. He clenched his jaw, muzzling the pain for the moment.

Dedrick continued in a tense, hushed voice. "Not only does their Tome exist, but the letter we recovered outlines its location, as well as some of its contents."

"Such as?"

"The Formula. Instructions to build the Simulorb. Information about the Salvation Light."

El Boffo pounded the table so hard that a glass tipped over and poured wine on the floor, right before Bunyan's eyes. "I *knew* it could be found! All these years we've been feasting on scraps! Now we'll have the mother lode! Ha! Where is it?"

Dedrick started to cough. The cough worsened and worsened until it was quite violent. At last, when he had finished coughing, he took a drink of water.

El Boffo asked again. "Well? The location."

"From the looks of it, not far," said Dedrick. "The Tome is potentially right here in the Windy City."

El Boffo pounded the table again, three times hard. *Thump! Thump! Thump!* "Then we'll get it tonight! We'll build it before the gala after all!"

Beneath the table, the pain from Bunyan's foot had at last grown unbearable. He arched his spine and subtly slid his foot out from under him . . . *Ah.* There. A bit of relief.

El Boffo went on, radiating intensity. "Money is no object. I'd trade my whole Wondertorium for it. We'll steal it if we have to. I want it right now!"

"It's not that simple," answered Dedrick. "The letter doesn't reveal the location of the Tome overtly. Clearly, the author was afraid of the book being discovered. He disguised the location in a riddle."

"Well, did you ask Niebuhr the answer to this riddle?"

"He claims he couldn't crack it. Apparently he only received the letter recently."

"Did you rough him up?"

"Mad Dog did, yes. But the doctor was steadfast. He swore he could not solve it."

Under the table Bunyan grimly imagined the kind of "roughing up" that might have occurred. Dr. Niebuhr was a slight, old man. He was also in charge of watching over Lucette.

"That hunchback," muttered El Boffo. "That sneaky little rhyming hunchback!"

Bunyan still hadn't gotten enough relief. Ever so slightly, as quietly as possible, Bunyan fully extended his foot to the rear and—

The linen flew up.

"I *thought* I heard something," said El Boffo, looking under the table and right in Bunyan's face. "And that *smell*. Lump!"

Discovered, the enormous Bunyan rolled out onto the floor. Once he'd stood up to his full height, he towered over the seated El Boffo and Dedrick.

"You again?" said El Boffo. "Don't you ever take the hint?"

"I guess not. Dedrick, good evening."

Dedrick sat dumbstruck.

"How long have you been under there?" demanded El Boffo.

"A few minutes, sir."

El Boffo looked at Dedrick in disbelief. "Just how the hell did he get in this room?" He turned back to Bunyan. "Well, what have you heard? All of it?"

"If there is a riddle you need solved, perhaps I could help. My wife, who I told you about today, she and I used to play these riddle games. You see, all through our courtship, we would trade—"

"Enough about your wife," El Boffo interrupted. "Are you some kind of *spy*?"

"Spy?"

El Boffo picked up a bell on the table, then rang it violently. "Garçon!"

"Please, sir," Bunyan pleaded. "If you just let me look at the riddle, there's no downside. I'm telling you—I have a *gift* for riddles."

As he waited for the help to arrive, El Boffo stroked his mustache. To Dedrick, he said, "Where is the letter?"

"In a safe at the Bubble."

El Boffo continued to smooth his mustache down on both sides with his fingertips, as if several ideas were clicking together in his mind at once.

"I heard zare was a disturbance . . . ," said Benedict Souslatable, rushing into the room. When he saw Bunyan standing in his dirty apron, Benedict's jaw dropped. "Do not worry, sir. We will expel zis clodhopper tout de suite!"

"Wait a second," said El Boffo. "Just wait."

El Boffo reached into his pocket and pulled out a cigar and a lighter. As he puffed it to life, he leaned back in his chair. "I must say, there is something that intrigues me here. Three times, this man has turned up. At the Fight Barn. At the Wondertorium. Now here. I'm not an easy man to get to. And I do admire a man of grit."

El Boffo blew out a grand cloud of smoke. "I'll cut a deal with you, Lump Master. If you solve this riddle for me, if we get that Tome, and if we build the Simulorb, I'll give you what you want. I'll bring it back to Lump Town."

The legendary investor looked so enthralled, it was as if his entire body were suppressing a series of small, inner dynamite blasts. "But just know, you're going to have a bit of competition finding the answer. To win, you're going to have to outsmart my Bubble."

CHAPTER 25

THE BUBBLE

Behold," said El Boffo to Bunyan an hour later, standing at the entrance of a room as large as a warehouse. "My Bubblemen."

The so-called Bubble was filled with row upon gridded row of seated, identical, handsome, athletic, suited, well-groomed men. Stunned for a moment by the sheer homogeneity, Bunyan struggled to discern any differences among the Bubblemen. Upon scrutiny, he spotted a few. Some had glasses, some did not. Some had dark hair, some blond. Some wore black shoes, some brown. As for their skin tones, there were indeed several varieties: cream, vanilla, eggshell, pearl, ivory, bone, frost, porcelain, olive, and parchment. Each Bubbleman had his own workstation, divided by small walls from which often hung degrees from famous universities: Swagmore, Harberth, Ruler Academy, the Scion Institute, St. Forebear's.

"There's only one kind of aristocracy in America," said El Boffo, brimming with pride as he led Bunyan through. "An aristocracy of *merit*."

They passed a buffet of salmon and deviled eggs, toast and jam, rolls and coffee.

"We have everything here. Food, bed, exercise equipment. We find it's most sound, in fact, if the Bubblemen never leave the Bubble. The outside world just . . . *confuses* them."

Two Bubblemen, each wearing scarves bearing the insignia of

their alma maters, filled up their plates and Bunyan overheard a snippet of their encounter:

"I presume the reunion at the Cottage Club was chummy?"

The second Bubbleman grimaced. "Bit of a sticky wicket. Lost to Colonial Cloister at homecoming. Even worse, the Queen Anne façade is crumbling."

"Surely the Steering Committee can find a donor at the Stuffy Jacket?"

"Unclear. I'd say the façade's got the chance of a high note at the froshy a cappella."

"Blast. What's next? A wall with no ivy?"

Bunyan turned to El Boffo, who was shaking hands, waving, and engaging in brief, cordial back-and-forths with well-wishers.

"What do these Bubblemen do?"

"They buy and sell, of course. Companies. Commodities. Stocks. Debt. Politicians. Information. Advice."

"Advice?"

"Oh yes. Great margin on advice. *Anything* can be bought and sold, and my Bubblemen figure out how."

Just then, one young Bubbleman approached El Boffo and the pair spontaneously launched into song while marching energetically in lockstep:

Go, Harberth men, be hale, be brave!
Prevail against Swagmore!
Go, Harberth, run! Go, Harberth, fight!
And score! Score! Score!

After a hearty laugh, El Boffo turned once again to Bunyan. "Boiled down, I'm in the business of one thing: making very fine judgments about my fellow human beings. And these Bubblemen are the harvest of my most discriminating selections."

As a group of Bubblemen surrounded El Boffo, Bunyan had to weave his way around a few desks to keep up.

He passed a workstation where two trim, well-groomed men studied a photo of a dead cow.

"Their tongues get so swollen," said the first in a hushed tone. "Locusts eat the hide. Then they attack."

"Any cure?"

"None that we know of. Over a dozen ranches reported Metal Meat outbreaks just this week."

Bunyan's ears perked up. What they were describing sounded just like the disease his father's cows had, back on the old homestead.

"That's why they're bringing the cows into the city—slaughtering them for meat before they can get sick."

"There's *got* to be a way to short this market—"

Noticing Bunyan lingering, the Bubblemen abruptly cut off their conversation. One slid a book across the desk, hiding the photo from view.

Bunyan noticed that on the cover of the book was a photo of a sprawling, palatial estate, complete with turrets, balconies, and stone walls. Trying to make small talk, he said, "What's that, the Mansion Book?"

One Bubbleman looked at Bunyan with a mix of befuddlement and hostility. "The Mansion Book is for the entry-level staff. On this floor we have the Castle Book."

Bunyan eventually emerged at the front of the room, where El Boffo had mounted a small stage. Dedrick rang a bell and at once the Bubblemen stopped work and raised their eyes.

"Friends, brothers, Bubblemen!" shouted El Boffo. "It is so *enriching* to see you!"

Whoops and hurrahs. "Boff your life!"

"Now, of course, I would love to hear your updates from the Silk Trail. The Rectangular Trade. The Spice Circuit." Different pockets of Bubblemen shouted back as their groups were singled out. "But today, I have a different task for you."

Behind El Boffo, Dedrick had written out the entirety of the secret letter on a large blackboard. El Boffo wheeled this blackboard to the front of the stage.

"Somewhere, hidden in the words of this poem, is the location of an important object. This evening, whoever can solve this puzzle shall bring home a rather *timely* reward."

El Boffo took off his watch, glittering with gold, and held it in the air.

"This watch to the winner," said El Boffo. "Or cash equivalent, if you'd like."

He turned to the blackboard and read aloud:

Dear Doctor,
I write to you in urgency, I write to you in haste,
I write to you without a second left of life to waste.
I write to you in secrecy, without identity.
(That said, I have a hunch you'll have a hunch who I may be.)

You used to unlock mysteries upon a board with chalk,
While I myself collected trash, and on three legs I walked.
I write to you amid a quite impossible conundrum:
My dearest love is trapped, you see, and I must go and get them.

We were the first to study Lump, the strange miracle stone.
And all that we found we wrote down in our enormous Tome.
We documented much: the raw, the Pure, the orb, the Light;
We also documented silverdark and toxic blight.

For years we've hidden all our work, for years we lived in silence,
For years we bore the constant threats of spies and covert violence.
At last I speak because it seems my life will soon be lost,
Belatedly, I tell the truth, at whatever the cost.

And so I share our research on the dangerous Lump stone,
Seven hundred pages, most of which is hardly known,
Seven hundred leaves with rows of facts and numbers filled,
Seven hundred pages, friend, that just might get you killed.

For in my Tome is coveted and fearsome information,
Of rabid beasts and darkened plants and also of Salvation.
You'll read of a machine that's quite seductive in its might,
You'll read about a Formula that makes a magic Light.

I write to you in code, Doctor, to thwart more greedy men,
In hopes that you and only your discerning acumen
Shall find the hiding place. For buried here, within this poem,
Is a map pointing the way to our much sought-after Tome.

If you find it, I beg you, shout it from the rooftops!
Tell the papers, every one! Yes, even tell the cops!
For though the Pure may make the old and sick feel fine and well,
It also might turn planet Earth into an ashen hell.

So seek, Doctor, seek at the shrine of my adopted people!
Seek and find beneath a terrifying living steeple!
None but a native genius finds the book that we did hide.
A mind of great perimeter shall make these words their guide:

To the northwest starts the path of the grove,
Round its southern edge, seek the root of
Eternal wind chill.
Excavate and you will
Open secrets spoken hereof.

"Well, get after it," announced El Boffo to the room. "Time's a-wastin'!"

Instantly, the Bubblemen burst into a flurry of activity. Scores crowded around Dedrick's chalkboard, jotting the poem down, barking orders.

"Get me a thesaurus!"

"Find a cryptologist!"

One Bubbleman drew a circle on a large piece of paper and proceeded to decorate the perimeter with the letters of the alphabet. Another wrote the final limerick backward, underlining patterns he saw in it. Still another unfolded a map of the Windy City and began marking *X*'s all over it in red pencil.

"It's about the *churches*," he muttered with conviction.

Up onstage, El Boffo lit a cigar beside Dedrick. "I'll bet they have it in ten minutes. If the Bubblemen can't solve it, it's unsolvable. They're the crème de la crème."

Bunyan himself wrote down a copy of the poem and walked off to an unoccupied desk in the corner, where he pushed aside a few papers, sat down, and studied.

To the northwest starts the path of the grove . . .

But as Bunyan tried to think, he found himself distracted, not by the language of the limerick, nor by the hubbub in the room, nor even by the prospect of winning El Boffo's glittering watch, but by . . .

A shoehorn.

The tool lay across the front of the desk, and Bunyan couldn't help but be taken by its craftsmanship. The long handle had been wrought to offer the illusion it was made of rope, an illusion so compelling that when Bunyan picked it up, he feared it actually might unravel like a piece of string. The shoehorn itself was cleverly and humorously made to look like a fat, flat tongue. The entire composition had wit, ease, and the light touch of mastery. On the back of the tongue was written in cursive, *Yan Hui's Blacksmithery.*

The wink of the Gleam shone about the name.

The rising banter and bickering of the Bubblemen woke him from this reverie. He needed to focus. He stared back down at the limerick.

To the northwest starts the path of the grove
Round its southern edge, seek the root of

He got up to pace, repeating the words to himself.

Eternal wind chill.
Excavate and you will
Open secrets spoken hereof.

Suddenly he had an idea.

Bunyan jammed the copy of the poem in his pocket, walked through the Bubblemen to the rear of the room, slipped out the door, and moments later was in the streets. He flagged a carriage and gave the address of John Henry's tenement.

CHAPTER 26

BRING 'EM IN COLD

Bunyan spoke rapidly, seated at John Henry's kitchen table. Polly stood behind, hand on her husband's shoulder.

"If we find the Tome, we both win," explained Bunyan. "I can save Lucette. You'll get El Boffo's watch, which you can use to pay Mr. V. But we've got to move fast. El Boffo's got all his Bubblemen trying to crack it."

"'To the northwest starts the path of the grove,'" said John Henry. "I wonder if that's the Western Grove."

"Right," said Bunyan. "And 'eternal wind chill'—that must mean the Windy City."

Just then, Bunyan heard a sound. All three turned their heads to see Newton snapping his fingers urgently from across the room. Polly went to him, lifted a map on the wall, and looked through a peephole out into the hallway. Immediately, she locked eyes with her husband, alarm in her face.

John Henry turned to Bunyan and said in a clipped voice, "Don't make a *sound*. Do exactly what I say."

Moving quietly into the bedroom, John Henry's family worked in unison, like they'd rehearsed this drill before.

"The window," whispered Newton.

"No time," said his father.

Newton and Polly together rolled up the map of the Great White

North. Along the wall behind it, John Henry tugged a board free, revealing a small enclosure. Into the crawl space squeezed Newton and Polly. Once they were in, John Henry replaced the board and let down the map, hiding them in the wall.

Knock knock knock knock. Someone at the door.

John Henry lifted up a floorboard. There at Bunyan's feet was a hole that looked half his size—shorter and narrower than his frame, like a child's coffin. John Henry gestured at it urgently. Bunyan pointed back at John Henry, as if to say, *No, you get in!* John Henry shook his head and pushed down Bunyan's shoulder.

Perhaps it is time to be small and humble.

Somehow Bunyan contorted his body, sucked up his belly, and twisted his legs to squeeze into the slot. Just as John Henry pressed the floorboard back down, the door to the apartment kicked open.

"John Henry!" came a voice from the main room. "Give yourself up! Don't make us bring you in cold!"

Pulaski and Lynch.

"Come on, John. We're not the enemy. We're just law-and-order guys. We're patriots."

"Surrender peacefully, and the woman and boy stay safe!"

Crammed beneath the floor, Bunyan heard a few more creaks above him made by John Henry. Then, silence. *Where did he go?*

The bounty hunters moved from the kitchen to the living room, then—*creak*—the bedroom door opened.

Beneath the floorboards Bunyan kept still, nuzzled like a bullet in the chamber. Pulaski and Lynch passed over him, just inches above. Through a slit between the boards, Bunyan could see their guns, up and ready.

Suddenly, Bunyan's view went black. Pulaski's shoe had stepped directly over Bunyan's eye.

"Come here a sec," said Lynch. "Take a look at this map."

If the bounty hunters found Polly and Newton, Bunyan was ready to spring up and attack. Yet it was just at that moment, *just* as Bunyan was straining his ears, that he felt an odd sensation . . .

A pinch on his foot. A wriggle. Then a rapid vibration, right on the spot where he'd found the hole in his boot. A moment later, Bunyan felt a scurry just by his head, a puff of breeze blitzing past his ear. Then a flick, like a shoelace, across his nose.

Rats.

"Looks like he's gonna make a run for the border," said Lynch. "Up in Smoke, as they say. Check out those suitcases."

"John Henry!" shouted Pulaski. "If I see that boy of yours, I'm gonna shoot! Last warning!"

Bunyan felt it again—the hot tickling. The wet, probing nose—*Oh God*—the rat had stuck its face in his boot and actually begun to *nibble.*

Bunyan shook his boot. No luck. The rat's head was lodged in. Squeezing his toes frantically in every direction, Bunyan tried to push out the rodent, but this effort was only met with more furious wriggling. Bunyan clenched his jaw, squeezed his eyes, then bit down hard on his tongue to try to mask the tickling sensation, but the rat was only growing bolder, darting its head in and out of Bunyan's boot, pressing its greasy little mouth right up against the flesh. Sweating, twisting, clenching his jaw, at last Bunyan jerked his leg up.

"Did you hear that?"

Bunyan bit down on his knuckle and silently screamed into it as sweat poured down his face. Again, the light went out in the crack over his eyes as the bounty hunters stood directly above.

That's when Bunyan felt the second rat dart through his hair, little claws gripping his scalp, the filthy tail again whipping across his nostril. Bunyan felt like a stick of dynamite about to explode—*I need to get out, Get Out, GET OUT—*

Again Bunyan shifted his knee up higher, trying to escape the rat below, but every time he pulled it up the rat seemed to just dig in more.

"It came from right under here . . ."

A wet nose sniffed by his ear. He was getting eaten at both ends—*NO!*

Bunyan snapped. He smashed his foot down hard as a piston against the wooden plank by his foot, twisting and crushing the meaty rat with all his weight.

"There! Right where you're standing!"

Bunyan heard a gun cock and was ready to make war with the bounty hunters, tear them to pieces with his bare hands . . . throw the board up in their faces—

"The plank is loose."

—when a finger entered the board, right by Bunyan's chin—

"Ready?"

—and Bunyan was about to leap up when suddenly—

"Ah!" Pulaski screamed and stomped his foot. "Ah! Ah! Ah! Something bit me!"

Lynch shot—*bang!*—and Bunyan felt the dust hit his face as the bullet struck the wood by his ear.

"Gall durn it!"

Pulaski ran into the kitchen, cursing as he washed the wound in a pail of water. Lynch followed him in.

"Whole place is a rats' nest!"

The danger gone for the moment, Bunyan realized he was sweating from head to toe, drenched as if he'd been dunked in a hot bath.

"Come on," said Lynch from the other room. "Let's just wait outside."

Seconds later, the front door slammed shut.

Yet Bunyan still heard footsteps.

Creak.

Had it been a trick? Had they only pretended to leave?

Creak. Creak.

Before he could react, the floorboard flew open and Bunyan threw up his hands, ready for a fight, and saw—

Polly.

"Where's John?"

Bunyan squeezed himself out of the floor, painfully stretching his Junk Foot, which had been twisted up in his brace. "I don't know. Last I saw him, he told me to get in here."

"Daddy?" Newton whispered, sounding worried. His glasses hung slanted on his face. "Daddy?"

Bunyan limped over to the bed, where he worked the dead rat from his boot sole.

Just as he did, one of the suitcases fell open. Out rolled John

Henry. How the muscular giant had curled himself up to fit in that tiny space, Bunyan didn't have a clue.

Polly and Newton embraced, but John Henry kept stern.

"Quick," he said quietly. "Out we go."

Again, in seemingly practiced movements, John Henry went to the window, where he unscrewed a protective metal grate and unleashed a rope ladder. Within a minute, all four had descended into the alley below.

After a brisk, silent walk down some back streets, they ducked into another alleyway. There at last John Henry picked up Newton, hugging him close. He kissed him all over the face.

"If you ever see those guys coming for you, don't trust a thing they say. Just run, you understand?"

Fear and obedience mixed in the boy's expression. "Yes, sir."

John Henry threw his arms around his wife but, after a moment, let her go.

"This is no *life* for you," he said. "I'm a curse on you both."

"No. You're a blessing, John. Always."

"Ten years you waited. And now, hunted like animals!" John Henry rubbed his face. "We're never gonna have a full life."

As John Henry hugged his boy again, Polly studied a sheet of paper. Bunyan saw it was the poem—she must have grabbed it in the commotion.

Suddenly, she looked up.

"I've got it," she said.

"Got what?"

Polly smiled. "How far is it to the Bubble?"

CHAPTER 27

THE LIVING STEEPLE

It was the wee hours of the morning when Bunyan, Polly, Newton, and John Henry arrived back at the Bubble.

The Bubblemen were arranged in every conceivable contortion of despair: heads down on their desks, gazing blankly at the ceiling, murmuring, pacing, crumpling up paper, then chasing after what they'd just crumpled up and smoothing it out for one last look, before crumpling it and pitching it out again.

One Bubbleman sneered to his officemate, "We've been to Holy Name, Old St. Patrick, Sacred Family. Nothing."

"My mind's like a dormitory without a view of the quad," said yet another as he bounced a tennis ball listlessly on the floor.

"I'm feeling less like the racket," answered his friend, "and more like the shuttlecock."

Bunyan approached El Boffo at the front of the room. "Sir, this is my friend Polly."

El Boffo was hunched over a piece of paper, chomping on a burned-out butt of a cigar, seemingly engrossed in solving the riddle himself. As Bunyan looked over his shoulder, though, he saw that El Boffo wasn't working on the puzzle but was building out something of his own:

E . . . ~~Excellent~~. Esteemed.
L . . . ~~Lucrative~~. ~~Lavish~~. ~~Lordly~~. ~~Lofty~~. Legendary.

B . . . Bountiful. Brilliant.
O . . . Opulent.
F . . . Famed. Famous.
F . . . Famed.
O . . . Ogust. Onorable. Honorable. O

Bunyan leaned over into his line of sight. "Excuse me, sir."

At last, El Boffo raised his eyes. "Sorry, what?"

"You may remember John from the fight the other night. This is his son, Newton, and his wife, Polly."

It took El Boffo a moment to realize who Bunyan was. "Oh, right."

Polly pointed down at the anagram. "How about *outstanding?*"

El Boffo gazed down at the final letter of his anagram. "Yes! Outstanding!" He scribbled it in. "It works!"

"Sir, we have the answer to the riddle," said Bunyan.

"Who does?" said El Boffo. "You?" He looked at John Henry. "Or him?"

Polly raised her index finger. "Me, actually. Could I use that chalkboard?"

Without waiting for a response, Polly walked onto the stage. Moments later, she turned the board over to a clean side, where she wrote out the final two stanzas of the poem.

"Excuse me," said Polly. She tried again, a little louder. "Excuse me?"

John Henry put his fingers in his mouth and whistled explosively. Every Bubbleman looked up.

"If you don't mind," Polly said, "I've solved the riddle."

With the Bubblemen looking on, Polly underlined a few words in the penultimate stanza:

So seek, Doctor, seek at the shrine of my adopted people!
Seek and find beneath a terrifying living steeple!
None but a <u>native</u> genius finds the book that we did hide.
A mind of great <u>perimeter</u> shall make these words their guide:

"The word *native* is the first clue," Polly began. "Thus, any shrine, any steeple, will likely be a holy site of an Indigenous people. The next clue is *perimeter*."

Moving on to the last stanza, Polly underlined several more words:

To the <u>northwest</u> starts the path of the grove,
<u>Round its southern edge</u>, seek the root of
Eternal wind chill.
Excavate and you will
Open secrets spoken hereof.

"When I first read it, I wondered if the author might be talking about the Western Grove," said Polly.

"That was obvious," scoffed one Bubbleman.

The man beside him offered a sarcastic, "Extra, extra."

"But even if that were true," Polly went on, "the question is *where* in the Western Grove? It's a vast wilderness, fifty miles by fifty miles."

Polly erased her previous underlines, then underlined the first and last letters in each line of the poem:

<u>T</u>o the northwest starts the path of the grov<u>e</u>,
<u>R</u>ound its southern edge, seek the root o<u>f</u>
<u>E</u>ternal wind chil<u>l</u>.
<u>E</u>xcavate and you wil<u>l</u>
<u>O</u>pen secrets spoken hereo<u>f</u>.

"This is where the 'perimeter' comes in." Polly pointed at the first T. "Start in the northwest perimeter of the *poem*, then follow it round the edge to the south. The trick is to turn the lowercase 'L' in the word *chill* to an uppercase 'I.' The two letters are written the same way."

She wrote the conclusion on the board:

TREE OF LIFE

"The Tree of Life was a place of worship for tribes who lived here long ago," said Polly. "It's also the X of your buried treasure. Excavate there and you'll find the Tome."

El Boffo walked up to the board and looked over her work. "And to think what I've been paying these dandies . . ."

Polly put down the chalk. "Great fortunes don't attract the most intelligent. They just attract those who want great fortunes."

"All right, it's solved," said Bunyan. "Give her the watch."

El Boffo turned to Dedrick. "How soon can we mobilize the Wrecking Crew?"

"First thing."

"Make it so." To Polly, he said, "We'll talk payment when I'm holding the Tome."

———————— ✦ ————————

At dawn they came to the Western Grove. In the rosy rays of morning light, the Tree of Life stood like no other.

The trunk was as girthy as a walled fortress, lacking any discernible form. Its middle was impossible to locate, as its bulging, multiplying trunks spread in every direction, melding somehow into a single gargantuan whole, the bark wrapping about it like an awkward skin over its formless torso. High up, the Tree of Life's branches sprouted an infinity of bright green leaves, and from these branches dropped tangled vines that dug into the earth below, hard as iron bars. Thirty feet in the air, wall-like roots emerged from the trunk and encircled the monstrosity like the flying buttresses of a living cathedral.

El Boffo, Dedrick, Bunyan, John Henry, Polly, and Newton stood in the vast clearing before the tree, in which no plant dared to grow. Behind them were arrayed ranks of the Wrecking Crew.

"What is that *smell?*" asked El Boffo, gagging. "Like eggs."

Dedrick coughed into his handkerchief.

"It's the tree itself, sir," said Polly. "The smell is part of its self-defense."

A redheaded woodpecker alighted on the tree and pecked into the bark. Within moments, a bright green sap began to leak, enveloping the bird's feet. The woodpecker flapped its wings to escape, but the lava had already hardened into a bulbous scab, trapping it. The oozing sap soon globbed over the bird's entire body, then stiffened, crushing the bird like a fist. The woodpecker gradually grew still, its beak cracked ajar, buried in the fresh bulb of rigid bark.

"More like Tree of Death," said Newton.

John Henry was the first to spot the strongbox, squeezed in at an angle among a tangle of hardened, elephantine roots. Closer to the tree, they could see the ghastly skeletons of deer, moose, and even the remains of some humans, all gripped in the tree's iron roots.

El Boffo approached. He was dressed in a kind of Nature-repellent suit: high boots, a sheathed knife, a protective helmet. A canister holding some mysterious fluid and a gas mask hung from his belt. Seeing Bunyan evaluating his outfit, El Boffo explained:

"Do not trust Nature till she is thoroughly tamed. She has been known to resist the milking." El Boffo shouted back to the Wrecking Crew. "Bring in the saw!"

At the command, six burly men, large as both John Henry and Bunyan, trotted up, carrying a giant-toothed blade. They wore masks over their faces to combat the smell, then took their position. El Boffo, back at a safe distance, lit a cigar.

"Take it down!"

The men vigorously pulled and pushed the blade, as if trying to slice into the wall of some organic castle. But the moment the blade penetrated, the green sap bubbled forth, covering the blade, stiffening about it, then crushing it. Soon, the saw looked like a mangled river reed in the mouth of a hippo.

El Boffo turned back to the Crew. "Get the horses!"

Twenty horses thundered up, drawing a carriage. The driver dismounted, unhooked the carriage, fastened hooks around the strongbox, then hitched the chain directly to the team.

"Yank it out!" shouted El Boffo.

The horses strained against their harnesses as up and down the line the driver whipped and scolded and prodded the animals. But the hooves only skidded in the dust.

"Look!" shouted Newton. "The vine!"

Along the ground, one of the Tree of Life's vines was slithering fast as a snake, threading along the chain. Before anyone could react, the vine caught the hoof of the rearmost horse, ensnared its leg, then spread beneath its belly and climbed up its neck, where it shot right into its ear. The horse wildly bucked and twisted, drooling blood, then collapsed on the ground as the gruesome vine exited its mouth, crawled round its snout, and plunged into its eye.

Panicked, the driver ran down the line to unchain the other horses, who broke off in terror, as behind them the new roots hardened over the dead beast and pinned it to the earth.

Horrified, Newton hid his face in his mother's dress.

Amid a cloud of cigar smoke, El Boffo smoothed his mustache. "Get the dynamite."

The team set the dynamite around the crevices of the tree, jamming every nook of the roots with the sticks. Then . . .

B-BOOM!

A concussive wave shocked the grove. Moments later, the screaming began.

The acid sap of the blasted tree rained from above and ate through the garments and into the flesh of the onlookers. Bunyan and John Henry scrambled for shelter beneath a nearby tree, where the two men formed a barrier around Polly and Newton. Members of the Wrecking Crew ran by in terror with gobs of skin half-melted off their limbs and sizzling with smoke. Others rolled on the ground, the very fabric of their clothes emitting a harsh hissing sound. El Boffo hid with Dedrick behind the wagon, his gas mask pulled tight around his helmet.

When the acid rain finally stopped and the smoke cleared, new growths had emerged over the trunk of the Tree of Life. The bright green slime slathered over the damaged bark and within moments new buds sprouted. Bolstered by its newly formed skin, the tree swelled to an even wider girth than before. The strongbox was now further hidden from view.

El Boffo looked on with a sneer. "We'll burn this whole forest to the ground if we have to. We'll burn it so not a single green leaf grows for another thousand years."

"Yes, sir," said Dedrick.

The Wrecking Crew brought in picks, kerosene, cannons. By late afternoon, the entire Western Grove was covered in a haze of hot, poisoned, stinking smoke. But nothing worked. The Tree of Life was more a fortress at dusk than it had been at dawn.

A ring of cigar butts encircled El Boffo's feet. His gas mask hanging from his neck, he hurled his last, half-smoked cigar at the base of the tree in disgust. A vine coiled about it and squeezed.

"Tell me something," said El Boffo with a scowl. "Just what *is* the purpose of Nature if it's of no use to me? Suitcase without a handle."

Bunyan approached. "You promised that if someone solved the riddle, they'd get payment. At least give them their payment."

El Boffo stared at Bunyan, John Henry, and Polly. "No Tome, no pay."

As El Boffo walked off, Dedrick coughed, then turned to the Wrecking Crew. "Clear out! We're finished here!"

CHAPTER 28

ALONE

Unable to safely return to their apartment, John Henry's family lay down beneath a tree in the dappled moonlight of the Western Grove, far from the ash, fire, and stench of the Tree of Life.

Bunyan himself was unable to sleep. He walked a ways off, till he arrived at a small clearing. There, he reached in his pocket for Lucette's lock of hair. By the moonlight he saw it was close to two-thirds silverdark.

He raised the hair to his nose and breathed in, trying to detect the sweet, faint, floral scent of soap by which he knew his wife. Pressing the lock against his nostrils, all he could smell was Lump.

He had nowhere to turn. More important, he had no one to turn to.

Bunyan heard a snap of a twig behind him and, thinking it was John Henry, looked to see—

The shadowy jaguar foot upon the forest floor. Bunyan bowed his head. He spoke with exhaustion.

"The Gleam has shown me a great deal. But still, what have I gained? I feel crazy. And look: I have nothing."

"*Hmmmmm.*"

"If only there was someone else who saw what I see! Someone who believed what I believe. But to keep chasing the Twisty Path alone . . ."

Bunyan turned slightly toward Moki, glimpsing the tip of the Chilali's great brown wing. The two were almost shoulder to shoulder. "If the Twisty Path and Beautiful Destiny were real," Bunyan asked, "wouldn't there be others on it?"

"Are not John Henry and his family here with you on the Path?"

"I suppose."

"And your mother, did she not teach you about it long ago?"

"She did."

"And what about the one you love?"

This gave Bunyan pause. "Lucette?"

"Isn't she trying to help you, even now?"

Bunyan was confused. "Lucette? Help me? How?"

"Before you left, didn't she show you something?"

Bunyan thought. "The riddle? *Bunyan Loves Lucette?*"

"Hmmmmm."

Suddenly, Bunyan remembered something more. His skin rose in gooseflesh as it came to him at once . . .

On Lucette's Dream Quilt there had been one patch she didn't understand. *A mysterious man with dark hair, seated in a chair. To his left lay a hammer, to his right, an anvil. In his lap lay an axe, which seemed to be glowing.*

On the streets of the Windy City he'd seen an axe glowing just this way in the shop window.

Then, the Bubble: the Gleam upon the shoehorn, *Yan Hui's Blacksmithery.*

And what had Lucette said about that patch?

I don't know what this one means yet. But I'm certain that axe isn't just an axe.

Suddenly, it felt as if Lucette were speaking to him directly from her silverdarkened sleep. She had foreseen it!

"It's the axe, isn't it?" said Bunyan. "The blacksmith . . ."

"Hmmmmm," answered Moki. And with a flutter of their wings, they were gone.

CHAPTER 29

A GAME OF CHECKERS

By late morning Bunyan, John Henry, and his family had arrived on the South Side of the Windy City, where they gazed up at a sign hanging from an arched, stone gateway:

YAN HUI'S BLACKSMITHERY

But the sign was the only part of the place that was intact. The front windows had been smashed. Inside they could see chairs tipped on their sides and debris scattered about the floor.

It was so hollowed out and ruined, they felt no hesitation in stepping inside. When John Henry pushed through the front door, hanging from just one hinge, it fell right off.

Inside, Bunyan saw tongs, hammers, and bolts scattered in the work area. Along the walls were numerous empty shelves, suggesting the place had been looted. In the rear were the blacksmith's forge, a few more scattered tools, and an anvil. In a dim corner, an American flag hung from a pole.

Behind the workshop was an attached living quarters with a stove and small kitchen. This too had been ransacked, with the drawers of a bedside bureau torn open. Clothes were strewn about.

Hanging crookedly along one of the walls was a framed newspaper story: "Yan Hui: America's Best Blacksmith?" The photo showed a line of people extending around the block to get into the once-handsome shop. Additional photos featured Yan Hui himself posing with several extraordinary pieces of metalwork: a lion's-head knocker; an ornate balustrade wreathed in lush grapevines; a woman's bracelet made of intricate interlocking spiral bands.

Polly stood before the smashed front window. "Maybe *they* can tell us what happened to him."

She pointed across the street to another shop, Liberty Metalworks.

They walked over and entered. An air of dullness pervaded the place. Though this, too, was a blacksmith's shop, none of the works displayed on the wall had the flair of the pieces Bunyan had seen in the photos of Yan Hui's work.

Behind the front desk, a gruff-looking white man eyed Bunyan.

"Something I can help you folks with?" He gave a deep, ripe stare to John Henry's family.

"We're looking for the blacksmith Yan Hui," said Bunyan. "I believe that's his shop across the street."

The man nodded toward John Henry. "They with you?"

"They are."

On the man's forearm, Bunyan spotted a tattoo.

"I'm afraid they're gonna have to wait outside."

Another white man came up from the rear of the shop and joined the stare-down.

"We'll be going in a moment," said Bunyan. "Perhaps you could just tell us what happened to Yan Hui."

"Should never have been here in the first place," said the second man. "Melting pot is overflowing these days."

"Do you know where he is now?"

"Last I heard he's playing checkers down by the train station. I believe he's finally made the right choice: to head back where he came from." This second man nodded toward John Henry's family. "Something maybe your friends should consider, too."

Bunyan turned to go. But after a few steps, he turned back. "Hey, can I see that tattoo?"

The man at the register extended his arm, displaying the F.O.L. abbreviation.

"You're missing a letter."

"What's that?"

"Fraternal Order of Liberty. There should be another O."

———————— ·•· ————————

At the train station, they searched the platform. From end to end it was covered in discarded newspapers and peanut shells. It smelled like engine oil and stale beer. Along one wall was a row of small tables and chairs.

"Listen, man," said John Henry. "This goose chase has to end at some point. My family, we got to get a move on—"

"Look down there," said Newton. "Is that him?"

At the far end of the platform, Bunyan saw a slender, middle-aged man with short, messy hair and a craftsman's unpretentious air. He looked like someone in the business of making things, rather than selling them. Bunyan recognized him from the framed newspaper article, back in the shop.

Yan Hui was in the midst of a game of checkers. His bearded opponent kept shifting his posture: hunched over, thinking, muttering, cursing, then moving a piece, then punching a little timer beside him, then clutching his beard, then cracking his knuckles and muttering more as he took another turn and punched the clock.

Yan Hui himself was all calm. When it was his turn, he would smoothly move a piece, tap the clock, then reach for his coffee mug and take a sip, returning the mug to its place as precisely as if he were an excavator on an archaeological dig, setting an artifact back among the ruins where he'd found it.

At last, all the red checkers were gone. The defeated man stood, looked one last time over the lopsided affair, then slapped a quarter on the table and walked off.

As Bunyan walked to him, crunching over the peanut shells, the station caller made an announcement. "Pacific Coast Express! Ten minutes!"

"Excuse me," said Bunyan, "are you Yan Hui?"

The man raised his eyes and took in Bunyan's face. "I am Yan Hui, yes."

Bunyan sat. "Good. Hello. It is a pleasure to meet you. And, well, I'm hoping you can help. My friend and I, we need to obtain a lockbox from beneath the Tree of Life in the Western Grove. Perhaps you could make tools for us, so we could get it out? We don't have much money, but we'll pay you what we can."

Without a word, Yan Hui began to pack up his board, pieces, and clock.

Bunyan pulled the lock of Lucette's hair from his pocket. "We're desperate, see? I'm on a mission for my wife. Once this hair goes dark, she'll die. We may only have a few days left. My understanding is that you are one of the best blacksmiths in America."

"Not for long." He stood.

"What do you mean?"

"My time in America is finished." Yan Hui put the quarter in his pocket, stood, and picked up his suitcase. "Sorry. Best of luck to you."

As Yan Hui walked along the platform, John Henry raced after him. "Excuse me, Yan Hui. My family needs your help, too."

Yan Hui didn't slow down. John Henry kept after him. "Perhaps I can make you an offer: if I can beat you in three games of checkers before your train comes, will you work with us?"

Yan Hui chuckled and shook his head. "Three games? I haven't lost a game in years. The train will be here in a few minutes."

"A few minutes should be all I need."

The great blacksmith stopped walking. "What's in it for me?"

"An encounter with a master."

Yan Hui gave John Henry a final once-over and then, apparently, decided the offer was too intriguing to pass up. He returned to the table, where his mug still sat, arranged the game, then set the clock so each player would have just ninety total seconds.

"Ready?"

"Begin."

Yan Hui went first, moving a piece, then tapping the clock. After only a few ticks, John Henry's finger flashed out and inched a piece forward, followed by his own push of the button. Fast as lightning, Yan Hui responded, in a single motion advancing his man and touching the timer. Back and forth they went: move-tap-move-tap-move-tap, so fast that Bunyan could hardly tell what was happening, or who was winning or losing. Suddenly Yan Hui jumped over one of John Henry's men, snapped it off the board, and said, "Ha!" But John Henry got him right back, grabbing one of Yan Hui's own, to which Yan Hui answered, "Mmhm!" as if John Henry had made an interesting point in a conversation. Then the blacksmith's hand flashed over the board to make another move, to which John Henry answered with a jump-jump.

In the previous match, Yan Hui had seemed in control, even bored. But face-to-face with a real competitor, he grew increasingly vocal, snapping up John Henry's pieces with a "Yes!" and a "Ha!" and a "How about *that!*"

Yet even to Bunyan's novice eyes, the game appeared to be turning in John Henry's favor, with his black king hopping backward across the board, wreaking destruction over the red pieces, till Yan Hui's army had dwindled to a sorry few.

"The Petersburg Blockade, eh?" said Yan Hui.

John Henry looked on stoically.

At his next turn, Yan Hui's hand extended over the board, then he pulled it back. He reached out again, tentatively, then recoiled. As the seconds relentlessly ticked by, he reached for his mug and sipped. The clock expired. *Ping!*

"You're no beginner, I see," said Yan Hui, already setting up the pieces for game two.

"Work the rails long enough, you master all sorts of things."

"You're not the only one who's picked up some tricks on the tracks."

As the second game began, a train rolled into the station and cast a shadow over the men. It slowed to a stop with a belch of black smoke and a deafening squeal of its great iron wheels. The two players were oblivious. Bunyan looked on as they hunched over the board, rapidly sliding the pieces and striking the clock. Their hands moved so quickly, it was like they were two chefs taking turns tossing ingredients into a pot of soup.

This time, Yan Hui was even more vocal than before, with his "Ha!" and "Mmhm!" at every jump. "The Danube Gambit," he exclaimed at one point. "Too obvious!"

But just one move later, John Henry triple-jumped him, taking both of Yan Hui's kings with a cool *thump, thump, thump* across the board.

The blacksmith rubbed his chin, brooding. "So, it was not the Danube after all . . ."

After a long wait, he made another move, at which point John Henry scooped up two more pieces, flipping the second piece in the air with his thumb, then catching it and stacking it deftly into a pile of captured pieces.

As the seconds ticked by, Yan Hui extended his index finger in the air, mournfully retracing his missteps. *Ping!*

"Pacific Coast Express boards in two minutes!"

"One more win and you help us," said John Henry. "That's our deal."

Without answering, Yan Hui quickly set up the board for the third game. As this game began, Yan Hui kept quiet. He appeared worried, almost shaken, grimly shifting his pieces across the board as if toward an inevitable fate. John Henry, still as a statue other than the movements of his arm and index finger, deftly countered. Bunyan felt confident.

But just as the pieces were equally spread across the board, Yan Hui leaned in. With decisiveness, he executed a double jump to the back row.

"King me," he said without lifting his eyes.

John Henry did so. The seconds passed. He was clearly stuck.

"You've got to move . . . ," said Bunyan under his breath.

John Henry shook his head. "He's got me."

Tick tick tick ping!

With no time left, John Henry nudged a piece forward with all the enthusiasm of a man pushing a friend to the firing squad.

Yan Hui acted without hesitation. *Jump, jump, jump, jump.* A quadruple. Not a single piece of John Henry's remained on the board. Bunyan's heart sank and he put his hand on his friend's shoulder.

"Pacific Coast Express! All aboard!"

Quickly, the great blacksmith swept his pieces into a sack, then packed up his board and clock. He picked up his suitcase and held out his hand.

"Best game I've had in years."

John Henry extended his hand and shook. "Agreed."

With that, Yan Hui hustled over the trash-strewn platform toward the train, then stepped onto a carriage.

Bunyan ran after him. "Wait!" He caught up just as the train whistle blew. "I'm begging you." Still a bit ashamed of the words, he blurted them out anyway. "You are part of my Beautiful Destiny."

The phrase seemed to catch Yan Hui's attention. He studied Bunyan closely.

"Last call!"

With another grand belch of coal-black smoke, the train lurched into motion. Yet the wheels had not made one full rotation when Yan Hui hopped off, suitcase in hand.

"Come on," said Yan Hui as the Pacific Coast Express pulled away without him. "Those on the Twisty Path must help each other."

———— • ————

An hour later they were back in Yan Hui's place. They'd stopped by the store and bought a few items: bacon, flour, butter, milk, coffee. Yan Hui set up the chairs around the kitchen table. In the midst of the near complete wreckage of his home, he went through his cabinets and found enough leftover ingredients to whip up some breakfast.

"I have spent years wondering if I would ever meet another man who believed in the Beautiful Destiny like me."

Bunyan hardly knew where to start asking questions. "When did you begin to follow it?"

The energetic blacksmith poured pancake batter on a griddle, then laid the bacon in his frying pan. "I first heard of Chilalis in the Far East. The story was that in America, Chilalis were seen by everyone. This lit my mind on fire. Imagine that—a nation filled up by those dreaming of the Beautiful Destiny! I wanted to be part of it."

He fed more wood into his stove, then put on water for the coffee. "My father didn't want me to leave our hometown. He had this little jade shop—it had been our family trade for generations. But in that small village, I felt, well, I felt nothing at all! There was a great numbness upon my soul. It was as though I knew all that waited for me if I stayed—what people I'd meet, what feelings I'd feel, what fates I'd encounter. I had nightmares of being suffocated.

"And yet, of course, I delayed. Delay is part of the Twisty Path. First, a person hears and denies. Next, they hear and listen. Third, they understand the truth but do not act. Then they act and fail. Finally, they act and transform their lives. No amount of coaxing can make a fruit ripen before its time!

"So I waited, caught in that sickness of self-denial. But one morning, passing by the harbor, I thought to myself, *I know I am going to get on one of these boats one of these days, so why not today?* I bought my ticket and went."

Yan Hui turned over the sizzling bacon with his tongs. "My first years in America were dark. I didn't find any others who believed in Chilalis, for one. The only job I could get was as a cook on El Boffo's tracks. That's where I picked up checkers. You know what I was like back in those years? A crab! Crawling sideways through my life, scuttling along the dark seafloor."

Yan Hui did an imitation of a shuffling crab, then flipped a few pancakes.

"Eventually I drifted to the Windy City and one day passed a blacksmith's shop. I saw an old man, working with his hands, and suddenly I was spellbound. My feet were so planted to the ground, an earthquake couldn't have budged me. Everything about the scene captivated me: the glowing fire of the forge, the tools arranged on the table. It reminded me, perhaps, of my own father's workshop. Well, that very night, the Chilali came. What was a dead end became a crossroads.

"The next day I walked into the store and met the old master, Obadiah. I begged him to just let me sweep the floors. At first he refused, but then I told him about my belief in America. My belief in Chilalis. My belief in the Beautiful Destiny. He said to me then what I said to you earlier. 'Those on the Twisty Path must help each other.' Obadiah had given himself to the Path, too.

"At first, it was all menial tasks. Sweeping floors, cleaning tools, feeding fires. But that was fine. With a true vocation, you've got to love the *guts* of a thing. Not just the flower and the fruit, but the sap, the roots, the bark. Everything."

At last, the breakfast was ready. Yan Hui set down the pancakes, bacon, and coffee before Bunyan and John Henry's family.

Bunyan marveled at the perfection of the meal. The thin pancakes were spongy in the middle with a touch of crispiness round the edges. Air bubbles had risen through the dough to form tiny holes, and each flapjack resided in a sweet puddle of glistening amber syrup like a delectable, gleaming coin. The bacon was perfect, too: lean red streaks with white ruby curls of fat.

Yan Hui served the coffee in white porcelain mugs. This, too, was first-rate. The black fluid had a texture all its own, with a hot brown froth clinging to the inner rim. A splash of cream added motherly comfort to the brash drink, which washed the meal down with a bitter finish.

"Delicious," said Newton.

"Wow," said John Henry.

"Thank you," said Polly.

"Outstanding," said Bunyan, wiping his mouth with a napkin.

"I love the American breakfast," said Yan Hui, leaning back in his chair. "You see, people born in this country, they love America like they love a parent, or sibling—they had no choice in the matter. But me, I *fell* in love with America. I traveled across an ocean so I could *win* her love." He sighed, with a sad smile. "But of course, that was long ago."

Before Bunyan could ask why he was leaving this land if he loved it so much, Polly spoke up. She'd spotted an iron saltshaker on the table, finely wrought with berries and lifelike vines wrapping about it—something the looters had left behind. She took it in her hand.

"This piece is wonderful. I've never seen anything like it."

"I was very inspired the day I made that," said Yan Hui. "It only took an hour. Sometimes the ideas come so strongly, it is like a hurricane passing through a keyhole."

Bunyan felt a sharp pang in his heart, at first not knowing why. Moments later he realized the source of his pain: Yan Hui's remark about the hurricane passing through the keyhole had reminded him of Lucette's own description of inspiration—how she was a gateway for the Voice when she sewed the Dream Quilt.

"Remarkable that you are so accomplished, when you only started this vocation midway through life," said Polly.

"Yes, quite strange!" said Yan Hui. "But those who learn with love learn twice as fast. In this country, there's so much praise of the young and handsome. But for me, middle age is best. Even old age! When is fruit sweetest? When does the earth smell the richest? When is the world full of color? The harvest season. I wouldn't trade my middle age for all the loose limbs and fresh eyes in the world."

Yan Hui at last took a bite of his meal, which till now had been untouched. "Anyway, friends, tell me why you've come. What is this business with the Tree of Life?"

Bunyan sipped his coffee, then set it down before his broad chest. "In the Western Grove, buried beneath the Tree of Life, there is a strongbox. We need to excavate it."

"We were there with El Boffo yesterday," said John Henry. "He attacked it with saws, horses, dynamite, kerosene. None of it worked."

Yan Hui raised his eyebrows. "The Tree of Life will resist all conventional approaches. Against it, the straight path will always fail."

"Do you think it's possible, using tools you make, to get the box out?"

"Nearly impossible, therefore intriguing. It's a metal box?"

"Yes, with locks."

"Perhaps the perfect hammer, then. And for the wood, perhaps the perfect axe . . ."

Yan Hui trailed off. Suddenly, a strange look came over his face.

"What is it?" said John Henry.

He stared into his thoughts as if into a revelation.

"Are you all right?" asked Bunyan.

"I feel it," Yan Hui muttered, setting down his fork. "The hurricane is coming, even now."

Within moments, Yan Hui was at his forge.

CHAPTER 30

SPIRIT ARMOR

In the ransacked smithery, Yan Hui rummaged among his things, found the equipment he needed—hammers, clamps, and punches—and laid them on his table. He pitched coal onto his open-faced forge and lit the flame. Next, he found more tools under his bench—goggles, gloves, and tongs. Back at the forge, he stirred the coals and puffed the bellows.

In the corner, Yan Hui found two unshaped billets—one big, one small—and buried the slabs in the fire pot. As the metal soaked in the heat, he went to a pile of wood in his yard and selected two rails of knotless hickory. He outlined both handles, each forty inches long.

Bunyan was struck by how the blacksmith seemed lost in his work, even while covered in sweat, grime, sawdust, and soot. It was an ecstasy of vocation that Bunyan knew, at least in a small way, from times he'd been lost in his work at the gear at the Factory.

Finished with the handles, Yan Hui drenched them in oil for hardness. By now, the unshaped billets had grown bright yellow in the forge. Yan Hui pulled out the smaller of the two and took it to the anvil. With his hammer, he beat it into shape as hot orange flakes flew into the air, then settled on the floor by his feet, where they cooled to a deep gray hue. The anvil clanged like a bell with the rhythm, and soon the rough shape of an axe head was born. Back into the forge it went, buried in the smoldering coal.

The master craftsman then pulled out the second billet, three times the size of the first. Again, he beat the edges, but this time into the shape of a clean block. Using his punch, Yan Hui drove a hole through the hot mass to form the eye for the shaft. Flipping the piece with his tongs, he pounded the edges into shape. This would be John Henry's hammer.

Back to the axe. Yan Hui again drew out the roughly beaten metal and pounded the blade into a clean arc. Once done, he plunged it into a fat tank of cool oil, which blasted up flames in response. When it had quenched, Yan Hui carried the axe head to his whetting wheel and, amid the spitting sparks, ground the blade sharp.

In the early evening, Yan Hui hung the heads on the handles and drove a wedge into the top of each so there was no gap in the eye, a flush fit.

He handed the axe to Bunyan. "It's so sharp it can split a hair. The blade will never dull. The shaft cannot splinter, even under the wheel of a train."

Next, he gave John Henry the hammer. "The head is harder than any nail, harder than any stone. It will never break or dent."

Bunyan looked at the axe's clean geometry in awe. Its cheek was polished as a mirror. The blade was fine as a razor. The varnished, straight-grained handle met the head in a perfect wedlock of wood and steel.

At a pile of firewood in Yan Hui's backyard, Bunyan set up a log. As he held the new axe in his hands, a calm joy spread through his body. It was a feeling of—how can it be described?—*home*. Not a home he had ever been to, but a home he was heading toward.

Just as he was about to bring down the axe, he saw it. Glinting there upon the log's face was a molten dollop with the unmistakable silvery hue of the Gleam. Bunyan whipped the axe down on just the spot. The wood split in two, as if the opening were already there.

Bunyan set up another log, saw the Gleam again, chopped again, success again. As he chopped and chopped, the pleasure of his body unfolded. His nostrils felt larger, taking in the thick springtime air. His skin seemed more alive, feeling the humid warmth of the swollen night. The Gleam shined all over the axe.

"Holding this, it's like I can see my way more clearly than ever before."

"Perhaps it is your Spirit Armor," said Yan Hui.

"Spirit Armor?"

"My old master, Obadiah, explained the concept to me before he passed away. It is hard to see the Twisty Path under any circumstance—some are born seeing it, but most have to learn over a lifetime. Spirit Armor is an object that helps a person see the Path, even in times of anxiety. Obadiah's Spirit Armor was his anvil. For me, it is the forge. For you, perhaps, it is this axe."

Just then, Bunyan heard a clanging sound. There in the small yard in the dimming light, he saw Newton pitching stones to his father, with John Henry swinging his enormous hammer and pelting the rocks far into the air like a baseball player.

John Henry came over to Yan Hui. "Finest hammer I've ever held. Not too heavy, not too light. Easy to grip, like an extension of my arm. How did you do it?"

"Practice. Only practice! When I was a beginner I did work that was noisy, complicated, and large. Over time I've learned to do what's most difficult: to make what is useful, simple, and just the right size."

"It has such a strange quality," said John Henry, admiring the tool. "It's as if it wasn't even made. It's like it's always existed."

Yan Hui took the hammer back in his own hands and studied it. Approving of his own work, he returned it to John Henry. "My job is to hide myself, to make it seem as if I was never there at all. I'm glad you like it. But I see a troubled look on your face. Why?"

Bunyan saw the consternation as well as John Henry set the hammer down against the house.

"Years ago, a fortune teller told me a hammer would be the death of me . . ."

But before he could say more, Newton came up to his father, asking for dinner.

Yan Hui affectionately rubbed the boy on his head. "I know just the thing."

After another quick trip to the store, Yan Hui soon had made a meal of roast chicken, fingerling potatoes, and coleslaw, a personal recipe he'd refined out on the tracks.

"You're quite a cook," said John Henry.

"Stay on the tracks long enough, you master all sorts of things you never planned to master," said Yan Hui.

Afterward, Polly took Newton to bed upstairs as Yan Hui poured Bunyan and John Henry some tea.

"I almost forgot," said Yan Hui. He disappeared into the next room, then returned with two leather sheaths. "To strap the tools across your back."

"How much do we owe you?" asked Bunyan.

Yan Hui shook his head. "It's enough reward for me to simply help someone along the Path. Though many know about the Path, so few continue to the end, once they confront the Bitter Test."

"The Bitter Test?"

"Even if a person has met a Chilali, has followed the Path, has gained their Spirit Armor, and is surrounded by the like-minded, still the Twisty Path can ask the impossible."

"Have you faced the Bitter Test?"

"I have faced it." Yan Hui took a sip of his tea. "And I shrunk away."

"What do you mean?" said John Henry.

"America isn't what I dreamed it was when I first came. I had imagined a place of boldness, where all countrymen chase the Beautiful Destiny together. But it's become a nation gripped by fear. Americans worry: Who can come here? Who has the right to stay? They find no brotherhood in those who look different from themselves—even if their beliefs are the same. Long ago I came here, believing in America's dream. But I do not think that dream believes in me. My Bitter Test is to stay in this country, which does not want me. But given what's happened"—he gestured to his ruined shop—"I've decided I must go."

John Henry nodded with understanding. "We met the F.O.L. across the street today."

"Yes, they are here. They are everywhere, more and more by the day. Myself, I am getting too old to fight. I came here, I worked hard, I played by the rules. But still, they want me out. Back in the Far East

I will be welcomed. I will look and speak like my countrymen, and so I will live in peace." He sighed. "It is not the blades, bombs, and bullets of adversity that kill the spirit. In the end what bleeds you dry is the little thorn of doubt. I have doubts about my dream."

"But surely there are some who believe as you do," said Bunyan. "As *we* do."

Yan Hui seemed resigned. "Obadiah used to say, 'Each person who chases the Beautiful Destiny causes another to chase it. Each person who gives up causes another to give up.' But at this point, I am simply too tired to live without sleep, too worn down to live in fear."

John Henry nodded toward the flag, hanging in the dark corner. "But you still have that."

"Years ago, I fell in love with that flag—not for what it has stood for, or even what it stands for now, but for what it yearns to stand for one day." Yan Hui sighed. "Anyway, the Bitter Test comes for all who give themselves to the Path. I hope you face it better than I."

"How will I know when the Bitter Test has come?" asked Bunyan.

The blacksmith sipped his tea thoughtfully. "You will know it by your fear."

Polly returned from putting Newton to bed. "We shouldn't stay in the Windy City much longer. We'll need a strategy for the Tree of Life."

"It's tricky, of course," said Yan Hui. "If you fail in your first attempt, the Tree of Life may overgrow the box, sealing it up forever. These two should train first so they are prepared."

"I'm afraid there's just no time," said Bunyan. "We have to go at dawn."

That night, Bunyan could hardly sleep. He tossed and turned as he held Lucette's lock of hair in his hand, now fully three-quarters dark. What would he do without her? Even in the lowest moments of his life, through Lucette's eyes he had always seen high and far, to vistas and beyond mountaintops.

Before sunup, they said goodbye in Yan Hui's yard.

"When this business is done," Bunyan said, "perhaps I could see you again. There's much you could teach me about the Twisty Path."

"Another westbound train leaves today," answered Yan Hui. "When I am on the platform, I will see where the Path leads."

CHAPTER 31

SIDE BY SIDE

By noon they stood in the Western Grove. Polly and Newton kept a safe distance as Bunyan and John Henry plugged their noses with wax to block out the stench of the gargantuan Tree of Life. The pair had made torches of cloth and kerosene, then put on leather smocks given to them by Yan Hui to guard against the acid sap.

Axe in hand, Bunyan advanced to his position among the roots. John Henry held two torches. His hammer, for now, was still strapped on his back. There amid the poisonous, predatory vines, Bunyan glanced about for the Gleam.

Then he saw it—there—on the bark of one of the roots that had grown over the strongbox.

"Ready?" he said.

Bunyan felt the heat of John Henry's torches looming just behind him.

"Go!"

Bunyan raised Yan Hui's axe and whipped it down. Hard as the bark was, the axe's blow sank in deep, and Bunyan yanked it back out quick, then whipped it down again, just where he saw the Gleam. The toxic green sap began to flow and cling to the axe head.

"Back!" shouted John Henry.

Bunyan pivoted as John Henry angled in quick with the torches and scalded the bark anywhere the sap leaked, then burned Bunyan's axe head where the green ooze clung so it fell away. Bunyan slid back into his spot and hacked with abandon.

Chop! Chop! Chop!

"Back!" yelled John Henry again as he ducked in and charred the tree's wounds. Back and forth they went, working in tandem, soon breaking through the first root. Bunyan spotted the silvery light of the Gleam closer to the strongbox.

Chop! Chop! Chop!

In and out they went, hack and char, hack and char, as Bunyan swung the axe and John Henry jammed the torches into the leaking slime.

"Wait, hold still," said John Henry as he grabbed Bunyan's arm. A splatter of sap had eaten through the axe man's leather gear and a small bud dug in below the skin. John Henry ripped it out of his flesh as Bunyan hissed in pain, then with another "Go!" the pair pivoted quickly back to work before the deadly tree could heal its wounds. After a dozen more chops, they'd reached the box.

"Switch!"

Bunyan sheathed his axe on his back and took the torches from John Henry, jamming both flames into the Tree of Life's cuts.

Now John Henry moved in, hammering fast—*Whop! Whop! Whop!*—his huge weapon flashing and pounding on the locks of the strongbox. Bunyan witnessed for the first time the true ripping power of his friend, who cranked the hammer down with the force of three men in an unrelenting rhythm, smashing the lid, not missing once, denting it, bludgeoning it—*Whop!*—till the first lock snapped free. Without a break in his swift motion, John Henry trained his eyes on the second lock and demolished it. *Whop! Whop!*

Bunyan kept clear of the hammer swing, then called, "Back!" and stepped up to plug the torches into the crawling green sap. After only a few seconds, a new pustule would swell, drip, and harden into bark if Bunyan didn't jam fire on it first.

The second lock burst, leaving just the third. They were close now, and Bunyan's spirits rose to see his friend's skill. Not one in a thousand could have whopped that hammer but once with the force John Henry unleashed for three score strokes in a row, precise with his aim every time. The way a kid might pick up a stick on the forest floor and slap it against a tree for fun, that's how easily John Henry drove his hammer against that last lock until—*crack!*—the strongbox sprung open.

John Henry lodged his tool into the maw of the box, wide enough for Bunyan to reach in. "Go!" Bunyan pitched the torches and dove into the hole amid the oozing sap, sliding both arms into the darkened crack of the box till he touched the fat Tome inside. He pulled it free—"Got it!"—and both leapt away. But as they did Bunyan saw a curling vine wrapping quick about John Henry's calf, beginning to squeeze . . .

Bunyan pitched down the Tome and drew out his axe.

"It's *burning*," said John Henry, keeping his calm.

Aiming once and true, Bunyan whipped the axe head down, his chop brushing against the very hairs of John Henry's calf as it sliced the snaking vine, which fell away and withered. Taking off his leather smock, Bunyan wiped the acid clean from his friend's leg. Already John Henry's flesh had begun to blister.

"Look!" shouted John Henry.

The furious, predatory vines raced at them both. John Henry snatched up the Tome and the pair sprinted clear, only when at a safe distance looking back to see the fresh oozing sap seeping over the hole, crushing the strongbox forever into the ancient womb of the tree.

John Henry held the book in his arms:

THE PROPERTIES AND PROCESSING OF FIRE SEED
MBE & AH

"Come on," said Bunyan. "Let's get this to El Boffo."

———————————•———————————

In the lobby of the Palace Hotel, Benedict Souslatable called up to El Boffo's room. A minute later, Dedrick came down and led Bunyan, John Henry, and his family to the elevator.

"Top floor," said Dedrick.

But the white elevator attendant refused to push the button.

"Top floor," Dedrick repeated.

"They can't get on here."

Dedrick looked surprised. "You know me. Push the button."

"We are under orders to make an exception for you and you alone," said the elevator man. "El Boffo knows how to count his bucks. Elevators just have room for one."

"El Boffo's in an important race," Dedrick insisted. "When I tell him you slowed us down, even a minute, he won't be pleased."

"Let me be the judge of which race is important." The attendant extended his arm. "The stairs are around the corner."

A crowd had begun to gather—all white. Dedrick turned to John Henry's family. "I'm sorry about this. You'll have to take the stairs." He turned to Bunyan. "You can come with me."

Bunyan shook his head. "I'll walk."

After they had climbed forty stories, Dedrick waited for them on the penthouse level. Upon entering, Bunyan froze in awe. He had never seen anything like El Boffo's suite: marble busts, checkered floors, a hulking bouquet of fresh-cut flowers on the lacquered front table. Twin staircases spiraled to the upper floor, and a wall of grand windows offered a godlike view of the grimy city below.

The Lord of Lump Town sat Polly and Newton in the foyer, then motioned for Bunyan and John Henry—both still sweating from their hike—to follow.

El Boffo's office was cavernous. A dozen antique rifles hung on one wall, and a gigantic buffalo head protruded above the fireplace. Over the desk itself was an intricately painted coat of Old World arms, with an insignia written in cursive script below:

The Court Is My Fist
The Cash Is My Gun

Alongside El Boffo stood his lead scientist, introduced as Dr. Otto Lecker. Lecker was a handsome man with oiled, neatly parted hair and a fine wall of teeth. To Bunyan he looked less like a scientist and more like a dashing actor cast in the part of a scientist.

As Lecker looked through the pages of the Tome, Bunyan marveled at its intricate penmanship, sketches, tables, and diagrams:

Here was a model of the molecular structure of Lump; there was a neatly marked table called "Decomposition Rate Under Toxin Exposure." Another page was headed "Hypothesis on Regenerative Cellular Activity."

"Do we have what we need?" El Boffo had an air of urgency bordering on fury.

"Much of this appears extraneous." Lecker seemed overwhelmed. "The author was a rather discursive thinker . . ."

El Boffo repeated: "Do. We. Have. What. We. Need?"

Lecker flipped back to the table of contents and ran his finger down the headings.

Possible Replacement of Carbon Fuels, p. 133
Germs, Bacteria, Viruses. Universalities of Infection, p. 202
Conditions, Disorders, & Long-term Afflictions, p. 251
Elixir Salutis, Panaceas, Mithridate, Catholicons, Theriacs,
    Nostrums. A Compendium, p. 280

He turned the page and kept skimming:

Outline of Lump Refining Methodology and "the Pure," p. 358
Airborne Processing Particles and Smog, p. 395
The Sludge—Insolubility and Permanence, p. 406
Toxicity at Scale, p. 414
Deleterious Effects on Mammals, p. 429

And further down still:

The Simulorb, p. 620
The Formula and Chemical Reaction in Device Core, p. 634
Generation of the Salvation Light, p. 645
Risks of Combustion, p. 651

Lecker turned to page 634, moving his lips as he read, then at last stood up straight and rubbed his jaw.

"Well, of course we were quite close. We frankly were headed in this direct—"

El Boffo slammed his palm down on his desk. "Do we have the Formula or *not?*"

Lecker raised his head and offered a handsome if sheepish smile. "Of course, sir. We have it."

"The Wondertorium Gala is in three days. Can it be functional by then?"

"I think, yes, maybe." Lecker bent down and scanned the page once more. "Just a few minor adjustments. We'd need to load it with all the Pure we have."

"You'll have it all."

"We'd need to test—"

"You have three days. Go."

Lecker reached for the Tome but El Boffo grabbed his hand. "You're not taking this. Write down what you need. Dedrick?"

Dedrick, who had been seated at the rear of the room, stood. "Sir?"

"Take him to the library, make sure he is able to copy down what he needs. The Tome stays with us."

"Of course."

After Dr. Lecker and Dedrick left the room, Bunyan spoke up. "If it works, I assume we can transport the device to Lump Town right away? My wife is on the edge."

El Boffo drew out a fresh cigar from the box upon his desk. He lit it and walked to the window overlooking the Windy City, his hands clasped behind his back, radiating triumph.

"I have a feeling, Lump Master, that three nights from now, all of our problems are going to be solved. Mine, yours, everyone's."

"So, we'll take it straight there?"

El Boffo puffed. "My investors, perhaps, will be most happy of all."

"But bringing it to Lump—"

"Wondertorium first!" El Boffo snapped. Then he turned and gave Bunyan a gentler grin. "Once that light starts shining, boy, nothing else will matter."

El Boffo saw John Henry standing by a row of pictures on the wall.

"Well, Steel-Drivin' John! You always turned down my dinner invitations, eh? Happy we could finally meet."

John Henry didn't answer, engrossed as he was looking at one photo: a picture of a father and son on a railroad track, both dressed in bright, clean suits.

"That's me and my father," said El Boffo, approaching. "The railroad can be a great place for families."

"Is that so?"

John Henry moved along to the next photo, a portrait of a middle-aged El Boffo standing in the mouth of a cave with a team of miners holding shovels and picks.

"Giving Mother Cave," El Boffo said. "The place I first discovered Lump."

The magnate walked across the room to a safe, where he spun in a combination. "My family has been in America for six generations. It takes that kind of time to build up real wealth." He removed a sack of money. "How many generations has your family been here?"

"Twelve," said John Henry.

"Well then! Two great American families, each building up our fortunes!" El Boffo returned to his desk, where he took off his watch. "So what's it going to be, Steel Driver? The watch or the silver?"

"The silver."

El Boffo handed over the sack. "From one hardworking American family to another."

With that, El Boffo escorted them to the foyer, where Polly and Newton were waiting.

The magnate shook Polly's hand. "Clever work on the riddle. You just never know where good ideas will come from." Then he turned to Newton. "Well, my boy, what do you think of the place?"

"So high up," said Newton.

El Boffo winked. "I'm always the top story, anywhere I go."

"And so much *stuff*."

"It's the great project of this country, isn't it? Turning Nature into *stuff*."

El Boffo led them past the elevator to the stairs. There, John Henry took in the splendor of the palatial abode one last time.

"So, this is where it goes," he said.

"Where what goes?"

"The sweat of our brows."

"That's the wonderful thing about America," said El Boffo with a smile. "If you want to get ahead, all you have to do is work!"

CHAPTER 32

FIAT LUX!

Outside the Palace Hotel, Bunyan bid farewell to Polly and Newton, then turned to John Henry.

"I knew there was a way for us to work together."

John Henry grabbed a handful of silver from his sack. "Here, take this."

Bunyan pushed John Henry's hand back. "You'll need it for Mr. V and the Great White North."

"If it weren't for you I'd already be with the bounty hunters," said John Henry, again proffering the silver.

Again, Bunyan gently refused. "The Simulorb's enough reward for me."

"You're a determined man, Paul Bunyan." This time John Henry grabbed Bunyan's hand and forced him to take the silver pieces. "But so am I."

Seeing no way to avoid it, Bunyan relented and put the silver in his pocket.

John Henry glanced around, suspiciously, almost automatically, for the bounty hunters. "I'll be staying at Gabriel's Roadhouse. In three nights, I'll get the documents I need. Hopefully we'll catch our ship while you're at the gala."

Big as bears, the men locked in a hug.

Three days later, Bunyan arrived at the gala, dressed in the tux he'd bought with John Henry's silver. Lucette's lock of hair was in his pocket, now nine-tenths silverdark. There was still time.

At the door, Bunyan showed his invitation, which Souslatable had begrudgingly provided to him that morning. An usher handed him a complimentary pair of circular, green-tinted glasses and a schedule of the night's events:

7:00 Hors d'oeuvres and Champagne
7:30 Plated Five-Course Meal
8:30 Little Miss Windy City and the Wondertorium Choir
9:00 Special Presentation by El Boffo
10:00 "Auld Lang Syne" & Fireworks

Bunyan had been held up at the tailor—his measurements were a bit large—and arrived late. The program was already well under way. Around him, the Wondertorium had been transformed.

Just days before, it had been El Boffo's showroom; now its booths and exhibitions had all been wheeled away. From end to end, men in jackets and top hats and women in flowing gowns of rich hues packed the hall, all of them sitting around circular, linen-covered tables, the interior lit tastefully by gas lamps about the perimeter. In the air hung a stew of rich aromas, perfumes and luxurious colognes.

Across a stage at the fore hung a huge, blood-red curtain. Above, the Lump-powered hot-air balloon still floated, though darkly, unlit. Still higher, and only faintly visible through the glass dome, an American flag gently lapped in the late spring breeze.

Bunyan felt too anxious to sit. Standing along the wall, he watched as Darlene LaLibertay wrapped up her version of "My Country, 'Tis of Thee." After she finished, she lingered for a moment in her white dress, blowing kisses.

Then El Boffo strode upon the stage before the giant curtain.

"My oh my. That Darlene, she really does love her country, doesn't she? How about another round of applause?"

The crowd murmured and faintly clapped, chatting over their glasses of sparkling wine. It was just then that Bunyan noticed, tucked off to the side of the stage, only a dozen paces from where he stood, a wide metal control panel.

Dr. Lecker sat before it in his white lab coat. His hair was neatly parted as before, though there were bags under his handsome eyes. A gas mask sat on the empty seat behind him. He fussed over the different knobs and buttons, tweaking and turning them, as if still concerned over whether he truly trusted their functions.

Curious, Bunyan edged along the wall to where he could read the labels on the machine:

CORE PRESSURE • IGNITION ROD •
ROTATION SPEED • LUMINOSITY

Up onstage, El Boffo appeared to be a changed man. No duck-walking. No call and response. No Boffing your life. His habitual gusto seemed tamed by the power of this moment.

"It is so wonderful to see so many friends tonight. The Rocker-fords." He pointed. "The Van Hausers. The Buchanans." He waved. "The finest families in America are in this room. You have given me much. Tonight, at last, I shall repay you."

As the crowd grew still, El Boffo stroked his mustache thought-fully. "I suppose, ladies and gentlemen, that the journey toward one's life ambition is like the scaling of a dangerous mountain. As a young man you're enchanted, full of glorious dreams. You have delusions of grandeur, yes, but then again, no true grandeur was ever achieved without delusions of it first. As you begin, you go fast. Soon, you've outpaced your peers. But then . . . things change. Obstacles and mis-fortunes. Suddenly, right there in the midst of your ascent, you look around and realize you're all alone. The more practical have fled, the reckless have been wiped out, the dilettantes have found another hobby, and the well-wishers have all gone home."

The audience was completely silent, transfixed by the man onstage.

Mastering a bit of emotion, El Boffo cleared his throat. "It's then you taste true despair. For while you have come further than the rest, and much too far to turn back, still the summit is nowhere in sight. You swore it to the world, 'I shall do what has never been done!' But ambition has led you into a trap of your own devising . . . and everyone saw it coming but you.

"You thought you'd be collecting trophies! You dreamed your life would be a neat and well-paced fable of conquest! One certain step after another. But here you shiver, here you starve, clinging to a rock amid the howling winds. You presumed you'd be an inspiration. Instead, you're a cautionary tale, just someone much too stubborn, or much too stupid, to stop."

El Boffo clenched his fists before his face as if he were shaking someone by the lapels. "But it is here, my friends, it is *here* you must endure! It is here, in this solitary stretch of barren, frozen rock, with not a soul as your witness, when you have no reason to go forward but that promise you swore to yourself long ago, it is *here* that you must drive on to the finish!

"And so, you swallow your pain. You grip another ledge. Before the audience of only one, you scale that icy rock. Shorn of romance, shorn of delusion, your dreamed-of glory now tasting like a mouthful of dust, you go on. And with every hard-won inch, you tell it to the mountain: I shall get to the top, or die trying."

El Boffo allowed himself a smile at this, his humbled eyes genuinely meeting the gazes of the crowd. "Eventually, friends, you *do* get there. For in the end, if they never call you crazy, they'll never call you hero."

The great showman cleared his throat, swallowing another lump of feeling.

"What is behind this very curtain, ladies and gentlemen, is the *pinnacle* of human engineering. It is designed to meet the most universal of human crises: that of our bodies' vulnerability.

"You may have noticed my song selection in the program. 'Auld Lang Syne' has always been a favorite. The New Year, bidding farewell to the old, greeting the new. Yet tonight, it is *particularly* appropriate. For tonight, we say goodbye to our past and hello to the dawn of a new age for all mankind.

"Tonight, you see, is the moment our species *decisively* gains the upper hand over Nature. The road here wasn't always pretty, nor clean, nor guaranteed, nor without sacrifice. But from the ashes of these American plains, my friends, we shall rise and be healed.

"From time immemorial, Nature has made war upon our species. Its germs invade. Its parasites colonize. Its bacteria infest. Its microbes take up residence within us, and then these squatting, derelict tramps of disease make a feast of our flesh. Till now, we have been both helpless and hopeless to stop the onslaught, facing Nature's marauders with little more than our prayers and our tears.

"In the Far East, desperate physicians blended herbs to cure the hundred ailments. In the Old World, alchemists labored for millennia to combat pitiless plagues. The greatest minds in history have tried and failed to secure that one, universal panacea. Who knew, ladies and gentlemen, it would fall upon our generation to find it? To build it?"

He gestured grandly to the curtain behind him. "Tonight you will see a light that will eradicate all illness. Just minutes from now, the very fibers of this light shall scrub the edges of your cells and cleanse these foreign agents in your body. Weary as you are from decades of struggle with these unseen encroachers and vagabonds, you shall be purified. And my invention does not stop with disease. The Light has demonstrated the capacity to heal wounds, as well. To bind up the bleeding. To fortify the dying. Your scuffs and cuts, your rashes and trauma, every last indignity and snub of time shall be knit whole without a seam."

Once more, El Boffo stroked his mustache. "I shall send you forth, my friends, with a clean bill of health. My light will make you the titans you were in your prime, as fearless of the future as you were upon a time."

El Boffo rubbed his hands together. "So then, shall we begin?"

The crowd of America's finest families offered a rousing cheer. "Heal us!" someone shouted.

"When you entered tonight, you were given a pair of green-tinted glasses. May I ask you to put them on?"

Across the packed hall, attendees fit on their glasses. At the side of the stage, Bunyan did, as well. A thousand green eyes trained themselves upon El Boffo, who turned to face the curtain.

"Ladies and gentlemen, behold, the Simulorb!"

As the curtain drew aside, the crowd gasped.

Suspended several feet above the stage was a hefty globe of glass, about the size of a man's chest. Iron bands and rivets held it together in a crude hashwork of latitude and longitude. The device itself hung from a thick chain attached to a large, horizontal gear about twenty feet up. To the rear stood a cluster of interconnected copper tubes and tanks. The complexity and bulk of the supporting equipment contrasted with the lone orb, hanging like the pendant of a god.

For a moment, El Boffo appeared caught in silent admiration before the star he had forged.

"Tonight, you will see a mesmerizing light. A miraculous light. A medicinal light. Only let the light touch your skin, and you shall be cured."

El Boffo put on his own green glasses and turned to Dr. Lecker. "Commence rotation."

As Dr. Lecker adjusted the knobs, the gear above the stage began to turn, and with it, the Simulorb below. Gaining speed, the iron bands of the globe became a blur.

"Excuse me, if I could just squeeze by," whispered someone beside Bunyan.

Bunyan moved aside as a man ducked past him and edged closer to the stage. Behind this man rapidly came a second, this one pulling a woman by the hand. "Sorry, pardon us."

As the decked-out denizens of the Windy City started a slow rhythmic clap, Bunyan noticed that many in the far back of the room were likewise leaving their seats and creeping forward.

Clap. Clap. Clap.

When the Simulorb had gained sufficient speed, El Boffo shouted back toward Lecker, "Ignition Rod!"

A few in the crowd stood and pointed as a trapdoor opened in the stage, and from the hole emerged a gigantic metal pole. The tip glowed white, like a superheated fire poker, and rose up toward the fast-spinning Simulorb, as if to impregnate it.

Clap! Clap! Clap!

"Sorry, excuse me."

"Coming through."

Still more passed Bunyan along the wall as the crowd by the stage swelled.

"Down in front!" said one man. "Please, my father is ninety years old."

Up onstage, half consciously, El Boffo gently clapped along with the crowd—

Clap! Clap! Clap! Clap!

With the glowing-hot rod just inches from vanishing into the spinning sphere, El Boffo held out his arms toward the Simulorb as if he would embrace it—

Clap clap clap clap clap clap!

—and at last the rod dipped in and El Boffo shouted over the whirring machinery, "Fiat lux!"

As the white-hot rod penetrated the dark hole of the device, the Wondertorium crowd fidgeted and buzzed in frenzied excitement, a sound interrupted only by a shouting match that had broken out on the other side of the hall, as two women struggled to get close.

"I was *standing here!*"

"Get back!"

"Look!" El Boffo pointed. "The *light!*"

As the Ignition Rod withdrew, Bunyan saw a golden light born within the whirring device.

"Brighter, Lecker!" shouted El Boffo over his shoulder "Brighter!"

Bunyan watched as Lecker adjusted the pressure gauge and the light of the Simulorb grew closer to white, illuminating the Wondertorium itself as if it were day.

"Stop pushing!" someone shouted.

"We need to get up, too!"

"We paid for this seat! I'm an original investor!"

"We all are!"

Amid the jostling, Bunyan was tall enough to have a clear view of the device, whose light had begun to mellow and turn gold. It seemed to be reaching out for him, bathing him, dipping into his very cells with ethereal fingertips . . .

"Hey, watch it!"

"I was here!"

More shouting from the front as a man hopped up onstage, next to El Boffo.

"You can't be up here." El Boffo only now seemed to grasp that a mob had formed. "Please! Everyone, return to your seats!" But even as he said that, three others jumped up on the stage. "No, no! If everyone could please be civilized!"

But it was too late. People were climbing up one after the other, drawn toward the golden light, swarming about the structure like shipwrecked, sea-strewn passengers about a life raft. As more stood onstage, they blocked the Simulorb's light, which thereby intensified the fight to get closer.

"I can't see at all!"

"Hey! You! Get down!"

A punch was thrown. Two men in tuxedos wrestled on the stage floor.

"No, no!" El Boffo's voice had grown unhinged with dismay. "Stop this! This is a great moment! Salvation is for everyone!"

El Boffo pushed through the people to Lecker.

"Why is it not working?" he said to his chief engineer. "Where is the Salvation Light?"

"I don't know. I just don't know . . ."

"Then make it work!"

As Lecker fiddled more frantically with the controls, the throng grew more restive.

"Barbarian!"

"Thug!"

Suddenly, the light in the room wobbled. The Simulorb began swinging from side to side.

"She's fallen in!" someone shouted.

"She's by the Ignition Rod!"

A scream.

The Simulorb careened back and forth like a wrecking ball, shoving part of the throng off the edge of the stage, where they tumbled like lemmings from a cliff.

Bunyan felt a sharp increase in heat and turned his head away from it. Moments later, he heard El Boffo shouting at Lecker.

"Shut it off!"

The swaying Simulorb crashed into another man, knocking him, too, into the hole in the stage down by the superheated rod.

"Shut it off!"

Dr. Lecker dove beneath the control panel. "I'm trying!"

Chaos had overtaken the stage as half the mob was trying to climb up onto it, while others fled the wildly swinging globe.

"If you would all just return to your seats!" El Boffo shouted. "If you could all remain calm!" To Lecker he said, "Just pull the emergency shutoff!"

Lecker emerged from under the panel and shouted back at El Boffo, "I already pulled it!"

Horror filled Bunyan's heart. It was not going to work, was it? The Simulorb was not going to Lump Town. It was not going to save Lucette . . .

Amid the swelling heat, Bunyan saw a service door at the rear of the stage and ran for it. He pushed through into the cool air outside and threw his green glasses on the ground as he jogged across the street, where he mounted the stone stairs of the post office opposite to look back.

Hundreds now poured from the Wondertorium, red-faced, sweating, panicked. From one exit a pair of men carried out an unconscious woman; at another a woman pushed an elderly man out in a wheelchair. A third door jammed with too many trying to squeeze through at once, as above, in the glass dome of the Wondertorium, Bunyan could see light growing brighter and brighter till—

BOOM!

The blast struck Bunyan, knocking him clean off his feet. His ears rang. He tried to stand but fell.

As he attempted to orient his mind, tiny shards of glass began to fall. He caught a potent whiff of Lump—that sweet and sour scent, like bread that promised to nourish but never could—and at last he raised his eyes to behold a sight he could scarcely believe:

The Wondertorium had erupted into a blazing inferno.

Where its majestic dome once had soared, there was only a rim of twisted metal beams. The Lump-powered hot-air balloon had been punctured and impaled diagonally on jagged glass amid the currents of streaming fire. From the entrance could be heard a chorus of screams, as people dashed, scrambled, and scattered across the road.

Regaining himself, Bunyan sprinted down the post office steps. On the way, he picked up a trash can, and as he arrived on the other side of the street he hurled it at one of the Wondertorium's ground-floor windows, shattering it. He kicked out the glass that remained, then reached a hand in for those trapped inside. Out they came, hobbled, bleeding, charred.

"There's a man down there at the next window!"

Bunyan looked to see someone banging frantically from inside. He lifted a giant Wondertorium sign off the building wall, an advertisement that said in huge letters, *TAKE IT!*

"Duck down!" he shouted.

Bunyan launched the rectangular board at the window, where it sliced straight through the glass. Hot air shot from the gap and Bunyan spied the man crouching amid the wreckage, his jacket pulled over his head. Bunyan kicked in the glass, yanked him free with one arm, and the pair tumbled back into the street together. As he stood, he saw who it was:

Dedrick.

The Lord of Lump Town got to his feet and brushed himself off as behind him, flames leapt from the room where he'd just been trapped. Without a word, stone-faced as ever, Dedrick vanished into the throng as Bunyan took in the wider scene:

Flames gutted adjacent storefronts—the Saloon, the Hat and Cap Boutique, the Law Office, and the Stenographer's. Tilting back his head, Bunyan could see, toward the top of the Wondertorium, the steel beams of the dome had begun to melt and sag, as tornados of fire leapt and twisted toward the heavens.

Suddenly, one entire side of the Wondertorium buckled into the building beside it, like a drunk friend slouching into his companion. A flaming beam rolled off the roof, trailing black smoke. Onlookers scattered clear just as it violently thumped down upon the rear of a horse-drawn wagon.

Firemen came clanging down the street and within seconds of parking their wagons were pumping tanks of water on the blaze, as the medics treated the wounded lying on the sidewalk and the rest of the crowd gawked at the scope of the disaster.

Up by the river, a water-bucket line had formed. One person passed a bucket to the next, who passed it to the next, all the way to the Wondertorium doors. Not knowing how else to help, Bunyan took his place in the water line, as the mood in the streets turned from panic to mourning.

It was then that Bunyan heard the most improbable sound: *singing.*

Back on the post office stairs, the Wondertorium Choir had assembled, their faces lit up orange with the blaze. Leading them was none other than Darlene LaLibertay, who rallied others to join in.

"Please, won't anyone sing?" There were tears on her face. "Won't you sing for this great man?"

And one by one, more and more joined in.

> *Should old acquaintance be forgot*
> *And never brought to mind?*
> *Should old acquaintance be forgot,*
> *And auld lang syne?*

Horses and dogs ran wild in the streets, as here a family loaded up a wheelbarrow with suitcases, and there, out on the river, a ship burned, rocking with flames as if possessed by ghosts. As Bunyan passed bucket after bucket of water, the song went on:

For auld lang syne, my dear,
For auld lang syne!
We'll take a cup of kindness yet,
For auld lang syne!

A scream rose from the crowd as a blast descended thunderously from the heavens, and Bunyan gazed up to see the sky suddenly filled with color—*Pink! Blue! Red! Green!*—bursts and eruptions, snaps and blasts—*Orange! Purple! White! Turquoise! Fireworks!*

No doubt these were meant to be seen through the glass dome of the Wondertorium during the gala finale, after the Salvation Light had bathed and cured the wealthiest in America. The conflagration must have set them off. One after the other, their colors slammed into the inky night, just above the American flag, which still flapped atop the broken dome, amid the torrents of black smoke.

Passing another bucket, Bunyan spied two men having an argument on the corner. Though both were disheveled and blackened by ash, Bunyan knew right away who they were.

El Boffo shouted in Dedrick's face as Dedrick listened in silence. El Boffo gestured up at the burning Wondertorium, then poked his finger in Dedrick's chest.

At last, Dedrick stalked off, as above the fireworks boomed and Bunyan passed another bucket of water toward the ruined Wondertorium, and Darlene stood high over them all, her face streaked with tears as the choir sang over the din:

For auld lang syne, my dear,
For auld lang syne!
We'll take a cup of kindness yet,
For auld lang syne!

CHAPTER 33

SHINE

Hours later, Bunyan stood on a hill in the north of the Windy City, overlooking the devastation. The air smelled of Lump as the spreading fire ate the guts of the city. He took the lock of Lucette's hair from his pocket, now nearly silverdark to the tip.

It was too late.

Soon, life would be as it had been before: he and his mother, alone on the Earth, helpless and poor, driven before the wind and scattered like chaff into the cracks. With Lucette, just for a little while, he'd felt he'd been invited to the great banquet of life.

He'd gotten his axe from the boardinghouse where he'd been staying since he parted from John Henry. The morning train left in a few hours. If he returned home quick enough, he could say goodbye to his wife while she still breathed. Bunyan had just one stop left to make: Gabriel's Paradise Roadhouse. On the porch stood a half dozen armed Black men.

"Is Gabriel here?"

"Who's looking?"

"I'm Paul Bunyan, friend of"—he almost said John Henry but didn't want to name his hunted friend—"Steel-Drivin' John."

One of the men went inside. To Bunyan's surprise, a few moments later, Gabriel rushed out looking stressed. He glanced up and down the block, then craned his head round to the back alley.

"Keep an eye out," Gabriel said to the men. He motioned to Bunyan. "Come on, quick."

Inside the Roadhouse, the dance floor was deserted, the stage empty.

"What happened to Paradise?" said Bunyan.

"Paradise is always moving. Paradise knows how to hide."

Bunyan followed Gabriel up the back stairs. "I only came to let you know that if Steel-Drivin' John ever sends me a message, you can forward it to me in Lump Town. I—"

"*Sends* you a message?" said Gabriel. "Your man's here right *now.*"

At the end of the upstairs hallway stood two heavily armed Black men, shotguns across their chests. Bunyan followed Gabriel through the door into a tight room. Round a table sat three people Bunyan hadn't expected to see for years to come, if ever:

John Henry, Polly, and Newton.

"Now, listen, all of you," said Gabriel. "Last time this white boy showed up, he had two bounty hunters on him. Things are hot enough as it is. Don't need it any hotter."

"He's straight," said John Henry.

"I thought you were supposed to be in the Great White North?" said Bunyan in disbelief.

"I thought you were supposed to be at the Wondertorium."

"The Simulorb blew up. What about Mr. V?"

"They got to him." Gravely, John Henry explained: "We went to him tonight as planned. But the F.O.L. was there. They'd stormed the Black docks. It was a riot."

"A riot?"

Gabriel looked out the window and in both directions. He pulled his head back in and drew the curtains.

"All America's a riot," he said. "Five Points Brawl, Broad Street Burning, Bricks and Sticks Battle, Cotton Gin Killings, Paha Sapa Slaughter, Far East Expulsion, Sugar Cane Fracas, Mulatto Melee, Tenement Rumble, Black Belt Bombing, the Buffalo Hangings, the White Night. The story of America's the story of a brawl. I used to think it was just dreamers versus takers. But look closely and you see the truth: every fighter's got a dream. Dark dream or bright dream, either way, it's my dream versus yours. That's why F.O.L.'s spreading quick. The past is slipping by and the bottom's rising up. If they can get to Mr. V, they can get to anyone."

"What about the money from El Boffo?" asked Bunyan. "Couldn't you pay someone else to help you?"

John Henry reached in his pocket and took out a crumpled sheet of paper:

WANTED: JOHN HENRY

A.K.A. "STEEL-DRIVIN' JOHN"
ESCAPED CONVICT TRAVELING WITH WIFE AND SON
SEEKING PASSAGE TO BIG SMOKE

$$$$$ FOR THEIR APPREHENSION $$$$$

DEAD OR ALIVE!
PULASKI & LYNCH, 111 ADAMS ST., THE WINDY CITY

"Who's gonna help us now?" said John Henry. "These are all over town."

Gabriel shook his head. "Getting hotter by the minute."

Bunyan rubbed his face with his hands. The Simulorb, gone. Mr. V, gone. Lucette, soon to be gone. His job, his reputation, his gold bar, and his home, all gone.

"What about you?" said John Henry to Bunyan. "Where to?"

Bunyan dug his hand into his beard. "The train to Lump Town leaves at dawn, so I'll be—"

Knock. Knock. Knock.

Everyone in the room turned toward the door. Bunyan watched as Gabriel went to it, opened it a crack, and talked to a man outside.

John Henry picked up his hammer, which was leaning against the wall. Following his lead, Bunyan unsheathed his axe from his back.

At last, Gabriel shut the door and turned back into the room. "Someone's come for you."

"For me?" said Bunyan.

"For both of you. Well-dressed. Face like a wood carving. Says he's your old boss from Lump Town."

"*Dedrick?*"

"You know him?"

"I know him. He works for El Boffo."

Gabriel pulled his gun from his belt, cocked it, and opened the door. The Lord of Lump Town walked into the room.

"How did you find us here?" Bunyan asked, incredulous.

"It's my job to know things." Dedrick's clothes were filthy, burned, ripped, but somehow, he retained his habitual air of self-possession.

Gabriel kept his gun pointed at Dedrick from a few feet away. "Who are you?"

"Just a man getting by."

"Living on the top?"

"Came from the bottom."

"Where exactly?"

"One Twenty and Tenth, round about."

"Where'd you get soup?"

"Toby's."

"Dinner?"

"Couldn't afford dinner."

"What'd they call you?"

"Shine."

"Never heard of you."

"Guess your shoes didn't need shining."

"Father and mother?"

"I was my own."

Gabriel pulled up a sleeve to show his wrist, where his prison cuffs had scarred him. "Ever been?"

"Never, by the grace of God."

Gabriel released the hammer on the gun, stuck it in his belt, and stepped to Dedrick almost nose to nose. "And why should I believe you're straight?"

"Hear my story, then decide."

"And what story is that?"

"Same as yours, I'll bet. Working twice as hard for half as much. Carrying a load no one can see. Obeying all the rules, yet every day the scapegoat. Walking on that wire, one slip from the pit."

"Walking white-topped mountains—I bet it does get slippery."

"Just trying to stand up straight."

"On whose shoulders?"

"You can't help a drowning man unless you're on the raft."

Gabriel reached out and touched Dedrick's fine lapel on his suit. "Right, *brother*. Seems like you're on the raft. Now tell me who you've helped."

"I'm about to help, if you'll let me talk."

After another long stare, Gabriel relented. He pulled out a chair. "All right. Start talking."

Dedrick sat at the table and loosened his tie.

"What's this about?" asked John Henry.

Dedrick answered, "You need to get to the Great White North with your family?"

"Yeah."

"And you"—Dedrick turned to Bunyan—"need to help your wife."

"Right."

Suddenly, Dedrick let out a great cough. He coughed for a long time, so much that at last Gabriel went to the door and said to one of his men, "Get him an iced tea."

Dedrick wiped his eyes, cleared his throat, and regained himself. "I believe I can help you both."

"Did El Boffo send you?" said John Henry skeptically.

"El Boffo doesn't know a thing about this. If he did, we'd all be in danger. In fact, what I'm about to say is information he would kill for."

One of Gabriel's men came back with the iced tea. As Dedrick drank, Gabriel told his men to wait outside.

"Well, you gonna help these boys or what?" asked Gabriel.

As the Windy City burned, Dedrick quickly told his tale.

From the day I was born, this city swept me along like rubbish, one alley to the next. I've always been the junk this city couldn't throw away.

When I started shining shoes I was so poor I had to steal rags. That's how much of nothing I had—I had to steal just to work. Hungry? Get that bread. Beat up? Get that bread. Run off the block? Get that bread. No place to sleep? Get up, boy, and get that bread.

Still, I had a knack for it. Shining was the first time I'd ever pushed and seen the world budge. By seven in the morning, I had lines around the block. I woke up with fear every day: fear about customers, fear about cops, fear about competition. Fear crushes nine out of ten. I turned mine into fuel.

I had a dream: a beautiful, creamy-white bank statement. I could see it, hovering before my eyes: a crisp, clean page, my name on top, and below it rows of black, juicy numbers. Every night, in the alleys among the squabbling critters, I saw that clean, hard cash. One day, somehow, I knew I'd make it mine.

Back then, white men came to my neighborhood for three things—get high, get laid, or get shined. One day El Boffo showed up. The next week, he came back again. After a third shine, he hired me. He said he liked to work with "PhDs."

"I never set foot in school," I told him.

"'Poor, hungry, driven,'" he said.

So, life threw me the ball. You can bet I didn't fumble. I showed up at six in El Boffo's office and worked till midnight. Sundays, holidays, no days off. I never told him I slept in the streets. He never asked.

After some years, an opportunity came up: run the Factory in Lump Town. El Boffo needed someone with three qualities: You had to not mind dirty work. You had to be tight-lipped. You had to be patient for the gold, believing one day it would come.

At that point, I was already doing well. If a Black kid from the South Side just breaks even, he's already won a kind of war. But with the Lump Town offer, at last I saw the path to that creamy bank statement. I would have run that Factory if it were at the bottom of a swamp.

So I came to Lump Town. I oversaw every aspect of the Factory.

I oversaw hiring, too. I learned to spot PhDs. I needed men who'd never talk and never leave.

One day El Boffo summoned me to his office here in the Windy City. That's when he told me about the real purpose of Lump Town. He told me about the Simulorb. About the Salvation Light.

See, El Boffo's scientists hadn't been able to build the device just yet. He was running out of money. He needed help. He needed information.

El Boffo laid a gold bar before me. "If you can get me the information that leads to the Salvation Light, this is yours. No questions asked."

That damned gold bar. Sometimes I think he's put that exact same gold bar in front of a thousand people, never once actually giving it away.

Well, if I worked eighteen hours a day before, it was now twenty-two. I'd have worked twenty-five if I could have. In a back room at the Factory, I mounted maps, photos, articles. I hired trackers, detectives, spies. My search parties spanned coast to coast trawling for tips, deposits, rumors, anything. We twisted arms, and not just arms. The war for information isn't pretty. Years passed with only dead ends.

This year, El Boffo gave me an ultimatum: Find the information that makes the Simulorb work, or it's the end of the road. No Lump Sum, no mansion, no gold, no nothing.

Desperate, I turned the screws on my trackers. I threatened some. Others, I offered bonuses out of my own pocket. The only good lead I ever got was in roughing up Dr. Niebuhr. You see where that led us. After tonight, it will take El Boffo years to build another Simulorb, if he ever makes one at all.

A few hours ago, El Boffo put an end to it. He fired me, right there on the curb. Not that I was surprised. I'd worked by his side for decades, but I knew his heart. Hard as a ball bearing.

And so, with no friend, no future, and no fortune, I walked back to the Palace Hotel.

But fate had one more card to play.

CHAPTER 34

FAREWELL

In the tight back room on the second floor of Gabriel's Paradise Roadhouse, Dedrick finished his story:

———— • ————

When I got back to the Palace Hotel, the concierge stopped me.

"There's someone here to see you."

Entering a private dining room, I saw a man in a creased leather jacket, jet-black hair in a long ponytail, wearing a dusty fedora. I knew him right away.

It was Running Deer.

His father was Chief Swallow, someone we used to deal with in the old days, a man who helped us, through a bit of paperwork, to originally get access to Giving Mother Cave. In the war for information there are eyes all around. Over the years, Running Deer had now and then kept an eye on the First Foot tribe in exchange for pay.

El Boffo had once mentioned in passing that it wasn't he who discovered Lump, nor was it his scientists who originally discovered its properties and potential. The ones who first brought Lump to his attention were a true odd couple: a Native woman named Bright Eyes and a hunchbacked janitor at the university by the name of Axl. El

Boffo spoke dismissively of them; said they were crazy, incompetent, uneducated. No match for his team of scientists, at any rate.

Desperate as I was, this scrap of information returned to my mind a few months ago. I sought out Running Deer and offered him a bonus if he could somehow, some way, find Bright Eyes and Axl and draw any Lump-related information from them before my deadline. The pair was hostile toward El Boffo, so I instructed Running Deer to spy on their comings and goings, sift through their trash, even break into their home if need be.

———————•———————

Dedrick drew a letter from his jacket pocket and smoothed it on the table.

"Bright Eyes and Axl are married now and live on the First Foot lands. Running Deer broke into their home a few weeks ago. There, he found this."

Bunyan and John Henry read:

Oh, Axl!

Eureka! Eureka! Eureka! A dream of the healing fire, sprung from dormant embers of my soul! At last—at last!—I have pinpointed the source of the Salvation Light. We were so wrong before—what we wrote in the Tome, all wrong! And yet the answer was hiding in plain sight! And how did you pick this week of all weeks to buy provisions in town? I can't wait for your return—I'm bursting to tell you right now! I have all I need to test it, except for a drop of Pure. Racing off for Giving Mother Cave. Will produce it there! Half an ounce is all I need! Oh, Axl! A light that cures our people!

—BE

PS: Have S-lorb with me!
PPS: If I'm not back when you return, come quick to GMC!

"Running Deer gave this to me a few hours ago. It appears the race for knowledge at last has been won, but not by El Boffo. It's been won by the Indian and the janitor."

"Giving Mother Cave . . . ," said Bunyan, remembering the photo from El Boffo's office.

Dedrick went on. "It's been abandoned for years, ever since El Boffo left it. It's a lethal maze under the earth, with miles of tunnels, some natural, some man-made. Much of it has already collapsed. After he found this letter, Running Deer waited at the home of Bright Eyes and Axl for a few days. When they didn't return, he went to the cave itself. Not far from the cave's entrance, he stopped at a pit of poisonous snakes. There, he beheld a strange sight: the old hunchbacked janitor was outside the cave's mouth, pacing and muttering to himself. Stranger still, Running Deer heard a deep bellowing coming from the mine. He said it was like the cry of a great, wounded beast. Afraid to go further, he turned back."

Dedrick produced a second piece of paper from his jacket pocket and unfolded it.

"Running Deer drew this map for me. To access Giving Mother Cave, you will have to travel here, up a narrow valley called the Gorge. Finding them there is the only chance we have left."

Bunyan, John Henry, Polly, and Newton all looked over the map, absorbing the tale.

"Why come to us with this information, and not El Boffo?" asked Polly.

"For one, this man saved me from the inferno tonight." He nodded at Bunyan. "Beyond this, El Boffo and I are finished. But there is another reason I come to you, more urgent still."

Dedrick burst into another fit of coughing. When the coughing was finally through, he pulled up his shirt to show the skin beneath. There, just beside his belly button, was a deep bruise. Bunyan looked closer: its hue was silverdark.

"The Stucks can overtake a body in moments, as it did with Lucette." Dedrick's eyes had fear in them. "But the disease can also creep more slowly. Either way, I don't have long. If El Boffo gets to it first, there's no way he'll use it on a man like me."

Dedrick coughed again, then finished his iced tea. To Bunyan, he said, "If you obtain the Simulorb, I will pay your mother's debt in full. I've managed to save enough over time."

Next, he turned to John Henry. "I understand you need to get across the border with false identities for your family."

"Right."

"I've hired my share of trackers. I know a thing or two about how people disappear. Get me the device and I'll get you what you need."

"Passage across? Papers, too?"

"Everything."

Gabriel, still standing by the window, shook his head. "Still don't know what to believe. Here's a man who took gold from the top year after year. A taker all the way."

"I had my eye on gold but never got much." Dedrick tucked his shirt back in. "I've done my share of wrong, that's clear. I'll do some good before I'm through."

With that, Dedrick went to the door. "Be warned, it's only a matter of time before Running Deer's intelligence gets to El Boffo. If you go, go soon. I'll wait back in Lump Town. There are bruises and coughs among the residents, too, more than you might imagine. You're not just on a mission for your wife anymore. You're on a mission for every last one."

———————•———————

At dawn, Gabriel had the carriage waiting.

Outside, John Henry laid his hands on Newton's shoulders.

"When I come back, we'll go to the Great White North. We won't have to run anymore."

"I know, Dad." Newton fixed his glasses on his face.

John Henry let out a long breath. "Let's go over it, all right?"

The boy nodded. Bunyan listened from a few steps away, standing beside Polly.

"What are the stages of life?"

Newton answered, "To seek. To learn. To build. To preserve. To give."

"And what are we when victorious?"

"Full of mercy."

"What are we in the face of defeat?"

"Full of resolve."

"What are we in the face of cruelty?"

"Full of worth."

"And what are we in the face of the Lie?"

"Full of clarity."

"What's a man without the Code?"

"A jellyfish."

"And who are you, deep down?"

"The good story."

"The world is full of pain."

"But I am full of spirit."

John Henry crouched down and hugged his boy. "You will be better than me. Smarter than me. Stronger than me. Happier than me. Safer than me. You will live the full life. You know that?"

"Yes, Dad."

John Henry rubbed his boy's head and kissed him on top of it. "I know you, son, inside and out."

"I know you, too, Dad. Inside and out."

John Henry stood and went to Polly. "It would have been easier if you'd married another man."

"I chose right."

"I've seen so much bad, I wouldn't believe there was any good in the world at all, if not for you."

Polly stroked her husband's cheek. "The good is what I remember. The good is what I keep. The good is where we're headed."

Bunyan watched as this pair gazed deeply into each other's eyes, passing strength between them. They kissed, then hugged, then kissed again.

Last of all, John Henry shook Gabriel's hand. "Keep them safe."

"Paradise is always one step ahead."

Bunyan climbed into the waiting carriage and hid himself in a long crate of corn, room enough for his body and his axe. John Henry hid in a sack of potatoes with his hammer.

Soon, they were on a train bound west for the Gorge.

CHAPTER 35

TESTED IN
THE GORGE

As the train raced west across the plains, Bunyan could see Lump's blight upon the country more clearly than ever before. Though they were hundreds of miles from Lump Town, Bunyan saw the dense smog, invading the sky, blocking out the sun.

From the train station near the First Foot reservation, the two men followed Running Deer's map into the Gorge.

At the outset, Nature was still lush. In the springtime air, they waded across streams and passed through flowered meadows. The breeze blew thick as perfume. Far away, rocky peaks clustered with pines soared up into the blue dome of sky.

On the first day, Bunyan's foot chafed in his brace, but he hid his pain from John Henry, limping and forcing himself along. That night, they camped by a stream and ate roasted fish. In the light drizzle, John Henry used some rope and a sheet to make a tent. After John Henry fell asleep and the rain cleared off, Bunyan looked up at the stars and watched the fireflies pulse in the grove.

Then he heard a faint, low noise, coming from further up the Gorge.

brrraaaawwwww

The voice was haunting, almost human.

Bunyan took his harmonica from his pocket and gently played till he was tired. At last, he fell asleep. But in the middle of the night, Bunyan awoke with a start.

John Henry was shouting. "No! No! No!"

Bunyan grabbed his axe and hopped up, ready to fight. By the dim moonlight, he saw John Henry was caught in a nightmare.

"Listen to me!" he shouted. "It's a lie! Listen!"

Bunyan stirred his friend awake. John Henry's eyes were wild.

"The judge was banging a gavel. He said, 'Guilty! Guilty!' They dragged Newton to prison in chains!" John Henry trembled in fear. "If I die, who will protect my boy?" Gradually the great hammer man grew more calm. "I can't stay here. I've got to get back to my family."

"I understand," said Bunyan. "But at least wait till morning when it's clear."

In time, they slept. At dawn, they turned over their boots for scorpions and shook out their blankets for snakes. When they finished packing up, John Henry turned to Bunyan.

"Come on," he said. "Let's keep going."

"Not heading back?"

"Came this far already," he answered. "Ain't hardly gonna die."

With the morning dew wet on their boots and their great tools strapped to their backs, the pair continued deeper into the Gorge, as the valley narrowed and bald bluffs rose on either side. Here, Bunyan noticed the first tinge of silverdark in the grasses along the stream, runoff from the mining at Giving Mother Cave years before.

Bunyan's Junk Foot was tighter than it had been in years. Still, he hid the pain from John Henry, limping along behind. In the evening he took off his boot and saw his foot was covered in blood. As John Henry slept, he soaked Old Junk Foot in the chilly river waters. Again he heard the low moan, full of fury, full of anguish.

brrrraaaaaaawwwwwwwww

In time, Bunyan lay by the fire to sleep. But again in the middle of the night, he awoke to see John Henry flailing about, his arms in the air.

"Do me instead!" shouted John Henry, still in his sleep. "Do me!"

Again, Bunyan shook his friend awake. Again, John Henry looked about in terror.

"They whipped him with Black Betty! Newton had no one to protect him. He's just a child!" John Henry rubbed his face, clearing his thoughts. "I can't be away a moment longer."

"All right," said Bunyan. "But at least wait till morning so you can see the way."

The next morning Bunyan awoke almost too stiff to move. His whole body ached. Legs. Back. Arms. Rigid as a corpse, he tried to bend over and unbuckle his wood and leather sock. He couldn't even reach it.

Bunyan crawled to the stream, plunging his foot into the icy water—boot and all.

John Henry walked up from behind. "All right, let's see that foot."

Bunyan was embarrassed but had no choice. He could hardly stand, much less hike. Crouching by Bunyan, John Henry carefully worked off the boot, revealing the swollen, bleeding mass beneath. Taking the battered foot in his lap, he studied it. "How did this happen?"

Bunyan let out a long sigh. "It was a cattle stampede when I was twelve, the one that killed my father."

"You fought me in Throttlecock's ring with a foot like that?"

"I had needs bigger than my fears."

"How do you treat it?"

"Lucette used to drive her elbow in. Like this." Bunyan showed him.

John Henry shook his head. "You should have shown me earlier."

"I wanted you to believe you were with a man's man."

John Henry drove his powerful thumbs into the swollen muscles, massaging them. "You know what makes a man's man?"

"What's that?"

"Doing whatever it takes. And sometimes that means being strong enough to say you're weak."

John Henry worked his hands into the muscles for a long time, till they were loose. When he finished, he gingerly fit the brace on Bunyan's foot.

Bunyan stood and walked about the camp. The skin was still chafed, but the foot itself felt good.

"All right," Bunyan said. "I think we can make it to the cave today. You coming with?"

John Henry nodded. "I got needs bigger than fears."

The two walked on through the narrowing Gorge. The signs of Lump poisoning grew more prevalent. Though the sky was blue above, the trees were petrified and silverdark. By evening, they came to a pit of rattlesnakes upon the path, just as Running Deer had described.

But these squirming snakes were not like any Bunyan had ever seen. They, too, had turned silverdark, contaminated by Lump.

A mouse darted between Bunyan's legs. One of the silverdark snakes struck it, fast as lightning, biting into its belly. In the mouth of the snake, the mouse gradually froze in place, paralyzed by the venom.

"We need to go around." John Henry scanned the high bluffs. "Above."

Bunyan took the lock of Lucette's hair in his hand. It was almost completely silverdark. "No time."

"How's your foot?"

"Loose. But we can't run through that."

The ditch of snakes squirmed and hissed.

John Henry examined the walls. "Maybe we can lean against each other. Take footholds along the edges."

John Henry hammered a nail into the rock and tied some of his rope there, so if they got across, they could use the rope on the way back.

The two men faced one another and pressed their palms together, clasping hard with their fingers. Along each side of the crevice there were small outcroppings, some just the width of a finger. Leaning their full weight against each other, they balanced on these tiny protrusions, forming a human bridge across the pit. They worked themselves along, sweat dripping from their faces down to the deadly gulf, coaching each other all the way.

"There's a ledge just ahead, lift your foot."

"There's a rock jutting out, use that."

Arms strong as iron pipes, these two giants worked in unison, moving inch by inch over the crevice. Halfway across, one of the reptiles poked its head from a crack in the rock, darting its tongue just by Bunyan's heel, then oozing like slow waterfall down the ridge, directly onto Bunyan's calf.

"Careful," said John Henry. "Lean hard on me. Then shake it off."

Pressing all his weight against John Henry, Bunyan slowly lifted his Junk Foot, gave his leg a kick, then watched the silverdark snake slip off. He slammed his foot back on the wall just in time to keep their balance.

"Almost there," said John Henry. "Easy does it."

Legs aching, arms trembling, this two-man bridge resumed its shuffle astride the chasm till at last they leapt onto a small plateau beyond the snakes, where they collapsed to the ground, exhausted.

There, John Henry hammered a second nail into the wall and tied off the rope, so they would be able to get back across more easily.

Evening had come.

Debris cluttered the clearing. Rusted old pots, hammers, and picks lay strewn about. Here was an old section of rail track, there a tipped-over mining cart. A few petrified silverdark trees clung to the crags. There was more recent debris, too: a few empty tins of beans and salted beef.

Wooden boards blocked entry to a cave, over which hung a sign:

GMC MINE

DANGER OF COLLAPSE

NO ADMITTANCE

From within came pained bellowing:
brrrraaaaaaaaaaaaaawwwwwwwwww

"These cans are from the last few days," said John Henry. "Let's hope the janitor is still here."

"We'll wait for him tonight," said Bunyan. "Let me try to find wood for the fire."

Bunyan walked across the crag looking for any kindling not yet turned silverdark. His imagination ran wild: Could it be that here, in this very cave, was a working Simulorb that could save Lucette? But what was this tortured creature that lurked within?

Just then, as Bunyan picked up a stick, he heard a flutter of wings, and saw . . .

The tip of the brown wing, just at the edge of his field of vision. Bunyan sensed Moki there, crouched upon a rusted mining cart.

Instinctively, Bunyan knelt. He spoke quietly to the being. "In the Windy City, Yan Hui told me that to reach the Beautiful Destiny, one has to pass through the Bitter Test. Is that true?"

"*Hmmmmmm.*"

"Tonight I need straight answers," said Bunyan. "I'm afraid of what waits for me down there."

"But haven't you prepared yourself, passing through each of the steps of the Twisty Path?"

"The steps . . ."

"Haven't you learned to follow the Path with courage? Then with humility? Then with companionship?"

"I suppose."

"What is left, then, but faith?"

Again, Bunyan heard the animal bellow, more furious than before. *brrrrraaaawwwwww*

His mind filled with horrific images of his father, dead in the mud. His sighed.

"I just need to know . . . ," Bunyan whispered, "can I defeat it?"

Moki flapped their wings and landed on a rocky crag, just behind Bunyan. The being spoke closely in Bunyan's ear. "Against the Bitter Test, what can a person do, but let the mystery within confront the mystery without?"

Bunyan bent down to pick up another stick for the fire. When he raised his head, Moki had vanished.

CHAPTER 36

THE RHYMING
SCIENTIST

By the time Bunyan returned, it was night. The moon was up. From the mouth of the cave, he heard shouting.

"Get up! Get up!"

John Henry had fallen asleep and was again caught in a nightmare. "Not yet!"

Bunyan stirred his friend awake.

"I was deep in a cave—this cave! I had my hammer in my hand. I was lying there . . ." Bewildered, John Henry stood. "I've got to get back. I can't stay a second longer."

"But wait till morning . . ."

John Henry shook his head. "For a long time, I wondered what I was—pigeon or lion. In the end, I'm neither. I'm a family man. No more, no less." Bit by bit he seemed to return to the world from his private horrors. "Every man has his limit, just as every man likes to tell himself he doesn't."

John Henry looked Bunyan in the eye. His face appeared full of things he wanted to say, things that were of no use to say. At last, he took Bunyan's hand and shook it, though Bunyan was too stunned to shake it in return. "You're a great friend, Paul. I've just got to look after my own."

He laid Yan Hui's hammer against the rocks. In the blue moonlight, so bright as if it were day, John Henry headed back down into the Gorge, where the rope led across the pit of silverdark snakes.

As Bunyan watched him go, he slumped against the rocks, too exhausted to consider what he might do next. Soon, he was asleep.

———————————•———————————

"Oi, mate. Rise 'n' shine."

Bunyan opened his eyes to see a shotgun barrel pointed at his face.

It was day. As Bunyan rubbed his eyes, he saw the gun was held, somewhat shakily, by an elderly white man in a dirty shirt, ragged pants, and beat-up boots that went up high over his knees. His long white hair was in a ponytail, where a single feather hung downward from it. On his back was a distinct, egg-shaped swelling. He spoke with a ripe cockney accent.

"Just what are you doing at Giving Mother?"

Trying to gather his wits, Bunyan propped himself up on his elbow. "Sorry, I'm on a mission for my wife."

"Wife's not here, is she?"

Bunyan could see the man's arms trembling with the weight of the gun. He seemed to be having a good deal of trouble even standing up.

"I mean no harm," said Bunyan. "Are you . . . the janitor?"

At that, the man lost his strength and nearly fell over. He stumbled back a few steps and caught himself against the rocks, where the gun clattered to the ground.

"Blimey. The notes. The spies. The word's got out. Here strangers come and ask what I'm about." He looked over at Bunyan. "Janitor in trade. Scientist in vocation."

Palms in the air, Bunyan slowly got to his feet and tried to ease the tension. "Listen. I'm from Lump Town. I understand there is someone here, a student, a Native woman, who has made the Salvation Light." Carefully, Bunyan produced the lock of hair from his pocket. "My wife has a disease called the Stucks. Once this all turns dark, her time is up. The Simulorb is her only hope."

Seeing the lock of hair, the man's eyes widened. "So love brought you through silverdarkened snakes." He winced and grabbed his side. "Ah! This age. This wound. This frame. These aches!"

Something struck Bunyan about the way he spoke—a rhythm to it. "If it's true your friend, your wife, has the Light, perhaps she could help me."

"Before we run down to our deaths together, let's be civil first and meet each other. The name's Axl." With his cockney accent it sounded like Axe-O. "And you are?"

"Paul Bunyan."

He winced again, grabbing his side. "Similar problem we have then, innit?"

"How's that?"

"I'm prepping here for my one final run. Once more unto the breach and then I'm done. The Beast is cruel and huge. He's trapped my wife. Thrice he's chased me. Next time it's my life."

As Axl finished speaking, he crouched with a groan and picked up his cane. Bunyan could see he had a few spots of blood on his shirt.

"Are you hurt?"

"A mighty gash I got when I went in. Healing up, before I go again."

Once more, the speech struck him. "Sorry," said Bunyan. "Are you speaking in rhymes?"

"Ah, you noticed. Yes, an old habit. Calms me when my heart beats like a rabbit. I have within an inner rhyming fountain. One could call me a doggerel mountain." Axl grimaced as he stretched his hunched back. "Some have hand-eye coordination. I have mind-mouth coordination."

"How long has your wife been down in the cave?"

"Three weeks full. And maybe that's enough. But Bright Eyes, she is clever and she's tough. Deep inside there is a sheltered space. If she survives, she hides out in that place."

Bunyan looked into the blackness of the cave. "Is there a way around the Beast?"

At this, Axl's eyes brightened. He shuffled to the cave entrance, reached through the boards, and produced a large sack.

"If it eats tranquilizer from this sack, the sleep's so deep we'll walk out on its back."

"Why not poison him?"

"On the first try, he ran me down the hall. Shot him next time—didn't work at all. Third time, I tried poison—wouldn't eat. Our last hope's this sleepy and sweetened treat."

Bunyan nodded. "Right. So, we'll drop the sack in his path. We'll find Bright Eyes. We'll bring out the Simulorb."

Axl took a drink from a canteen hanging over his shoulder. "May I ask, friend, how you knew I was here?"

"Spies," said Bunyan. "The war for information."

Looking vexed, Axl muttered, "Running Deer, I'll bet. He found her note. Or no, the lines to Niebuhr that I wrote." He shook his head. "Spilt milk." Axl screwed the cap back onto his canteen and felt his injured side once more. "Glad you're here. Gird up. Ready yourself. Given my gash, I sure could use the help."

Bunyan secured his axe over his back, then picked up his lamp and the sack of tranquilizer. Before they walked into the cave, they heard a great bellowing once more.

brrrraaaaaaaaaaaawwwwww

Bunyan stared through the boards over the dark entrance of Giving Mother Cave. "Before we go in, tell me: do you think she has it? I mean . . . a Simulorb that works?"

Axl smiled wryly. "To crack Lump's mystery, you must be wise. And no one's wiser than the great Bright Eyes. I reckon she's done it."

His cane in one hand, Axl strapped his gun over his shoulder, fixed his long ponytail, then stepped through the boards. From the darkness inside he poked his head back out and flashed his bushy white eyebrows.

"And away we go."

─────────── · ───────────

Axl edged nimbly down the steep incline, impressive for his old age. He held a lantern before him, leading the way into the pitch black along the old tracks. Bunyan followed behind, filled with primal fear.

"Why is it no one has come to help you?" Bunyan slipped on the rubble and skidded down a few feet before he grabbed the track to steady himself. "Why is it you must find Bright Eyes alone?"

"The First Foot, they no longer will come down," said Axl. "'Twas holy once, but it's accursed now."

At last, they arrived at the bottom. Axl lifted his lantern before the wall. There Bunyan saw an enormous, carved image of what looked like a female goddess. She sat with her legs crossed and her arms held out on either side of her body, as if making a gift of the earth below.

"Giving Mother, she is. For ages the First Foot gathered Fire Seed here." Axl held his lamp up so it lit the carving more clearly. "That was before it was called Lump."

Bunyan stood transfixed by the penetrating stare of Giving Mother, lit by the yellow globe of Axl's lantern light. She seemed at once full of pity for the earth's infinite terrors, yet also full of acceptance for the same. Raising his own lamp, Bunyan noticed several scrawls of graffiti across the bottom. Miners' names. Crude epithets. Puerile etchings.

Axl sighed. By the light Bunyan could see tender puffs of flesh beneath his eyes, soft as eggs. "This place was majestic, before El Boffo came."

They heard a faint, distant bellow.

brrraaaaaawww

Looking into the darkness of the mine, Bunyan recalled that sound, heard when he was a child so long ago. He asked, "What is the Beast?"

"Beneath our progress lurks terror and loss. The Beast leaps from that place of pure chaos."

Before them, three corridors extended deeper into the earth. Axl flashed his eyebrows once more. "And away we go."

Advancing down one of the shafts, they took several quick turns.

"You're sure you know the way?" asked Bunyan.

"Over time, I've come here for supplies. The Rotunda is where we'll find Bright Eyes."

The pair came to a two-way fork and turned left, then a three-way fork and took the middle passage, then advanced down a narrow set of stairs.

There, Axl stopped before a huge iron door. It leaned at an angle off its hinges, open just a crack.

"What's here?" said Bunyan.

Axl leaned against the cavern wall and caught his breath. "Unspeakable of unspeakables. Untouchable of untouchables. The dump of Lump. Of all the dunghills, slag heaps, scrapyards, and sewage pipes of the world, this one is the worst. Dead bodies with the Stucks went in there. They poured Sludge over it all. A toxic gravy, fathoms deep. It's called the Hole."

In the dim light, Bunyan peeked through the crack. Dark was all he saw. His mind filled with horrors as he imagined the waste-filled pit of Sludge-drowned corpses beyond.

Axl once more resumed the journey, finding his footing with his cane. "And away we go."

In this portion of the mine, stone walls had been built up, forming tighter, man-made corridors. Bunyan stepped over primitive processing tools, an old crank and a gear. There were chains and tipped-over carts. They turned left, went down a set of stairs, right at a fork, then across a bridge under which dark waters flowed.

Suddenly, a thunderous bellow echoed down the corridor.

BRRRRAAAAAAAAAWW

"No more chitchat, man. Not one more sigh," said Axl, hushed. "Keep close and quiet now. The Beast is nigh."

Again came the noise. Closer still. Bunyan's palms began to sweat. He whispered, "Just tell me, what is it? What kind of animal, do you reckon?"

Axl quietly answered. "He's sick and covered in a buggy wool." Axl held the lantern by his face. "Can't say for sure. But my guess is: a bull."

At that word, *bull*, Bunyan seemed to be thrown back to his youth . . . *The thundering of the hooves, the shaking of the earth. The cry for his father. And then . . . the Gleam!*

Bunyan thought he heard a noise behind him. Quick, he spun round to see . . .

Only dark.

Bunyan sensed the Beast looming, just beyond the reach of the light, ready to leap forth out of the fabric of the dark, the same breed of diseased animal that crushed his father long ago . . .

"Pssst!"

Up ahead, Axl had lowered his lantern toward the floor. There, Bunyan saw a single locust.

Axl whispered, "He's close, but we are nearing the Rotunda. Don't trip, don't fall, don't make a single blunder."

But in that very instant, Bunyan felt a rumbling underfoot, then heard the guttural roar, coming for them just behind—

BRRRRAAAAAAAAAAAWWWWWWWW

Axl darted away from the galloping hooves as Bunyan's terror spiked and the Beast was almost upon them—

"Quick, mate! In here!"

Axl dove into a hole along the floor and Bunyan scrambled in behind.

"Your light," whispered Axl.

As the pair crouched side by side, each man snuffed out his lamp.

CHAPTER 37

BRIGHT EYES

In the cramped crawlspace, Bunyan heard the Beast . . . hooves walking heavily over the ground . . . a liquid snort . . . a buzzing insect horde . . . and again he was a child, caught in those final moments when the locusts swarmed him . . . with his father reaching into the cow's mouth, saying, *You have to soothe their pain . . .*

Sniff. Sniff. Snnnooooort.

The gargantuan, diseased creature loomed just an arm's length away. As Bunyan trembled, his body pulled into a ball, the Beast bent down, sniffing in the dark, bugs twitching on his snout.

BRRRRRRRAAAAAAAAAAAAAAWWWW

At that eruption of sound, the air clouded with a furious storm of critters shooting into the crawlspace and bouncing about Bunyan's ears, cheeks, neck, arms, and legs. Bunyan's palms were slick with sweat as he covered his face and squeezed his eyes shut, pulling himself tighter into a ball.

And then, after a few more sniffs, mercifully, the Beast stalked slowly away and the locusts withdrew.

Sweat poured down Bunyan's hair and over his armpits and chest. His shirt was soaked. He could feel his blood pounding in his veins beat after beat after beat.

"Out we go," whispered Axl.

As Bunyan squeezed himself out, he felt his arms trembling.

"Have you got the tranquilizer?"

Bunyan nodded.

"Oi. Have you got it?"

Realizing Axl couldn't see him nod in the dark, Bunyan muttered, "Yes. It's here."

Axl lit his lantern again and shined it on the mine floor. "Quick. Empty it."

Bunyan poured out the contents, a sticky mass of hay and goo.

Axl slung his shotgun over his back. There was a quiver of emotion in his face. "By my reckoning, she is just ahead. Let's go find out if she's alive or . . ."

Without finishing, the old man advanced over the old cart tracks. Here, at last, the corridor was too narrow for the Beast to follow.

Axl vanished down a stairwell. Moments later, Bunyan heard a cry. Whether it was one of pain or joy he could not say. Bending so as to not hit his head, he carefully made his way down the stairs and entered the Rotunda.

The room was wide and spacious, with a high, domed ceiling of rock. Along one wall flowed a small creek. On the opposite side of the room stood a man-made stone wall. Rail tracks ran directly into that wall, as if somehow, where the wall stood, there once had been an open passage. Along another wall sat an old metal machine—it looked like a miniature version of the purifying vats Bunyan operated at the Lump Town Factory.

Just at Bunyan's feet was the lantern, tipped over on the floor. Bunyan picked it up, raised it high, and beheld an astonishing sight:

Before him knelt Axl, with a woman lying across his lap. She wore a wool, high-necked dress, and her dark hair fell across her chest. Her body appeared limp, though her position suggested life. As Bunyan stepped closer, the woman weakly held up her hand.

"Please," Bright Eyes said quietly. "Not too much . . ."

Axl, meanwhile, kissed her head, caressed her face, then kissed her head again. Murmuring sweetly to her, he seemed to be filled with infinite kisses that he could not suppress. He took her hands and kissed her fingers and knuckles, too.

"Three times I failed, yet found you in the end. I'll never leave your side, never again."

She reached up and weakly slung her arm about his neck. Axl bent so their foreheads touched. Her body curled into his, as if a sculptor had carved them from a single block.

"Here. I've got food. Drink." Axl reached into his pouch and produced a piece of bread. Bright Eyes took it and ate.

Bunyan was amazed. Here they were! The pair who had written the Tome. The pair who had solved what El Boffo's teams of scientists working for so many years could not.

Bright Eyes slowly chewed the bread and drank sips from the canteen.

"Oh, my love," said Axl gently. "How did you survive this dark?"

Her answers came slowly at first, as if each thought were making a long journey to the surface, a fish summoned from the depths of a lake. "A bit of water each day. A bit of light. Only just enough. I knew you'd come."

She ate more bread, took more sips, slowly built her strength. Though she had been lying here in the dark on the very edge of survival for weeks, her large eyes shone with an almost sublime inner strength.

At last, these eyes made their way to Bunyan. "Who is this?"

Axl caressed a long strand of her hair, tucking it behind her cheek. "He's on a trek like mine, but for another. Those who love the same will find each other."

"And where is the one he is seeking? Also in this cave?"

"In Lump Town. She has the disease. The Stucks."

At that, Bright Eyes turned sharply to Axl. "Why does he come here?" She struggled to sit up. "What does he know about us?"

"It was the letter you left. The word is out."

Bright Eyes sat up, troubled. "No, no . . . then they will come . . . they all will come . . . just like for my father . . ."

Axl kissed her again on her forehead. "You're living, love. That's all I need to know. The Beast will soon be sleeping. Then we go."

But Bright Eyes remained vexed. "The device is not for him. I will not tell him. I will not help him. He will not take it."

"Let's not debate this now. Be calm and drink. Let's focus on one thing: build up your strength."

But suddenly, Bright Eyes seemed to have regained all her strength at once. She got up on her feet, supporting herself on the wall. Axl worked himself to his feet, too, using his cane.

"Never, never, never!" said Bright Eyes, filled with sudden passion. "I will not let this man take it! Will there never be an end to taking?"

"Careful . . ." Axl reached for her hand. "This man is not one for you to attack. He helped me here, and soon he'll help us back."

Bunyan pulled the lock of hair from his pocket. "My wife is sick. Almost gone. Only the Salvation Light can help her now."

Bright Eyes raised her gaze to him. Her face held a tight fury Bunyan could hardly understand. "So, I help you . . . But who will help the First Foot?"

Suddenly, she lost her balance. As she fell to the ground, she rolled awkwardly. Bunyan went to her to help her up. As he did, he saw, hanging from a chain on her neck, a glass and iron sphere designed in swirling, arabesque detail, about the size of a tangerine.

Bunyan and Axl together led her gingerly to an outcropping of rock along the wall, where she sat.

Bunyan remained entranced by the object, still hanging outside her dress—its elegance, its beauty.

"Is that it?" he asked in awe. "The Simulorb?"

Bright Eyes quickly tucked the device back into her dress. She kept her hand upon it, where it hung over her heart. "The Simulorb is not for you. It will never be for you. The Simulorb is for the First Foot alone."

Bunyan was too confused to put his thoughts together. He had braved the Gorge, escaped the Beast, risked his life, and at last come here, only to be rebuked?

He had half an instinct to simply yank it from her neck, sprint from the Rotunda, and see if he, alone, could make it back to the outside.

"But we can bring it to her," he pleaded. "There's still time!"

Bright Eyes didn't answer.

Axl himself seemed curious. "Have you truly done it, my love?"

She sat back on the outcropping of rock, exhausted. "All I needed was a drop of the Pure. I made it here with that machine."

"And the Formula?"

Bright Eyes nodded. "We were so close, and yet so far."

Bunyan intervened. "Well, if the device is working, then there's no sense in waiting. A few days is all I need. Once I raise her up, you can have it back. There are lives at stake. Not just my wife, others in Lump Town, too. I'll make any deal you want."

Bright Eyes glanced at Bunyan coldly. "A deal. Always another deal . . ."

"Yes. Money. Anything." Bunyan thrust the lock of hair before her eyes. "Look!"

But as he stepped toward her, Bright Eyes got on her feet, and, supporting herself on the wall, she walked to the creek and dangled the device over the water.

"I would rather drop it in here and see it wash away than give it to you."

"Drop it rather than save lives? Axl said you were a doctor!"

"I am indeed a doctor. And what are you?"

Bunyan sputtered. "What am I? I don't know. I'm just . . . a man . . ."

"See? That's just it. You don't even *know* what you are."

Axl went to her. "Bright Eyes, please. Stay calm. Come back and sit. You'll need your strength to venture from this pit." He took her gently by the arm and helped her back to the rock outcropping. "This man has been trustworthy from the start. He comes here with a full and earnest heart."

"A full heart and a desire to take. Like all his kind."

"My kind? I am not of any kind. I'm just a man trying to save my wife."

Bright Eyes took another sip from Axl's canteen. "Just a man," she said. "Just a *white* man."

Bunyan ran his hand through his hair. The trio seemed to have come to an impasse.

At last, Axl spoke. "It's a tale ugly and brutal, what we know. The scars of hidden wounds that rarely show."

"Then tell it to me," Bunyan begged. "Tell me so I can try to understand."

"You could never understand," said Bright Eyes.

"But try! Then I will tell you my side and let's see where we end up. There must be a way to bridge this gap."

Axl caressed his wife's hand. "In coming here I think he's rightly earned at least the chance to hear how you were spurned. It's a debate your father would have loved. Let both sides speak, then see if you are moved."

Bright Eyes took another bite of bread. After a long silence, she answered. "It is not a custom of my people to speak very long about oneself. I will tell him, so he knows. But I will never make a deal. My father's name was Iron Eye. I have iron in me, too."

And so, deep in the earth, as this trio waited for the Beast to fall asleep, Bright Eyes told Bunyan the true story of Lump.

CHAPTER 38

THE WHITE MAN'S MEDICINE

I will never forget the day my father gathered the chiefs and showed them the white man's medicine.

My father, Chief Wallace, had gone to the Windy City, where he purchased an electric battery and a lightbulb. Back at our home, he insisted the chiefs sit around our dining room table.

"The white man has taken nearly everything from us," my father said. "We are like driftwood in his current, potatoes in his wheelbarrow. But why does the white man succeed so much? Is it his guns? His laws? His money? No. It is none of these things."

My father raised the lightbulb over his head. Then he switched on the current and the bulb began to shine.

"All the white man's medicine, even his power to make light shine with the touch of his finger, comes from one single thing: his willingness to sit in schools and read books."

For the First Foot, this was a time of sighs, horror, and blame. The buffalo were dead. The people were sick. We'd become strangers in our own country. No one felt certain about the way forward. No one but my father.

"It is up to you," he told the chiefs, "if you will live with your eyes open or closed. But my mind is made up. We must trade our knives and bows for saws and plows. Our children must read and study. The white man is not born better by nature, but his way of life has become the way of the world. The First Foot have a choice: assimilation or annihilation."

My siblings and I looked on from the next room, as did my white mother. We watched for the chiefs' reaction.

Chief Manypenny stood up. He was my father's oldest and most loyal friend from childhood.

"I have tried to farm as you advised us," he said. "But still, my crops don't grow. I am afraid that if the First Foot try to cross the river to the white man, we might get halfway across and drown. The most dangerous place in a river is halfway."

My father nodded. "I understand. But the path backward leads nowhere. Staying put gets us nothing. Though crossing a river is dangerous, danger is better than nowhere and nothing."

A second chief, No Fences, then stood. He was younger, with a scar on his face, and he was frightening to us kids. Rumors swirled that he had killed white settlers and kept a pile of their shriveled scalps in his teepee.

"Whites are like leeches," said No Fences. "Once they get on the land, you can't pull them off without bloodshed." No Fences rubbed his hands together, like he was squishing a hard-boiled egg into a paste. "When the white man comes for me, I'll rub him out."

"Have you seen the coffee mill gun?" answered my father. "The white man just pours bullets in the top and turns a crank. A hundred shots a minute! A child could kill an entire herd of buffalo from the top of a passing train."

"I have a fearless spirit," said No Fences. "It is spirit that decides the battle. Besides, it's them who started these wars."

My father nodded respectfully but stuck to his point. "When I was young, I admired men who can fight. Older now, I admire men who can change. It takes someone to start a war, yes. But it also takes someone to start a peace."

A third chief, Spotted Corn, was the oldest at the meeting. He had two long braids of gray hair, which lay over both shoulders. Small pockets of creased flesh hung below his chin. Slowly, he stood. He had a high, scratchy voice.

"Before the whites, we had no guns, we had no houses, no doors, no keys, no locks. We had no school, no church, no laws, no money. Yet we also had no poverty. We had no jail, no slaughter, no theft, no hunger. No one was without a home. In old times, we had none of the white man's things, and yet we had all we needed."

My father tried to interject, but Spotted Corn kept going.

"The First Foot used to know every rock, tree, and creature on this land. We grew corn, squash, and beans, and we hunted buffalo as we pleased. We were here before they came, and we knew how to live. The old ways are good enough for me."

My father answered, as always, with a lively spark in his eye. Though he considered everyone's point of view, he always believed he could convince anyone. "Chief Spotted Corn, you have been one of our greatest leaders. But let me tell you something about this new nation that is forming. *Every* person who comes to America gives up their old ways. Even the whites do! And so, just like all Americans, the First Foot must become something different to live in this new nation."

My father then handed the lightbulb to Chief Swallow. Chief Swallow was from another tribe, the Snake River People. They were our rivals and enemies, but like I said, my father believed he could convince anyone.

Chief Swallow held the bulb in his hands as my father turned it on and off, on and off. Chief Swallow was so stunned by it, he threw it back on the table.

At that, No Fences got up to leave. Even though he was younger than my father, he spoke to him without respect.

"Hey, Chief Wallace, remember when we used to call you Iron Eye? Where is Iron Eye now? I would never marry a white woman, or let a white woman bear my children like you have. It's a shame, what happened to you. You wandered in the white wilderness and you got lost." He looked over at me, my siblings, and my mother and smirked. "I am he who the white man calls 'unsavable.' I'll never change."

When the chiefs had gone, my father was undeterred.

"Within any struggle," he said to us, his children, "there are really three struggles. First, the struggle with one's opponent. Second, the struggle with one's allies. Third, the struggle with one's self. The most bitter of the three is often with one's allies."

He gave me a hug. "The people are in pain, but we can learn to change. Change is made from pain, like pots are made from clay."

My father ran the general store on the reservation and saved enough money to send us east for school. We had heard that the whites forced some children, in other tribes, to go to school and learn the white ways. Whites were the "parent nation," and we were the "child nation." But my father didn't need to be forced—he actively wanted us to go. I was the oldest and went first.

We rode horses to the train station. There, my father said to me, "You have a great light inside you. You won't be able to hide it for long."

I was very shy and didn't believe him. "I don't think there is any great light in me, Father."

"Oh, but I'm certain of it!" he said with a spark in his eye. "When you hold a firefly in your hands, you can hide it. But if you have a torch in your hands, it cannot be hidden. You must hold it above your head! You, Bright Eyes, have a torch. One day the world will see."

When I arrived, I found the Windy City overwhelming. Where I came from, the man-made parts of life were small, temporary, feeble. All that was most beautiful was not man-made. But in the Windy City, it was the opposite. There, if you could not find beauty in the man-made, you would find no beauty at all. Strange as it was, I knew I could bear it, for I had been raised in the wilderness. If I could bear walking in snow for days without food, so hungry I gnawed on my moccasins, I could bear any troubles of the man-made world.

The only school that would take me in those times was a school in the Windy City for Black children. There, I left behind my name Bright Eyes and went by Mary. The first day, they asked me how old I was. It was funny, for I didn't even know. The First Foot had no calendars. So they just made up an age for me, based on how I looked.

They put me in a boardinghouse with the Black girls. As I learned about their history, I came to realize I shared something with them. All the other races in America had come to America by choice— all but ours. We Natives had our homeland stolen. The Black folks, meanwhile, had been stolen from their homes.

I was quiet and slow to make friends. But I absorbed all my teachers taught me, sometimes without even writing it down. I won memory games, solved puzzles, and figured out equations.

My curiosity flourished. I was so filled with questions. Like, why did water flow upward in a building's pipes? How did a clock know the time? And the old question of my father, how did the electric bulb shine bright?

My teachers couldn't answer all my questions. I found it quicker to just read about them myself. Yet each book I read led me to other books. Within, behind, and beyond each mystery lay more mysteries still. My learning did not quench my need for knowledge but only made me thirstier. I sometimes grew frustrated I couldn't read books faster! I wanted to absorb the entirety of the library in an instant. Soon I was beyond the other students.

After my first year of school, I returned to the First Foot reservation to find an outbreak of measles. We sent for white doctors, but none came.

My father, who had such bright visions for my future, asked me what I wished to do, once I got older. "Will you travel the world? Will you teach in the Windy City? Will you become a translator? A lawyer? A writer?"

"I will become a doctor," I said. "And I will build a hospital here on the reservation."

"You would need a good deal of money for that. Maybe you could work somewhere where there is already a hospital."

"The reservation is where I will be needed," I said. "So, that is where I'll stay."

My father laughed. "It's like I said—you hold no firefly, Bright Eyes. You hold a torch!"

A few years later, I graduated first in my class at my school and enrolled at a new women's medical school in the University of the Windy City. There again, I was the only Native student. But this time, there were not any Black girls—only whites. I was side by side with daughters of bankers, statesmen, and tycoons.

One of the families helped me purchase what I needed to fit in. I had worn fur, and beads on my buckskin dress. Now I wore blouses and shiny black shoes and rode in buggies along boulevards. I had slept in teepees through gusting blizzards and called to birds with my whistles. Now I ate ice cream in skyscrapers and heard violins at the theater. I came from a place outside of time. Now time ruled my life by the minute.

The white girls ignored me, or worse. Some of them whooped and did a dance around me, saying, "Time to skin the buffalo!" I never raised my hand in class, for fear they would make fun of my accent. I fit in nowhere. I was too much a First Foot to be white. But back on the reservation, I had become too white to be a First Foot.

My father tried to comfort me. "Just remember your calling to build the hospital," he said. "Let your calling be your shelter."

The classroom and the library were the only places I felt at home. Books always welcomed me. I began to audit courses in chemistry, physics, engineering, and mineralogy.

One night I was working late in the library. Needing some fresh air, I'd gone for a walk outside. When I returned, a man was standing at my table, a mop in one hand, looking at my notebook.

"Excuse me, what are you doing?" I said.

"Very close, you were," said Axl.

I'd been mapping a molecular structure and he pointed out my error. We struck up a conversation. I soon learned Axl had wished to enroll at the university, but due to complications with his spine, he never got the chance.

The next night, Axl found me again. Leaning over his bucket, propped up by his mop, Axl revealed himself to be a true polymath. He could speak about mathematics, crystallography—even literature. He always kept me laughing with his little jokes, poems, and riddles, which seemed to float into his mind with no effort at all. We spent hours talking. It was as if we were starved for conversation.

"How is it you are not a professor?" I asked him. "You're smart enough to be the dean of this school."

"They could never get over the hump, as it were," he said with a wry smile. "But even if they won't have me, I still can dream." He gestured up at the books lining the walls. "My own Everest is to one day publish a book."

It disgusted me that they had made Axl an outcast for his affliction. I told him so.

Axl only shrugged. "Hobbled to the world, perhaps. But in the arena of knowledge, I am a gladiator without limit. My relationship has never been with stature, but with excellence. The university can keep the first from me, not the second."

From then on, Axl met with me every day.

One time, he showed me a newspaper. The railroad baron El Boffo was running a contest. Anyone who could present him with a new, profitable source of energy, to be purchased by El Boffo Industries, would receive the prize of one gold brick.

"One gold brick," said Axl. "With that, you could build your hospital."

I immediately thought of the ancient fuel of the First Foot, Fire Seed. For generations we'd dug it up from Giving Mother Cave to start our fires. It burned slow, nothing like oil and gas. Thus far, white people had ignored it.

A month later, I traveled back home. Axl came with me.

Things had grown worse in the village. This time, an outbreak of tuberculosis. Again, the white doctors did not come. On top of this, there was a new problem: alcohol. My father forbade it, but bootleggers and whiskey peddlers camped out at the reservation's edge.

Despite all this, I recall it as one of the happiest summers of my life. Axl spent time with my family and began to learn our language. He spent most nights up late smoking a pipe with my father. The pair took to each other. They shared a kindred zeal for life. Axl seemed more at home with the First Foot than he ever did at the university.

Before we left for school again, we went to Giving Mother Cave and got some Fire Seed—what you now call Lump.

Back in the Windy City, Axl had a small workshop of his own. There, we began conducting experiments. We heated Lump, melted it, spun it, pressurized it. We recorded all our results in the Tome, filling page after page with calculations, equations, predictions, and data of all kinds.

We worked relentlessly, so much that Axl's hands often ached. My eyes hurt from staring into microscopes. This went on for months. Yet we were tireless—I was motivated by the hospital, Axl by publishing the results. Lump was all we discussed. Our minds were like knives, cutting through the matter, all our power concentrated along a single blade. Discovery begat discovery, and iteration influenced iteration.

Lump's fully reduced state of the Pure proved to be highly potent, more combustible than oil and gas. The problem was the Sludge. In those early days, we dumped the Sludge in the woods behind Axl's home. We soon saw what blight it caused: the ferns, grass, and trees turned silverdark. One day, we found a dead squirrel. We dissected these flora and fauna in Axl's lab, and in time we came to the dispiriting conclusion that Lump Sludge was alarmingly toxic, even in small amounts. On a large scale, the damage to Nature would be unthinkable. Perhaps irreversible.

One evening I looked over our collection of dead critters and plants, all turned silverdark. I remember being in a foul mood. For weeks I'd had a sore throat, a running nose. A cough, as well.

"We need to stop," I said. "We're manufacturing poison."

Axl agreed—though he had tears in his eyes. As it so happened, we had a bit of the Pure left. We decided to use it for one final experiment.

It almost didn't happen, because when Axl reached for the beaker of Pure, he spilled it across the table, where it mixed with some of the dirt from the plants we'd laid out. The beaker dropped and shattered on the floor. As I picked it up, I cut my finger.

At any rate, once we'd gathered what Pure remained, we poured it in our primitive Simulorb and began the normal process of heating, pressurizing, and spinning. Given that this was our last experiment, we accelerated our device to the limit.

And that's when we witnessed the miracle.

The Simulorb was made of temperature-resistant glass. Normally, we could observe the Pure glowing orange, red, and yellow with heat inside. But this time, it was . . . how can I describe it? It was as if the device emitted a *physical* light. It began to glow with a kind of golden *broth*, a substance that passed through me and that my cells themselves could drink.

The Light lasted only a few moments, then vanished. After, we gazed about the lab, astounded by what we saw:

Upon the table, the silverdark plants we'd brought in had been restored—they had turned green! Two squirrels, while still dead, had lost their silverdark shading. Their fur was new again.

More shocking still was how I felt. Young. Like a child. There was ease and newness in my limbs, like my body was a clear pane of glass. Stranger still, I looked down at my finger, which had been bleeding just a moment before. It had entirely healed over—not even a scar.

"My hands," said Axl.

Axl's hands often ached from his incessant writing in the Tome, so much that they trembled. He held them up.

"There is no pain," he said in awe.

It was only then that I realized yet another strange thing: my nose was entirely dry. My throat wasn't sore. The illness I'd struggled with for weeks had vanished.

We immediately and carefully recorded all we had observed about this final experiment in our Tome. That night we were too excited to sleep—had we made a discovery that would change the world?

We were in a bind, we knew. We were grappling with the true paradoxical nature of Lump. It empowered as it polluted. It cured as it killed. It contained the power of both death *and* life. Lump was a devil's bargain.

"Flip a coin," Axl said. "On one side the panacea. On the other, venom."

Close to dawn, at last I returned to my boardinghouse to sleep. In bed, I thought of my father. He had encouraged me to learn the white ways and to engage with the white world. When I awoke I hatched a plan. I told Axl and he agreed.

We would write at once to El Boffo.

A meeting was arranged. Our strategy was to tell the famous magnate as little as possible. Not till we had won his contest and gotten the gold bar would we reveal any of the critical details.

At the Palace Hotel, El Boffo sat behind his desk with his chief engineer.

Axl and I spoke about the purification process. About the Simulorb. We discussed heating, electricity, even the potential for weapons. We told him about the Light. At the same time, we were forthright and adamant about the risks.

"Fire Seed must be handled with the utmost care," I said. "On a small scale, and in trace amounts, its harm is de minimis. But at an industrial scale, it could devastate the planet. If you developed it, you would have to experiment thoroughly to find a clean purification process. At this point, we are not even sure one exists."

El Boffo excused himself and conferred privately in an adjacent room with his engineer. Then the pair returned.

"Have you published any of this?" asked the engineer.

It was a secret, we said.

"And the location of this substance?"

Also a secret.

"May we borrow your Tome, to review it?"

"Only if you give us the gold and declare us the winner," said Axl.

Again, the two conferred. Then El Boffo spoke apologetically.

"I'm sorry, but it all just seems too risky. We have doubts about the science. After all, neither of you even has a degree. And of course, El Boffo Industries is concerned about any harm to Nature."

After the meeting, Axl and I were crestfallen. There would be no gold bar, no hospital, nor any world-saving technology. Perhaps, at any rate, Axl could publish the Tome and fulfill his ambition of putting out a book, even if it was a book about the impossibility of safely processing Fire Seed at scale.

Then, three weeks later, I got a telegram from my father:

An army has surrounded Giving Mother Cave. They have guns.
Mining equipment. We hear dynamite. They say Giving Mother
Cave is now the property of El Boffo.

CHAPTER 39

A CLOSING HEART

As they huddled deep in the Rotunda of Giving Mother Cave, Axl took a moment to sneak up the stairs. After a minute, he returned.

"Good news, my friends. The Beast, it took the bait. Let's hope it snoozes now. Till then, we wait."

Axl had hardly finished his rhyme when the diseased animal lamented from the labyrinth beyond.

BRRRAAAWWWWW

The Beast was very close and far from sleep.

After a sip of water and a piece of bread offered by her husband, Bright Eyes went on, speaking with grace and precision.

Panicked, I left the Windy City for the First Foot lands. Axl came with me. At Giving Mother Cave we saw cranes, rubble, and ash. The Gorge had been littered with picks and spikes, trucks and trash. Worse still, they were already refining Lump, right in the open air.

El Boffo himself was there.

"What are you doing?" I ran at him in a blind fury. "How did you find this place?"

"Ah, the hunchback and the Indian," he said. "How did I find you? It's simple. I have eyes all around."

"This is not your land! You cannot be here!"

El Boffo produced a piece of paper. "I beg to differ. Chief Swallow signed this. We have a treaty."

"Chief Swallow has no authority. The Snake River People are not First Foot!"

"It's all so confusing, isn't it? There's beavers and deer on the land. Do they have to sign, too? Anyway, the deal is done. Chief Swallow has already been paid." El Boffo read from his so-called treaty. "Three barrels of sugar, two pallets of coffee, a thousand bullets, and fifty rifles. Oh, and four crates of bourbon."

"*Bourbon? For land?*"

A blast of dynamite shot from inside the cave and spit debris in the air. I looked around myself with an ever-increasing sense of horror. This once majestic place of crystal-clear streams and bighorn sheep would soon be wrecked, blackened, toxic . . .

All because of me.

That night, my mind was in disarray. Axl sat by my side as I wept and told my father everything. I was ashamed, terrified, inconsolable. All my good intentions! All my life I'd heard whites call Natives "incompetent." The only thing we are competent enough to do, it seems, is sign treaties giving away our land.

"How could he just take?" I said. "Take when we say no?"

Axl shook his head. "Power doesn't feel itself. Only the victim feels. Injustice doesn't know itself. Only the victim knows. Between the tree and the axe, only the tree remembers."

"But where is his soul?"

"Bloodhounds could not find it." Axl was grim. "There is but a small difference between a criminal and a capitalist. A criminal parts with his conscience as a habit. A capitalist parts with his but for a fortune."

My father was resolute. "I will fight this alongside you," he said to me. "I have acted as an American. I expect to be treated like an American."

A knock came on the door. El Boffo stood outside with a few tough-looking white men. He took off his hat politely.

"Ah, Chief Wallace. The famous Iron Eye. I'm sorry if there has been a misunderstanding. Do you mind if we come in for a parley?"

At our kitchen table, El Boffo laid out his offer. "We should not approach this as antagonists. In my opinion, we should be partners. We would compensate you handsomely, Bright Eyes, if you would only show us that Tome."

I was too furious to put my thoughts into words.

"Why would my daughter give you a thing?" answered my father. "She trusted you once, telling you about Fire Seed. Look where that got her! But rest assured, you'll see the Tome. You'll see it when we publish it. Then all of America will learn about your trickery. They'll see how you play with poison."

El Boffo nodded and calmly lit a cigar. "Actually, I don't think she will be publishing anything."

One of his thugs produced a sheaf of papers from his bag and laid it on the table. "As of one week ago, I have patented all technology related to Lump. I have ownership rights over all Lump development, anywhere in America. I have patented devices, too."

"You don't have any devices," said Axl. "You only heard about this barely a month ago."

El Boffo blew out a cloud of smoke. "We recently paid a visit to your workshop, hunchback."

"Don't call him that!" I could have spit in his face.

"Although we did not find your Tome, we found plenty. *Your* inventions"—El Boffo patted the papers on the table—"are now *my* inventions. It's all gone through the courts. An expedited case."

My father always spoke calmly in heated moments. "All my life," he said, "I have tried to be part of the new America, to make peace with the new America, to learn from the new America. I have encouraged my own people to take part in this new America, too. I even worshipped the God of the new America. I *am* American. And I plan to have the justice of an American."

"Well, that's just the thing. By my lights, where we sit now, it's not *quite* America, is it? And you, the First Foot, you're not *quite* Americans. To most Americans, to *real* Americans, to American *courts*, the First Foot are, well, invisible. And this means your land is, to put it bluntly, here for the taking."

"You cannot take," said my father, raising his voice. "You will not take."

One of the men sitting next to El Boffo had a tattoo of a pyramid on his forearm—white on top, black on the bottom. El Boffo reached over and patted the man, right on this tattoo.

"If any of you should speak about Lump publicly, if you so much as send a single letter about it, rest assured, I will find out. The battle for information is a deadly one. And it's one that I will win." El Boffo mashed his cigar in a pot of my mother's flowers that sat on the table. "As a wise Indian once told me, 'All is fair after a warning.'"

El Boffo stood to go, but my father followed him to the door.

"We have taken ten steps toward you, while you don't take one toward us. Every bridge we build, you knock it down. One day, the shoe will be on the other foot. God is watching."

"Yeah," said El Boffo. "Let Him watch."

That very night, my father settled on a plan.

"I will ride first thing to the newspapers. We will publish the whole story. The world must know what this man has done. What he is about to do."

Axl and I wrote down all we could remember about the hellish side of Lump, enough to alarm the world. At dawn, my father rode.

After one day, my father did not return. Then two. Then three. Then four. Every day, I grew more and more sick with premonition.

Then, a week after he left, I received a letter. On the front was written our home address. On the rear were the initials "F.O.L."

The letter read:

Your father can be found by the end of the stone wall, near the post office, thirty miles south.
Do not speak about this matter ever again.

In the envelope was a feather my father often wore in his hair. There was blood on it.

I rode with Axl and my brother to find my father's body. Of his condition, I will say nothing more.

As we loaded him onto our wagon—my father, visionary; my father, leader; my father, left in a *ditch*!—in the distance, we saw two white men on horseback. Watching.

At the funeral, Chief Manypenny spoke. "Iron Eye was like one straddling two ice floes in a river. He held them together as long as he could, and finally, he fell. But his strength was unlike any. No one else could have held on so long."

As we buried my father, I remembered his words: *When you hold a firefly in your hands, you can hide it. But if you have a torch in your hands, it cannot be hidden. You must hold it above your head! You, Bright Eyes, have a torch. One day the world will see.*

I felt no torch then. Everything I touched had turned to ash.

In time, I returned to the Windy City. Axl took me to see his workshop. El Boffo's men had indeed ransacked it. The tables had been turned over, the papers taken. Our devices had been taken, too, including our Simulorb prototype.

The one thing they did not steal was the Tome. Axl had locked it in his janitor's closet before we left. Under the cover of night, Axl fled to the Western Grove and hid the book in a lockbox under the Tree of Life.

After, we wrote a letter to El Boffo. "The Tome is destroyed. You will never hear from us again. We will never speak about Lump. Please, leave us in peace."

For me, that made an end of it.

A few years later, I finished my studies and returned to the reservation. Axl came with me.

The deterioration on the First Foot lands was abject. Disease.

Starvation. El Boffo's men had destroyed and abandoned Giving Mother Cave. They left the Gorge a poisoned junkyard filled with Sludge and silverdark snakes. My mother had passed. My three siblings had moved away.

Alone on this desolate land, I felt bereft. Without Axl, I would have lost all hope.

Axl always liked to say, "Those who love the same will find each other." He and I—we loved the same. I was not the most conventional woman to love. From a young age, I was ambitious, mission-bound. I was no housewife. I had no desire, nor room in my life, for children of my own. I didn't want to be a caretaker to a handful; I wanted to be a caretaker to a people. Axl understood this without debate, without even a question. To an outsider, perhaps, we appeared an odd couple. But we knew exactly how to love each other. I could ask for no better companion.

Since we had no funds for the hospital, Axl suggested we see patients in my childhood home. Bit by bit, year by year, our hospital grew. There are days now when I see fifty patients. In warm weather, I ride from dawn to dusk, visiting each far-flung home.

Much has changed since my father first brought back that electric bulb. Chief Spotted Corn died, Chief Manypenny, too. No Fences went west. Before he left, he said to me, "You see? Those who make peace are treated worst of all." We never saw him again. Alcohol is everywhere now, especially among our men. I understand why. A person starts to drink when they feel the paths walked by their ancestors lead to nowhere.

Over the years, many white people have passed through, bound west. They tell me about their destiny to settle America. They tell me that the whites are a great people.

Yet I wonder: when will their idea of greatness include listening to the conquered? Perhaps pity for the conquered is a luxury they can't afford. Whites call themselves brave, but look how brittle they grow when the other side talks. We have *lived* this history. Yet the white man can't even bear to *listen.*

I think of how weak the whites were when they came to this land, long ago, arriving on our shores like a foundling. We welcomed this infant, sheltered him, fed him, and taught him how to survive. Yet now the foundling has grown so strong, he drives us from our own home.

Sometimes, First Foot children come to me and ask, "Will the whites put back what they have taken from Giving Mother Cave?" Or they ask, "Can you cure Giving Mother, Doctor? Giving Mother is sick, too." I do not have answers. Here on the reservation the First Foot have come to understand Nature's old iron law: the strong take what they can and the weak bear what they must.

And so, I might have lived out my life, tending to our sick, if it were not for that dream I had some weeks ago about the Light.

Why Lump was on my mind, I cannot say. I had read in the newspaper that El Boffo would announce his new device. Also, I had gone rummaging in the basement recently and come across some of Axl's old machines. Who knows what was the trigger?

In this dream I saw, with startling clarity, as if frozen in time, those first moments when we saw the Light. With a strange, unlimited power of perception, I cataloged each aspect of the room. And there, I spied one crucial detail that had escaped us both till now.

Sitting up in my bed, I began to sweat. My heart beat fast. I was filled with a white heat of a breakthrough. It felt like *youth*! I hadn't thought of Lump—not scientifically—in twenty years, but suddenly all my calculations appeared fresh in my mind, as if I'd thrown open some locked vault of memory.

I got my notebook and wrote it down. There! Yes! The Formula! Clear as day! And oh—it was so simple! Axl and I had often remarked upon this very point: how the struggle for insight is long and convoluted, but Nature's truth is always elegant and clean.

We had been wrong by a hair. We had been wrong by a mile.

That morning, I dashed off the letter to Axl, who had gone to town for several days to get hospital supplies. Then I went to the basement. Axl, ever the tinkerer, had built another Simulorb some years ago, much smaller and more manageable than the first. I grabbed it and rode straight for Giving Mother Cave, approaching by the secret path the First Foot know, behind the Gorge.

Here in the Rotunda, I found a bit of Lump. I purified it. Unable to wait, breathless with excitement, I mixed the Pure according to the new Formula and put it in the device.

Then, for the second time in my life, I beheld the Salvation Light.

I rushed for the exit of the cave, but the rest you know. The Beast trapped me, and here we are.

———————•———————

You have asked me to help save your dying wife. You are shocked that I say no. Now that you've heard my story, you might guess why that is so.

I say no because of El Boffo, this man who wrecked our land, this man whose ambition was unchecked by any empathy, any honor, anything at all; this man who lied to us and killed my father, who spied on me for decades and spies upon me still. If you take this device from here, no doubt he will track it down. He will take what is not his and he will go unpunished yet again. America is filled with forgiveness and second chances for a man like him. It hasn't given a first chance to a people like ours.

I say no for what white people have taken from the First Foot. What you discovered was already ours. What you filled was already full. What you christened already had a name.

I say no because of *how* you took. You took in the name of God, took in the name of science, took because only your conscience stood in your way; in other words, nothing stood in your way at all. You crushed us with disease, then guns, then laws, then drink. And last and most of all, you crushed us by simply looking the other way.

Chief Swallow's sugar is all gone, but his treaty still remains. The inheritance of the First Foot used to be the earth itself. Today it's just a sad, old tale of times that won't come back. As our chiefs are known to say: White people made a thousand promises to the First Foot, and you only kept one—you promised to take our land, and you took it.

And yet after this, after all *this*, you dare to come to me and say, "Let me take but one thing more." For generations we were invisible, and now you say, "It's *me* who suffers. Won't *you* see *me*?" After ignoring our cries, you say, "But hear *my* cry!" As if the weight of one man's woe could match the desolation of generations! You ask for mercy, but my mercy's just another thing to which you feel entitled.

I loved my father. Yet at this moment, I feel no understanding of him at all. He took steps toward the whites, and what did it get him? A sudden death in a shallow ditch. I've had twenty years to turn over my grief, and each year my heart's door closes a bit more.

And so, for the stories you've heard, and those you haven't, I say no. For the nights you slept and the nights we wept, I say no. For the good you said and the bad you did, I say no.

I say no because I want one, single, simple, solitary thing that is only for my people and my people alone. Just *one thing* for the First Foot that the whites can never touch. Just *one room* you cannot enter, one time that the good is *only* for us—no division, no demands, no debate.

El Boffo worked for years to generate the Salvation Light. Why? So he could give it to his own. I only want the same.

This once, I want a miracle for the First Foot. This once, I want the fruits of this land to be ours again, like they were in times gone by, when our inheritance was the earth.

CHAPTER 40

THE BEGGAR

What could Bunyan say?

Bright Eyes' story had been told masterfully and without hesitation. Her quiet, firm manner made her facts seem like the only version possible, as if hers was the story the world *itself* would tell if the world could speak. Her judgments, too, seemed polished, like they were stones turned over in her mind by years of thoughts, stones smoothed by the endless tossing of waves.

What argument could win? Bunyan was not wanted here. Generations of his own kind had preceded him. And though Bunyan's personal tale was full of misfortune, it now seemed to add up to so very little. Sitting before him was the only woman in the world who could possibly help him. Yet to her, he was a pariah.

Still, he told his side of things. He detailed his past: diseased cattle, dead father, locked-up mother. He talked about his grim life: Lump Town and the gear, Lucette and the Stucks. He recounted his journey through the Windy City: John Henry, the Tree of Life, the Wondertorium. He explained how he came to Giving Mother Cave: Bright Eyes' letter to Axl, which was found by the spy Running Deer. He talked, too, about the Gleam and the Chilali.

But when held up against the history of the First Foot, it all seemed so weightless, even to his own ears. When he finished, the

Rotunda stayed silent for a time, other than the gentle sound of the running creek. At last, Axl spoke.

"Paul, I want to ask about your father's death. You said his bulls went mad. What was the location of your family ranch?"

"South and east of here. Not far from the Big Muddy River. North of Cow Town."

"And the cattle had locusts on their fur, stiff tongues, too . . . much like the Beast in this cave?"

Bunyan sighed. "It must be the same disease. The Beast even makes the same sickening sound."

"And how long ago was that?"

"Fifteen years."

Axl exchanged a glance with Bright Eyes, though her own expression showed little.

"Lump pollution poisons all," Axl said. "But it has a particularly terrible effect on cattle. In livestock, Lump disease is now called Metal Meat. The beef turns gray."

"My family's cows had gray meat, too." Bunyan guessed where Axl was going. "But if you're saying Metal Meat is caused by Lump—if you're saying Lump poisoned my family's cows—that's impossible. My father's farm was nowhere near Lump Town."

Axl pointed his cane at the creek flowing through the Rotunda. "The waters here run out to tributaries bound south. In time, they empty into the Big Muddy." With pity, Axl went on. "The waste El Boffo first dumped into these waters twenty years ago would have made its way downstream. If your father's ranch was near the Big Muddy, the Sludge from Giving Mother Cave would have been in his soil."

Horror and insight, terror and clarity, pity and outrage, all mixed within Bunyan. He saw his father, there in his mind's eye, his arm in the mouth of the cow. *You must soothe their pain.* He felt light-headed. He got up to pace but then leaned against the wall to steady himself.

"It was Lump?" he muttered. "Lump all along?" He tugged at his beard as he peered into his memory, the entire story of his life taking on new meaning. "It wasn't my father's fault. It wasn't bad cattle.

It wasn't bad luck. It was Lump . . . It was him . . . El Boffo. Always him."

Bunyan let out a scream at the realization—one part grief, one part laughter. His voice echoed through the cave.

"All of it!" he shouted. "My father, dead! My mother, in prison! My wife! The Stucks! My foot! My *life*!"

"Lump is the great accelerant," said Bright Eyes. "It accelerates health, accelerates disease. Accelerates civilization, accelerates extinction. With one hand it gives, with the other it takes. But what it takes is so much greater."

Suddenly furious, Bunyan turned to her. "Then how can you say we are not on the same side? Look at what Lump has taken from you. Look at what it's taken from me!"

Still, Bright Eyes stayed silent.

Bunyan dropped to his knees before her, his hands clasped. He went on, almost unhinged. "Bright Eyes! Listen! I hear your story and it boils my *blood*! We are *both* caught in a history we did not write. My people, your people! My history, your history! But we are not that. We are *us*. Just us! Here! Two people!" He beat his chest desperately. "I am not them. I am just one man. I am me! And I just want to save my *wife*."

Sitting on the outcropping of rock, Bright Eyes maintained her same stony expression. It seemed to Bunyan that all his words had fallen upon her like a meaningless rain.

In time, she glanced at Axl. "If the Beast is sleeping, we should go."

"And the Simulorb?" Axl said.

"He will not have it."

Bunyan's heart sank.

Sitting on the stool of the old Lump machine, Axl didn't get up just yet. His chin rested on his hands, which were stacked on the top of his cane.

"Before we go," said Axl, "could I ask, what is the Formula?"

"I will not say it in front of him."

Axl got up—groaning a bit as he did—and walked, using his cane, to where his wife sat. There, she whispered in his ear. As Axl listened, he nodded, then murmured as if confirming some calculation in his mind, then, at last, his mouth showed a faint, almost beatific smile.

"Of *course*," he said when she'd finished. "The answer is so clear. So impossible to foresee, yet so intuitive once seen. The contradiction, as ever, was only apparent. In the end, the mysteries unite."

Using his cane, Axl walked back to the stool. As he passed Bunyan he put a hand on his shoulder. "Off your knees. Sit."

Bunyan got off his knees but did not sit. He stood against the wall of the Rotunda, massaging his temples, at a loss.

"To tell the truth, I did not think I would hear the answer about the Formula, not until the world beyond," said Axl. "I'll tell you my image of heaven: It is a beautiful, long, wood table, and around it sit the great thinkers of history. There is a seat for me along the side, and together, to pass eternity, we unpack the mysteries of the universe, day after shining day. It was there, in the library of the angels, that I believed the mystery of the Light would be revealed."

Axl smiled and shook his head. "Of course it would be you to solve it, my love. All these scientists, working round the clock, stuck at the ledge! But you found the bridge across, connecting known and unknown. And it works?"

Bright Eyes nodded. "I have seen the Light. Here in this very room."

Axl shifted his weight on his stool, hissing with a bit of pain. "Old age has come for me, at last. Much as we contemplate time, still, it surprises us. As we ponder, time plunders, I suppose. And yet, I am content. For I had but three ambitions for my life: to be part of a great discovery, to know a great love, and to publish a book. Two out of three is enough."

Bunyan took in the man's age as he had not before, lit as Axl's face was by the lantern at his feet. He saw the creases on his forehead and the delicateness of the skin that hung down flatly from his sharp cheekbones. Clearly older than his wife, Axl seemed like a squat, skeletal autumn tree, covered in curled leaves. A strong gust of wind might have shorn away what life remained.

"Of the trio of ambitions, love did appear to be the most unlikely. The orchard of knowledge is infinite; each generation need only step to the next tree. But love, well. It is no guarantee. Many go without, or settle for a meager match.

"I don't think I ever told you, Bright Eyes, but the night we met, I cried. Yes. I went home and wept. For I thought, *Here is a woman who could love just as I love.* Love, I think, can be learned only through example. My parents gave love to me; that same love I knew I could give to another. But appearing as I do, well, I was unsure who might desire such an offering. Yet that one night—the most consequential of my life!—when I saw your molecular equation in the library . . . your math is not often wrong, but thank goodness it was then! If not, I might still be at my mop."

As Axl spoke, his eyes shined. He struggled to steady his voice and to keep his expression firm. Bright Eyes watched her husband with a stitch in her brow. His words drew up emotion in her, too.

"Now, why am I going on about love?" Axl continued. "Bear with me, for I will in time arrive at the point. It concerns your father. He was called great by a great many, and for a great many reasons. Myself, I had my own reasons for thinking he was so.

"See, when I met Chief Wallace that first summer, I was, by that point, exhausted with the human gaze. I avoided eye contact. My appearance, I knew, could trigger a bevy of hidden judgments: a muzzled bias, a well-meant pity, a savage epithet.

"But when I met your father, his eyes were so different. On the first day, he did not look at the swelling on my back. On the second day, no again. As we sat together each evening in rocking chairs, I kept waiting for him to squint or frown, or to put forth the inevitable question. He certainly had witnessed the feelings between you and me.

"It was I, at last, who forced the topic. At the train station, the day of our departure, I said to him, 'As Bright Eyes' father, I can imagine you have concerns about my back. I would understand it if you did.' Mind you, I had a speech prepared for him, with many fine arguments and noble sentiments designed to convince and reassure. I was going to say, 'Chief Wallace, a man can neither make his body nor mend it—all he can truly mend is his ways.' And 'There is a tyranny that lurks behind the notion of normalcy.' And even 'Do not judge a book by its cover.' But none of this speech making was necessary. When I mentioned my back, your father didn't miss a beat. He cut me off and quickly answered. 'Axl,' he said. 'What worries my daughter worries me. What does not worry my daughter does not worry me.'

"Of all the deeds and sayings of your father, the great Iron Eye, none showed me the depth of his soul more than this.

"At any rate, and to the point: One day that same summer, your father hurt his arm unloading a wagon. That evening, he sat on the porch with me. He was in a foul mood from his injury, and he spoke sharply to your mother—something he never usually did. 'I want my pipe,' he told her. 'You don't want your pipe,' she answered back. 'You want your tea.' He nodded, knowing she was right. He turned to me and said, 'When I am weak, those who love me best know me better than I know myself.' She brought him tea, and, indeed, he enjoyed it. It was a small comment, but I have often thought of it. When we are weak, those who love us best know us best. In pain, sometimes, we cannot see ourselves.

"And now, to the matter at hand. I know you, Bright Eyes. I have known you at your most expansive, magnanimous, and openhearted. Your whole life, you wished to be seen for who you are: not as a Native, not as a woman, but as an individual. As Bright Eyes. And your whole life, in your firmness of character, you wished to offer to others this same treatment—seeing them in the fullness of their selves—even if the same had been so often denied to you.

"Before us sits a brokenhearted man, telling a story from a broken world. He has white skin, yes. But there is more to his story. Far more. His is a story of pain, of wandering, and of steadfast love. Your father once said that within any struggle there are truly three: the struggle against enemies, against allies, and against self. To me, this man Bunyan is an ally.

"Of course, I understand your refusal. Your reasons are clear and clearly stated. The Simulorb is yours, the Formula is yours, the choice is yours. You have heard no a thousand times. You have a right to say no in return.

"But my question to you is this: Is it the strongest Bright Eyes who says no? Is it the most brilliant Bright Eyes who refuses? Is it the most courageous Bright Eyes who now decides? I have seen the grandness of your soul, I have seen the weak find comfort at your hands, I have glimpsed your spirit on the mountaintop. A harsh decision shows power. But mercy shows both power and greatness."

Axl's eyebrows floated up into the middle of his forehead as emotion filled his face. "My love for you is as true today as it was long ago. My heart is filled with that vital blood that keeps it firm and fresh. In a thousand years of searching, Bright Eyes, I could not find a truer pairing. And in all our life together, I have never admired you more than I do at this moment. Yet there are times when even the best of us are trapped within, and can only see the way forward by trusting blindly in those who love us. Indeed, over the years, I have trusted your judgment through my own bouts of misery, not understanding your wisdom till the pain had long passed.

"Here, then, is what I believe: that you, not cornered, that you, not starved, that you, not so worn down with cares, that you, at your very best, would find mercy for this man."

Bright Eyes' lips twisted up and a tear fell down her cheek. Axl stood and went to her, and they embraced for some time. At last, she spoke.

"These weeks I lay here in the dark, I heard my father's voice, like murmurs from the water. I have so much to tell him when we meet."

Axl caressed her cheek. Her hair.

"It has been so very, very hard," she said, "and for so very, very long."

"I know," said Axl. "I know."

She looked up at him. "Am I not myself?"

"You are partly yourself. Yet there is more."

She searched her husband's face. "What, then, should we do?"

Axl took her hand and kissed it. "Escape from this cave. Help this man. Then return, and for all the rest of your days, help the First Foot."

Bright Eyes buried her face in Axl's side. In time, she wiped her cheeks and stood to face Bunyan.

"I trust Axl with my heart, my life, and my soul. If he says mercy . . . then mercy it shall be."

———— ◆ ————

Within minutes, the three had ventured up the stairs from the Rotunda into the corridor of the old mine shaft. Axl led the way, holding his lantern. Behind him walked Bright Eyes, then Bunyan. The Beast was nowhere in sight.

Axl's nerves had returned, and so had his rhymes. Talking to them over his shoulder, he said, "Quick, stay close. It's slippery and steep. Can't say how long my drugs will make it sleep."

The trio pressed on through more lefts and rights, over a bridge and under slumping beams. At last, Bunyan saw a faint light ahead. Then the carving of Giving Mother. His heart rose. Moments later they were on the landing with a view up the shaft.

Yet as Bunyan peered up the incline into the blinding sunlight, he saw someone seated at the top.

"Oi, mate," said Axl. "Friend of yours?"

As Bunyan squinted, he saw a man stroking his mustache, holding a pistol.

"Oh no . . . ," muttered Bunyan.

"The hunchback and the Indian," the man said, twisting the sound of that last word. "At long last, we meet again."

CHAPTER 41

THE HOLE

There at the top of the shaft, silhouetted by the light in the mouth of the cave, was the Darwin of Debt, the Bismarck of Business, the Napoleon of Net Worth. He sat hunched forward with elbows on his knees, holding the gun limply in one hand as he looked down at Axl, Bright Eyes, and Bunyan.

"Did you know that you are trespassing?" he said in a light conversational tone. "Giving Mother. The equipment. Everything here, it's all mine. Still mine. Always mine. Funny thing is, even though it's mine, I've never actually been down there. Not past that little carving, anyway." El Boffo shook his head and mused. "What a woman, Giving Mother. Me and my boys had our way with her, I promise you that. Sometimes you just have to *take* a woman."

Next to Bunyan, Bright Eyes was muttering half consciously, "No, no, no, no, no . . ." She tried to step back into the labyrinth, but just then, out from the shadows emerged a second improbable visitor.

"Don't take another step."

Mad Dog Mahoney, solid as a barrel of bullets, stepped forward.

"You . . . ," said Bunyan.

"It's not your turn," said Mad Dog with a crooked smile. "It's never gonna be your turn."

"Clear the way and let us go in peace," shouted Axl, up to El Boffo. "Be decent now, you owe us that, at least."

El Boffo scratched a scab on his forehead, an injury no doubt from the Wondertorium fire.

"Me, owe *you*? I think it's the other way around, hunchback. *I'm* the one in debt. This old hag sucked my wallet dry." He sniffed with a grimace. "That *smell*. It's like the perfume of an ex-wife. Alluring, once upon a time. But now it's just, suck, suck, *suck*."

El Boffo picked up a bit of rubble, studied it, then pitched it away. "Nature, in the final measure, is one of three things: cow, snake, or toilet." He held up three fingers in succession. "You can milk it. You can kill it. Or you can flush it. Whichever it is, I do the deed and get out quick."

Axl set down his lantern, hooked his cane on his belt loop, and slid his shotgun off his shoulder, holding it with two hands. "We're coming up."

"Be careful, intruder," said Mad Dog.

"Be careful, indeed. " El Boffo added, "I'm a law-and-order guy, see. I'm well within my rights to just shoot you for being on my land. Furthermore, I've got an extra reason to be upset, considering what you've been up to, hunchback."

"Stop calling him that!" shouted Bright Eyes.

El Boffo rose and took a step down the shaft. "Yes, *hunchback*, I found out about the letter you wrote to my Lump Town professor. Trying to tell the world about the Tome. Trying to scare everyone."

"Stop there!" warned Bunyan.

But El Boffo kept coming. "And *then* I hear from Running Deer that you and the Indian are working on the Simulorb, a device that has a patent in my name! Just how am I supposed to feel?"

By now Axl's shotgun was pointed at El Boffo.

Mad Dog took another step toward him. "You shoot, you die."

"Please," begged Bright Eyes.

Bunyan noticed she had her hand directly over her chest where the Simulorb hung behind her dress.

El Boffo was halfway down. "I tell you, hunchback, the *only* thing that is going to put me in a forgiving mood is that device. Give it to me and no one gets hurt."

Bunyan tried to intervene. "We already told you. We don't have it."

"And you! Lump Master! What a disappointment. We could have been a team. But then you went and aligned yourself with these ... noncitizens."

"Your gun!" shouted Axl. "Pitch it down!"

Arriving at the bottom of the shaft, El Boffo looked at Bright Eyes, who still clutched the hidden Simulorb where it hung. He smirked. "What a pair of outcasts. It's moving, really, how you found each other. But the truth is"—he cocked his pistol—"unprotected wealth is a provocation."

Bang!

A gunshot. Bunyan instinctively scanned his own body to see if he'd been hit. He hadn't. He looked at Bright Eyes, El Boffo, Mad Dog, all still standing, and then—

Axl tumbled down. He dropped the gun, which landed at Bunyan's feet. Blood pumped from a hole his chest.

Bang!

Axl's body jerked at the second shot.

Mad Dog quickly stepped over the body and ripped Axl's shotgun away.

El Boffo lowered his firearm, the tip smoking. "It's a shame it had to come to this." He turned to Bright Eyes. "If you want to save your hunchback now, you will have to produce the healing device. I know that you have it."

Bright Eyes shrieked. "Axl! My Axl!" She dove upon the body of her husband, cupping his head. "No!"

In shock, still alive, Axl blinked and coughed blood, which leaked from his mouth. Bunyan knelt by him and put his hand over one of the wounds, trying to stop the gush of blood, but it oozed through Bunyan's fingers out onto the cavern floor, mixing with the hairs of Axl's long white ponytail.

"I'll heal you," said Bright Eyes. "I'll save you!"

She reached into her dress and removed the device, pulling it over her head. She held it over him, where it dangled, dim and unlit.

"There it is," said El Boffo quietly. "Finally ..."

Yet even as she laid her fingertips on the globe to ignite the Light, Axl yanked her arm down.

"No." He coughed. "It's done. Go quick."

"I have to heal—"

Yet with another burst of strength, Axl shoved her arm away. "Run!"

"I won't leave—"

Axl grabbed her neck with his good arm and pressed her forehead against his. "Whatever happens, my love, just don't . . . let him . . . *take it!*"

Axl's arm then slid off her neck, and in the next moment the life seemed to pass from his eyes.

"No!" shouted Bright Eyes.

El Boffo advanced, eyes fixed on the device where it lay on the ground beside Bright Eyes, still attached to her fingers by the chain. He set down the lantern, knelt, and reached across Axl's body, muttering, "Just to hold it . . . after so very long . . ."

But as his fingertips extended, Bright Eyes suddenly snatched it up, leapt to her feet, and dashed down the nearest shaft, back into the heart of Giving Mother Cave.

El Boffo raised his gun and fired off a quick shot. *Bang!* An echo. Then, silence.

Mad Dog stared down the shaft, stunned.

"Well, go get her!" El Boffo shouted.

Snapping up his lantern, Mad Dog ran after Bright Eyes.

El Boffo stood. Looking down at his knee, and seeing the fabric of his pants covered in Axl's blood, he scowled. Then he aimed his gun at Bunyan.

"I should just kill you. Unless you know where she might have gone."

Bunyan thought quick. In a moment, he had a plan.

"I think I do. There's a cavern deep inside called the Rotunda. I can show you."

El Boffo kept the gun up. "Leave your lantern here. Hands up. No sudden moves."

Bunyan headed into the shaft, his hands raised on either side. El Boffo's lantern shined from behind as the pair stepped through the lugubrious dark of the abandoned mine and Bunyan tried to recall the way Axl had shown him.

"I can't believe men actually *worked* down here," said El Boffo, following along. "Look at these slumping beams. Might have fallen at any moment. How much farther?"

"It's just up ahead."

Farther underground they went. "Obtain this device for me, Lump Master, and you'll get what's coming to you. I don't mean the gold bar and a mansion. I mean Lord of Lump Town. The Castle Book. You'll be happy with the deal we make."

Limping along in the dark, Bunyan felt the pain in his Junk Foot. Instead of answering, he just clenched his jaw.

The pair came to a fork and Bunyan went down the left-hand passage. At a three-way fork, he chose the middle, heading toward a set of stairs.

"It's just down here."

At the bottom of the stairs, they stood before a huge iron door, hanging heavily from its hinges. It was open just a crack.

Bunyan turned to El Boffo and raised his finger to his lips.

"She's in there," he said quietly. "Turn your lamp down. I'll go first."

Bunyan bent down and hoisted up the iron door, opening it just enough that he could squeeze through. Stepping into the dark, he was struck by the most powerful stench of Lump he'd ever encountered— that old, breadlike scent that promised to nourish but never could. Underfoot, the sticky, indestructible Sludge sucked at his boots. It hadn't evaporated or decreased a bit in the years since the mine was abandoned.

By the faint light coming from El Boffo's lantern behind him, Bunyan glimpsed, just ten paces away, the edge of the unholy pond. The evil effluvium. The unflushed swamp of Sludge. Here, a corpse's arm. There, a floating back. There, a skeletal head, slicked with goo, Sludge in the sockets. None of it decomposed. All of it preserved in eternal tarlike slime.

In horror, Bunyan wheeled back around, swallowed, composed himself, and took a few steps back toward the door.

"I've spotted her, just around the corner," he whispered to El Boffo. "Let me take the lantern."

El Boffo hesitated.

Bunyan showed him the Sludge on his boots. "I don't want you to fall into this stuff. Just keep one hand on my shoulder. Promise me you won't shoot her. Just take the Simulorb and go."

Again, El Boffo hesitated.

"Please."

"All right," El Boffo said at last. He handed over the lantern. Bunyan turned it down low, just to the pilot light.

"The moment I turn the light up, be ready to grab her. Got it?"

"Try anything and I shoot." El Boffo cocked the gun. "Go on."

Bunyan stepped through the door into the dark, El Boffo's hand on his shoulder just behind.

"Where is she?" whispered El Boffo after a few steps. "I can't see a thing."

Bunyan didn't answer. After ten sticky steps, he judged they were at the edge of the Hole. That's when he asked his first question.

"Did you know the Sludge is indestructible?"

"Yes. Where is she?"

"Did you know it flowed from this very cave, out into the rivers of America?"

"I know everything. God, the *stench of it.*"

"And did you know Sludge makes the cows sick, so they attack their owners?"

"You know what they say about omelets."

Bunyan felt certainty pass over his heart.

"My family once had a ranch outside of Cow Town," he said. "Our herd got sick from Lump. Those same sick cows killed my father."

"Where is that *Indian?*"

At that, Bunyan turned the lantern up to full blast. El Boffo raised his gun, ready to fire, but as his eyes adjusted, confusion took hold.

Before them extended the putrid, silverdark bog of Lump, the eternal sewage of wasted corpses, with its limbs and skulls and carts and debris slathered in murk. The liquid burial stew of glistening goo extended below the low roof of the cavern, forming a silent, toxic tableau of motionless rot.

"There's a saying of yours," said Bunyan, "'Mankind can engineer itself out of any crisis. Especially one of its own making.'"

El Boffo muttered, "What . . . is . . . this . . . place?"

"It is the crisis of your own making," answered Bunyan. "Now, get yourself out of it."

With that, Bunyan grabbed El Boffo by his back and his belt and, with all his might, hurled him headlong into the Hole. With a thudding splash, the magnate flopped in the Sludge, thrashing about on the surface as he tried to stay afloat in the stringy slop. Snatching up the lantern, Bunyan raced toward the door as El Boffo screamed a burbling, drowning scream and sunk into the sucking muck.

Two shots rang out—*bang! Bang!*

The bullets ricocheted off the rocks as Bunyan arrived at the huge, heavy door, squeezed through to the other side, then shoved it as far closed as he could, sealing El Boffo in.

Alone in the corridor of the shaft, Bunyan caught his breath. As the screams of the plutocrat subsided, he raised the lantern.

"Bright Eyes!" he called down the corridor. If he could only find her, they could escape with the Simulorb. "Bright Eyes! It's Paul!"

Echoes. Silence.

Bunyan proceeded into the dark along the tracks, holding the lantern before him. He passed one empty rail cart, then another.

And that's when he heard the sound.

BRRRRAAAWWWWWWWWWW

CHAPTER 42

THE BITTER TEST

The Beast was awake.

Bunyan hustled away from the sound and at the next intersection he swung the lantern in both directions and found the corridor empty. He raced down the hall one way. Dead end. He walked back to where he thought he'd been. Now it was an unfamiliar fork.

He heard a man's voice. More like a garbled shout—

"No! No!"

A rumbling underfoot—

Bunyan ran toward the sound, ducking deeply under a sagging beam, then—

BRRRRAAAAWWWWW

The entire cavern seemed to shake and dust fell from the ceiling as a locust shot past Bunyan's face. Another bug struck his leg. Bunyan crawled and hid behind an empty iron track cart, heart racing, sweat pouring down his back.

In the next moment, a barrage of locusts filled the air, so thick it blotted out the light of the lantern, a storm of missiles blasting down the hall, followed by the mighty moan of the Beast mixed with a man's scream—

Gunfire. *Crack crack crack!*

A high-pitched scream. "No! No!"

BRRRRRRRAAAAAAAAWWWWWW

Keeping utterly still, Bunyan listened as the snorting Beast mauled its victim. Then came a dull *thud* against the cavern wall.

Shot through with fear, Bunyan sprinted into the maze of halls, running left, then right, haphazardly and without a plan, as the lantern swung wildly before him. He hit another dead end of man-made stone wall, turned back, then went left again, but there the cave had freshly collapsed, blocking the way, so he wheeled back around and raced up a set of stairs, where—

Bunyan stopped in his tracks.

There, on the cavern floor, was the mangled, gutted body of what had once been Mad Dog Mahoney. The Beast had torn the torso in half from belly to shoulder. The innards of the three-time Lump Master glistened in the lamplight, and blood slicked the ground like oil. A carpet of locusts blanketed his skull, broken open like a pomegranate.

Just then, a fresh swarm of bugs blitzed Bunyan's face like bullets zipping through the dark. Bunyan held up the lantern and the bugs bounced off its glass case—*ping, ping, ping, ping*—and there he beheld, at the opposite end of the corridor, the vision of his deepest nightmare.

"Easy," Bunyan tried to say, though no sound came from his mouth. He backed up, half-tripping over Mad Dog's corpse. "Easy . . ."

Insects wriggled and flitted over the Beast's snarling, snorting face, and its stiff tongue hung to the floor. Strings of blood and drool twisted from its buckteeth.

BRRAAAAAWWW

Bunyan backed down the narrow, man-made corridor, but within only a few steps he was at another dead end, with earthen walls and rubble surrounding him on three sides. His spirit went slack and the locusts pelted him and the Beast bucked on its bloody hooves, its massive head wide as a man's body. It lowered its protruding, razor-sharp horns, then on it came, rumbling down the corridor as the floor shook like an earthquake and the Beast tore through the remains of Mad Dog, tossing the body aside like a rag doll, and Bunyan's hands groped behind him again, finding only the dead-end wall as the giant closed in, tongue dragging low—

BRRRAAAAAAAAAWWWWWW

—and Bunyan dropped his lantern, which skittered over the ground as he reached for his axe behind him, but as he pulled it from its sheath, it slipped right from his sweaty palms, and at the last moment he raised up his trembling arms, helpless before the very manner of creature that had once slain his own father—

BRRRRRRAAAAAAAAAAAAAWWWWWWW

—but just as Bunyan braced to block the blow, he heard a shout, then a clang, then the crash of the Beast striking the wall at full speed. The horde of locusts shot in every direction, up and down and back and forth, as if their hive had been broken.

Had he been mauled? No.

Was he hurt? Somehow not.

Bunyan scrambled on all fours to grab his lantern, thrusting it forward into the storm of critters.

The Beast lay upon the ground, stunned. And there—how could it be? A rusted rail cart had struck its head. One of its enormous horns had punctured the side of the cart and was now stuck in it. The wounded Beast tried to stand but collapsed, bleating in pain.

Standing over Bunyan, a tall figure reached down with one hand.

"You came back," said Bunyan.

"Friendship over fate," said John Henry.

The great hammer man pulled Bunyan up and in an instant Bunyan had picked up his axe and the pair was running blind through the cloud of locusts, batting them with their hands, when—BRRAAWW—they heard the frustrated Beast struggling to gain its feet and dislodge the horn as it bashed the iron cart against the walls.

A support beam overhead snapped.

"Watch out!" shouted John Henry.

The two dove forward as dust and rock spit down the passage behind them and the shaft collapsed.

Holding up his own lantern, John Henry pointed at the wall. On it was a faint white line.

"When I came looking for you, I left these markings. It shows the way back to the entrance."

John Henry led the way, his hammer in one hand and a lantern in the other. "Get your axe ready," he said over his shoulder. "The Beast may find another way around."

Bunyan held the flawless axe Yan Hui had forged as the pair advanced, following the chalk markings along the labyrinthine walls. They made two quick turns, then hurried beside the flowing stream, back toward the entrance of Giving Mother Cave.

Bunyan's wooden brace had come unbuckled and Old Junk Foot throbbed in his boot. Kneeling, he refastened it.

"What about the Simulorb?" Bunyan asked. "Bright Eyes is still down here."

"No time. The ceiling's caving in."

John Henry held his lantern up beside another marking, then took a few steps toward the exit, but this time Bunyan didn't follow.

"Hey," said John Henry. "Come on."

But Bunyan didn't budge. He stood motionless in the corridor, staring at his axe.

Its head, somehow, had begun to glow.

The axe had turned the very hue of the Gleam, a molten, shining silver. Holding it before him, Bunyan swung the axe in the direction of John Henry. In that direction it dimmed. He swung it back in the opposite direction, from whence they'd come. There, it churned with inner light.

"Do you see it?"

John Henry nodded. "I see it."

The corridor rumbled. Whether it was from the Beast or from another shaft about to collapse, Bunyan couldn't tell.

"I have to follow it."

"You want to go *back*? Paul. Listen. The Beast has knocked out one beam after another. We'll be flat in a minute!"

Bunyan closed his eyes. The words of Moki passed through his mind:

Against the Bitter Test, what can a person do but let the mystery within confront the mystery without?

The cave shook again. Dust spewed. But Bunyan did not go toward the exit. Instead, he stepped in the direction lit by the axe—

back toward the Beast, deeper into the cavern. As he did, the axe
glowed brighter. Another step. Still more it glowed.

BRRRAAAAWWWWW

The Beast was somewhere near. Bunyan guided his axe toward the
sound and it gained power yet again. He spoke to Moki in his heart:

Why to the Beast? What should I do?

John Henry called to him from behind.

"The Beast is up ahead, man! We can't go down there!"

Bunyan turned to him sharply, his face lit by the axe. *"Do you
believe?"*

For a long moment, John Henry stared at his friend. He looked at
the glowing axe head, then back to Bunyan. At last, he nodded.

"All right, man. I'm with you."

At that, Bunyan headed deeper into the mine, more quickly and
more confidently now, descending a stairway, then back along the
underground waters and by the rail tracks as the pain of his Junk
Foot faded and the axe grew brighter still. At each stairway and fork,
Bunyan swung the axe one way, then the other. It would dim here,
then erupt with a swirling light there.

BRRRRRRRRRAAAAAAAAAAAWWWWWWWWWWW

The Beast was almost upon them.

Bunyan spoke to Moki again. *What am I to do? Kill it? Tell me!*

Bunyan swung his axe down one corridor—dim. Down another—
dim. It glowed furiously down the third hallway. Then, just as Bunyan took a step forward, John Henry grabbed his arm.

"Look."

Clinging to the stone wall was a locust, long as a finger. Beside it
suddenly landed a second, third, and fourth.

John Henry spoke quietly. "There. Up ahead."

As Bunyan slowly rotated, pointing his axe before him down the
shaft, the very light of the tool now lit up the face of the monster.
Fifty paces up, wide as the corridor itself, its horns and hooves glistened with blood.

Bunyan saw more:

The Gleam. Unmistakable. Bright. It shined directly upon the

Beast's drooling mouth. Visions of death invaded Bunyan's mind—
his father facedown in the mud.

BRRRRRRRRRAAAAAAAAAAAWWWWWWWW

Axe raised before him, shining bright, Bunyan clenched his jaw.
He took a step toward the animal. The axe glowed brighter. Another
step, brighter again.

John Henry followed just behind him, his hammer high.

And still another step Bunyan took, as the axe grew furious with
light and bugs shot past his ears. Before him, the Beast crouched,
pawing the ground, preparing to charge, as Bunyan thought back to
that day long ago, the very last moments his father was alive . . .

Soothe their pain . . . Be gentle . . . Gentle to the last . . .

The Beast dug at the stones with its hoof and blew strings of blood
from its nose as pus twisted from its mouth, and Bunyan gripped the
shaft of his brilliant axe before the brutal predator, which now com-
menced its drive, and Bunyan crouched low and ready—

Soothe their pain . . .

"Paul!"

—and as the Beast hurled forward, gobbling up ground, filling
the narrow shaft like a locomotive, brushing the walls on either side,
rumbling and roaring, closing in fast, Bunyan's eyes locked upon the
gleaming mouth as he cocked the axe so far back it grazed the base
of his spine—

Soothe their pain . . .

—and the Beast was just ten strides out when Bunyan finally
understood, and, knowing what to do at last, he whipped the glowing
axe head low across the corridor, directly into a wooden beam holding
up the mine. It stuck clean, leaving Yan Hui's handle extended horizontally across the hall, directly in the path of the charging thing—

BRRRRAAAAAAAAWWWWWWWWWW

"Get back!" shouted Bunyan to John Henry, and the two dove
away as the Beast clattered into the axe handle, carved so expertly by
Yan Hui that even now it did not splinter, and down went the huge
animal, tripping in its stride, skidding forward, tumbling two times
over, and crashing into the wall.

Bunyan leapt upon the Beast, throwing his full weight upon its neck, with one arm pinning down its horns. He shoved his hand deep into the suffering animal's mouth, remembering his father's lesson:

There are boils and blisters beneath the tongue, you have to clean them so the bull can breathe . . .

"Pin him down!" shouted Bunyan.

John Henry threw himself on the back of the Beast, holding it in place as Bunyan kept reaching deep into its mouth by its molars, where he felt the clusters of blisters. Bunyan scooped out a handful of slime, flung it on the ground, then reached in for more. The smell made him retch but he didn't stop. The Beast's eyes were open now, searching, stunned by the sensation of Bunyan's hand. The diseased animal looked confused, wounded, like a newborn calf fresh into the world.

"Easy, babe . . . I've got you now . . ."

It seemed like the slime would never end as Bunyan drew out scoop after scoop, flinging it away as the Beast began to quietly bleat—

brrrraaaawwwwwww

"I know it hurts, babe . . ."

The Beast tried to stand, but John Henry kept it pinned.

Bunyan scooped out still more of the Metal Meat slime, then, when most was gone, he tore the blisters off the gums and pulled the dead flesh off the roof of the mouth, then the tongue, too, just as his father had patiently done years ago, trying to comfort his poor, sick herd.

Be gentle to the last.

At last, the Beast relaxed. Its body loosened.

Brrraaawwwwwww

Suddenly, the cloud of locusts dispersed into the air. The bugs rose in a single swarm and shot down the hallway and into the darkness like an airborne river. Their absence revealed the Beast's raw hide, whose eaten fur looked like a map of the diseased earth. A shudder of relief passed through the mighty, wounded animal.

Brraawww

The sound was meek. He shuddered with relief.

At last, Bunyan stood. "You can get off him now."

John Henry still had his full weight on the Beast. "You sure?"

Bunyan nodded. The moment John Henry got up, the animal hopped to his feet. Bunyan rubbed him between his bloody horns.

"Come on, babe. We've got to get out of here."

Bunyan could tell instantly the animal was as intelligent as he was strong. He saw gratitude in the bull's eyes.

"Let's go," said John Henry as more dust fell from the ceiling. "The roof is coming down!"

CHAPTER 43

THE COLLAPSE

Bunyan wrenched his axe free from the beam and sheathed it on his back. The pair ran for the exit, following John Henry's chalk lines. The bull galloped behind, running at Bunyan's heels, as a corridor thunderously collapsed to their right and spit rocks into their path. Suddenly, they heard a plaintive moan.

"Help!"

"Bright Eyes!" shouted Bunyan.

John Henry ran toward the sound and moments later found the source.

"I'm here!"

The sound was coming from behind a wall.

"Stand back!" said John Henry. "I'm knocking it down!"

Quickly, the Steel-Drivin' Man unsheathed his hammer, aimed, and in a single blow put the tool through the wall. Two more strikes and the wall crumbled. As Bunyan cleared off the rubble, John Henry reached round and helped Bright Eyes leap free.

"The Beast!" She pointed in terror.

"He's on our side now," said Bunyan. "Which way to the exit?"

"The path to the entrance is gone," said Bright Eyes. "The only way out is through the Rotunda."

Taking Bunyan's lantern, Bright Eyes led the way. The bull—

beastly no more—kept up behind. But just as they arrived at the stairway to the Rotunda, a gunshot rang out.

Bang!

"Stop right there!"

Bunyan turned. The figure standing in the hallway was shocking to see.

El Boffo was dripping, head to foot, with Sludge. Boots, pants, shirt, jacket, even his white hair, all of it glistened silverdark, as if he'd been dunked in a vat of tar. The slime even slathered his mustache in glop. He might not have been visible at all in the mine shaft without the light of Bunyan's lantern reflecting upon him.

"Put the lamps on the ground," he said. His gun was up. "Slowly."

They set the lanterns down.

"Good," said the gunk-soaked magnate. "Put the axe down. Hammer, too."

They did.

"Lay the Simulorb before you."

Bright Eyes didn't move.

"Now!" shouted El Boffo.

She reached into the pocket of her dress, pulled the Simulorb out, and laid it on the cavern floor.

El Boffo tapped the chamber of his revolver.

"You know what I've loaded in here?" His tone was sharp. Furious. "Lump-laced bullets. They'll give you the Stucks. Not in a matter of days, either. Not in a matter of hours. You'll be silverdark in a minute."

As El Boffo went on, only the whites of his eyeballs and teeth were visible amid the coating of gunk. "I guess you could say this is my true calling—destruction. Lump is indeed the miracle substance— miraculous in its ability to choke off life. Get on your knees, all three of you."

They knelt. El Boffo slowly approached, picked up one of the lanterns, then the Simulorb. He held the device before his eyes. Then he kissed it.

Sliding the orb in his pocket, he leveled the gun at Bunyan.

"And to think, Lump Master, you will die just like your father. A sick cow by your side."

"Please." Bunyan knelt with his palms in the air. "At least spare them."

"No, I can't spare anyone." El Boffo pulled a string of Sludge off his mustache and flicked it away. His voice hardened. "Because the fact is, *I* am a great man of history. And you"—he waved the gun barrel at the trio—"you are the rabble. The great men walk upon the rabble."

It was just at that moment that the enormous, wounded bull stepped in front of Bunyan, John Henry, and Bright Eyes. There, the animal began to scrape at the ground with his hoof.

brrrraaaaaaawwwwww

El Boffo scoffed. "Behold. A snake in a toilet. I'll shoot you, too."

The scraping continued as the bull readied the charge.

"You mound of rancid beef—"

BRRRAAAAWWWWWW

Bang! Bang! Bang! Bang! Bang! Bang!

El Boffo unloaded all of his Lump-laced bullets into the hide of the bull.

Yet in the silence that followed the bull did not budge. Rather, he stood just as tall as before.

A moment later, he leapt toward his prey.

El Boffo turned to run, but the bull gained on him stride for stride, even as the Columbus of Capitalists dove round the bend in the cave. Bright Eyes, Bunyan, and John Henry could only listen to the shrieks as, out of sight, the bull carried out his bloody, bone-crushing work. After several thumps against the cavern wall, finally, the screaming stopped.

What followed was a bellow triumphant.

BRRRRRRRAAAAAAAAAAAWWWWWWWWWWWWWW

Bunyan ventured up ahead. There, on the slick, sticky surface of the ground, a mix of blood and Sludge, he pulled the Simulorb out of the pocket of the dead man.

He turned to the bull. "Atta boy, Babe."

brrrawww

The cavern rumbled.

Altogether, they rushed to the Rotunda. There, the stairway was too narrow for the bull to enter. John Henry made quick work of the situation, wielding the hammer Yan Hui had forged. In five quick strikes upon the stones, he'd knocked the doorway wider and made room for the bull.

Down they went together, entering the deepest cavern as the earth shook beneath. A huge piece of the ceiling thudded on the ground with such force it caused all of them to stumble. The fallen rock blocked the underground river, which rushed upon the ground, washing over Bunyan's boots.

"How do we escape?" said Bunyan.

Bright Eyes pointed across the floor. "See that wall, where the tracks go under? On the other side is a shaft that leads to the surface. They built the wall there to hold up this room. If we knock it out, the Rotunda will collapse."

John Henry splashed across and set about blasting at the stones. Round and round his hammer went, quick like lightning, but he'd only made a dent when a roar came through the Rotunda door. Beyond, the rest of the labyrinth had caved in.

Bunyan crouched before the mighty bull, his head at eye level. "All right, Babe. You see that wall over there where my buddy's got his hammer?"

The bull glanced across the room.

"We're gonna run at it, me and you, and you're gonna blast straight on through. Got it?"

The bull reared up on his hind legs.

Brrraawwww!

Bunyan knew he understood.

"John! Come on! Bright Eyes, get behind!"

John Henry sheathed his hammer and positioned himself on the other side of the bull. Bright Eyes took the spot behind Bunyan, who rubbed the great bull under his jaw.

"We're right behind you, Babe, all right?"

As the rising waters flowed over their ankles and the ceiling rained down stones, Bunyan turned to John Henry.

"Came this far already," he yelled.

Together they shouted, "Ain't hardly gonna die!"

"Go, Babe, go!"

BRRRAAAAWWWWW!

The bull charged, splashing over the ground with every stride, as Bunyan, John Henry, and Bright Eyes rushed alongside the creature right up to the wall and—

CRASH!

—for a moment, all was dark. Bunyan was covered in debris. He'd landed on top of the bull with John Henry tangled beside him. The bull shook off the rubble and Bright Eyes pointed above.

"Light!"

Before them, a long stairway led to an opening high up. Through it, they could see a sliver of bright blue sky.

As the earth shook on every side, Bunyan helped Bright Eyes onto Babe's back, then the two men hopped on, too. Bunyan slapped the bull's hide and shouted, "Go on, Babe!" and the bull leapt forward, racing up the ancient corridor as the cavern collapsed behind, one beam after another, and the walls rattled and the dust spit and chased them faster and faster as they climbed toward that point of sky and Giving Mother Cave sealed off behind them—

"Almost there!"

—and they clutched the tufts of fur on the bull's broad back as he galloped faster. With one final leap into the air the trio shot from the hole and into the blinding light of the day and Bunyan, Bright Eyes, and John Henry toppled off the bull onto the green grasses as the cave convulsed with a thunderous rumble and exhaled its final blast.

Lying on the ground, Bunyan laughed. Beside him, John Henry laughed. They stood and embraced.

"You came to get me," said Bunyan. "Why?"

"Had needs bigger than my fears."

"But the curse—that you'd die in a tunnel with your hammer."

John Henry clapped Bunyan on the cheek with affection, then kissed him on the forehead. "Tunnel's gonna get me one day, I reckon. Till then, the world is mine."

Kicking about on the grass nearby was the bull. In the daylight, he looked pathetic, with all his fur eaten, and his blistered, swollen tongue hanging low. Yet the creature was joyful, bucking with glee.

Bunyan then spotted Bright Eyes, kneeling upon the ground, her forehead upon the earth. Bunyan went to her.

"My Axl," she said.

Bunyan sat beside her as Bright Eyes wiped tears from her cheeks.

"I only wanted him to see our device work once more. He would have loved to see that Light again."

"At least he learned the truth."

Bunyan took the Simulorb from his pocket and handed it to her. She stared down at it.

"It is as much his work as mine," she said.

After another moment, Bright Eyes stood. "We don't have much time. We can still save one life with this."

With that, Bunyan approached the intelligent bull, still bucking joyfully about on the grass.

"All right, Babe," said Bunyan. "You think you could handle one more run, down to the train station?"

Brrrawww!

CHAPTER 44

LUCETTE

It was late afternoon when the train pulled into Lump Town, with its gridded streets, volcanic stacks, and ashen tracks. Bunyan, John Henry, and Bright Eyes ran to Bunyan's house, where a crowd had gathered around his door.

"I need to get in! I have the cure!" He passed a member of the Filter Brigade. "Am I too late?"

"They tried to keep us out, but we forced our way in this morning," the woman said. "She hangs by a thread!"

The trio pushed up the stairs to the small bedroom, where Bunyan saw Dr. Niebuhr, a bandage on his face, sitting by the bed. Seeing his wife again, Bunyan's heart nearly shattered.

Her face, neck, and hands all bore the deepest, uniform hue of silverdark. The only sign of life was the slow rise and fall of her breath beneath the Dream Quilt.

Bright Eyes pulled the Simulorb from her pocket. With her fingertips, she carefully turned the top, three full rotations.

Through the glass, Bunyan saw the device's intricate gears begin to rotate. Slowly, the golden light was born, mellow and warm. As the inner wheels and cogs spun faster, the light grew yet richer and more lustrous, shining upon the faces of those around the bed. Its reflection gleamed in Lucette's iron-hued skin.

"Help me undress her," Bunyan said. "Use the scissors. Careful not to budge her!"

John Henry pulled the Dream Quilt off as Niebuhr took scissors from his case and cut through Lucette's clothes down to her undergarments, revealing her silverdark frame.

Now Bright Eyes lowered the device over her skin, moving it back and forth, across her arms and belly.

"Look . . ." Niebuhr grabbed Bunyan's arm. "The Light."

Bunyan raised his eyes to witness: the Salvation Light was born.

It was different from any light Bunyan had ever felt. It was palpable, thick, warm, and Bunyan's skin welcomed it, thirsted for it. The rays seemed to pass straight through him, cleansing his cells like a river passing around stones. Soaking in the rich, thick Light, he felt his bones and muscles mending, as if they were drinking a golden milk.

The crowd of Lump Towners had formed a line that stretched from the room, down the stairs, through the kitchen, and into the street.

"She is shining a light upon the body," whispered those on the stairs.

"They're passing a device over her limbs," said those in the kitchen.

"They're curing her!" said those in the streets.

Yet even as the aura washed over them all, Bunyan's mind began to unravel. For still, Lucette did not budge.

Bunyan laid his mighty hand over the silverdark hand of his wife, which felt cold as a quarry rock. He bent by her ear and whispered, "Lucette, I have come back for you. Now you come back to me."

It was just then that he felt the slightest of stirs. He couldn't tell if it was his imagination. Yet when he looked down at his hand, he saw her fingers—*there!*—had curled about his own.

"She moved!" said John Henry. "I saw it!"

Immediately, the word passed down the stairs: "She stirs!"

And into the kitchen, "She lives!"

And down to the street, "She's saved!"

Now Dedrick came sprinting in from the Factory, where he arrived at the edge of the crowd and pushed his way up the stairs to the threshold of the bedroom.

"Shine it here!" Bunyan said to Bright Eyes, who passed the Light close to Lucette's fingers.

Bunyan caught his breath . . . She blinked.

"Lucette!"

He put his face close to hers and brushed her cheek with his knuckle. Feebly, her eyes focused on him. Then she whispered, barely audible . . .

"Paul . . ."

And that is when it happened—oh, miracle of miracles! All at once, like an inky tide withdrawing from a bright beach, the silverdark receded from her skin. Here, it vanished from her face; there, from her legs; here, from her arms; there, from her neck; there again, from her hands and fingers.

"Astonishing," whispered John Henry, who stood at the bottom of the bed.

"Incredible," muttered Dr. Niebuhr.

And still the Light chased out the dark, as the natural color of Lucette's brown hair raced from the roots to the tips. Even her lips— so leaden moments before—turned lush and pink.

Bright Eyes herself could not resist the emotion of the moment. Her face, too, trembled as she witnessed the might of her invention.

Bunyan and John Henry carefully helped Lucette sit up. She coughed to clear her throat. Bunyan placed the Dream Quilt round her shoulders as Bright Eyes continued to shine the light on all the exposed skin, down to the soles of her feet.

Weak and delicate, but alive, so very alive, Lucette looked curiously over her body.

"My arms," she said. "They are so heavy . . ."

"She speaks!" The word passed out of the room.

"She rises!"

"She lives!" they shouted in the streets.

Bunyan laughed and sobbed at once. Holding her, he said, "How do you feel?"

A look of trouble passed over Lucette's face. "Such things I saw . . ."

"Tell me."

Lucette now laid her head on her husband's shoulder and stitched her brow with wonder as she spoke:

"I rose up, out of this body, out of this room, over the land, into the sky and far beyond. I was not alone, but side by side with other souls. We were so many, like bright raindrops rising together."

Bunyan pressed his mighty arms around his wife. "And then what did you see?"

"I rose higher still, past purple galaxies, blood-red stars, and meteors of ice. Then came darkness—a silence too vast for words! An emptiness so wide and deep! Far off I glimpsed, a speck at first, then growing as I rose to it, a light that marked the final boundary. Soaring through the void, in time I arrived there, that distant place where I came face-to-face ..."

She gasped, as if in fear.

Bunyan held her firm. "Darling ..."

"It was the Voice, Paul! At last, the Voice I'd yearned so long to know! It was so beautiful, and yet ... so awful! The Voice was ... *wrestling with itself*!

"I saw, on the one hand, its annihilating power, so absolute it could crush the Earth to dust in an instant. I saw the breadth of its empire, where eternal laws and logic reigned unchecked over tracts of ice and fire, end to end. And I was afraid.

"And yet I saw more! Much more! For in that ghastly quiet I heard a sound; within that void of dark I saw a growth of green. It was life! Tender, murmuring life! Rebellious life! Here and there, and there and here, it bred and multiplied! Impossible to suppress! Ungovernable! Inexplicable! In that reign of frigid darkness, I saw life, defiant!

"In awe I watched these two sides of the Voice bound in struggle: the thread of death woven through each life, the reign of death upset by sprawling births. And though these opposites tried to overwhelm the other, they could not. They mixed and intermingled ceaselessly. I saw the dark was vaster than the light. But the light was more eternal than the dark."

"She speaks of visions!"

"She speaks of dreams!"

"She's seen the world beyond!"

Lucette shuddered. "Around me, I saw soul after soul rising into the Voice and merging with it forever. At last, it was my turn. I felt myself heading across the final boundary . . ."

"Lucette . . . ," whispered Bunyan as he caressed her hair.

"Yet on that edge, the Voice spoke. 'Why do you hesitate, young one? Do you see what lies before you? Knowledge? Union? Return?' I was afraid to speak the truth within my heart. Still, I said, 'I am not finished yet. For there is one I desire more than knowledge, more than union, more than return.'

"The Voice said, 'And who is this one?' I answered, 'He has trekked across the earth to raise me up. He returns to my side, even now! He is the one I love with all my heart!' To this, the Voice answered, 'And what do you wish to do with him, this one you love with all your heart?' I said, 'I wish to go with him freely into the green world, to follow the twisty paths, the slow paths, the backward paths, the roundabout ways, as long as it be side by side.'

"For a long time, I watched the Voice churn and churn, destroying itself, giving birth to itself. At last, it spoke again. 'Then go with this one you love into the green world. Follow the twisty paths, the slow paths, the backward paths, the roundabout ways, as long as it be side by side. For you are not finished yet.'

"Then I began to fall away, even as souls rose past me. Back I fell, across the void, past blue planets and whirling stars, falling and following the sound of your words, which called me across space and time."

Bunyan's face was wet with tears.

"I came back for you," said Lucette.

Bunyan held her close. "I came back for you."

"So warm," said Lucette.

"So warm," answered Bunyan.

The room erupted in cheers. "They embrace!"

"They embrace!"

"They embrace!"

Bunyan pressed his cheek to his wife's and buried his nose deep in her neck. He drew in a long, full breath, and the sweet, faint, floral scent of soap—the smell by which he knew her—filled his nose, filled his body, and filled his soul up to the brim. As all Lump Town clapped and whistled from the streets below, Bunyan took Lucette's chin upon his knuckle, raised it up, and kissed her lips.

Oh, wondrous night! Oh, beautiful night! The night the true Light shined on!

It was wondrous for all in Lump Town, as one after another, the inhabitants took their turn standing before Bright Eyes' device, which healed all their wounds, both known and unknown.

Dedrick was among the most grateful, as he exposed his silverdark bruises to the Light and so was freed from the scourge of the Stucks. Soon Lump Town would be shut down, and El Boffo Industries would go bankrupt. But Dedrick would act quickly. He would take wealth from El Boffo's safe and distribute it, share by share, to those who had worked in his Factory all those years.

Oh, improbable night! Oh, liberating night! The night the pure Light shined on!

It felt improbable for John Henry, who would soon return to the Windy City under the cover of night. Dedrick would help him, just as he'd promised, to gain papers and passage to the Great White North.

There would be fog on the water the dawn he departed. Standing by the brilliant, beautiful Polly, the long-journeying, far-traveling man would hug his friend Bunyan, there on the docks.

"You ain't no jellyfish," John Henry would say.

"And you. You're a lion."

Bunyan would crouch down before Newton. "So, what will you do when you get free?"

"I'll tell you what," the boy would answer. "We're gonna live that full life!"

Oh, astonishing night! Oh, gratifying night! The night the clear Light shined on!

It was astonishing for Bright Eyes, who would return to the First Foot, the Simulorb in hand. Dedrick would give her the last of the

Lump Town Pure and for years to come, the First Foot would come to her hospital, where she would heal them with her device.

Bright Eyes would mourn her late husband and in time compile their research, which she would publish as a book.

THE PROSPECTS AND PERIL OF FIRE SEED, A.K.A. LUMP
By Dr. Mary Bright Eyes and Axl Hummingsworth

Just as Axl had dreamed long ago, the book bearing his name would be carried in every library, university, and store in the land.

Oh, staggering night! Oh, breathtaking night! The night the pure Light shined on!

It was staggering for Bunyan, of course, who felt the power of springtime birthed in his heart. As he looked into Lucette's living eyes, it was as if, within him, ten thousand buds stirred in their roots and the birds broke from every branch.

Dedrick saved a portion of gold for him, and with it, Bunyan paid off the family debt to get his mother out of prison.

Outside the jail, Sue asked, "Did you ever let them crush your spirit?"

"I never did."

In time, Bunyan traveled west, searching for the bull he'd battled in Giving Mother Cave. He found the sorry creature near the train station, close to where he'd left him. And what a surprise! That poor animal, once covered in locusts, had healed, and his hide had grown back a different color.

"Look at you, Babe! You've turned blue!"

Brrraawwwww! exclaimed the happy bull, who from that day on became Bunyan's trusted companion.

In the months to come, Bunyan would seek out Yan Hui as well, to discuss with him the many mysteries of the Twisty Path. Yan Hui had decided to stay in America, after all.

"We are on the Twisty Path together, you and I," the master black-smith would say. "We can't give up now, when our dreams are almost born."

And Bunyan would etch a name into the handle of his axe:

THE PATHFINDER

For Bunyan was no longer a beat-down man in a hard, hard world, fearful of the Gleam. He would become a lumberjack, working among the trees in the primeval American woods, with the joy of a true calling in his soul. And Bunyan made a rule: for every tree he chopped down, he would plant another, to ensure the world would be more green than dark.

Oh, majestic night! Oh, miraculous night! The night the new Light shined on!

For years to come, Bunyan would recall how Lucette sat like a risen queen, cloaked in the glorious Dream Quilt.

For on that night, after the Lump Towners had been healed, Bright Eyes herself went to the window and threw it open wide to hold the Simulorb up high, so its Light filled the streets below. It was just as Chief Wallace had foretold, so many years ago:

When you hold a firefly in your hands, you can hide it. But if you have a torch in your hands, it cannot be hidden. You must hold it above your head!

The Light shined through the dust and smog, down to the American flag hanging from the Bunyans' doorway. The Light shined on to Christ Trunk and over the dark waters of Moses Creek. The Light shined out yet farther, to the gates of the Factory, where the iron letters read:

THE FUTURE IS IN YOUR HANDS

And from there, the Light shined up to the silverdark woods, where dwelled that majestic being, Moki, the Chilali.

The Chilali waits for all of us, up ahead at the crossroads, in the moment when we can choose the straight road or follow the Twisty Path to the Beautiful Destiny.

Within each one of us there is at least one great journey. Moki had guided Bunyan along the first steps of his, yet there was still so much to be known and so much more to be done . . .

For the fight is never finished and the hope is never gone.

ACKNOWLEDGMENTS

Thank you to my editor, Anna Kaufman. You are one of a kind and utterly brilliant at your craft. I am not alone in this judgment (we writers talk amongst ourselves). You grasped the spirit of this work from the first time you saw it, and for that I will always be grateful.

Thank you to my agent, and fellow Thoughtful Bro, Chad Luibl. Your steady hand and reliable insight through this project were immeasurably reassuring. I always knew you had my back—a priceless fact in this precarious world of writing.

Thank you to Tina Pohlman. You were instrumental in this project's early stages in countless ways. You were enthusiastic when I got it right, patient when I got it wrong. In all things you went above and beyond. This book would likely never have made it into the world without you.

Thank you to my wonderful team at Pantheon. The mojo y'all have is rare, special, and, best of all, joyful. Thank you to my production editor, Kathleen Cook. Thank you to my copy editor, Aja Pollock. Thank you to my proofreaders Suzanne Anderson, Jane Elias, and Jennifer Rodriguez. Thank you to my cover designer, Mark Abrams, and my cover artist, Chris Wormell. Thank you to my interior designer, Nicholas Alguire. Thank you to Demetri Papadimitropoulos and

Kate Lloyd, my publicists. Thank you to my marketer, Sarah Pannenberg. Thank you to the assistant editor, Ellie Pritchett.

Jenna Blum, your influence on my evolution as a writer can't possibly be overstated. In your class—a remarkable collection of talented, warm, enthusiastic people—I learned my craft, found my artistic blind spots, and honed what I believed and did not believe about how to tell a story. Your generous mentorship, endless cheerleading, and relentless faith are simply a fact of my life now. And of course, you were on the phone with me that one night, shepherding me through my one great breakthrough on this book. On we go, shoulder to shoulder in the crusade.

Joe Moldover, you are a brilliant critique partner and fellow story theorist. You've been there every step of the way, my brother in the trenches. When things got rough, you always took the call. I often felt you understood my work even better than I understood it myself. We got drafted into the league together, and we'll be bonded for life.

T. M. Blanchet, my fellow fantasy accomplice—thank you for reading this book more than any other person on earth. Your editorial eye could find a needle in a haystack.

Thank you to my circle of close friends in the writing community here in Boston. Each of you left a distinct mark on this book: Hillary Casavant, Tom Champoux, Cathy Elcik, Jennifer De Leon, Chuck Garabedian, Julie Gerstenblatt, Edwin Hill, Alex Hoopes, Sonya Larson, Kirsten Liston, Kimberly Hensle Lowrance, Jenna Paone, Kris Paull, Jane Roper, Whitney Scharer, Grace Talusan, and Adam Stumacher. I can call to mind without hesitation an insightful comment or two each of you made along the way that ultimately influenced this tale.

Thank you to my patient, loyal friends who read and offered feedback on this manuscript in its early, unwieldy, adolescent days: Jim Frew, Meredith Hendrix, Andrew Gerstenblatt, and Matt Clarke. Tom Buckingham and Grant Catton, thank you for your support through the years.

Thank you to Devin Ross for the career coaching, and for always being available to me, even when you didn't have to be.

John Jaynes, thank you for your feedback on metalworking. Allison Grinberg-Funes and Danielle Benaroche Gottesman, thank you for your guidance on checkers. All mistakes that remain are my own!

Thank you to Rhys Davies for the amazing map at the front of the book, and for being such a wonderful collaborator.

Thank you to the communities at GrubStreet and Odyssey Writing Workshop, whose classes helped me refine this story.

Thank you to the historian Joe Starita for his two wonderful works, *A Warrior of the People: How Susan La Flesche Overcame Racial and Gender Inequality to Become America's First Indian Doctor* and *"I Am a Man": Chief Standing Bear's Journey for Justice*. The real-life figures of Starita's two books influenced the depictions of my fictional characters Bright Eyes and her father, Chief Wallace. The La Flesche family (which includes the aforementioned Susan La Flesche; her sister, Susette La Flesche, a.k.a. Bright Eyes; and Chief Joseph, a.k.a. Iron Eye) is one of astonishing accomplishments, one of the great families of American history. While the characters in this book are creations of my imagination, and not meant to be literal analogues to the real people, their incredible lives inspired me, and I would encourage anyone interested in this remarkable family to research them further, through Starita's works and beyond.

Thank you to Erin Kelly for her Pulitzer Prize–winning book, *Chasing Me to My Grave: An Artist's Memoir of the Jim Crow South*, which features the story and artwork of the late Winfred Rembert, with contributions from his wife, Patsy Rembert. Winfred Rembert is a genius, and that book is a classic. It's also where I first heard the phrase "cain't to cain't," used here with permission.

Thank you to the team that supports the *Thoughtful Bro* show at A Mighty Blaze. The pandemic was terrible, but we Blazers created something special within it. Caroline Leavitt—thank you for all the encouragement, the early read, and the killer blurb.

I'd like to thank five teachers whose insights on the subject of storytelling left an indelible impression on my craft: Robert McKee, Chris Vogler, Michael Arndt, Jeanne Cavelos, and K. M. Weiland.

I would recommend these five to anyone interested in how to construct a meaningful story.

To my parents, Tom and Patsy, and everyone in the Cecil, Bussmann, and Orraca-Tetteh families who have been watching this journey unfold, thank you for being there for me and for showing me what's most important in life.

To my four awesome children, Henry, Wyatt, Aubrey, and Ronan: you listened to the original version of this story at bedtime. Your laughter and snores were the most blunt and honest feedback I've ever received. You may not be ready to read this book quite yet, but one day when you're wondering, "What's Dad really all about?" you'll find in these pages a kind of answer.

And Dede? From day one, you saw the vision. You never doubted, even when I did. As Blink 182 said, "Always I know, you'll be at my show. Watching. Waiting. Commiserating." It's been ride or die from the jump, Fishie. And you *know* we still ridin'.

Mark Cecil is host of *The Thoughtful Bro* show, for which he conducts interviews with an eclectic roster of award-winning, debut, and best-selling storytellers. Formerly a journalist for Reuters, he is Head of Strategy for the literary social media startup A Mighty Blaze. He has taught writing at GrubStreet and the Writers' Loft. Originally from Worcester, Massachusetts, he lives outside of Boston with his family. This is his first book.

A NOTE ON THE TYPE

The text type in this book was set in Jenson, a font designed for the Adobe Corporation by Robert Slimbach in 1995. Jenson is an interpretation of the famous Venetian type cut in 1469 by the Frenchman Nicolas Jenson (c. 1420–1480).

Typeset by North Market Street Graphics
Lancaster, Pennsylvania

Printed and bound by Berryville Graphics
Berryville, Virginia